Dare to believe in . . .

ANSWERED PRAYERS

Also by Danielle Steel

DANIELLE STEEL

ANSWERED PRAYERS

A Dell Book

ANSWERED PRAYERS
A Dell Book

PUBLISHING HISTORY
Delacorte hardcover edition published November 2002
Dell mass market edition / October 2003

Published by
Bantam Dell
A Division of Random House, Inc.
New York, New York

Library of Congress Catalog Card Number:
2001058252

ISBN 0-440-23672-X

Manufactured in the United States of America
Published simultaneously in Canada

OPM 10 9 8 7 6 5 4 3 2 1

To my very wonderful children,
who are the answers to my prayers,
Beatrix, Trevor, Todd, Samantha,
Victoria, Vanessa, Maxx, and Zara,
and Nick who was not only the answer
to my prayers, but has my prayers now,
and my heart, as he always will.
I love you all, with all my heart and soul.

with all my love,
Mom/d.s.

ANSWERED PRAYERS

1

FAITH MADISON LOOKED SMALL AND SERIOUS AND STYL-
ish, as she set the table, tossed a salad, and glanced into
the oven at the dinner she'd prepared. She was wearing
a well-cut black suit, and at forty-seven, she was still as
slim as she had been when she married Alex Madison
twenty-six years ago. She looked like a Degas ballerina,
with her green eyes, and her long straight blond hair,
which she had knotted into a sleek bun. She sighed, and
sat down quietly in one of the kitchen chairs.

The small elegant brownstone townhouse on East
Seventy-fourth Street in New York was deadly quiet,
and she could hear the clock ticking, as she waited for
Alex to come home. She closed her eyes for a minute,
thinking of where she had been that afternoon. And as
she opened them again, she could hear the front door
open and close. There was no other sound, no footstep
on the hall carpet, no shout of "hello" as he walked in.
He always came in that way. He locked the door behind
him, set down his briefcase, hung his coat up in the
closet, and glanced at his mail. In time, he would come

looking for her. He would check her small study, and then glance into the kitchen to see if she was there.

Alex Madison was fifty-two years old. They had met when she was in college, at Barnard, and he was in business school at Columbia. Things had been different then. He had been enchanted by Faith's open easy ways, her warmth, her energy, her joy. He had always been quiet and reserved, and cautious with his words. They married as soon as she graduated, and he got his MBA. He had been an investment banker ever since. She had worked as a junior editor at *Vogue* for a year after graduating, and loved it, and then stopped when she went to law school for a year. She dropped out when her first child was born. Eloise had just turned twenty-four and had moved to London in early September. She was working at Christie's, and learning a lot about antiques. Faith's other daughter, Zoe, at eighteen, was a freshman at Brown. After twenty-four years of full-time mothering, Faith had been out of a job for the past two months. The girls were gone—and she and Alex were suddenly alone.

"Hi, how was it?" Alex asked as he walked into the kitchen looking tired. He barely glanced at her and sat down. He'd been working hard on two IPOs. It didn't even occur to him to touch her or to hug her. Most of the time, he spoke to her from across the room. He didn't do it out of malice, but it had been years since he'd come home from the office and given her a hug. She had no idea when he'd stopped. She'd been so busy with their daughters that she didn't notice, until one day she realized that he didn't touch her when he came home anymore. She was always doing homework with the girls, or bathing one of them, when he came home at night. But it had been a long, long time since he'd been affectionate with her. Longer than either of them knew or cared to remember. There was a chasm between them now that they had both long since accepted, and she felt as though she were looking at him from a great distance as she poured him a glass of wine.

"It was all right. Sad," she said, as he glanced at the paper, and she took the chicken out of the oven. He preferred fish, but she hadn't had time to buy any on the way home. "He looked so small." She was speaking of her stepfather, Charles Armstrong. He had died two days before, at the age of eighty-four. The rosary had been that day, and the casket had been open so Charles could be "viewed" by family and friends.

"He was old, Faith. He'd been sick for a long time." As though that not only explained it, but dismissed it. Alex did that. He dismissed things. Just as for years now, he had dismissed her. She felt lately as though she had served her purpose, done her job, and been dispensed with, not only by her children, but by her husband as well. The girls had their own lives now that they'd left home. And Alex lived in a world that didn't include her, except on rare occasions, when he expected her to entertain clients, or go to a dinner party with him. The rest of the time, he expected her to amuse herself.

She saw women friends sometimes in the daytime, but most of her old friends still had children at home and were pressed for time. In the past several months, since Zoe left for college, Faith had been spending most of her time alone, trying to figure out what to do with the rest of her life.

And Alex had a full life of his own. It seemed eons since she and Alex had sat for hours at dinner and chatted about the things that were important to them. It had been years since they had gone for long walks on the weekend, or gone to movies and held hands. She could barely remember what that had been like with Alex. He seldom touched her, and rarely spoke. And yet, she knew he loved her, or at least she thought so, but he seemed to have almost no need to communicate with her. It was all shorthand and staccato words, silence suited him better, as it did now, as she set his dinner down in front of him, and brushed away a stray lock of blond hair. He seemed not to notice her at all, and was engrossed in something he was reading in the paper. It took him a long time to answer when she spoke again.

"Are you coming tomorrow?" she asked gently. Her stepfather's funeral was the next day. He shook his head as he glanced up at her.

"I can't. I'm going to Chicago. Meetings with Unipam." He had been having trouble with an important account. Business took precedence over all else, and had for a long time. He had become a very successful man. It had bought them the townhouse, and their daughters' educations, an unexpected amount of ease and luxury that Faith hadn't expected to enjoy. But there were other things that would have meant more to her. Comfort, laughter, warmth. She felt as though she never laughed anymore, and hadn't in a long time, except when she was with the girls. It wasn't that Alex treated her badly. It was more that he didn't treat her at all. He had other things on his mind, and he didn't hesitate to make that clear to her. Even his lengthy silences told her that he would rather think than talk to her.

"It would be nice if you were there," Faith said cautiously, as she sat down across the table from him. He was a handsome man, and had always been. At fifty-two, he had grown distinguished as well, with a full head of gray hair. He had piercing blue eyes, and an athletic build. One of his partners had died suddenly of a heart attack two years before, and Alex had been careful about diet and exercise since then. Which was why he preferred fish to anything else, and was pushing the chicken she had cooked around his plate. She hadn't had time to be creative. She had been at the funeral parlor with her stepsister, Allison, all afternoon, while people came by to pay their respects. The two women hadn't seen each other since Faith's mother's funeral the year before, and not for ten years before that. Allison hadn't come to her brother Jack's funeral two years before Faith's mother's. There had been too many funerals in recent years. Her mother, Jack, now Charles. Too many people had disappeared. And although she and her stepfather had never been close, she had respected him nonetheless, and it saddened her to think of his being gone. It felt as though all the familiar landmarks were fading from her life.

"I have to be at the meeting in Chicago tomorrow," Alex said, looking intently into his plate. He was only picking at the chicken, but he hadn't bothered to complain.

"Other people go to funerals," Faith said quietly. There was nothing strident about Faith. She didn't argue with him, didn't fight. She rarely disagreed with him. There was no point anyway. Alex had a way of removing himself. He did what he wanted, usually without asking or consulting her, and had for years. He operated like a separate entity from her most of the time, and what motivated him was business and the demands it put on him, not what Faith wanted him to do. She knew how he worked and what he thought. It was hard to get behind the walls he put up around himself. She was never entirely sure if it was a defense, or simply what made him comfortable. It had been different when they were young, but it had been this way for years. Being married to him was a lonely place, but she was used to it. She only felt it more now because the girls were gone. They had provided all the warmth she needed for years. It was their absence she felt now, more than his. And she seemed to have drifted away from many of her friends. Time and life and marriage and kids had somehow gotten in the way.

Zoe had left for Brown two months before. She seemed happy there, and had yet to come home for a weekend, although Providence was close enough. But she was busy with her friends, her life, her activities at school. Just as Eloise was happy in London, with her job. Faith had been feeling for a while that they all had fuller lives than she, and she had been wrestling with trying to decide what to do with her own. She had thought of getting a job, but had no idea what kind of work she could do. It had been twenty-five years since she'd worked at *Vogue*, before Eloise was born. She had also thought about going back to law school, and had mentioned it to Alex a couple of times. He thought the idea was ridiculous, at her age, and dismissed it out of hand.

"At your age, Faith? You don't start law school again at forty-seven. You'd be nearly fifty before you graduated and passed the bar." He said it with a look of utter contempt, and although she still thought of it from time to time she didn't mention it to him. Alex thought she should continue doing charity work, as she had for years, and going to lunch with her friends. All of which had begun to seem meaningless to Faith, particularly now with the girls away. She wanted something with more substance to fill her life, but she had yet to find a plan that seemed sensible to her, and one she could convince her husband would be worthwhile.

"No one is going to miss me at Charles's funeral," Alex said conclusively, as Faith cleared his plate, and offered him some ice cream, which he declined. He was careful about his weight, and was very trim and in good shape. He played squash several times a week, and tennis on weekends, when the weather in New York allowed. They had rented a weekend house in Connecticut when the girls were small, but they hadn't done that in years. Alex liked to be able to go in to the office, if he needed to, on the weekends.

She wanted to tell him that she would miss him at her stepfather's funeral the next day. But she knew there was no point. Once he made up his mind, one way or another, he could not be swayed. It never occurred to him that she might need him there. And it wasn't the nature of their relationship for her to portray herself that way. She was capable, and well able to take care of herself. She had never leaned heavily on him, even when their children were small. She made good decisions, and was sure of herself. She had been the perfect wife for him. She never "whined," as he put it. And she didn't now. But she was disappointed that he didn't want to be there for her. Disappointment had become a way of life for Faith now. Alex was almost never there when she needed him. He was responsible, respectable, intelligent, provided well for them. And the emotional side of him had vanished into thin air years before. They had wound up with the same relationship his parents had. When she had met them, she had been shocked by how cold they were, and unable to express affection for each other. His father had been particularly remote, just exactly the way Alex had become in time, although Faith had never pointed out to him how similar to his father he was. Alex wasn't demonstrative, and in fact it made him uncomfortable when others were, particularly Zoe and Faith. Their constant displays of affection always made him uneasy, and even more distant and critical of them.

Of the two girls, Zoe was the most like her, warm, affectionate, good-natured, with a sense of mischief about her, reminiscent of Faith when she was young. She was a terrific student, and a bright girl. But it was Eloise who was closer to her father, they had a kind of silent bond that was more comfortable for him. She was quieter than her sister, and always had been, and like Alex, she was often far more critical of Faith, and outspoken about it. Perhaps because he was. Zoe was always quick to come to her mother's defense, and to stand by her. She had wanted to come to Charles's funeral, although she wasn't close to him. He had never had any real interest in the girls. But as it turned out, she had midterm exams, and couldn't get away. And there was no reason for Eloise to come all the way from London for her stepgrandfather's funeral, after he had never given her the time of day. Faith didn't expect it of them, but it would have been nice if Alex could have made the effort to be there.

Faith didn't mention it to him again. As she did with a lot of other things, she let it go. She knew she wouldn't win the argument. As far as he was concerned, she was perfectly capable of going alone. And he knew, just as his daughters did, that Faith and her stepfather had never been close. His loss was more symbolic to her. And what Faith didn't verbalize to him was that it was more painful because it reminded her acutely of the others who had gone before. Her mother, her brother, Jack, whose death had devastated Faith when his plane went down on the way to Martha's Vineyard three years before. He was forty-six years old at the time, had been an excellent pilot, and the engine had caught fire. The plane had exploded in midair, and it was a shock she had only just recently begun to recover from. She and Jack had always been soulmates and best friends. He had been her sole emotional support, and a source of comfort for her throughout her childhood and adult life. He was always forgiving, never critical, and fiercely loyal. They were two years apart, and growing up, their mother had always said they had been like twins. Particularly when their father died suddenly of a heart attack when Faith was ten and Jack twelve.

Faith's relationship with her father had been difficult, nightmarish in fact. It was something she never talked about, and which had taken her a good part of her adult life to resolve. She had worked on it with a therapist, and made her peace with her past as best she could. Her earliest memories were of her father molesting her. He had been sexually inappropriate and abusive with her starting when she was four or five. She had never dared to tell her mother about it, and her father had threatened to kill her and her brother if she told. Her deep love for her brother had kept her silent until Jack had discovered it when he was eleven and she was nine, and he and his father had had a huge fight over it. And he had told Jack the same thing, that he would kill Faith if either of them told. He had been a very sick man. It had been so traumatic for both of them that they had never talked about it again until both of them were grown, and she was in therapy, but it had formed an unseverable bond between them, a love born of compassion, and a deep sadness in each of them that it had happened at all. Jack had been tormented by the fact that he hadn't been able to shield Faith from the nightmare their father had inflicted on her physically and emotionally. It tore Jack apart, knowing what was happening and that he was helpless to turn the tides. But he was only a child. And a year after he had discovered it, their father died.

Years later, Faith had tried to tell their mother about it when she was in therapy, but her mother's denial mechanisms had been insuperable. She refused to listen, believe, or hear, and insisted repeatedly that what Faith was saying was a vicious lie, created to malign her father and hurt them all. As Faith had feared all her life, her mother blamed her and retreated into her own fantasies and denial. She insisted that Faith's father had been a kind and loving man, who adored his family and revered his wife. She had somehow managed to canonize him in the years since he had died. It left Faith with nowhere to go with her memories, except to Jack, as usual. He had gone to the therapist with her, and dredged up painful memories for both of them. Faith had sat and sobbed in his arms for hours.

But in the end, Jack's love and support had helped her put old ghosts to rest. Her memory of her father was of a monster who had violated the innocence and sanctity of her life as a child. And it took Jack years to get over the fact that he couldn't keep it from happening to her. It was a painful bond they shared, and a wound they both fought valiantly to heal. And Faith had finally made her peace with it, in great part thanks to Jack.

But the scars had taken a toll nonetheless. Both of them had sought out difficult relationships, with people who were cold and critical of them. They managed to match their mother's coldness in their mates, and found spouses who blamed them for anything that went awry. Jack's wife was neurotic and difficult, and left him several times, for reasons that no one could understand. And Alex had kept Faith at arm's length for years, while blaming her for whatever problems came along. Their choices were something she and Jack had discussed often, and although they both understood what they'd done eventually, neither of them had ever been able to turn it around. It was as though they had chosen situations that reproduced many of their childhood miseries, so that this time they could win them over and make the outcome different, but they had chosen people who couldn't be won, and the outcome in each case was as disappointing as their childhood had been, though less

traumatic at least. Jack handled it by being a peacemaker and tolerating almost anything his wife dished
out, including frequent abandonment, so as not to anger
her or risk losing her. And Faith had done much the
same thing. She rarely if ever argued with Alex, seldom
challenged him. The lessons her father had taught her
ran deep. She knew in her heart of hearts that she was to
blame for everything. It was her sin, not his, and somehow her fault. Her father had convinced her of it. And as
awful as it had been, his final punishment had been to
abandon both of them when he died. Faith had somehow sensed, or feared, that she was to blame for that
too, and it made her careful not to do anything in her
marriage that would make Alex leave her. In some part
of her, she had spent a lifetime trying to be the perfect
little girl, to atone for the sins no one but her brother
knew about. She had thought about telling Alex the
truth about her childhood over the years, but never did.
At some deep, unconscious level, she was afraid that if
he knew what her father had done to her, he wouldn't
love her anymore.

And in recent years, she wondered if Alex ever had.
Perhaps he loved her in his own way, but it was a love
based on her doing as he said and not rocking the boat.
She had sensed early on that he couldn't have borne
hearing the truth about what her father had done to her.
Her dark secret remained with Jack and his was the only
unconditional love she'd ever known. It was mutual between them. She loved him totally and unconditionally,

as he did her, which made it even harder for her when he died. His death was an almost unbearable loss for her, particularly in light of everything she didn't have at home.

It had been difficult for both of them when her mother married Charles when Faith was twelve and Jack fourteen. Faith had been suspicious of him, and fully expected him to do the same things her father had. Instead, he ignored her entirely, which was a mercy for her. He was not a man who was comfortable with women or girls. Even his own daughter was a stranger to him. He was a military man, and he was hard on Jack, but he was at least able to demonstrate some affection for him. All he did for Faith was sign her report cards and complain about her grades, which he seemed to think was expected of him. It was his only role. Beyond that, Faith didn't exist for him, but that was comfortable for her. She was amazed when he didn't initiate sexual practices with her, she had expected them, and was stunned when he showed no interest in her. The relief she felt made up for the coldness Charles always exhibited to her, and everyone else. That was at least a familiar style to her.

Charles had won Jack over eventually by doing manly things with him, but he had never paid any attention to Faith simply because she was a girl. She had scarcely existed for him. It was Jack who had been her only male role model, her only sane bond to the masculine world. And unlike their mother and Charles, Jack had been affectionate and loving and happy and warm, just as Faith had been then. The woman he married was much as their mother had always been, distant and un-emotional and cold. She seemed unable to warm up to him. They had separated several times, and in a fifteen-year marriage they never had children, because Debbie couldn't stand the idea of them. Faith could never un-derstand the attraction he'd had for her. But he had been devoted to her, in spite of their difficulties, always made excuses for her personality, and saw things in her no one else did. She had stood stone-faced at his funeral, and shed not a tear. And six months after his death, Debbie had remarried and moved to Palm Beach. Faith hadn't heard from her since. Not even a Christmas card. In a sense, she was yet another loss, however little Faith had cared for her. She was a surviving piece of Jack in a way, but had disappeared.

In truth, Faith had no one now, except Alex and her two girls. She felt as though her own world were grow-ing smaller and smaller these days. The people she had known and loved, or even cared about, were leaving one by one. If nothing else, they had been familiar to her, like Charles. And in the end his sanity and wholesome-ness, even if cool and aloof, proved to be a safe place for her. And now they were all gone. Her parents, Jack, and now Charles. It made Alex and the girls even more pre-cious and important to her.

She dreaded Charles's funeral the next day. She knew it would remind her of Jack's funeral, if nothing else,

and that in itself would be hard enough. She was thinking about it as she walked past the study where Alex
liked to read at night. He was poring over some papers
and didn't look up at her as she paused in the doorway.
He had a way of isolating himself, of letting people
know he didn't want to be touched or disturbed. It
made him unreachable even as he sat across a room
from her. The vast distance that had grown between
them over the years couldn't be bridged. Like glaciers,
they had moved imperceptibly, each of them moving
slowly away from the other, and now all they could do
was look at each other from the distance and wave.
There was no way to get close to him anymore. Alex had
successfully isolated himself, while living under the
same roof with her. And she had long since given up.
She simply accepted it, and went about her life. But the
emptiness that she felt now that her daughters were
gone was overpowering. She still hadn't found a way to
fill the void, and wondered if she ever would, as she
watched Alex put his papers away without saying a
word to her, and then she moved silently toward the
stairs.

He followed her to their bedroom half an hour later.
She was already in bed, reading a book Zoe had recommended to her. It was an amusing novel, and she was
smiling to herself as he walked into the room. He looked
tired, but he had done most of the reading he needed to
do for his meeting in Chicago the next day. He glanced at
her, and went to change, and a few minutes later, he

slipped into bed next to her. It was as though there were an invisible barricade down the middle of their bed. It was a Maginot Line neither of them crossed, except in dire necessity, once every few weeks, or even once a month. Making love was always one of the few times when she felt closer to him, but even that was ephemeral. It was more like a reminder of what they had once shared before they had gone their separate ways, than anything they shared now. Their lovemaking was brief and perfunctory, though pleasant at times. It was a reflection of their reality, not the realization of the dreams they had once shared. It simply was what it was, and nothing more. Remarkably, due to good therapy, she had no sexual problems, despite her father's early travesties. But due to the lack of communication and warmth between her and Alex, their lack of sexuality was sometimes a relief to her.

And tonight, as he got into bed, Alex rolled over on his side and turned away from her. It was a signal that he wanted nothing more from her that night. They had had dinner together, he told her where he was going the next day. He knew where she would be. And she knew from his schedule that she was going to a business dinner with him the following night, after the funeral. It was all they needed to know about each other, and were able to share. If she needed something more, some gesture of closeness or affection in her life, she would have to get it from the girls, and she knew that. It was what still made her miss Jack all the more. With the marriages they each had respectively, they had needed each other, for coziness and solace and warmth.

Faith had loved her brother desperately, and she thought it would kill her when he died. It hadn't, but a part of her had wandered like a lost soul since that day, as though it had lost its home. She couldn't tell her daughters or anyone else the kinds of things she had shared with Jack, and always had. There had never been anyone else like him in her life. He had never disappointed her, or failed to be there for her. He had never forgotten to make her laugh, or tell her how much he loved her, and she had done the same for him. He had been the sunshine in her life, the heart, the life preserver she had clung to at times. And now with Alex snoring softly next to her, and her daughters having moved away, Faith quietly turned off the light, and felt silently adrift in a lonely sea.

2

ALEX HAD ALREADY LEFT FOR CHICAGO WHEN FAITH woke up with the alarm at eight o'clock the next day. The funeral was at eleven, and she had promised to pick up her stepsister in the limousine. Allison was fourteen years older than Faith, and at sixty-one, she seemed a thousand years old to her. She had children who were nearly Faith's age. The oldest of them was forty, and Faith scarcely knew them. They all lived in Canada, in the north of Quebec. Allison had never had any particular bond to her stepmother, nor to Faith. She was already married and had children herself when her father and Faith's mother had married. And her stepsiblings, Faith and Jack, were of no great interest to her.

Allison and her father weren't close, for the same reason he hadn't been close to Faith. Charles Armstrong had no particular use for girls. He'd been a graduate of West Point, and career army. He'd been forty-nine when he married Faith's mother, and recently retired. And he had treated his stepchildren like West Point cadets. He inspected their rooms, gave them orders, meted out punishments, and had left Jack out in the rain all night once for failing a test at school. Faith had let him in her window and hidden him under her bed, and in the morning they had splashed water on him so his clothes would be wet, and he'd sneaked back outside when the sun came up. Charles hadn't caught on to it, but there would have been hell to pay if he had.

Their mother had never intervened on their behalf, just as she hadn't in their previous life. She avoided confrontation at all costs. All she wanted was a peaceful life. She'd had a difficult, emotionally barren first marriage. And two years of dire financial problems when her husband died and left her drowning in debt. She was grateful that Charles had rescued her, and was willing to take care of her and Jack and Faith. She didn't care that Charles seldom spoke to her, except to bark orders at her. All he seemed to want from her was that she was there and cleaned his house. And all he wanted from Faith and Jack was for them to follow orders, get good grades, and keep out of sight. It had helped set the stage for both of them to marry people who were as removed and unemotional as Charles and their mother had been, and Faith's father before that.

Faith and Jack had talked a lot about it the year before he died, when he and his wife had separated yet again. He and Faith had both been aware of the parallels in the relationships they had. They had married cool, aloof people, who were neither affectionate nor warm. Although Alex had seemed affectionate at first. But he had cooled rapidly by the time Eloise was born. And it had been a progressive cooling process after that, it was just the way he was. Faith no longer resented it, but accepted him as he was.

Alex was also far more sophisticated than Charles had been. Charles had been more of a rugged man's man, a West Point man to the bitter end. But in some ways, over the years, Alex had begun to remind her of Charles. Her mother had been long suffering. It was her defense to keep the world at bay. She managed to convey that life had disappointed her, without saying it in words, and yet she did what was expected of her, and had been married to Charles for thirty-four years when she died. She never seemed happy to Jack or Faith. It was not a marriage Faith would have wanted, and yet in an odd way, it was the one Faith herself had now. She wondered why she hadn't seen that when she and Alex married. And Debbie, Jack's wife, was just as cold to him.

Their history was what had made Faith determined to be overtly affectionate with Zoe and Eloise. She had gone to great efforts to go overboard the other way, and with Alex as well at first. But he had made it clear over the years that affection was something that not only made him uncomfortable, but that he didn't need from her. He needed an orderly life, a great career, a handsome house, and a wife who was there for him, doing what he expected her to do, while he conquered the business world. But he didn't want the little frills and

flourishes and warmth Faith would have liked to offer
him. So instead, all the love that came bubbling out of
her, she lavished on her brother and her girls.

The limousine was waiting outside the house, when
Faith left at ten-fifteen. She was wearing a black dress
and coat, black stockings and high-heeled black leather
pumps. Her blond hair was swept back in the same bun
she had worn the day before, and the only jewelry she
wore was the pair of pearl earrings that had been her
mother's and that Charles had given her. Faith looked
sedate and subdued and dignified, and beautiful, and
despite what she wore, she looked younger than her
years. There was something open and kind about her
face, and she had an easy smile and gentle ways. When
she wore blue jeans and her hair down, she still looked
almost as young as her girls. Whatever sorrows she had
had in recent years had not appeared on her face, and as
she slipped onto the backseat of the limousine, she was
thinking of Jack. He would somehow have managed to
be irreverent, even about this somber day. He would
have made it easier for her, and found some subtle levity
or absurdity that he would have whispered to her. Just
thinking of it, as they drove to Allison's hotel, made her
smile in spite of herself. He had been full of mischief
right up to his untimely and unexpected end.

Jack had been an attorney in a Wall Street law firm,
and had been much loved by his colleagues and friends.
Only Alex had found him undignified and had issues
with him. The two men were at opposite poles on every

subject, and Jack had found his brother-in-law tedious, although he rarely said as much, out of deference to her. He knew there was no point discussing it, Faith didn't like his wife either, and talking about it just made it more awkward for him. Their spouses were a taboo subject most of the time, except when they themselves chose to bring it up. And Jack was wise enough to offer as little criticism as possible, out of his deep love for her.

Allison and her husband were waiting outside the hotel when Faith stopped to pick them up. They looked like solid, decent older people. They had run a large prosperous farm in Canada for forty years. They had three sons nearly Faith's age who helped them run it, but hadn't come to the funeral, and a daughter who had stayed home because she was ill. Allison and her husband Bertrand seemed uncomfortable with Faith. She was sleek and citified, and although Allison had known her since she was a child, they had scarcely seen each other once adults, and their lives were centered in different worlds.

They inquired about Alex, and she explained that he had to fly to Chicago for the day. Allison nodded, she had only met him a few times, and he was like someone from another planet to her. They had been of no interest to him, and he had made no effort to talk to them when they met, and again when he saw them at Faith's mother's funeral. He knew that Allison meant little to Faith. They were virtually strangers to each other after being related for more than three decades, and Faith couldn't help wondering as they drove to the church if they would ever see each other again after today. She had no real attachment to her, and knowing that increased her sense of loss again. Allison was yet another person who was about to slip away from her. Her entire life seemed to be a peeling-off process. No one was entering her life anymore, everyone was exiting. Jack, her mother, Charles, her daughters in their own way . . . now Allison . . . she had begun to feel in recent months as though everything in her life now was about loss. And Charles's death, however timely and appropriate at eighty-four, seemed like yet another blow. Another departure. Another person moving away from her, abandoning her.

She and Allison and Bertrand said little to each other on the way to church. Allison seemed quiet and composed. She and her father rarely saw each other, and had never been close. She told Faith she wanted to invite people to come back to the hotel afterward, if there was anyone she wanted to include. She had taken over a large sitting room, and ordered a buffet, which Faith thought was a nice touch, and thoughtful of her when she offered it. It would be nice for their parents' friends.

"I'm not sure how many people I'll know," Faith said honestly.

The obituary they'd given to the newspaper had said where the funeral was, and she had called a number of her parents' friends. But many of their old friends were gone, or in convalescent homes. Charles and her mother had lived in Connecticut for many years, and had had a number of friends there, but after her mother's death, Faith had moved Charles into town, to a care facility, and he had been ill for most of the past year. His death had come as no surprise to any of them. But it was hard to say how many people would come to his funeral service. Faith suspected that attendance would be pretty thin. They were going to the cemetery immediately after the funeral, to bury him. And she and Allison agreed that more than likely by one-thirty they'd be back at the hotel. They anticipated greeting people at the hotel for the remainder of the afternoon, and Allison and Bertrand were flying back to Canada at eight o'clock that night. Faith and Alex were going to a business dinner, which would be a good diversion after a depressing afternoon.

All three of them were surprised, as they entered a side door of the church, how many people had actually come and were already sitting in the pews. Charles had been a respected member of the community in the small town in Connecticut where they had lived. Surprisingly, Faith always felt, people had been fond of him, they thought him decent and upstanding, and even interesting. He had been stationed in some exotic places in his youth, and often had tales to tell, although he didn't share much of that with his wife or stepchildren. But people beyond his immediate circle had always thought well of Charles. He was not nearly as chilly to them, and made considerably more effort with them, which had always seemed odd to Faith. Particularly since he and her mother hardly ever seemed to exchange more than a few words, and she could never understand what her mother had seen in him, other than that he had been a solid citizen, and at one time a nice-looking man. But as far as Faith was concerned, her stepfather had been utterly without charisma or charm.

The service began punctually at eleven o'clock. Faith and Allison had chosen the music the day before, and the casket stood a few feet from them, under a large spray of white flowers. Faith had used her own florist for the flowers in the church, and offered to pay for it, and Allison was relieved. The service was a simple one, he had been Presbyterian, although Faith's mother was Catholic, and they had been married in the Catholic Church. But neither of them had been staunch about their faith, although Faith was, and Jack had been as well. They had often gone to mass together right up until the time he died.

The sermon was brief and impersonal, as seemed appropriate. Charles wasn't the kind of man about whom one would wax poetic or tell anecdotes. The minister listed his accomplishments, talked about his West Point background, his military career, and referred to Allison and Faith. He got confused, and assumed they were both Charles's daughters, but Allison didn't seem to mind. Everyone sang "Amazing Grace" at the end, and as they did, Faith felt tears begin to slide down her cheeks. For some reason, she had just had a vision of

Charles when he was young, one time when they were
children and he had taken them to a lake, and was trying to teach Jack to fish. Jack had had big bright eyes,
and had looked lovingly at Charles for one of the rare
times he did, when Charles wasn't berating them, and
all she could see in her mind's eye, was Charles standing over Jack, showing him how to hold the pole, and
Jack grinning from ear to ear. . . . It made her miss Jack
far more than Charles, as she closed her eyes, and could
almost feel the August sunshine from that day on her
face. It made her heart ache thinking back to that time. It
was all gone now, part of a lifetime of memories.

She couldn't stop the tears as they continued to slide
down her face, and a sob caught in her throat, as the
pallbearers from the funeral home slowly rolled the casket away, just as they had Jack's three years before. His
friends had been his pallbearers, and he'd had so many
of them. There had been hundreds of people at his funeral, and for Faith, the memory was only a vague blur.
She had been so distraught that day that she could
hardly remember it, which was merciful. But as she
watched Charles's casket roll slowly down the aisle,
it brought back agonizing memories for her, particularly
as she followed Allison and Bertrand down the aisle.
They stopped in the vestibule as the pallbearers took the
casket to the hearse, and Charles's three surviving relatives waited to shake hands with friends.

They were halfway through the hundred or so
mourners who had come, when Faith heard a voice

behind her that was so familiar, all she could do was stare. She had been shaking the hand of a woman who had been one of her mother's friends, and before she could turn, he said a single word.

"Fred." It brought a smile to her face in spite of the circumstances, and she was beaming as she turned. There was only one person in the world who had called her that, other than Jack. In fact, he had created it, and Jack had adopted it. It had been her nickname for all of her growing-up years. He had always said Faith was a stupid name for a girl, so he had called her Fred.

Faith turned with a broad smile and looked at him, unable to believe that he was there. He hadn't changed a bit in years, although he was the same age as Jack, and two years older than she. At forty-nine, Brad Patterson still looked like a kid when he grinned. He had green eyes the same color as hers, a long lanky body that had always been too thin, but seemed more reasonably so now. She had always told him he had legs like a spider when they were kids. He had a smile that stretched across his face irresistibly, a cleft chin, and a shock of dark hair that had not yet begun to go gray. Brad had been her brother's very best friend from the time he was ten. Faith had been eight the first time she had laid eyes on him, and he had painted her blond hair green for St. Patrick's Day. She, Jack, and Brad had thought it a terrific idea, although her mother had been considerably less amused.

Brad had come up with a million plots and pranks

over the years, he and Jack had gotten into everything, and been inseparable for a dozen years. They had gone to Penn State together, and only separated finally when they both went off to law school. Brad had gone to Boalt at Berkeley, and Jack to Duke. Brad had fallen in love with a girl out there, and eventually stayed on the West Coast, and then somehow real life intervened. He married and had kids, he had twin sons roughly the same age as Eloise. And as time went by, Jack flew out to see him once every couple of years. But Brad stopped coming east. It had been years since Faith had seen him when he came to her brother's funeral. They had both been devastated and spent hours talking to each other about him, as though by telling everything they remembered about Jack they could bring him back to them. Brad had come back to the house with her, and met Zoe and Eloise. The girls had been fifteen and twenty-one then. Alex hadn't been terribly impressed by him, he thought him too West Coast, as he put it, and was dismissive of him, mostly because he was Jack's friend. But Faith didn't care, all she wanted to do was cling to him. She and Brad had exchanged letters for a year, and lost touch again finally. His own life seemed to devour him. She hadn't seen him since Jack's funeral, and hadn't heard from him in nearly two years. She was stunned to see him standing there, at Charles's memorial, and couldn't imagine how he had come to be there.

"What are you doing here?" The smile they exchanged could have lit up the entire church.

"I was in town for a conference, and saw the obituary in the paper yesterday. I thought it would be a decent thing to come." He smiled at her just as he had nearly forty years before. He still looked like a boy to her, and in her heart he always would be, no matter how old he got. Their youth was all she saw. He was one of the three musketeers she and Jack had formed with him. And she smiled up at him, grateful that he had come. It made it easier for her suddenly, and made her feel as though Jack was also in their midst. "And I knew I'd see you here. You look great, Fred."

He had teased her mercilessly as a kid, and she had had a crush on him when she was about thirteen. But by the time he left for college three years later, she had gotten over it, and was dating boys her own age. But he had remained one of her best friends. It saddened her that they had lost contact finally, but it was hard to maintain their friendship over distance and time. All they had was history, and the enormous affection she still felt for him. They both treasured endless memories of the years they had shared growing up.

She invited him to the hotel afterward, and he nodded, his eyes seeming to drink her in. He looked as moved to see her as she was to see him.

"I'll be there," he said reassuringly. He had seen her crying as she sang "Amazing Grace," as he had as well. He couldn't hear the hymn anymore without thinking of Jack's funeral three years before. It had been one of the darkest days of his life.

"It was nice of you to come," she said, smiling up at him, as people on the receiving line moved around them to shake hands with Allison and Bertrand.

"Charlie was a nice old guy," Brad said benevolently. He had some fond memories of him, fonder than Faith's. But he and Jack had done things with him Faith had never had the chance to do, like deer hunting, and fishing at the lake. He had been good about things like that, and it would never have dawned on him to include Faith. "Besides," Brad added, "I wanted to see you. How are your girls?" he asked, and she smiled again.

"Great. But gone unfortunately. Eloise is in London, and Zoe is a freshman at Brown. How are the twins?"

"Terrific. They're spending a year in Africa, chasing lions around. They graduated from UCLA in June and took off right after that. I want to go see them one of these days, but I haven't had time." Faith knew he had gone out on his own a few years before. He was doing some sort of community legal defense work, working with minors convicted of felonies. Jack had told her about it just before he died, and she and Brad had talked about it at the funeral. But she didn't have time to ask him about work now, Allison was signaling to her that they had to leave for the cemetery. Faith nodded and looked back at Brad.

"I've got to go. . . . Will you come to the hotel afterward? The Waldorf." She looked like a kid again as she reminded him, and he smiled. He wanted to wrap his arms around her and give her a hug. Something in her eyes told him she'd seen hard times. He wasn't sure if it was Jack or something else, but there was something powerful and sad in her eyes that tugged at his heart, like when she was a kid and she looked sad. He had always felt protective of her and still did.

"I'll be there." Faith nodded, and two people came between them and offered their condolences as they shook her hand.

Brad signaled good-bye to her, and then drifted off. He had some errands to do before he went to the hotel. He didn't come to New York often, and he wanted to stop at a few favorite haunts, and go to a couple of the shops he liked. He would have preferred to go to the cemetery with her, to offer his support, but he didn't want to intrude. He knew it would be hard for her, because of Jack. Funerals and cemeteries were all too familiar to her now. And he realized as he watched her get into the limousine and drive off behind the hearse that he hadn't seen her husband with her. He wondered if something had happened between them—if they'd split up—and if that was the sadness he'd seen in her eyes. He and Jack had talked about it after Faith had married, neither of them had been enthused about Alex. He had always seemed distant and cold to them, even then, but Faith had insisted to Jack he was a great guy and warmer than he looked. And Brad was no longer close enough to her now to ask how things were. But he found it odd that Alex wasn't there.

The brief interlude at the cemetery was perfunctory

and grim. The minister read several psalms, and Allison said a few words, while her husband stood silently by. And then each of them left a rose on Charles's casket, and walked away quietly. They had agreed not to stay while it was lowered into the ground. It would have been too sad. Only a handful of people had come, and half an hour later, they were on their way back to the city again. It was a brilliantly sunny October day, and Faith was grateful at least that it hadn't rained. It had poured the day they'd buried Jack, which made it that much worse. Not that sunshine would have helped. Nothing would. It was without question the most agonizing day of her life.

Burying Charles was different for her. It was quiet and sad. It made her think of her mother, the marriage they'd had, and the childhood she and Jack had spent with them. Based on her experience with her own father, Faith had been afraid of Charles at first, when her mother had married him. She wasn't sure what to expect. But she had been relieved to find early on that he had no sexual interest in her, although he had been unyielding and stern. He had often shouted at them. The first time he'd done it, she had cried, and Jack had held her hand. Her mother had said nothing to Charles in their defense. She had never wanted to make waves, and hadn't stuck up for them, which seemed like a betrayal to Faith. All her mother had wanted was for everything to work, no matter what it took, whether she had to sacrifice herself or Faith or Jack. She deferred to

Charles about everything, even her own kids. It was Jack who had always protected Faith. He had been her hero all his life until the day he died. It made her think of Brad again, and how pleased she was that he had come. Seeing him at the hotel was something to look forward to, as she tried to turn her thoughts away from painful memories. There were far too many of them.

The car pulled up outside the hotel, and Faith and Allison agreed to let it go then. Faith could either walk or take a taxi home, and Allison and Bertrand were going to take a cab to the airport at six o'clock. All they had left to do now as part of Charles's funeral was spend a few hours with his friends. As they walked into the hotel, Allison was still holding the folded flag they had taken off his casket at the cemetery. It made her look like a war widow, Faith thought, as they walked across the lobby, and took the elevator upstairs.

The room Allison had rented for the afternoon was simple and elegant. There was a grand piano in one corner, and a buffet covered with sandwiches, cookies, and cakes. There was coffee, and a waiter offering people drinks and wine. What she had provided to eat was basic but adequate, and the first people began to arrive almost as soon as Faith hung up her coat. And she was relieved to see that Brad was the third one there.

She just stood and smiled at him for a minute as he crossed the room to her. It made her think of how gangly he had been as a kid. He had always towered over her, and when she was really young, he used to throw her in the air, or push her on the swing. He had always been part of the furniture of her childhood and teenage years.

"How did it go?" he asked her, as a waiter handed him a glass of white wine and he took a sip.

"Okay. I don't do funerals anymore, if I can help it. But I couldn't avoid this. I hate cemeteries," she said, with a fleeting frown, and they both knew why.

"Yeah, I don't like them much myself. Where's Alex, by the way?" Their eyes met and held, he was asking her more than just that, and she sighed and then smiled.

"He had to go to Chicago to see clients. He'll be back tonight." There was nothing critical in her tone, but Brad thought he should have been there, for her. It annoyed him on her behalf that he wasn't, but he was also glad. It gave him time alone with her, to talk and catch up. It had been far too long since they'd talked.

"That's too bad. That he's in Chicago, I mean. How's everything else?" He perched on the arm of a chair, and was almost the same height as Faith as she stood and they talked.

"Okay, I guess. It's weird having both of the girls gone. I don't know what to do with myself. I keep saying I'll go to work, but I don't have any marketable skills. I was thinking of going back to law school, but Alex thinks I'm nuts. He says I'm too old to go back to school, or pass the bar."

"At your age? Lots of people do. Why wouldn't you?"

"He says by the time I pass the bar, no one will hire

me anyway." Just hearing her say it annoyed Brad. He had never liked Alex anyway.

"That's nonsense. You'd make a great lawyer, Fred. I think you should." She smiled in answer, and didn't try to explain to him how impossible it would be to convince Alex of that. He was a stubborn man.

"Alex thinks I should just stay home and relax, take bridge lessons, or something like that." It sounded deadly to her, and Brad agreed. As he looked at her, he was remembering her long blond hair when she was a kid, and wished he could pull the pins out of her bun, for old times' sake. He had always loved her hair.

"You'd be bored to death. I think school is definitely the right idea. You ought to look into it." It was exactly what Jack would have said, and it sparked her enthusiasm again, as a fresh group of people walked in, and she went to greet them. She recognized several faces, and thanked them for coming, and a little while later, she came back to Brad.

"So what's Pam doing these days? Are you working together at all anymore?" They were both attorneys, and had met at law school, although Pam had been a year ahead of him. Jack had gone to their wedding and been best man, but Faith had only met her once. Pam had seemed hard and more than a little daunting to her, but smart certainly. Brad had definitely met his match in Pam.

"Hell, no," Brad grinned. "She's still working in her father's firm. He keeps threatening to retire, but he's seventy-nine and hasn't yet, so I don't know if he ever will. She's a litigator and she thinks I'm insane for what I do."

"Why?" What he did had sounded both interesting and noble to Faith. According to what he'd said the last time they met, he was defending a wide assortment of kids accused of some fairly major crimes.

"No money, for one thing. Most of the time I'm court appointed, the rest of the time I don't get paid, or not enough, according to her. I work days, nights, and weekends. She thinks I gave up a cushy job in her father's firm to hang around in county jail with a bunch of kids who are allegedly unsalvageable. The nice thing is that some of them actually do turn their lives around, if they get a break. It's interesting work. And it works better for me. You can come and clerk for me one summer if you go to law school," he teased. "You'd have to work for free of course, or you could pay me, that would work." They both laughed as they wandered to the buffet, and Allison introduced them to a couple Faith had never met. The crowd had begun to thin by midafternoon, but Allison thought they should stay till five out of courtesy, in case others arrived late. It gave Faith a chance to spend more time catching up with Brad.

"So what else, Fred?" Brad teased as they sat down again, after eating egg salad sandwiches with watercress, some strawberries, and petits fours. "Any misdemeanors? Felonies? Parking violations? Affairs? You can confess to me, I'm bound by confidentiality," he said, and she laughed. He realized as he sat with her, how much he had missed seeing her in the last several years. It was so easy to drift apart with distance and time and busy lives, his at least. And yet the moment they were together, it was as though nothing had changed. And if anything, Jack's absence brought them closer together and provided a tighter bond. "So, what's the deal?" he pressed.

"No deal," she said, crossing her legs, as they faced each other. He was still an incredibly handsome man, she realized, as she looked at him. All the girls had always been crazy about him, although it was always Jack who had gotten the best girls. He had had irresistible charm, and in some ways, Brad was shy. Faith had always loved that about him. "You'll be very disappointed. No misdemeanors or felonies. I lead a pretty boring life. That's why I want to go back to school. I've been out of a job since Zoe left for Brown. Alex is busy all the time. Ellie's gone too. That's about it. I do some charity work from time to time, organizing fundraisers. I can do that in my sleep."

"What about affairs, Fred? You've been married for a hell of a long time. Don't tell me you've behaved all this time!" He'd done the same thing to her when they were kids. He'd always wormed all her secrets out of her, with his big brotherly way, and then teased her about them afterward. But this time she truly had nothing to tell.

"I told you. I lead a very boring life. And no, I've

never had an affair. I don't think I'd have the guts, too complicated, besides, I've never seen anyone I want. I've just kept busy with the girls. It sounds embarrassingly dull, doesn't it?" She laughed and he grinned, his green eyes locked on her.

"You must still be madly in love with Alex then," he said, and she looked away thoughtfully and then back at him. It was odd, all the same intimacy was still there between them, even after all these years. She trusted him, who he was now, and all he'd ever been to her. And he was standing in for Jack in a way. In some ways, at certain times, she had been even closer to Brad than to her brother. She and Brad were very similar. Jack had always been more outgoing than either of them, and more outrageous at times. She and Brad had always had a lot in common. And she had told him things in the past that she hadn't even told Jack.

"No," she said honestly, "I'm not in love with him. Not 'madly,' as you put it. I love him, he's a good person, a good father, a good man. We're good friends. Actually, I'm not sure what we are anymore. I think his work is his first love, and he doesn't need anyone close to him, he never has. We live in the same house, share children, go out together to business dinners, and see friends occasionally. Most of the time, we go about our own lives. We don't have much to say to each other anymore." He realized then that that was the sadness he had seen in her eyes.

"That sounds lonely, Fred," he said quietly, although

his own life was no better than hers. He and Pam had scarcely been more than acquaintances for years. Things hadn't been going well between them when he went out on his own professionally, and she had yet to forgive him for leaving her father's firm. She viewed it as an abandonment, and a betrayal of sorts. She had taken it personally, and couldn't see that what he was doing was better for him. It was diametrically opposed to everything she wanted and believed, for either of them. Making money, lots of it, was far more important to her.

"It is lonely sometimes." She didn't want to tell him it was lonely all the time. It didn't seem fair to Alex to say that, and it sounded pitiful to admit that to Brad. "He's a very solitary person, and we have different needs. I love people, being with the kids, I used to love seeing friends, going to movies, hanging out together on weekends. We kind of lost all that. Alex can't see the point in doing anything unless it's related to his work." Even his golf games were with clients, or people he wanted to get to know, and do business with eventually.

"God," Brad said, running a hand through his hair and sitting back in his chair, with an agitated look. He hated to think of her living that way. She deserved so much more, which was what Jack had always said, and Brad agreed. "He sounds like Pam. All she cares about is how much money we make. And frankly," he smiled at Faith sheepishly, "Scarlett, I don't give a damn. I mean sure, I wouldn't want to see us starving to death. But that's not going to happen. She makes a fortune at her father's firm, she has some very, very major clients. And he's going to leave the whole shebang to her when he retires, or dies, whichever comes first. We have more than enough put away. We have a great house. Terrific kids. What the hell more could we want? How much more do we need to make? The beauty of it is that I can afford to do what I want. I don't have to gouge clients, or do boring tax work for them. I love what I do, that means a lot to me. I think Pam is embarrassed by it, because I'm not making the kind of money she thinks I should. And in the end, who gives a damn except Uncle Sam on April fifteenth? We've got more than enough to leave the kids, and we live very comfortably. I figured it was time for me to give back. Someone should."

"It makes sense to me," Faith said thoughtfully. It sounded like he'd made the right decision, for himself at least. But it also sounded as though it had created a big rift between them.

"For Pam, it's all about status and prestige, who you know, what other people think, what clubs you belong to, what parties you get invited to. I don't know, maybe I am getting old, or weird, but I'd rather sit in a jail cell talking to some kid than go to a boring black-tie dinner and sit next to some old bag who doesn't work and doesn't have a goddamn thing to say." He looked heated as he talked about it, and Faith smiled at him.

"I think that's me you're talking about. I think that's the best argument I've heard for going back to school."

"Maybe it is," he said honestly. "I don't know. I just

knew I had to do something better with my life than estate planning, or listening to people whine about their taxes, and try to help them preserve their fortunes for their kids, who need to get out and make a living anyway, and probably never will. I think I might have killed someone if I'd stayed." He had hated the years he'd worked at her father's firm and longed to get out.

"I get so bored with nothing to do all day," Faith confessed. "I feel like I'm wasting my life. The girls have their own lives, Alex has his work. I don't know what to do with myself now that I'm not taking care of them. All I have to do is show up and cook dinner at night. I can only go to so many museums, and have lunch with so many friends."

"You definitely should go back to school," he sounded firm. "Unless you want to go back to work."

"And do what? I haven't worked since before Ellie was born, and I was really only a glorified gofer then. You can do that at twenty-two, you can't at my age. It doesn't make sense. The trouble is I'm not sure what does anymore. But Alex is going to have apoplexy if I go back to school."

"Maybe it threatens him," Brad volunteered, as Faith thought about it. "Maybe he likes knowing you have nothing to do and are dependent on him. I think that was part of it with Pam. I think she liked knowing I worked for them. It made me feel claustrophobic as hell. I'd much rather screw up and go down the tubes on my own."

"I'm sure that won't happen," Faith said reassuringly. "It sounds like you're doing fine, or at least you're doing the right thing. And it doesn't sound like the money is really an issue for either of you." It was a nice position to be in.

"The money is a major issue to her. It's how she measures herself, by her success, and the money she brings in. I don't think that in the end that's what counts. When I die, I want to know I made a difference to someone, that I changed a life or two, that I saved a kid, and kept them from destroying their lives. I can't tell myself that by saving tax dollars for people who have too much money anyway."

"I think Alex and Pam may be twins." Faith smiled at him. She had always loved his values and views, even when they were kids. And she was sorry when Allison reminded her that they had to give up the room at five o'clock, and she was leaving for the airport at six.

"I think it went off pretty well," she said to Faith. They all looked tired, but a lot of Charles's old friends had come by, and it had been an afternoon of affection and respect.

"You did a lovely job," Faith said, wondering suddenly if they would ever see each other again, and although they had never even been friends, thinking about that saddened her. "Charles would have been pleased."

"I think he would," Allison said, as both women got their coats, and Bertrand signed the check. He had insisted that they wanted to pay for it. Faith had paid for the flowers at the church, which had come to almost the same amount.

Brad walked to the elevator with them. Allison and Bertrand were going upstairs to pick up their things. And Faith had to go down to the lobby to get a cab.

"When do you leave?" Faith asked Brad as they waited for the elevator with Allison and Bertrand.

"Tomorrow morning," he said as the up elevator arrived and Faith and Allison embraced, while Bertrand held the door for them.

"Take care of yourself, Faith," Allison said. She appreciated everything Faith had done for the past two days. They both had the same sense that their paths might not cross again.

"I will, you too. Call me sometime." They were the words of people who had nothing to talk about, but who shared a sliver of history.

They got in the elevator and Faith waved as the doors closed, and she turned to Brad after they had, with tears in her eyes. "I'm so tired of losing people . . . of saying good-bye . . . and people who leave my life and never come back." He nodded and took her hand in his as their elevator came, and they rode in silence on the way down.

"Are you in a rush to get home?" he asked as they crossed the lobby to the Park Avenue doors.

"Not terribly. We're going out tonight, but not till eight o'clock. I have time."

"Do you want to have a drink somewhere?" he asked even though they had just spent the entire afternoon eating and drinking in the room upstairs.

"What about walking me home?" It was twenty-four blocks, a decent walk, and she wanted some air. Brad liked the idea, and they went through the revolving door and headed north up Park Avenue arm in arm.

They were quiet for a little while, and then both spoke at the same time.

"What are you going to do now, Fred?"

"What are you working on when you go back?"

They laughed and he answered first. "I'm trying to get a kid acquitted who accidentally shot his best friend. Possibly not so accidentally as it so happens. They were both in love with the same girl. He's sixteen, and charged with attempted murder in the first degree. It's a tough case, and he's a nice kid." It was routine stuff for him.

"I can't compete with that," she said, as they walked in easy stride side by side, in spite of his long legs. He was remembering how to adjust his steps to hers. They had gone on a lot of walks together in the old days. "Actually, I'm not doing a thing."

"Yes, you are," he said easily, and she looked surprised. "You're going to call Columbia and NYU and whatever other school appeals to you, and get the catalogs and registration forms for the law schools. You'll have to find out about the exams you have to take. You have a lot to do."

"You've got my work cut out for me, don't you?" She looked amused, but she had to admit, she liked the idea, and so did he.

"I'm going to call you next week and find out how much progress you've made. And if you've dropped the ball, I'm going to raise hell with you. You've got to get off your ass, Fred. It's time." He had walked back into her life as a stand-in older brother. Just like the old days. She didn't disagree with what he was saying to her, but she still didn't know how to sell Alex on it, or if she could. And she also didn't know if she was brave enough to defy Alex entirely. That didn't seem like a good idea, and challenging him had always frightened her. Some lingering memory of her father's criticisms and betrayals of her had always made her hesitant about standing up to men. At some deep, hidden level, she suspected she was afraid. The only men who'd never frightened her were Jack, and of course Brad.

"Do you have e-mail, by the way?" He was matter of fact as he asked, as they moved into the Sixties. It was getting dark, and Park Avenue was brightly lit, as people went home from work.

"Yes, I do. I just bought a laptop so I could e-mail Zoe. I'm getting pretty good."

"What's your address?"

"FaithMom@aol.com."

"You should change it to Fred," he said, smiling down at her. "I'll write to you when I get back to San Francisco."

"I'd like that, Brad," she said, it would be nice to stay in touch with him this time. She hoped they would both make the effort. If he had time. His life was far busier than hers. "Thank you for being there today. You made it a lot easier for me."

"I had some good times with Charlie a long time ago. I figured I owed it to him." She still had trouble thinking of Charles in that context, but clearly he had been a lot more interested in Jack and Brad than he had ever been in her, or Allison. "And I wanted to see you." His voice became gentler as they walked along, they were half-way to her house. "How are you doing without him?" They both knew who he meant, he was talking about her brother.

"Not so great sometimes," she said, looking at the pavement as they walked, and thinking of him. He had been such an extraordinary person. There had never been anyone else like him, and never would be in her life again. "Other times, better. It's weird, sometimes I'm fine about him for months, and then all of a sudden, it hits me. Maybe it will always be like that." She had spent a lot of time alone, wrestling with her grief, since he died. That had been another thing that had isolated her from friends. Grief was a solitary thing. And she had often gone to church alone, to pray for him. It was comforting. She had tried to talk to Alex about how much she missed her brother, but it made him uncomfortable, and it was awkward discussing it with him. He didn't like hearing about it. She had gone to see a psychic once, who had "channeled" Jack, and Alex had had an absolute fit when she told him, and forbade her to ever do it again or discuss it with him. He said it was a sick thing to do, and the psychic had taken advantage of her. But actually, Faith had liked it. She had gone back two more times, and never told Alex. And as they walked, she told Brad about it. He wasn't convinced of its veracity either, but saw no harm in it if it made her feel better. There seemed to be nothing wrong with it, to him.

"I miss him too, Fred," he said gently. Brad was a gentle person. "It's so odd thinking that he's gone. I still can't believe it. I go to call him sometimes, I reach for the phone, when something funny happens, or I'm upset, or bothered about something, or need advice . . . and then I remember. It doesn't seem possible. How does someone like Jack just disappear? He's the kind of guy who should have lived forever. Do you ever hear from Debbie?" For reasons of her own, she had also vanished. She had maintained no contact whatsoever with Jack's family. Faith didn't even know where she was now, other than in the vicinity of Palm Beach. Or at least that was where she'd gone when she left, and then vanished.

"I never hear from her," Faith answered. "I don't know that I ever will again. I think she knows I never liked her, although I tried for Jack's sake. She really jerked him around." She had threatened to leave him regularly, separated from him repeatedly, and never appreciated what a terrific person he was. It had irked Faith constantly, although Jack had defended Debbie staunchly to Faith for all the years that they were married. "I always thought their relationship was sick. I don't know why he put up with it. She hardly said two words to me at the funeral, she left town two weeks later without saying good-bye, and Jack's lawyer told me that she had remarried. She used the insurance money to buy a house, and then married some guy. I think Jack got a raw deal from her."

"I always thought so too. I think it's too bad they never had kids."

"She probably wouldn't have let me see them anyway," Faith said unhappily, and then looked up at Brad again. It was so nice talking to him about Jack, and life, and old times. "Are you really going to e-mail me?" she asked, looking young again, and he wanted to tell her to take down her hair so she'd look like the Fred he had always loved. She was the little sister he had never had, and had always been. And in some ways, she still seemed like a kid to him, and he felt protective of her.

"I told you I would." He put his arm around her again and held her close as they walked. She was almost home.

"You won't drift away again? I miss you when I don't hear from you. There's no one left from my childhood anymore, except you."

"You'll hear from me, Fred. I promise. But I want you to look into schools too. The world needs more lawyers like you." They both laughed at that. And a few minutes later, they were standing outside her house. It looked elegant and respectable, with freshly painted black trim against the brick, and a narrow clipped hedge out front.

"Thank you for coming today, Brad. It's weird to say, but it actually ended up being a nice day. It's a funny thing to say about a funeral," but it had meant a lot to her to spend time with him. She was happier than she had been in a long time. She felt comfortable and at peace, and safe, and loved, almost the way she had been as a little girl, when she was hanging out with him and Jack. They were the only thing about her childhood that she had loved.

"I think Charlie would have enjoyed himself if he'd been there. I'm glad I went. It's been a long time since you and I talked. Take care of yourself. I worry about you." He looked down at her with concern, and she looked up at him with a brave smile.

"I'll be fine. Have a safe trip back to California, and don't work too hard."

"That's the part I like best," he admitted to her. Other than his sons, it was the only thing that really meant something to him in his life. He didn't have a lot of common ground left with Pam, and was no longer sure he ever had.

Brad gave her a big hug then, and hailed a cab, and she watched him get in and drive away. He rolled down the window just before they turned the corner, and gave her a last wave. Faith wasn't entirely sure she would hear from him again. He had drifted out of her life several times. After law school, and again after Jack's funeral. But at least they had shared this one lovely day. And in an odd way, it had been like sharing a visit not only with him, but with Jack. She was still smiling to herself when she turned the key and walked into the house.

She could hear Alex moving around upstairs. She hung up her coat, and walked slowly up the stairs, thinking of Brad.

"How was it?" Alex asked her, as she walked into their bedroom, and she looked at him with a smile.

"Nice. Everything went fine. Allison rented a room at the Waldorf, and a lot of people came by afterward. A lot of his friends, and my mom's. And Brad Patterson, I hadn't seen him since . . . in a long time."

"Who's that?" Alex looked distracted. The television was on and he'd been watching the news. He was standing in his boxer shorts and socks, buttoning a freshly starched white shirt. And as he talked to her, he knotted his tie.

"He's a friend of Jack's. His best friend, in fact. We grew up together. You met him at Jack's funeral. He lives in San Francisco. You probably don't remember him." There had been so many people there, and Alex never paid close attention to details like that, or people who were of no use to him. Brad would have fit into that category for him.

"No, I don't. Will you be ready in time?" He looked concerned. It was an important evening for him. It was a dinner party given by one of the senior partners of the firm, for a new client they had just signed. And he didn't want to be late. But Faith seldom was.

"I'll be ready in half an hour. I'll take a quick bath, and do my hair. How was Chicago?"

"Tiresome. But necessary. It went all right." He didn't ask her anything about the funeral, but she wasn't surprised. Once he knew he wasn't going, he had swept it from his mind.

She walked into the bathroom then, and as promised, emerged half an hour later, wearing a black silk cocktail dress and a string of pearls, with her makeup on, and her hair combed straight down her back. She looked more like one of his daughters than his wife. They both had Faith's blond hair. Alex looked her over appraisingly and nodded, and didn't say anything. It would have been nice to hear him say she looked beautiful, but he hadn't done that in a long time.

They left the house five minutes later, and hailed a cab. The dinner party was ten blocks down Park Avenue, and Alex didn't say anything to Faith as they rode downtown. She didn't notice. Her mind was a million miles away. She was thinking about Brad. It had been so nice talking to him all afternoon. She hadn't confided in anyone that way in such a long time. Not since the last time she had talked to him, when Jack had died. It made her feel suddenly as though someone was interested in her life, her worries, her fears, the things that mattered to her. She had found in him the family she had been longing for and felt she had lost in the past few years. It reminded her of something she forgot at times these days, that someone cared about her, and she was loved.

3

ALEX WENT BACK TO CHICAGO THE FOLLOWING WEEK, and surprisingly he actually made an effort to spend some time with Faith over the weekend when he got back. They went for a walk in Central Park on Saturday, and then had an early dinner at a nearby restaurant on Sunday night. Alex spent the day in the office on Sunday, but it had been a surprise when he offered to take her out after she got back from church. He rarely spent time with her on weekends anymore, and she was touched that he had. He was planning to be in Chicago again the following week.

Faith called Zoe on Monday night, and asked if she had some spare time. Faith had been missing her a lot, and suggested she come up to visit, and Zoe was thrilled. She and her mother had always been close. She suggested that Faith come to Providence on Tuesday night. She wanted to stay at the hotel with Faith, although she had two roommates she liked. And Faith was smiling when she hung up and booked a room.

On Tuesday night, Faith got off the plane, took a cab

into Providence, and checked into the hotel. Zoe arrived half an hour later, with a small overnight bag, and the two looked more like sisters than mother and daughter as they chatted and laughed and hugged, and sprawled out comfortably in the cozy room. They went out to dinner that night, and Faith told her about Charles's funeral, and seeing Brad. She had told both her daughters endless stories about growing up with him and Jack, and Zoe could see easily how happy it had made her to see her old friend.

"I talked to him about going back to school," Faith told her over dessert. She and Zoe had talked about it before Zoe left for Brown, and she thought it an excellent idea. But she hadn't heard anything about it since, and was glad to hear that her mother hadn't abandoned the possibility. She knew that she needed something to do with her life.

"I think it's a great idea, Mom," Zoe encouraged her. She knew how lonely her mother had been ever since she and Ellie had left home. "Have you done anything about it yet?"

"I thought I'd get some catalogs, and check into the tests I'd have to take. I'd have to prepare for the LSAT. I'm not even sure I could pass, let alone get into law school." She looked nervous about it, but excited as well, and Zoe was thrilled. Faith looked happier and more animated than Zoe had seen her look in months. "I could take some general law courses at the NYU School of Continuing Education, and a prep course for the

LSAT, which I'd need. I haven't decided yet, but it would be fun, and a lot more interesting than the bridge lessons Dad thinks I should take." She smiled ruefully at Zoe.

"Good for you, Mom." And then the pretty blonde, who was the image of her mother, frowned. She knew all the obstacles Faith would have to face. And Faith did too. "Have you told Dad?"

"Not yet. We talked about it a while back. He wasn't too pleased." It was a modest understatement of the facts, as Zoe knew.

"There's a surprise. Not. The Iceman doesn't like the idea of you being independent, Mom. He just wants you to sit around the house, waiting to take care of him."

"That's not a nice thing to say about your father," Faith said loyally, but they both knew it was true. "He actually suggested I do some more charity work. He likes it when I keep busy."

"As long as it's not something that threatens him." She was surprisingly astute. "And you've done enough charity work. You've taken care of all of us, now you need to do something for you." Zoe was always quick to champion her mother's cause, and she and her father had had a running battle for years. She said openly that all her father cared about was his work. As far as she was concerned, her father had been a nonparticipant in their family for most of her life. She was well aware that her mother had always been there for them. She and her older sister had heated arguments over it. Eloise had always hotly defended their dad, although she loved her mother too. But Zoe spoke openly about how emotionally unavailable their father was, and she thought that their mother had gotten a raw deal. "I really want you to do it, Mom. I'm going to bug you till you do."

"You and Brad," Faith smiled. "What if I don't do well on the test? I may not even be able to get in. You have more faith in me than I do in myself. We'll see." And she still had to talk to Alex about it. That was key.

"Those are just excuses, Mom. You'll get in. I think you'd make a great lawyer. And don't let Dad talk you out of it. If you make up your mind, there's nothing he can do to stop you. He'll just have to adjust to it."

"Maybe I should let you discuss it with him," Faith teased. But she was grateful for the vote of confidence and the support. Zoe had always been her staunchest supporter in the family.

Faith asked her about school then, her classes, and her friends. They were the last people to leave the restaurant, and went back to the hotel and talked for hours. And that night, they slept together in the king-size bed and Faith smiled at Zoe as she drifted off to sleep, thinking how lucky she was. Her daughters had been the greatest gift Alex had given her. And she was hoping to go to London to see Eloise soon. She had promised to come home for Thanksgiving, and Faith was thinking of going over for a few days after that. She had nothing but time on her hands. But that would change if she actually went back to school.

Zoe left the next morning at nine o'clock. They had just enough time for scrambled eggs and English muffins and a pot of tea, before Zoe gave her mother a hug and a kiss and dashed off. And at ten o'clock Faith was on her way back to the airport, lost in her own thoughts. On the way home from the airport, she asked the driver to take her to NYU. She went to the law school, and got an armload of flyers and catalogs, and some information about the tests she had to take, and then she stopped at the School of Continuing Education and got their brochures too. And she called Columbia when she got home.

She spread out the information she'd gotten on her desk, and sat staring at it with a look of awe. It was one thing to get the catalogs and another to get into the school, and she still had no idea how to convince Alex to agree. Zoe thought she should present him with a fait accompli, but Faith thought that was inconsiderate and rude. He had a voice in the matter too. It was a big commitment for her to make, particularly if she went to law school next fall. She would have homework and exams, and hours of studying to do. She wouldn't be as available as she had been, and she knew it would be a big adjustment for him. She was still thinking about it when she glanced at her computer and saw that she had mail. She assumed it was from Zoe, clicked on the mailbox, and was surprised and pleased to see that it was from Brad.

"Hello, Fred. How are you? What's new? Do you

have the catalogs yet? If not, get off your ass right now and head out the door. I don't want to hear from you till you've done your research. No time to waste. Maybe you can start taking classes in January. Hurry up!

"Otherwise, how's by you? It was good to see you last week. You look better than ever. Is your hair still as long as it used to be? I'll be happy to paint it green anytime you feel the need, St. Paddy's day or not. Pink for Valentine? Red and green for Christmas? I thought the green looked pretty good, if memory serves.

"Have been swamped since I got back. Working on the case I told you about. The poor kid is scared to death. I have to get this one off. No small feat. What kind of law interests you by the way? I think you'd be great as a children's advocate, unless you want to go for the big bucks of course. In that case, you should talk to Pam. Corporate law is interesting, though not my cup of tea, but maybe yours.

"Have to get back to work. . . . Off to school with you. Take care. Keep me posted. Love, Brad."

Faith sat smiling as she stared at the screen, and hit the reply button immediately. She was very proud of herself that she already had the NYU catalogs on her desk and could report that to him. She felt like a kid as she typed her message to him.

"Hi, Brad, just got back from Providence. Had a great time with Zoe last night, dinner, chatter, lots of giggles and hugs. She seconded your idea. I stopped at NYU on the way home—you'd better be proud of me!!—and picked up the catalogs, thousands of them, and all the info I need. Called Columbia and asked for theirs. Not sure if I should apply to more schools. In any case, I've held up my end. Will read the catalogs carefully this week. Alex is in Chicago. I still have to tell him. I'm not sure how he'll react, or actually I am. He'll go through the roof. He may put his foot down, and then what? Not worth starting World War III over my law career. That may be the end of it. We'll see.

"I like your idea about children's advocacy. Sounds good at least. Not sure what it entails. But I have always had a soft spot for kids. That's putting the cart before the horse at this point. First, Alex. Then exams, applications . . . will I get in??? What if I don't??? Feels like high school again." She had suffered the agonies of the damned with Zoe the year before, while she waited to hear from her first-choice colleges. Brown had been her favorite among all of them, and she was thrilled when she got in. Alex had wanted her to go to Princeton, Harvard, or Yale, and was crushed when she turned down all three of them to go to Brown. He had gone to Princeton and wanted her to go there, but Zoe was adamant, although her father called Brown a "hippie school." Zoe just laughed at him. It had been "everyone's first choice," according to her.

"Otherwise, nothing new here." She continued her e-mail to Brad. "No news from Eloise. I assume she's fine. She loves London. I want to go over and visit her, while I have the time. I'm going to be seriously tied down if I start school." Just talking to him and Zoe about it, the plan was becoming real. "If you come to New York again, give me a call. In the meantime, this is fun. Send me another e-mail when you have time. I know how busy you are, so don't worry about it. Anytime will do. Much love, Fred." She smiled again as she signed her name.

And she was rifling through one of the catalogs when her computer spoke up and told her "You've got mail" again. She smiled and clicked on the icon again. He must have been sitting at his desk when her e-mail arrived, because he had already answered her.

"Good girl! Now read the catalogs, and sign up for some classes at Continuing Ed next term. It can't hurt and will get you in the mood. And screw Alex. Fred, he cannot make your decisions for you. He has no right to stop you, if this is really what you want to do, and I think it is. He'll get used to it. If you had a job, you'd be busy and tied down too. You can't just sit there, wandering around the house, waiting for him to come home so you can wait on him. You need a life too! He has his. Now it's time for yours! Have to run. More soon. Sign up. Be good. Love, Brad."

It was fun hearing from him, and writing to him. She deleted their exchange, particularly the "screw Alex," which sounded like something Jack would have said to her. She spent the rest of the afternoon reading the catalogs. But she didn't say anything about it to Alex when he called her from Chicago that night. Something as delicate as suggesting that she go back to school had to be handled face-to-face. And when he came home on Friday night, he looked drained.

Faith had to be registered with the law school data assembly service by December first. Her law school applications were due on February first. Their answer would come in April. She had filled out the forms to sign up for two general law classes in January and an LSAT prep crash course that started very soon and lasted eight weeks, in time to take the LSAT after Christmas. But she had not yet sent the forms in. She really wanted to talk to Alex first. And he was in no mood to do anything but eat and go to bed when he got home. He went to the office on Saturday, and stayed until late that night. It was Sunday before she felt she could broach the subject with him. He was reading the Sunday *Times,* and the football game was on, droning away on the TV, as she brought him a cup of soup and a sandwich. He didn't look up from the paper, or say anything to her, as she sat across from him, nervously thumbing through the Book Review and the Sunday *Times* magazine.

"I saw Zoe this week," she began, as he turned the sound up on the TV. "She looks great and she loves it there," Faith went on, trying to make herself heard.

He answered without looking at her. "I know, you said. How are her grades?"

"Fine, I guess. She has midterms soon."

"I hope she's doing the work, and not just playing up there." She had always been an outstanding student, and Faith wasn't worried about her. She was looking for an opening to discuss her own education with him, but it wasn't easy between the television and the newspaper. He seemed mesmerized by both, and he had a stack of reading next to him. She was going to have to jump in at some point, he wasn't going to turn his attention to her unless she forced him to. She waited another five minutes, and then did.

"I want to discuss something with you," Faith said cautiously. She could feel her palms sweat, and hoped he would be reasonable. It wasn't easy to talk to him sometimes, and she was beginning to wonder if she should wait, when he finally focused on her, and took a long sip of the soup.

"Good soup."

"Thanks. I was talking to Zoe about NYU." She took the leap, and felt as though she were diving into cement. She could see why Zoe called him what she did. He seemed like an iceman at times, even to her. Faith told herself that it wasn't that he didn't care about them, it was that he had more important things on his mind. It was what she had always told herself, and the girls. Alex wasn't easily approachable, for any of them, except maybe Eloise, who seemed to have a knack with him. But it was up to Faith to convince him now. No one else was going to do it.

"Is she thinking of transferring?" He looked shocked. "I thought you said she was enjoying it. I told her she should have gone to Princeton or Yale."

"No," Faith said quietly. "It isn't about her. It's about me."

"What about you?" He looked blank. And suddenly she could see Brad and Zoe standing over her, and telling her what she had to do.

"I'd like to take some classes at NYU." It was like dropping a bomb on him, Faith knew.

"What kind of classes?" He looked instantly suspicious of her.

"Some general law classes at the School of Continuing Education. They sound very interesting," she added, feeling nervous. He was staring at her, and he looked anything but pleased.

"That's ridiculous, Faith. You don't need to study law. What would you do with it? Why don't you take a class at the museum, that would be much more interesting for you." He was trying to head her off before she said her piece. But she knew she had to forge ahead. All she could do now was pray that he'd agree. The nature of their marriage had been such that, for twenty-six years he had had veto power over everything she did. And it was too late to change that now. It had started out as mutual agreement about many things, and over the years it had become clear to everyone that Alex ran a dictatorship. Ultimately, he had the final say, and made the rules. Because of her own psychological history, she had accepted it that way.

"I've taken a lot of classes at the Met, Alex. I want to do something more interesting." She had just pulled the pin on a hand grenade. All she had to do now was throw it at him.

"And then? What's the point of that, Faith?" He knew the answer before she answered him, but he wanted to hear it from her.

"I want to apply to law school for the fall." She said it with quiet strength and no apology, as she held her breath.

"That's absurd. We've had this conversation before. A woman your age can't go to law school, Faith. No one will hire you when you graduate. You'll be too old."

"I'd like to do it anyway. I think it would be fascinating. And maybe someone would hire me. I'm not that old, after all," she said, doggedly pursuing the goal she had finally set for herself, no matter what he thought.

"That's beside the point. Do you have any idea how much work is involved? You're going to be locked in this house studying for the next three years. And then what? You get a job and work fourteen hours a day? You won't be able to travel, you'll never be able to go out at night. You'll be telling me that we can't entertain or go anywhere because you have exams. If that was what you wanted to do, you should have thought of it before the girls were born. You could have finished law school when you started, but you didn't. It's too late now. You just have to face it."

"It's not too late. The girls are gone, Alex. I have nothing to do. And I can juggle my schedule and studying so we can still go out at night. We never travel together anymore, except for a few weeks in the summer, and I can get away then. I promise you, I'll do my best to manage it so it won't interfere with you." She looked imploringly at him, to no avail.

"That's impossible!" he exploded finally. "There's no point being married if you're going to be locked up for the next three years. You might as well go to jail, or medical school! I can't believe how unreasonable you are. How can you even suggest a thing like that? What's wrong with you?"

"I'm bored to death," she said quietly. "You have your work and your life, Alex," she said, quoting Brad. "I'd like mine too. My old friends either have jobs or kids still at home. They're all busy, and I don't want to take bridge lessons, or do charity work, or take courses at the Met. I want to do something real. And I've already done a year of law school. If they give me credit for it, it might knock off a year."

"It's too late for all that," he growled at her, slamming his empty soup mug down next to him. He seemed to be visibly threatened by what she had proposed. Perhaps he realized it meant that she would have a life of her own, and he would have less control.

"It's not too late. I'm forty-seven years old. I'll be fifty when I pass the bar."

"*If* you pass the bar. It's not easy to pass, you know." He was implying that she wasn't capable of it, which was another form of control. The implications of what he'd said weren't lost on her. But she forced herself to stay calm. She knew it was the only way she would win.

"Alex, this is important to me." The way she said it silenced him, but not for long.

"I'll think about it, Faith. But I think this is a harebrained scheme." He looked immensely irritated then, and turned the sound on the television up so loud that there was no way to talk to him. But at least she had told him what she wanted to do, and she knew that now she had to let him think about it. What he decided in the end was another matter. But she could argue about that with him then. And Zoe was planning to talk to him about it too. She wanted to give her mother a hand convincing him, since it was so important to her that Alex agree. She felt she needed his approval before she could allow herself to do what she wanted to.

Faith retreated quietly into her study, and clicked on her e-mail.

"Bulletin from Hiroshima," she began her e-mail to Brad. "I dropped the bomb. I told Alex. He's furious. He doesn't think I'll get into school, pass the exams, or the bar. Says it's a complete waste of time, and major inconvenience to him. I'm not winning any popularity contests here. And I don't think he'll agree. I'd still like to do it, but really can't if he's opposed to it, that wouldn't be fair to him. I am married after all, and he has a right to expect something from me. Alex says that I'll be too busy studying to go out at night, or travel with him, which is actually a pretty reasonable point, particularly once I start law school. It's a constant grind. Anyway, we'll see. I may be signing up for bridge lessons after all. More soon. Hope all is well with you. Love, Fred."

She checked her computer that afternoon, but there was no answer from him until late that night. Alex hadn't spoken to her all afternoon, and they had eaten dinner in icy silence. And shortly afterward, he'd gone to bed without saying a word. He was leaving the house at four A.M. to fly to Miami, for meetings he had scheduled there for two days. Faith had crossed the line, as far as he was concerned, and it was clear to her how angry he was. He was punishing her.

It was nearly midnight in New York when Brad's e-mail came in. "Dear Fred, Never mind what's fair to him. What about what's fair to you? This is not the Dark Ages . . . or is it??? He reminds me of Pam, and all her arguments when I decided to go out on my own. You have the right to pursue your dream. It's not fair of him to stand in your way. I understand his concerns, but I am convinced that you could handle it well. And although he won't admit it, I'm sure he is too. It probably threatens him. So don't give in! Don't give up. As your self-appointed older brother, I forbid you to take bridge lessons. Go to school, like a good girl!!! Hang tough.

"I'm in the office, working late. We have a hearing tomorrow on a new case. A fifteen-year-old accused of raping an eight-year-old girl. I hate cases like this. Court appointed. Seems like a decent kid, but he clearly has some serious problems. Heavy-duty abuse at home.

Kids do what they learn and what's been done to them. I'll call you sometime this week, and we can talk about how things are going there.

"Talk to you soon. Love, Brad."

He was right of course. Faith knew it. But it was easy for him to say, and harder for her to live with. She was married to Alex after all, and he was still visibly angry at her when he woke up the next day at three A.M. for his trip. Faith got up, as she always did when he left town, and made him coffee and toast. But due to the hour and their conversation the day before, he said not a word and glowered at her before he left at four. They didn't have time to discuss her academic plans again, but he had made it obvious that he considered it an act of war. She was upset about it all morning, and called Brad in the office that afternoon. It was nice to hear his voice. He had just come back from court.

"I'm glad you called me," he said, trying not to sound distracted. There were a thousand things going on, but he was concerned about her, and wanted to give her support. "I've been worried about you all day."

"Given what you have on your plate, I feel guilty for even calling you." But she was suddenly very grateful to have him back in her life. It was the kind of call she would have made to Jack. She wanted to bounce her thoughts and feelings off him, and hear what he had to say.

"He's being totally unreasonable, Fred. You know it as well as I do. How have you let him get away with this for all these years? You're not his slave for chrissake, he doesn't own you. You're married to him. He has to hear what you want too."

"No one's told him that yet," Faith said, smiling ruefully as she listened to Brad.

"Then you should. I don't know another woman who would put up with that from him. Pam would kill me if I told her what to do. We have some pretty rotten arguments, and we fought for months when I left her father's firm, but she still respected my right to do what I needed to do. She didn't like it, but she knew that in the end she had to suck it up and live with it. You can't let him tell you what to do."

"He always has. That's what he expects," she said, embarrassed by the admission.

"Then move him into this century, Fred. That's your job here. He may consider it bad news, but slavery is dead."

"Not for him," and then she felt instantly guilty for what she'd said. "I shouldn't say that. He's just used to running things at the office, and he expects to do the same at home."

"Listen, I would like to be King of California, or maybe even President of the United States, if it weren't such a rotten job, but that's not likely to happen, in either case. We'd all like to run the world if we had the chance. But we can't just run each other. What kind of life are you going to have if you don't do this? What are you going to do for the next forty years? Stay home and watch TV?"

"I think that's what he has in mind." She sounded discouraged, she knew Brad was right. But he didn't know Alex. He would make her life miserable if she didn't do what he said. He always did.

"He can't do that to you. You can't let him. And I won't let you. I think I came to Charlie's funeral for a reason. I think Jack sent me to you to kick your ass."

"Now there's an appealing prospect," she said, laughing. "Maybe you're right."

"What would Jack say if you told him about this?" Brad asked. It was an interesting question, and he knew the answer before she said the words.

"He'd be mad as hell. He hated Alex. And Alex didn't think much of him. They were always at each other's throats."

"For good reason, if this is what Alex did to you when Jack was alive. You didn't answer my question. What would Jack say?" He wanted her to think about it. He knew her brother would hold more sway than he.

"He'd tell me the same thing you did. Go to school."

"I rest my case."

"You don't have to live with Alex."

"Maybe neither should you. If he can't behave like a civilized, decent human being, he doesn't deserve you. And I think Jack would have said that too."

"Probably. But look at who he lived with. Debbie

made Alex look easy to live with. She was a lot more unreasonable than he."

"Look, all I want is for you to be happy. You didn't
look happy to me when I saw you. You look bored and
sad, and lonely. If this is what you want, go for it. More
than anything, you need a dream. We all do. This is
mine out here. I've never been happier in my life than
since I opened this office." The only trouble was he still
had to go home at night, but he didn't say that to Faith.
If he could have slept at the office, to avoid Pam, he
would. Things had reached an almost intolerable level
of late. He and Pam were what the English called "chalk
and cheese." It was not a good combination, but his parents had had an ugly divorce when he was in his teens,
and he did not want to do the same thing. So he had
made his peace with his differences with Pam. It was
Pam who was nipping at his heels these days, complaining about everything he did, and arguing with him
about the fact that he was never at home. And she was
right. He didn't want to be. But he had no intention of
leaving her, and knew he never would. It was simpler
this way.

"Do I look as bad as that?" Faith sounded distressed.
"I'm not that unhappy, Brad. We just have differences
about some things."

"And he's never there. You said so yourself. He
didn't even come to Charlie's funeral with you. What's
that all about?" He knew more than anyone about marital stress.

"I told you, he had to be in Chicago. He had meetings at Unipam."

"So what? They could have waited a day. Charlie was only going to get buried once. You could have used the support."

"It was okay . . . and you were there."

"I'm glad I was. And listen, I can't criticize your marriage. My own is nothing to brag about either. All I'm saying is that if he's not there for you a lot of the time, he owes you one. He can't have it both ways. He can't do his own thing most of the time, and still expect you to sit home waiting for him. If he has a life, then you should have one too."

"He doesn't see it that way." She sounded discouraged.

"He will, if you refuse to give in. I promise. You have to stick up for yourself."

"It's not that easy," she said sadly. Alex had a will of iron, and he was going to torture her till she gave up, just as he had before.

"I know it's hard, Fred. But it's worthwhile. You have no choice. If you don't stick to your guns on this, your life will be miserable, and then you will feel old, and depressed. I think your mental health and well-being are at stake."

"You make it sound like life and death," she smiled as she sat in her small study and thought of him. He was a terrific friend.

"In some ways it is. I want you to really think about it."

"I will." What he had said to her made sense, she just didn't know how she was going to convince Alex. But maybe Brad was right, maybe with enough energy and conviction, she could. It was worth a try at least. "How's everything with you?"

"Busy. Crazy. I've got half a dozen new cases, big ones. We're up to our ears in shit."

"Lucky you. It sounds like fun," she said enviously.

"It is." They chatted for a few more minutes, and then he had to get off, but he promised to e-mail her or call her soon, and she knew he would. He had been so amazingly helpful in these last two weeks. He had given her focus and perspective and strength, as well as love and support. It was an unbeatable combination and she was grateful to him. And more than that, he had strengthened her resolve to tackle Alex—and win.

4

WHEN ALEX CAME HOME FROM MIAMI, HE WAS IN A dreadful mood. Faith knew enough not to question him about it. Obviously, the meetings had not gone well. She cooked dinner for him in silence, and as soon as he finished his last mouthful, he got up, went upstairs, showered, and went to bed. He hadn't said a single word to her while they ate. And it was only the next morning at breakfast that he asked her how she was.

"Fine," she said, pouring him a cup of coffee. She had made him oatmeal, berries, and muffins, and he seemed in a slightly better mood. "Tough trip?" He nodded, but did not volunteer any details. He was like that. When things didn't go the way he wanted, he never had much to say. And if they were going well, she could see it by his demeanor, but he kept the news to himself.

"I talked to Eloise in London," Faith offered, as he read *The Wall Street Journal.* He didn't seem to hear what she said, and it was a full five minutes later when he spoke from behind the paper.

"How was she?"

"Fine." Faith was used to his style, and knew what he was asking. "She's coming home for Thanksgiving, for the long weekend."

"Good." He put the paper down then, and stood up, as he glanced first at his watch, and then at his wife. "I don't have time to discuss it with you now, Faith. But I wanted to let you know that I've given a lot of thought to what we discussed."

"About what?"

"Your pipe dream about law school. I want you to know now, clearly, that I will not agree. You'll have to find something else to do." He didn't wait for her to comment but turned on his heel and walked out of the room. And the way he did it instantly infuriated her. In the past, she would have been crushed. But this time, for some reason, she was outraged, and she followed after him into the hall. He was putting on his raincoat, it was pouring outside.

"You can't just dismiss me like that, Alex. And it's not a pipe dream. It's a reasonable thing I want to do. I'm willing to put the work into it, and to make it work for us too."

He looked at her with an icy stare that had quelled her for years. "I'm not. I'm not going to live with a full-time student, and all the stress and nonsense that entails. You're my wife, Faith. You have an obligation to hold up your end of the deal."

"So do you," she shot back. "This isn't fair. Why can't you respect me as a person, and realize that I need something in my life, something intelligent to do, now that the girls are gone?"

"See a psychiatrist if you're having trouble adjusting to the girls leaving home. Don't go off half-cocked trying to recapture your youth. The truth is you can't."

"You act like I'm a hundred years old. I'm not."

"I'm well aware of your age, Faith. You're not a kid, don't act like one. You're not a child. This whole project is childish and immature. Act like an adult. Your daughters are gone. You're married. You have responsibilities to me. You can't fulfill them if you're in school." It was all about him. It always was.

"What are you worried about? That I can't handle an occasional dinner party because I'm in school? I'm not going to the moon for heaven's sake. I'll be here. I told you, I can make it work." She sounded desperate and was near tears. He had never before been quite as unreasonable as this. But she had never challenged him to this extent.

"You have no idea what you're talking about, Faith. Law school is all-consuming. You won't have time for anything else. And I have a voice in that."

"Don't I?" she asked, as tears burned her eyes.

"Not in this case. That's the end of it, as far as I'm concerned. Find something else to do." And with that, before she could say another word, he opened the front door and stepped out into the rain, as Faith stood staring at him. The Iceman. Zoe was right.

Alex closed the door firmly behind him, and Faith

went back to the cozy wood-paneled kitchen and sat down. Their breakfast dishes were still on the table, and all she could do was cry. Great, long, wracking sobs. She felt as though she had been put in jail. He acted as though he owned her, as though what she felt and wanted were of absolutely no consequence to him. She had never felt as powerless in her life. And she was still crying when she finally stood up and put the dishes in the dishwasher, and went upstairs to their room.

She stood for a long time, looking out the window at the rain. She was monumentally depressed. And when Brad e-mailed her that afternoon, she didn't answer. She felt as though she had failed him too. He expected so much of her, but he didn't know Alex. No one did. Not like this. Other people thought him reasonable and intelligent and thoughtful. No one but Faith and his children knew how ice cold he was, or could be. He had to have everything his way. Zoe had had countless arguments like this with him, and had eventually given up discussing anything with him. She had shut him out. Only Eloise seemed able to reason with him. He regarded their world as his fiefdom, and Faith felt like his slave. Brad was right.

Faith was depressed for the next two days, and they barely spoke to each other at breakfast and dinner. And finally, two days after Alex had issued his ultimatum, Brad sent her another e-mail.

"Hey, are you okay? You've gone very quiet. Something

wrong? I'm worried about you. Let me know you're alive. Love, Brad."

With a long sigh, she began typing on the keyboard, but there wasn't much to say.

"Lost the war. Alex told me that law school is out of the question. In his view, it conflicts with my responsibilities to him. He hasn't spoken to me all week. He laid down the law and that was it. And now I'm depressed. Besides, it has rained here all week. I'm miserable and feel like shit. Eating worms, I guess. Now what am I going to do for the rest of my life? Love, Fred."

His answer came back almost instantly. He was at his desk when her e-mail came in. And as soon as he read it, he was profoundly upset. He thought about calling her, but decided to e-mail instead.

"This sounds bad. Hang in, Fred. You're depressed because you feel like you lost control of your life. For good reason. You have. I'm not telling you what to do, only you can decide. But if you let him do this to you, give you orders and ultimatums, you're going to be depressed. Very. Do you feel like you can do something to take some of the power back? Whatever feels comfortable to you. You decide what and how much. But you have to do something. You can't be treated like a child. Or worse, a thing. He has to respect your needs too. And if he can't, you have to. High price to pay if you don't. I know, I've been there. It feels very high risk to challenge that, particularly with people like him and Pam. But if you don't, you lose you. Bad place to be.

"Figure out what you need to do to feel a little more in control, or a lot more if you prefer, and then hold your nose and jump. It's worth it. I'll hold your hand as best I can. Now get out your umbrella and go for a walk. Sounds like you need some air. I'm here if you need me. And if you kill him, I'll defend you. Justifiable homicide for sure. Open and shut. Love, Brad."

She smiled as she read it, and deleted it so no one would ever see what he wrote. The part about killing Alex might upset the girls, to say the least. And then she decided to take his advice. She put boots on, and a slicker, and left the house. He was right, she needed air, and it gave her time to think. She walked down Lexington Avenue and back up Fifth, along the park. She didn't realize it while she was walking, but she was gone for two hours, and it did her a world of good. He was absolutely right. She had to take back some kind of power. Alex was treating her as though he owned her, as though she were an object he had bought. And she was no longer willing to let him do that. It was a huge change for her. She had hoped he would be reasonable and agree, but since he hadn't, she knew now what she wanted to do. She was going to send in the forms for Continuing Ed and the LSAT prep. It was a start at least. She could decide later what she wanted to do about law school. But this way, she'd have a choice. The LSAT prep course was to begin the next week, and he didn't need to know. She still had three months to reason with Alex, take her LSAT, fill out her applications, and make up her own mind. Applying to law school would give her options, and just making the decision to go to Continuing Ed classes gave her a sense of control.

She mailed the forms that afternoon. As they dropped into the mailbox, she stood there in the pouring rain and smiled. There was a knot of angst in her stomach, but at the same time she had a lighter heart, and clearer head. She knew she had done the right thing. She ran back to the house and called Brad. He answered his inside line.

"I did it!" she said exuberantly, and he knew instantly who it was. She felt like a kid who had just won the spelling bee at school. First prize.

"What did you do?" he asked with a smile, as he leaned back in his chair, and tipped it on two legs.

"You were right. First, I went for a walk in the rain. A long walk. And then I came home, grabbed the forms, and sent them off. I just dropped them in the mailbox on the corner and I feel great. The LSAT prep class starts next week. I'm not going to say anything to Alex, I'll just go." She felt dishonest but powerful and much more in control.

"At least I did something to take back the power. I feel human again." She was amazed at how fast her actions had brought her relief from the crushing depression she'd been in.

"I'm glad, Fred. I was worried about you. You sounded pretty bad." Worse than that in fact. "And I'm so proud of you!"

"I felt like shit, and have for days. How are you, by the way? I'm sorry all I did was talk about me. I've been a mess all week."

"No wonder. His little speech was not exactly designed to make you feel great. I know, I went through it with Pam when I left her father's firm. Threats, ultimatums, guilt, accusations—I thought she'd leave me if I quit. But in the end, I knew I had to take the risk. If I didn't, I would have lost respect for myself, and my life would have gone right down the tubes."

"You're braver than I am," she said, impressed by what he'd done. Pam sounded like a piece of work, and was.

"You're doing okay. Give yourself an A plus for today. I'm really proud of you, Fred."

"Thank you, I'm proud of me too. If you hadn't said what you did, I'd still be sitting here in tears." He hated to think of her that way, and was glad if he had helped. "Thank you, Brad." She hadn't done anything conclusive yet to defy Alex, but she was spreading her wings a little bit. Just enough to revive her self-respect.

"You're welcome," he said gently. She made him feel useful and important. It was a good feeling, and made him feel closer to her.

"How's work?" She sounded cheerful and interested again, and felt alive.

"As crazy as ever. We go into trial for the kid accused of first degree next week. I have a lot to prepare."

"Think you'll win?"

"I hope so. He's counting on it. Me too. It's going to be tough. He's a good kid, he deserves a break on this. It wasn't premeditated, but the minute you put guns in kids' hands, anyone's hands in fact, shit happens and someone gets hurt. That's just the way it works. Anyway, don't get me started on that. So what do you do now, Fred? I hope you're not planning to tell Alex you sent the forms in."

"Not yet," she said honestly. She hated lying to him about the LSAT prep course. She was just going to disappear every morning for three hours, and he'd never know. He rarely called in the daytime, except to talk to her about a change of plans. And she'd be home by lunchtime every day. "There's no point fighting with him yet. We'll just drive each other insane. Maybe the LSAT will be too hard for me anyway. I'll see how I feel after I take the class."

"You'll do fine," he said, and meant it. She was one of the brightest women he knew, and she'd always done well in school, and had gotten into law school before.

But they both knew she'd have to face the music with Alex eventually, and there was no doubt in Brad's mind she would be accepted at law school. And then she'd have to decide. She couldn't believe how much better she felt since she sent in the forms to her classes. It had totally turned her depression around. She no longer felt powerless and defenseless.

"You did the right thing, Fred," he said gently. "I'd

better get back to work," he said regretfully. "I'd rather talk to you, but duty calls."

"Thanks, Brad. I'll talk to you soon," she promised. She puttered around the house for the rest of the afternoon and was in surprisingly good spirits when Alex came home from the office. She was singing in the kitchen while she cooked dinner.

Alex commented on it as soon as he walked into the kitchen.

"You're in a good mood. What did you do today?" he asked cautiously, as she smiled at him. He had expected more of the same tension they had had between them that morning. And instead, she seemed relaxed and sunny.

"Nothing much. I went for a long walk, and did a few errands," she said vaguely. She hated lying to him, but felt she had no choice.

"It rained all day," he said, looking suspicious, as though he didn't believe her.

"I know, I had a great walk in the rain," she said, as she put their dinner on the table. She didn't tell him about the conversation with Brad. There was no reason to. He had become her secret friend, and champion of her causes, just as he had been when they were children. It was harmless. And Alex wouldn't have been interested anyway. He never had any interest in her friends, unless their husbands were important. Her women friends were of no interest to him. Nor would Brad be, since he was only a childhood friend of Jack's.

Alex made no further inquiries into the cause of her good humor. Instead, he ate quietly, and she asked him how Unipam was doing. He seemed pleased that she had asked him, and gave her a brief summary of their progress. It was one of those rare nights when they actually talked to each other. And by the end of the evening, she actually felt closer to him, and had forgiven him for his attitude about her going to law school. She still had hopes of convincing him in the next few months. They went to bed early that night, and predictably when he opened up to her a little, she found herself snuggling up to him. They made love and it was, as always, somewhat perfunctory and not particularly creative, but it was comfortable and satisfying and familiar. It would have proven to him, had he thought about it, what a difference it made when he was warmer to her. And with a little more effort, they might have actually enjoyed each other. But their relationship wasn't something he thought about a great deal, and never had. Their marriage was just something he took for granted, just as he did Faith.

Faith started the LSAT prep class on Monday, and it was exciting and unnerving at the same time. There was an incredible amount of material to absorb. She couldn't imagine how she would pull it off in eight weeks. And every day, after the class she was back home by one.

The ensuing weeks before Thanksgiving passed without incident between her and Alex. She was being particularly careful not to irritate him, and he was pleased, and convinced she had seen the light. She had, but not the one he thought. And he was busy too. Alex flew to Boston and Atlanta, and made another quick trip to Chicago. Faith was occupied with her class. The two others she'd signed up for didn't start till January. And she was organizing Thanksgiving, and excited about seeing Eloise and Zoe. She talked to Brad once or twice, and he sent her infrequent e-mails. He was up to his ears in his trial, and she scarcely heard from him, until it was over, two days before Thanksgiving. And much to her delight, and his relief, his client was acquitted of first-degree murder. He was charged with manslaughter, and given three years' probation, and credit for time served in county jail for seven months before his trial. It was a major victory for Brad.

"That was a close one," he admitted to her in his first call after the verdict. "The jury was out for six days. The poor kid's mother was practically hysterical, and he was scared to death. So was I actually. It was hard to tell which way they'd go. There were a lot of very good arguments for both sides. All's well that ends well. They're going to have a very nice Thanksgiving," he said, sounding relieved. "What about you?"

"The girls are coming home tomorrow. I can't wait to see them. We're just having dinner here, the four of us." They had no extended family. Alex's parents had died years before, and now her family was gone too.

"What are you doing, Brad?" she asked, happy to hear him. She hadn't heard from him in several days.

And talking to him had become a habit in the last month, one she cherished. It was hard to believe he had disappeared from her life for so many years. It was like finding a long-lost brother, and she loved talking to him. He gave her sound advice, and an enormous sense of well-being. He was high on her list of things to be grateful for that Thanksgiving, along with her kids.

"Pam is giving an enormous dinner," Brad said, sounding tired, in answer to her question. It had been a grueling two weeks for him, during the trial, and waiting for the verdict, not to mention the hours of preparation that had gone into it before that. "I think she's got thirty or forty people coming. I lost track a while back. She invited a number of people from her office. Her father will be here of course, her stepmother, their children, some old friends. And a couple of people I've never met before, probably from her boards and committees. Pam loves having a lot of people around."

"What about you?" Faith asked softly. She had the kind of voice that always soothed him. She was one of those people who always brought peace and offered comfort. There was a motherly quality about her that had always touched him, and at the same time a naïve feminine side that made her seem younger than she was.

"Honestly? I'd rather spend it quietly with a few people I really love. But Pam would feel cheated if she couldn't turn it into a big event. That's just the way she is. I've got work to do in the office in the morning anyway. I have a lot to catch up on after being buried in the trial."

"On Thanksgiving? Can't you take the weekend off? You sound exhausted."

He smiled. "I am, Fred. Bone tired. But there are other kids counting on me. I can't let their cases slide for the holiday. I can use the time to get caught up."

"What about the boys? Are they coming home?"

"It's too far to come. Jason and Dylan are staying in Zambia. I can't blame them. I'm going to try and get over there to see them after the first of the year, if I can. It must be terrific. They just love it. Have you ever been?"

"No. Alex has. He went on a safari with a bunch of friends a few years back, and I wanted to go with him. But none of the other wives went. I took a trip to Bermuda with the girls instead."

"That's a little more civilized," Brad smiled. "What time will you be celebrating Thanksgiving?" he asked, yawning. She wasn't boring him, he was just blind tired after the trial. The letdown was always enormous. All he wanted to do was go home, take a shower, and crawl into bed. But he had wanted to call her first, and celebrate the victory with her. Oddly enough, these days he found himself worried about her, if they didn't talk or e-mail every couple of days.

"We usually have dinner in the middle of the afternoon, around three o'clock. It's kind of a weird hour, but the girls like it. And at five or six o'clock, we can go to a movie, or they can go out with their friends. What about you?"

"Dinner is at seven. We'll eat around eight. I'll call you before I leave the office. You'll probably be through by then, before I go home, rev up the engines, and meet Pam's friends." He made it sound like he was a stranger in his own house, and these days, sometimes he was. "How's school going, by the way?" She had e-mailed him about it several times and it sounded as though she was being challenged and having a good time.

"Great. But scary as hell. I haven't concentrated this hard in years." And whenever Alex wasn't around, she was studying at home.

"I'm proud of you, Fred," he repeated as he often did, and he was.

They hung up a few minutes later. Faith tidied up the girls' rooms that night, and put vases of fresh flowers in them. She wanted everything perfect for their homecoming, and she felt happy and relaxed when she went back to her own room. She started to say something to Alex, and then realized he'd fallen asleep with a book in his hands. She laid it gently on the night table next to the bed, turned off his light. He looked peaceful and handsome as he lay there, and she couldn't help wondering why he was so rigid sometimes, and so hard on her and the girls. And then suddenly she thought of Charles Armstrong. In some ways, Alex's views weren't so different from his. He had enormous expectations of his children, he wanted them to work hard, get good grades, and be successful. It was what Charles had demanded of Jack when he was young, although he expected far less of her, because she was "only" a girl. Alex had the same old-fashioned ideas, although he had modified them somewhat because he had daughters instead of sons, and he expected as much of them as he would have of sons. But he treated Faith in very much the same way that Charles had treated her mother, as though she didn't exist some of the time, and wouldn't understand what he did with his days, as though she were somehow less competent than he was. It was a subtle form of devaluation that irked her when she was a child. It had bothered her that her mother had let Charles treat her that way. And now Faith realized that she had done the same thing. She let Alex put her down, and criticize her, belittle her, and ignore her. Letting him forbid her to go to law school was something her mother would have done. And as she got into bed next to him, as he snored softly, she vowed not to let him do the same thing to her. The tides had slowly started to turn.

She couldn't help wondering if she had married Alex because he was like Charles. His silence and distance were familiar to her, although they hadn't been as noticeable in the beginning. But something about him must have struck a chord with her. What frightened her now was that she had become her mother, which was precisely who she didn't want to be. The main difference was that her mother had whined and complained and grown bitter, and eventually long-suffering. It was the last thing Faith wanted to happen to her. Her mother had seemed helpless in the face of Charles's domineering ways, which was an example Faith didn't want to set for her daughters. She wanted to model dignity and integrity and strength for them. But it had been a battle for her. One that Alex didn't want her to win. It had been a silent war between them for many years. The Iceman, as Zoe called him. The sad thing was that he wasn't entirely, there was a warm core in there somewhere, that Faith had known and loved in the beginning of their marriage. But the warm core had gotten covered with layers of ice over the years. It was hard to get to it anymore, and she only caught a glimpse of it occasionally.

As she drifted off to sleep that night, she hoped it would be a nice Thanksgiving. There was no reason for it not to be, especially with the girls there. She felt useful suddenly, being with them again. They needed her, or at least they used to, and they would now, if only for a few days. Just knowing they would be home made her feel happy, safe, and loved. It saddened her to realize that Alex no longer made her feel that way. The only joy she had left was her girls.

5

IT STARTLED FAITH TO SEE THAT BOTH ELOISE AND ZOE had grown into independent young women in the brief months since they had been away. Eloise had left for London in September, and Zoe for Brown in August, and both had changed dramatically in a remarkably brief time. Eloise suddenly looked stylish and sophisticated. She'd lost some weight and bought a new wardrobe in little shops in London, and she was crazy about her job. She had met lots of new people, and had a new boyfriend, a young Englishman who also worked at Christie's. And although she was happy to see how she was thriving, Faith felt a pang as she realized how empty her nest really was. And that it was going to stay that way. Eloise was talking about staying in London for two or three years, if not longer, and maybe taking a job in Paris or Florence after that. She loved what she was learning and the people she worked with. All was well in her world.

And Zoe absolutely loved Brown. It was everything she had hoped it would be. She had designed a curriculum for herself in fine arts, with a minor in economics. She wanted to run an art gallery eventually, or start a service to buy art for important collectors. She already had her goals in her sights, even at eighteen.

Faith was reveling in the excitement of having them both home. The house seemed full of noise and laughter again, doors were banging, the girls were running up and down the stairs, and she heard them in the kitchen late that night. Alex was already asleep by then. He and Eloise had had a long quiet talk in his den, while Faith and Zoe had chatted in her room. Faith tiptoed quietly down the stairs to join the girls.

"Hi, Mom." Zoe looked up at her with a grin. She was sitting on the counter eating ice cream out of the container with a spoon, while Eloise was sprawled in a chair, sipping a cup of tea.

"It sure is good to see you guys here," Faith smiled at them. "This house is like a tomb without you." Zoe offered her a spoonful of ice cream, and she took it and then kissed Zoe's long blond hair, which hung to her waist. Eloise had just cut hers short, and it looked well on her.

"What are you both doing this weekend?" she asked as she sat at the table with Eloise, and smiled at her. She was a beautiful girl, taller than her younger sister, though not by much. They both had Alex's height and his long, lanky looks, their mother's perfect figure, and faces like cameos. They had both been asked to model at various times, but neither had ever been interested in it, much to Faith's relief. She thought that a frightening world, full of people who would have exploited them, and dangers in the form of men and drugs. She was well aware that she had been lucky with both girls.

"I'm seeing all my friends," Zoe said delightedly, "everyone's home from school."

"Me too," her older sister said. "There's a bunch of people I want to see." Although some of her friends had taken jobs in other cities, or had gone to graduate school, many of them were still in New York. She had worked for Christie's for two years in New York before they'd transferred her. It seemed the perfect job for her.

"I wish you could both stay longer," Faith said wistfully. "It's so nice to have you home. I don't know what to do with myself without you."

"You should get a job, Mom," Ellie said practically, and Faith didn't volunteer that she was back in school, and preparing to take the LSAT in a few weeks. By then, Zoe had gotten on the phone with one of her friends, and didn't hear what either of them said.

"I might one of these days," her mother said offhandedly. "Daddy thinks I should do charity work or learn to play bridge."

"That would be nice," Eloise said, sipping her tea, not wanting to contradict what her father said. She usually agreed with him, on principle. She always had. She thought the sun rose and set on him. And in contrast, Zoe criticized nearly everything he said and did. She felt he had never been there for her, whereas Ellie thought him the perfect father. She was far more critical of Faith, and had battled ferociously with her during her teen years, unlike Zoe, who had been easy for Faith, and still was. Although they looked very similar, the girls had totally different personalities and points of view about everything.

The three of them sat in the kitchen for an hour, chatting about nothing in particular, and then finally Faith put the dishes in the sink, turned off the lights, and they went upstairs to their respective rooms. Faith got into bed next to Alex and she slept like a child that night, knowing that her girls were home. And she got up at the crack of dawn the next day, to make the dressing and put the turkey in the oven and get everything ready before the others came downstairs.

They had a late breakfast, and sat reading the paper in their pajamas, as Faith checked on the turkey, and set the table in the dining room. Zoe offered to help, and Ellie sat talking to her father. There was an easy, convivial atmosphere that they all enjoyed. And even Alex looked pleased to spend time with them. It was noon before they all went back upstairs to dress. They usually congregated in the living room at two o'clock on Thanksgiving Day, and ate at three.

And when the girls came back downstairs, dressed and made up, and looking very pretty, they sat next to their father and watched the football game with him. Ellie was a huge football fan, and told him she'd been to some rugby games with friends, but it just wasn't the same thing. Zoe went to help Faith in the kitchen then, and by three o'clock, the candles were lit, the table looked beautiful, and they were ready to sit down for the meal. They ate neither lunch nor dinner on that day usually. Instead, they picked at leftovers late at night, which was almost a tradition with them, after eating the enormous meal Faith prepared. It was a traditional Thanksgiving feast and looked like something in a magazine. The turkey was a golden honey brown, and there were sweet potatoes with marshmallows, spinach, peas, mashed potatoes, stuffing, cranberry sauce, chestnut puree, and pumpkin and apple pies for dessert. It was everyone's favorite meal of the year.

Faith said grace, as she always did, Alex carved the turkey, and everyone chatted animatedly. It saddened Faith a little thinking of years gone by when Jack and Debbie had been with them, and Charles and her mother. It was odd to think that they were all gone, and only the immediate family was left, but she tried not to think of it as she and Alex chatted with the girls. They talked about everything from business to politics to school. And they were already eating dessert when Alex looked at Faith and commented to his daughters with a derisive look that their mother had been thinking of going back to school. He said it as though it were something very foolish she'd been considering, and more than anything, he looked amused.

"She came to her senses fortunately. She had some crazy idea about going to law school, until I pointed out she's a little old for that. We'd have been eating peanut butter sandwiches for Thanksgiving next year, while she studied for exams," he said, and Ellie laughed, while Faith looked hurt, and Zoe glared at him. It was the kind of thing he did, and she hated. She detested it when he put her mother down, which he did frequently.

"I don't think it's a crazy idea, Dad," Zoe said bluntly, staring right across the table at him with a determined look. She wanted to put her arms around her mother and protect her from him. It made her furious to hear him diminish her. He had often done it to Zoe too. "I think it's a great idea." She turned to her mother then, who was looking upset. "I hope you're still planning to follow through on it, Mom." They had talked about it several times, and she wanted her father to know that she approved of the plan, and he looked annoyed as soon as Zoe spoke up, which meant nothing to her. She wasn't afraid of him. She had her own ideas.

"We'll see, sweetheart. Daddy thinks I wouldn't be able to do what I need to for him, although I think I could. We'll talk about it again sometime," she said, trying to move the conversation along, as Alex looked pointedly across the table at her.

"There's nothing to talk about, Faith. We resolved that some time ago. I thought we agreed." She didn't know what to say to him. She didn't want to lie to him, nor start a war with him on Thanksgiving, when the girls were home. And she wasn't ready to tell him she was already taking a class at NYU's School of Continu-

ing Education, studying to take the LSAT in December.
It was the wrong place and time to discuss it with him,
but he seemed to want to make an issue of it in front of
the girls, to drive the point home that he had the final
say in it. But Zoe quickly took the bait, even before Faith
could respond to him.

"I think Mom should go to law school. All she does is
sit here and wait for you to come home, Dad. That's
not a life for her. And you travel a lot anyway. Why
shouldn't she be a lawyer if that's what she wants to
do?" Faith was touched that she'd stuck up for her, but
she wanted to get them off the topic as soon as possible
before it turned into an argument, which it inevitably
would.

"She's too old to be a lawyer," Alex said stubbornly.
"And she has a job. A full-time job. She's my wife. That
should be enough for her. And I think she knows it is."
Alex looked sternly from Zoe to Faith, and Ellie stared at
the remains of her dessert, not wanting to enter the discussion if possible. She thought her mother should
get a part-time job or do volunteer work. Law school
sounded a little too demanding to her too.

"Alex, why don't we discuss this when the girls
aren't here," Faith said, looking pained. She didn't want
an argument to spoil the little time they had together,
particularly on Thanksgiving. But he looked pointedly
at her, and his voice rose a decibel.

"That subject is closed, Faith. I was just telling the
girls what you'd been considering. But it's ridiculous,

you know that. It's not an option, I just thought they'd be amused to know you'd thought of it." The way he said it humiliated her, and she rose to the bait in spite of herself, and snapped at him.

"It's not 'ridiculous,' Alex. I'm serious about it. And I think it's a damn good idea," she said, and he looked stunned, as Ellie began to look seriously uncomfortable. She hated it when her parents disagreed. And Zoe looked furious on her mother's behalf. She looked like a volcano about to erupt when her older sister intervened.

"I think it would be a lot for you to take on, Mom. My friends who are in law school all hate it, they're drowning in work, and can hardly keep up. Dad's right. You'd have a tough time being here for him." It seemed a reasonable argument against it to her, but it brought Zoe out with eyes that flashed at her.

"Then maybe that's a sacrifice Dad would have to make, for her sake for once. There's a novel idea." She glanced from Ellie to him, and Faith felt panicked at the turn the meal was taking. She looked at Zoe appreciatively, but tried to turn the tides before they all drowned in them.

"I think Daddy and I have to settle this on our own. But thank you, sweetheart. We don't have to decide this right now," she said, the eternal peacemaker, although her heart was pounding at what he'd said to her.

"We already did, Faith. The subject is closed."

"Then you shouldn't have brought it up," Faith said sensibly. "I wouldn't have. And no, actually, it's not closed. I sent the forms in for two classes at NYU's School of Continuing Education. I start in January." She didn't tell him she was taking the LSAT so she could apply to law school if she wanted to, and to see how she would do. But she could have kicked herself for saying even as much as she had. She didn't want to start a war with him and ruin Thanksgiving for the girls, but he had been so condescending and humiliating that she couldn't resist letting him know that he didn't have total control. But she instantly regretted it, as he slammed a fist down on the table, which made all the silver and crystal jump, and both girls. They were stunned by his vehemence, as was Faith. And whether she wanted it or not the war had started again. This was a power war with him, and he did not intend to lose.

"Withdraw them, Faith. Call the school. There's no point doing that. You are *not* going to law school, and that's final. I won't tolerate it!" She only wanted to take the classes to prepare herself for law school in the fall and get back into the rhythm of school. Besides, it was a more intelligent pursuit than lunches or shopping with her friends.

"Who the hell do you think you are?" Zoe shouted at him, as her father stood up, looking enraged.

"How dare you speak to me that way!" he shouted back at her, as tears filled Faith's eyes. She didn't want this to happen. She wanted everything to be perfect for them while they were there. And she felt as though this was all her fault, since they were arguing over her.

"Zoe, please!" Faith said gently, trying to calm her, but Alex was furious over what she'd said to him. It was the culmination of a lot of old battles between them. Zoe was always critical of him, and had been since she was a little girl. But this was the most outspoken she had ever been to him. She couldn't stand the way he spoke to and about their mother. And Faith had a hard time defending herself. Years of being criticized and dominated as a child had taken a toll.

"No, Mom," Zoe said, turning to her, her own eyes brimming with tears, "I don't know how you can let him talk to you that way. It makes me sick. And if you won't tell him to stop, I will." And then she turned to Alex, trembling with rage. "You're so goddamn disrespectful of her, you *always* are. How can you treat her that way? Can't you treat her like a human being, after everything she does for you, for all of us? When does she get her turn, to be treated with respect? And if she wants to go to law school, why the hell not? Frankly, I'd rather eat hot dogs next year, and know that she was happy."

Ellie piped up then, looking superior and irritated, as Faith wished she had a magic wand to make them all behave. "You always spoil everything," she said to her younger sister. "You're always picking on Dad."

"For chrissake, look at the way he treats our mother! Is that all right with you? Do you think that's what she deserves? Dad's not a saint, you know, El. He's just a man, and he treats Mom like shit."

"Stop it!" Faith shouted at them. They were all behaving abominably, and worse yet, they were doing it on her behalf. The meal was over by then, but it was ending on an ugly note that none of them would ever forget, and all because Alex had mentioned that Faith wanted to go to law school. She was furious with herself too for snapping at him and setting a tone that had been picked up by the girls. She felt she should have known better, and was devastated to have been the cause of a situation that had upset everyone. And without saying another word, Alex stormed out of the room, marched into his study, and slammed the door.

"Now look what you've done!" Ellie shouted at her mother and sister. "You've ruined everything for Dad."

"Bullshit!" Zoe shouted back at her. "You're always protecting him, but he started this. He put Mom down in front of all of us. How much fun is that for her?"

"You shouldn't have told him you sent the forms in for school," Eloise reproached her mother. "You knew it would upset him. Why did you tell him that?" She was in tears too.

"Because I was upset," Faith said apologetically, wanting them both to calm down. She hated it when they fought, particularly over her—and she always felt guilty when they did. "I was going to tell him eventually anyway, if I decided to go. I haven't made my mind up yet." She was torn between wanting to take a stand, and not wanting to upset them. She could still decide not to take the classes, or even the LSAT in a few weeks.

"You'd better go, Mom," Zoe railed at her. "I'll never forgive you, or Dad, if you don't. It's what you want to do, and you have as much right as we do, or Dad does, to do what you want."

"Not if it upsets your father that much, and creates this much havoc between the two of you." Faith looked heartbroken. Why did something so reasonable for her have to come at such a high price for everyone else?

"He'll get over it," Zoe said, glaring angrily at Eloise. She hated it when her sister stood up for their father, when he was wrong. Ellie always defended him, no matter what, which seemed unreasonable to her. "Mom has to have a life too," she said, as Ellie disappeared from the dining room. She was going to console her dad.

Faith was clearing the table then, with tears running down her cheeks. "I hate it when you girls fight," she said miserably, as Zoe put an arm around her and held her tight as Faith juggled the plates distractedly.

"I hate it when he treats you like shit, Mom. And he always does. He does it just to torture you in front of us."

"He doesn't torture me," Faith said as she put the plates down and gave Zoe a hug. "But thank you for defending me. It's not a good idea if it gets everyone upset. That's just the way he is," Faith said, forgiving him more easily than Zoe ever would. She had years of scores to settle with him, which would take her a lifetime to resolve. Faith hated that too, but she could never convince Zoe otherwise. Alex had been too hard on her for too long.

"He's arrogant and inconsiderate, and supercilious and disrespectful and cold," Zoe said, reeling off what she felt were his main faults, as Ellie walked back into the room. Her father had told her he wanted to be alone.

"And you're a bitch!" Eloise said from across the room.

"Girls! Stop it!" Faith shouted at them, and then gathered up the plates and left the dining room. It was a nightmarish end to what was supposed to be a wonderful afternoon. Zoe followed her into the kitchen then, and Ellie went upstairs to call her friends. Faith was crushed over what a disaster the afternoon had been.

"Mom, I hate to desert you and go out," Zoe said apologetically. "I was supposed to meet some kids at six o'clock." It was nearly that by then.

"It's all right, sweetheart. I don't suppose we're going to get all this sorted out tonight. I hope everyone will calm down by tomorrow."

"He'll be the same then, Mom. That's who he is."

"He's still your father, and I don't care how much you disagree with him, you have to show him respect."

"He has to earn it first," Zoe said, unwilling to relent. She had strong principles, and integrity, and the only respect she felt was for Faith. Her father had lost hers years before.

She kissed her mother, and ten minutes later, she left. And a few minutes after that, Eloise came downstairs carrying her coat and purse. She had made a date with friends, and she was anxious to get out. The atmosphere in the house was leaden after the explosion at the end of the meal.

"I'm sorry things got so difficult," Faith said sadly to her. She had wanted it all to be so perfect for them. She hadn't counted on the argument that she had caused.

"That's okay, Mom," Ellie said unconvincingly. She still looked upset. They all did.

"I shouldn't have reacted to what your father said," Faith said apologetically. She didn't say, as Zoe would have, that he shouldn't have goaded her by saying it. It had been a gesture of disrespect, whether Eloise admitted it or not. "It'll be all right."

"Yeah, I know. . . . I hope you don't go to school, Mom. It will upset Dad so much." And what about me, Faith wanted to scream. What kind of life will I have if I don't? No life at all.

"We'll work it out. Don't worry about it. Just go out tonight and have some fun. What time do you think you'll be home?"

"I don't know, Mom." She smiled. She was twenty-four years old, and she'd been living on her own in an apartment in London. She wasn't used to having her mother checking on her anymore. "Late. Don't wait up."

"I just wanted to know what time I should start worrying." She smiled. "Sometimes I forget how old you are."

"Just go to bed. I'll be fine." Zoe had said she'd be back by ten. And she worried about both girls when they were out. They were beautiful, and more vulnerable than they thought.

Eloise left a few minutes later, and Faith spent the next hour clearing the table and cleaning up the kitchen. The leftovers were put away, the counters were clean, the dining room table looked pristine again, and the dishwasher was going full force.

It was after seven when she turned off the lights and knocked on Alex's study door. There was no answer for a long time, but she knew that he was there. In the end, she cracked the door open and peeked in. He was sitting in a chair, reading a book, and glanced up at her with a frown.

"May I come in?" She was respectful of him, and his space, and spoke to him from across the room.

"Why? There's nothing to say."

"I think there is. I'm sorry things got out of hand. I got upset by what you said."

"You already agreed to give up the idea of law school, Faith. You went back on your word. And there's no point in your taking classes this spring. I assume they're law classes you signed up for?" She nodded and he looked sullen, angry, and cold. And she felt the same icy wind of disapproval she'd had from the men in her life since she was a child. But this time, she was determined to handle it differently.

"We didn't agree. You ordered me to do what you

told me to." She sat down in a chair across from his. It was a small, cozy wood-paneled room, with a leather couch, and two large leather chairs, and a fireplace Alex often lit on winter nights, but not tonight. He hadn't been in the mood. "Alex, this is important to me. I need a new purpose in my life, a reason to live, something to focus on, now that the girls are gone." She wanted to make him understand how much this meant to her, and hoped that then he would agree.

"You have a purpose. You're married to me. You're my wife." It was the only role he could see her in, and he had no intention of changing that now. It suited him, whether or not it was enough for her.

"I need more than that. You're a busy man. You have a life. I don't."

"That's a sad statement about our marriage," he said, looking glum. Her appeals were falling on deaf ears.

"Maybe it is," she said quietly. "Maybe it's a sadder statement about me. I need a purpose in life, a bigger one than I've got. Let's face it, I've been a full-time mother for twenty-four years, and I'm out of a job. That's tough."

"That's life. All women face that when their kids go away to college."

"A lot of them have jobs and careers. I want to be one of them. And all I can tell you is that I'll do my best not to let it interfere with you." She was pleading with him, but he showed no sign that he'd relent.

"Things are going to come to a bad pass with us, Faith, if you don't back off."

"Don't threaten me, Alex. That's not fair. I wouldn't do this to you. If this was important to you, I'd try and support you as best I could."

"It's important to me that you *not* go to school." They were each deadlocked where they were, and Faith had no idea how to resolve it with him, or get what she wanted. She hated to give up. There seemed to be so much at stake suddenly, not just whether or not she went to school. This was about respect and self-esteem, and a new life she wanted desperately, but their old life was far more comfortable for him.

"Can we shelve this for now?" She didn't know what else to do. All she could hope was that time would soften him, when he got used to the idea.

"I'm not going to discuss it with you again," he said, and then startled her by what he said next. "Do what you want, Faith. I suppose you will anyway. But don't expect my support. I'm a hundred percent opposed to your going back to school. I just want you to be clear on that. Do it at your own risk."

"What does that mean?" His veiled threat frightened her, just as it was intended to.

"What I said." She wondered if he would punish her in some way if she went back to school. But in her heart of hearts, she knew it was worth the risk. It was something she knew she had to do. No matter what. For once in her life, she was going to do something just for her.

"Do you want to come upstairs?" she asked him gently, grateful that he had backed off, even a little bit, although there had been an implied threat. Maybe this was the best he could do, and she was grateful that it wasn't worse. It could have been.

"No, I don't," he said, lowering his eyes to his book again and shutting her out, as he always did.

She got up quietly and left. She touched his shoulder as she went, and he did not respond. He felt like a statue when she touched him, and he said not a word. She went upstairs to take a bath, and then sat in her own small study, while she waited for Zoe to come home. She checked her e-mail, but there was no word from Brad.

Thanksgiving had been difficult certainly, and she'd won a victory. But at a high price. But at least, she consoled herself in the silence of the house, she'd won this round when he told her to do what she wanted. For once in her life, she intended to, and strengthened her resolve to proceed. It was going to be a brave new world for Faith. In truth, it already was.

6

BRAD STAYED IN THE OFFICE UNTIL FIVE O'CLOCK ON Thanksgiving Day. The boys were in Africa, and Pam told him she was playing golf with friends. Their friends were coming at six o'clock, and they weren't going to eat dinner till seven or eight. She had invited forty people, at least half of whom he didn't know. And he didn't even bother to object. There was no point. Pam did what she wanted to. The only difference his objections made was that she prepared better arguments to convince him. But in the end, perhaps because of lack of energy on his part, Pam prevailed. He preferred to save his energy for bigger things, like his work.

He got a lot of paperwork done, and caught up on a number of things. And in a sentimental moment, he wrote a long letter to his sons, telling them how proud of them he was, and that he was grateful for them. They were both terrific boys. He admired their spunk in going to Africa for a year. They were working on a game preserve, tending to injured animals, and assisting animals that were somehow in trouble in the wild. And in their spare time they had volunteered at a church in the village. Dylan was teaching kids and their parents how to read, and Jason was digging trenches for a new sewer system. Their letters so far had been full of enthusiasm and excitement for everything they'd done and seen. It was an unforgettable experience for them. They were going to be there until July, and he had promised himself and Pam that he was going to take some time off from work, and visit them for a couple of weeks. But so far, he hadn't had the time. And neither had Pam. She was far less enthusiastic than Brad about going to Africa. She was terrified of diseases, accidents on a trip like that, and bugs. Her idea of adventure travel was flying to L.A. and staying with friends in Bel-Air.

She and Brad had done some traveling over the years, but never to exotic places, usually to Europe, or somewhere in the States. They stayed in luxurious hotels, and ate at three- and four-star restaurants. Pam loved going to spas, when she had the time, and playing golf with business associates, or clients she was trying to woo to the firm. Almost everything Pam did was geared toward advancing herself somehow, either socially or professionally. She rarely did anything just for the fun of it. She always had a plan. And was totally unlike Brad. He had no social ambitions, no desire to run the world, no need for enormous amounts of money, and the only real passion he had was for his work. The rest went over his head. Pam teased him about it sometimes, and had tried to show him the ropes to greed and success. They were lessons that, much to her chagrin, he had refused to learn. And since he'd gone out on his own, and left the firm, she'd given up. Most of the time, nearly always in fact, they each did their own thing, which was a relief for Brad. The work she put into her social and business life exhausted him. He didn't give a damn about showing off, being in the papers, or impressing people in her world.

Brad sealed his letter to his sons, and told them he sent them his love. They had only called a few times in the past four months. There were no phones on the game preserve, only radios that connected to nearby farms, and the local town. In order to call home, they had to go into town, and wait for hours at the post office for a phone and an outside line. It sounded like being on another planet to him. But at least they wrote occasionally, and so did he. Pam kept sending them care packages with vitamins and insect repellent, purchased by her secretary, and so far, all but two of the packages had been stolen or lost. Somewhere in Zambia there were postal workers or customs officers who were taking her vitamins, and no longer plagued by bugs. But he figured the boys were fine.

He thought of calling Faith before he left the office, but when he glanced at his watch, he realized that they were probably about to sit down and eat. It was a real bonus for him to have found her again. She was a piece of his childhood, his history, a memory of a happy time for him. Things had gotten complicated for him after college. His parents had gotten divorced, and he had always felt that the acrimoniousness of the divorce had killed them both. His mother had died of breast cancer at forty-three, after being obsessed with the things Brad's father had done to her, and his father had had a heart attack two years afterward. They had become and remained bitter, angry people whose only interest had been doing each other harm. His father had refused to attend his ex-wife's funeral, as a final slight to her, and in the end the only one it had hurt was Brad. He had vowed to himself that he would never marry. And when he met Pam, and dated her, she had had a hard time convincing him to get married. And when she finally did, after issuing a tough ultimatum to him, he was equally determined never to get divorced. He didn't want his sons to feel the same anguish he had, watching his parents' pitched battle to destroy each other. When he said "for better or worse" when he married Pam, he had meant every word of it. He knew then that no matter what happened later on, he was married to her for life.

It made him philosophical when their paths slowly began to go separate ways, and she disappointed him again and again. He knew he was a disappointment to her as well. He wasn't ambitious enough in her eyes, or interested in the same things. By the time the boys finished college, or even when they started it, Pam and Brad had no shared interests at all, and few friends they both liked. Brad's values were entirely different from hers, and the only joy they still shared was their sons.

Brad turned off the lights in the office, and got into the Jeep he used for work. He had a Mercedes parked in the garage at home, but he seldom used it anymore. It was the wrong signal to send out for a court-appointed attorney, or one doing mostly pro bono work, defending indigent kids accused of violent crimes. The Mercedes embarrassed him, and he'd been thinking of selling it, although Pam had just bought herself a Rolls. The difference in their cars seemed symbolic, to him at least, of their differences in all else.

He didn't delude himself that he was happy with her. He hadn't had any illusions about his marriage in a long time, but he was entirely clear that he wasn't going to do anything about it, and never would. And that was comfortable for Pam too. He suspected she had brief affairs from time to time, and he had gotten involved with a married secretary for two years. But eventually she'd gotten divorced and wanted a deeper involvement with him. He had never misled her about his plans, and they parted ways and she quit on good terms. And she had since married someone else. Brad hadn't been involved with anyone since, and that had been three years before. He would have been lonely, if he'd thought about it, but he didn't allow himself to. He simply accepted what was, and stayed submerged in work.

But talking to Faith had added another dimension to his life in the past two months. He had no romantic notions about her, on the contrary, she was sacred to him, and he cherished the friendship they had. She seemed to understand him perfectly, shared many of the same points of view, and her own loneliness allowed her to reach out to him in ways that others wouldn't have dared. And in his head, she was still like a little sister to him, and that made him interact with her in a totally chaste way. He loved what he felt for her, and what they said to each other. He loved helping her, and being there for her. He was determined to do everything he could to encourage her to go back to school, and he hoped she would. He felt as though he was of some use to her, and that made him feel good. She was, in every sense of the word, his friend.

Brad drove into the driveway just after six o'clock. He had intended to get home by five and get changed, but it had taken him longer than he thought to wrap up. He knew it wouldn't take him more than a few minutes to shower and change, and he was startled to find, when he let himself into the house, that they already had guests. They were standing in the front hall in black tie, and looked surprised when he walked in, in jeans and a sweatshirt.

Pam introduced him to a dozen people he had never met, and he disappeared to their room. They still shared a room, and a bed, although they hadn't made love in five years. It didn't bother him anymore, he had sublimated all his sexual urges into other things. And the only thing that had just startled him about the people

he'd met was that they were in black tie. He had completely forgotten that Pam had made Thanksgiving a
formal event this year, which seemed ridiculous to him.
Thanksgiving, to Brad, was about families and people
you cared deeply about, sitting around a table, or near a
blazing fire. It only meant something if you shared it
with people you loved, or good friends, not strangers in
tuxedos and evening gowns, standing around, drinking
champagne. But he had promised Pam he'd play the
game, and he felt he owed it to her to try. He avoided
most of her social events, either intentionally, or because
he couldn't get away from work. So there were certain
events he appeared at religiously, Thanksgiving, her
Christmas party, the opening of the opera and the ballet
every year, and the symphony if she couldn't find anyone else to go with her. He always encouraged her to try.

He was in the living room half an hour later, in his
tuxedo, looking handsome and well groomed, and to
anyone who knew him well, bored to death. He was
talking to her father about two new clients they'd ac-
quired. They were major corporate entities, and had
been a real coup for Pam, as her father said. He was in-
ordinately proud of her. She had learned everything
from him, her business acumen, her legal skills, her
values, her ambitions, and her ability to get what she
wanted in almost any circumstance, whether right or
wrong. Pam was not a woman one could easily say no
to, or who accepted being turned down. She was easily
the most determined woman Brad had ever met. He had

learned not to lock horns with her, whenever possible, and when necessary to avoid being stampeded by her, he just stepped aside. It worked better for him that way, and had allowed their marriage to survive. His love for her had been a casualty to the way she treated him, but even after his feelings for her had died, he made every effort to keep the outer shell of their marriage intact. The inside, the soul of it, had long since died.

"Do you want me to introduce you to the people you don't know?" Pam asked generously as she came to stand next to Brad, and slipped a hand into her father's arm, and he turned to her and smiled.

"I'm fine. Your father and I were singing your praises. You've pulled off some major coups recently, from what he's telling me. You're doing a hell of a job." She looked pleased with his praise. Brad tried to give her credit whenever he thought it was deserved, although he didn't have a great deal of respect for the arena she competed in. She rarely returned the favor to him, and most of the time dismissed what he did, however important it seemed to him, or the rest of the world. She was also disturbed by Brad's influence over their sons. She thought their altruistic leanings were of no consequence, and she had been trying for several years to convince them to go to law school, and join their grandfather's firm. It would have been a huge victory for her. But so far, neither of the boys had been swayed, much to Brad's relief.

She was a pretty woman, though not in an overtly

feminine way. She was tall, athletic, with a strong, sinewy figure. She played a lot of tennis and golf, and was in great shape. And she had brown eyes, and hair as dark as Brad's. She looked more like his sister than his wife. And people had often said she looked like him.

Pam drifted away then from where Brad and her father were standing. And Brad made a minor effort before they sat down. He introduced himself to several people, and had two glasses of wine to make the evening more bearable for him. He spoke to a woman who played tennis with Pam. She ran an ad agency Brad had heard of, but as he listened to her, his mind began to wander, and he finally left her to join a small circle of lawyers standing near the bar. Brad knew almost all of them, and had worked with two of them at the firm. They were nice guys and the conversation was easy and familiar, unlike the two women he sat next to, when they were finally seated at the table. Both were extremely social, and were married to men Brad had heard about and never met. It was exhausting trying to keep the conversation moving. And after dinner he was relieved to slip away. The living room was full of sated, happy people, drinking brandy. And most of them looked like they were planning to stay all night. Pam was engaged in a heated debate at that point, over some recent tax law that was of no interest to him. And the kind of law he practiced was of even less interest to them.

Brad felt a wave of exhaustion wash over him, as he

slipped into his study, turned on the light and closed the door. He took off his black satin bow tie and dropped it on the table, and then sat down in his desk chair and sighed. It had been an interminable evening, and all he could think of was how much he missed his boys. He longed for the kind of holidays they'd had when they were little, when Thanksgiving still had some meaning to him, and it wasn't an excuse to invite forty strangers to the house. Pam used every opportunity to fill the room with people who were useful to her, rather than those who had real meaning in their life. Although there were precious few of those left, and he and Pam no longer shared common friends. His were defense attorneys and public defenders, hers were socialites and social climbers, and heads of corporations she wanted to lure to the firm. Brad knew that no evening was complete for her, unless she felt she had made what she referred to as a "score."

He glanced at his computer and wished that he could e-mail Jason and Dylan and wish them a happy Thanksgiving. Instead, he typed in Faith's e-mail address in New York. It was nearly two A.M. for her.

"Hi . . . are you still up? How was your Thanksgiving? You probably won't get this till the morning. I finally escaped. A total zoo. Forty people for dinner, in black tie. One can't help but be impressed by the absurdity, and emptiness, of spending Thanksgiving in black tie. I missed the boys. That's what holidays are all about. What about you? Peaceful and pleasant? You must be happy to have the girls home. I envy you. I'm working tomorrow. Two new kids in jail, and a third I think the county is referring to me. What happens to these kids way at the beginning? It would be nice if they didn't need me, and just had happy, ordinary lives, whatever that is. I felt so stupid tonight spending Thanksgiving with a bunch of strangers, all dressed up like waiters. Pam loved it. Wish I could say the same. Sorry to complain. Just tired, I guess. Talk to you soon. And happy Thanksgiving by the way. Love, Brad."

He shuffled through some papers on his desk, not wanting to go back out amongst the guests. He was planning to sneak up the back stairs and go to bed. He had a long day the next day. And Pam was used to his leaving parties early. He always did it discreetly, so as not to disrupt the guests, or make them feel they had to leave. He was sure that Pam and many of the others would be there till long after midnight. But he was delighted not to be in their midst.

He was just turning off the lights in his study, when his computer told him he had mail. He clicked the button, and saw it was from Faith. He smiled and sat down.

"Hi . . . nice surprise . . . I'm still up. Your Thanksgiving sounds very fancy. We were just the four of us, but it wasn't easy. It started out okay, the bird was good, everyone liked the dinner. And we got in a huge fight at the end of it about my going to school. Zoe shouted at her father, Alex had a fit, the girls got into an argument. Everyone went to their separate corners, and then both

girls went out with their friends, and Alex went to bed.
Zoe is home, Ellie is still out. The girls are furious with
each other, or were, and Alex wouldn't speak to me after
dinner. It's my fault really. He was dismissive about my
going to school, and I lost my temper and snapped at
him. That set him off, so he said some fairly harsh things,
and Zoe leaped to my defense. I shouldn't have reacted
in the first place, and then everything would have been
all right. I should know better. I'm an adult for heaven's
sake. He just hit a nerve, I guess. In the end, he said I
should do what I want, but the implication was that if I
screw up, I'm up shit creek. It's a victory of sorts, but not
at the expense of the girls getting along with each other.
They have so little time together, and dinner was a mess
in the end. I hope they patch things up before they leave.
Why do things always get so complicated? What happened to nice peaceful family Thanksgivings among
people who love each other, don't get mad at each other,
and say nice things? At least the girls were here. I'm
grateful for that. Sorry to whine. I was trying to wait up
for Ellie so I could apologize to her, but it's two A.M. and
I'm going to bed. Happy Thanksgiving to you too, big
brother. Love, Fred."

It made him happy to read it, and he felt sorry for her.
It sounded like a tense afternoon. At least he and Pam
hadn't argued for once. He knew better, and did his best
to avoid making scenes.

He was quick to type in a response to Faith, in case
she had not yet gone to bed. But knowing how quickly

he normally responded, she had decided to wait up for a few more minutes to see if she heard from him again. And of course, she did. Their e-mails were like a candy dish they passed between them, and neither of them could resist responding instantly, if at all possible, when they got the other's mails.

"Dear Fred, Sounds like a tough day. I'm sorry. But a victory too, if Alex gave you tacit 'permission' (I hate to acknowledge or endorse that he has that power over you) to go back to school. That's actually good news. The silver lining in this one. Sorry about the girls. Hard on them too, if Alex puts them in that position. If you're anything like you used to be, when you were soothing Jack and me during our occasional arguments, you are the ultimate peacemaker, and I suspect you still are. You can't fix everything for everyone, Fred. It's okay for them to disagree sometimes, or even to defend you against him. The important thing was that you were all together, and you stood up for yourself. That's good for them to see, even if it caused some dissent among the troops. They'll get over it. Most important, I'm thrilled he gave you the green light for school, if only because now you'll feel less guilty about it, and can actually do it. I think you should go to NYU law school next year.

"By the way, I keep forgetting to tell you. I have to come to New York in a few weeks. Right before Christmas. It's a national conference for criminal defense attorneys, and I thought I might pick up some interesting stuff. I'll only be there for two days, and I'll be pretty busy. Hope you can spare me a minute for dinner or lunch." What he was most grateful for this time was that they had maintained contact. In fact, they had formed a tighter bond than they had had for years. He was determined not to lose sight of her this time, for old times' sake, for Jack's, and for his. And she was grateful for it too. "I'll give you the dates and the schedule when I'm in the office," he continued. "It'll be fun to see you. Hope the weather isn't too miserable by then. I can't afford to get snowed in. Hard enough to get away for two days. Goodnight, Fred, it's back to school for you!!"

She smiled when she read it, and jotted off a few more words to him. "Thanks for the encouragement. You make the day seem like less of a fiasco. I've been upset all night over it. Can't wait to see you when you're here. I'll try to fit you into my busy schedule," she teased him. "I'll have my secretary let you know what day is good for me. Seriously, I'm entirely at your disposal. Just tell me when. Goodnight, have a good day tomorrow. Love, Fred."

He read it, smiled, and turned off his computer. It had been a long day, a boring evening for him, and a sad one for her. But at least they had each other. That was something. The cherished gift of friendship and brotherly love between two old friends. As far as Brad was concerned, it was what Thanksgiving was all about, and he was grateful for her.

7

THE ATMOSPHERE WAS STILL STRAINED BETWEEN ZOE
and Ellie when Zoe flew back to Brown on Sunday
morning. They all had breakfast together, and the two
girls appeared to be talking to each other, but Faith
couldn't help but notice that the exchanges weren't
warm. And she was especially sorry that they didn't
have time to patch things up further before they left.
Eloise was flying back to London that night. And Alex
disappeared before lunchtime to spend the afternoon
with a friend. He said good-bye to Eloise before he left.

"I'm sorry things got out of hand on Thanksgiving,"
Faith apologized to her. She was especially upset about
the rift between the girls.

"I still think Daddy's right, that you shouldn't go
back to school. It'll be too stressful for you, and you
won't have any time to spend with him." She always
thought of her father first.

"I need something better to do with my time than
play bridge or have lunch with friends." Faith continued to defend her ideas, but Ellie looked unconvinced.

And as she stood there, she looked tall and beautiful and cool. She looked a lot like Alex when he was younger. And she had that same distant, slightly removed demeanor. She had boundaries for people not to come closer, unless she invited them to. And in contrast, much like Faith, Zoe seemed to have none at all, or very few. And it struck Faith as she watched her, that somewhere in the middle of the two positions would have been good.

"It's going to upset him if you do it," Ellie warned her, and Faith nodded.

"I'll do my best to see that doesn't happen. And if it does, I can always quit." It wasn't a strong position to take, but she wanted to give herself room to move.

"I guess so," Eloise said vaguely. "Maybe you shouldn't start in the first place."

"I'm just taking a couple of classes," Faith said, and smiled at her. "Law school's not a sure thing yet." And she still had to get decent grades on the LSAT, or it would be irrelevant.

"Don't make any hasty decisions, Mom," Eloise warned her as though Faith were the child and not the mother. "Try to think of Dad too." All Faith wanted to do was remind her, when hadn't she? Everything she did with her life, and had, was in accommodation of him. But she realized that she didn't always let her daughters see that. It was something she did discreetly, as she planned her life around him. But she seemed to get no credit for it, from him, or the girls, Ellie at least.

Zoe was far more cognizant of the sacrifices her mother made.

Eloise went to finish packing her suitcase, and Faith made her a sandwich and a cup of soup before she left. No matter how awkward the conversations had been, or how stressful their Thanksgiving dinner, she was thrilled that Ellie had come home, and thanked her for it before she left.

"I'll see you in a few weeks," Faith said as she hugged her before she left. Ellie was planning to come home for Christmas, and had insisted her mother didn't need to come to the airport. She was perfectly capable of taking a cab to the airport by herself, and in fact preferred it that way. Alex would have preferred that too. Faith and Zoe liked companionship at all times. Eloise was very different from them.

The house was astonishingly silent once both girls were gone. It depressed Faith as she checked their rooms, stripped the beds, and washed the sheets. There was a cleaning person who came in three times a week, but as a motherly gesture, which still allowed her to take care of them, she preferred to do their rooms and laundry herself. It was all she could do for them. And as she wandered around the silent house, she was reminded of how empty her life was without them.

She was actually relieved to see Alex come home that night. He had spent the afternoon at a downtown maritime museum with a friend from Princeton who was asking him to be on the board. Alex said he had enjoyed himself, and he seemed slightly more pleased than usual to see Faith, which startled her. She wondered if he was lonely for the girls too. Their absence impacted everyone, even Zoe, who felt like an only child now when she came home, and didn't like it. But it was hardest of all for Faith.

Faith and Alex spent a quiet evening together. He told her about the maritime museum he'd visited, and the plans he had for that week. It was the longest conversation they'd had in months, and after their argument at the end of Thanksgiving dinner, and his vehemence about her not going to school, she was stunned. It also gave her a chance to share with him how lonely she was without the girls.

"You knew this would happen eventually," he said sensibly, seemingly surprised that it bothered her as much as it did. It was hard for him to conceptualize that this had not only been her heart, but her job for twenty-four years. Had he lost his, he would have understood. "You have to find other things to do. Going back to school just seems so extreme to me. And so pointless, Faith. Most lawyers want to retire at your age, not start their careers."

"It would open a lot of doors to me. Everything else seems so short-term, like a Band-Aid on a wound. This would be a whole new life. And who knows what I would actually do with it eventually. I'm not even sure of that myself." He still seemed not to understand, but he wasn't taking it quite as personally, which was a re-

lief. His talking to her about it made for a cozy evening
for them, and took the edge off her missing the girls. It
was one of those rare evenings that only happened to
them once in a blue moon. And for the moment at least,
he seemed to have forgiven her for wanting to go to
school. Or had put his own hatred of the project on hold.
For the time being at least. And his doing that created
some much-needed and unexpected warmth between
them.

For the next two weeks, Faith kept busy getting ready
for Christmas. She bought presents for Alex and the
girls. He took several trips, and they saw so little of each
other that the topic of her going back to school didn't
come up between them again. In the little she saw of
him between business trips and after work at night, all
he did was eat, say a few words to her, and go to bed.
She was busy getting ready for the holidays, and had
agreed to help organize a benefit for Sloan-Kettering for
the spring. She had already told them she might only be
able to help for the next few weeks. Once she started
school in January, she wouldn't have time to continue
working on it, but they said that worked for them. They
were grateful for whatever time she could give.

She and Brad were still e-mailing regularly, but after
Thanksgiving, their e-mails had been brief. He had two
trials to prepare, and a bunch of new cases he had to
evaluate. It was a crazy time for him. It was two weeks
after Thanksgiving when she was eating a yogurt in her
kitchen before going to a meeting at Sloan-Kettering,

and opening her mail haphazardly. The confirmation of her two law classes at the School of Continuing Ed was there. One of them was Constitutional Law, and the other was a more general class on the law in a broader sense. It had sounded very abstract to Faith. But it was nice getting the confirmation, and made her plans seem more real. And she mentioned it to Brad when he called. He promised to take her out and buy her a bottle of champagne to celebrate when he came to town, and she sounded pleased.

"When are you coming?" She had almost forgotten about his trip. Between joining the benefit committee, Christmas shopping, and her LSAT class, the time had slipped away.

"A week from today. The fourteenth. Till the six-teenth. I hope to hell you're free." He'd given her the dates once before, but he hadn't been specific about when he'd be free to see her, and he wasn't sure yet. But one thing was sure, he wanted to spend as much time with her as he could.

"We don't have anything planned. I'll check with Alex. He's been pretty busy at the office. Maybe you and I can go out to dinner, or at least lunch."

"You'd damn well better have time for me!" he warned.

"I will." They chatted for a few more minutes about school, and she spent the next two days worrying about the LSAT exam she was going to take. She was praying she would do well. She always underestimated herself, and had for years. Alex didn't help in that area. He put her down without meaning to sometimes, and at other times, he did it intentionally.

"When are you going to tell Dad that you're definitely going to take classes in January?" Zoe asked and was worried for her when they spoke of it. She knew how important it was to her mother to get his approval of what she did. And she was afraid that if her father didn't relent, her mother might not do it after all, which Zoe thought would be disastrous and depressing for her. She was as anxious as Brad to see her mother get a new lease on life, and go back to school.

"I'll do it this weekend. I hope he's in a decent mood."

"Me too," Zoe said anxiously. "I'll keep my fingers crossed, Mom. Just take a deep breath, and do your best. And no matter what he says, you have to do the right thing. That's what you would tell me."

"Yeah. I guess it is." She didn't sound convinced.

The conversation, when it happened, was almost as difficult as Faith had feared. They hardly saw each other on Saturday. Alex worked in the office all day, trying to catch up on assorted projects he had to complete by the end of the year, and they went to a dinner party that night. They were late getting there, and he was exhausted when they got home, and went straight to bed, and fell asleep.

She finally forced herself to broach the subject with him on Sunday afternoon. He was reading some papers he had brought home from work, and was sitting next to the fireplace in the living room. Faith brought him a cup of tea and sat down at his feet.

"Alex," she started cautiously. But she knew she had to jump in. He had to know what she was planning to do, and she didn't want to lie to him about it. Having it hang over her unresolved was making her feel sick. She knew what she wanted to do. "Can I talk to you for a minute?" He looked irritated by the interruption when he glanced at her.

"What's up?" He might as well have said "Make it quick." He wasn't in the mood to talk.

She decided to make it brief. "I signed up for the two classes at NYU. I'm starting in January. And you know how much that means to me." He knew she had sent the forms in earlier, but it was definite in her mind now that she would go. And she felt obliged to share that with him. There was an endless silence from Alex, as he looked down at her from where he sat. He said nothing for a long moment, and took a sip of the steaming tea. The pause seemed interminable to her. "I know you don't like the idea of my going back to school, but this isn't law school yet. We can see how this goes, and how manageable it is for us. I'm only taking two classes, and if we really can't handle it, we'll both have an idea by the end of the term. But, Alex . . . I really want to try. I'll do my best to make it a nonevent for you." She felt she owed it to him to make him part of the decision, and allow him to acquiesce, if he would.

He looked at her long and hard, and he knew her well. He didn't want her going back to school, but he also knew that if he said no, at this point, it would have an impact on them. There was no avoiding that now.

"I don't want to give you my blessing on this," he said finally, as she felt her stomach churn, "but I also don't want the responsibility of telling you that you can't. I think I'm going to have to leave this up to you, Faith. I think it's a foolish thing to do, and a genuinely bad idea. I don't see how you can make this a 'nonevent' for us. I think you're kidding yourself about that. If you do it right, it's going to impact your time, and your ability to spend time with me, or even the girls when they're home." But she had thought of that, and thought it was worth the inconvenience to all of them for the next few years, and all she had to do, she told herself, was be organized about her study time.

"I'd like to try," Faith said quietly, looking at him with imploring eyes. They would have melted any man's heart, but his. Alex was better defended than most, and was impervious to feminine wiles.

"Then do what you want. But even if you manage those two classes, which seems pointless to me, law school would be another story. It's a major event, and will demand all your time. Don't kid yourself about that. And I'm not going to put up with it," he said ominously, and then went back to reading his papers. The subject was closed. He didn't comment further, or congratulate her for her plans. He had neither approved, nor denied. He had put the responsibility on her, and she grabbed what she got and ran. She was more than willing to take full responsibility for what she wanted to do, and make every possible effort to make it work. She quietly left the room, went to her study, and picked up the phone. She called Zoe in her dorm and told her that she was going back to school. There was victory in her voice.

"Did Dad say yes?" She sounded stunned.

"More or less. Not in so many words." She sounded pleased. "He just said he wouldn't stop me, and he thinks it's a bad idea, but he left it up to me." Zoe gave a war whoop of glee. She was thrilled. And so was Faith. It truly was a victory for her.

She wrote an e-mail to Brad after that, telling him that Alex had not stood in her way. It was the best she could have gotten from him. It wasn't in his nature to lend more support than that, or recant on what he'd said. And it was good enough for her. He didn't have to be jubilant about it, just not demand that she withdraw or forbid her to go.

She made dinner for Alex after that. He never mentioned her plans again, or asked her about them. He was quiet that night, read his papers at the dinner table, and mentioned before he left the table that he was going to Los Angeles that week. He was leaving on Tuesday and would be gone for four days. He didn't tell her much about the trip, but assured her that he'd be back on Saturday, in time to attend a Christmas party they went to every year. Faith didn't question him, she just acknowledged what he'd said. She didn't want to rock the boat, and spoil the progress she'd made. She was in her study that night when an e-mail came in from Brad.

"I was playing tennis when your e-mail came in. Sorry, Fred. Bravo!! What did you do to him? What did you have to give up in order to get what you want, or would I rather not know? In any case, I'm happy for you!! Great news!! Can't wait to see you this week. I'll be in on Wednesday night, and out again Friday afternoon. Can you make dinner Wednesday night? I might be able to do Thursday night too. Won't know till I see the final schedule for the conference. I'll let you know as soon as I do. I'll call as soon as I get to the hotel. My flight gets in at five. I should be at the hotel after six. See you soon. Congrats again! I'm proud of you, Fred. Love, Brad." He was always warm and supportive, and she couldn't wait to see him. It had worked out perfectly that Alex was going to be away. She wasn't hiding seeing Brad from him, but it would have been harder to be flexible about time to spend with Brad, if Alex had been in town. His trip to L.A. had been perfectly timed.

She was madly busy for the next few days, and let the benefit committee know that she would only be available to work until mid-January, and after that, she would have to quit. They were understanding about it, and she spent a day in their offices. And another day Christmas shopping. Zoe was coming home that weekend, right after Brad left. It was going to be a hectic week. And she was planning to buy the Christmas tree with her. She wasn't sure yet when Ellie was coming home. She had been vague so far about dates. And on Tuesday night, she called home. It was nearly midnight for Faith, and early morning for her, before she went to work.

"Hi, sweetheart, what a nice surprise." Faith hadn't told her yet about getting into school. She'd been saving it till Ellie got home.

"I hope I didn't wake you up," Eloise said cautiously.

"Nope. I was just finishing our Christmas cards." She'd gotten a great photograph of the four of them the previous summer, on a sailboat off Cape Cod, and had used it as their Christmas card. She sent photographs of them every year, but it was getting harder and harder to get them all together. She was grateful she had this one. "When are you coming home?"

There was a brief pause. "I . . . uh . . ." Faith's heart sank as she heard the words. "I wanted to talk to you about something. I didn't know how you'd feel. I've been invited to go skiing in Saint Moritz." Anxiety and guilt dripped from her voice. Faith knew her daughter well.

"That sounds like fun. Pretty fancy doings. Anyone I know?"

"Geoff's parents rent a chalet there every year, and he invited me to go." Geoffrey was the boy she'd been dating for three months. Faith didn't think it was serious, at least Ellie hadn't said it was, but he sounded like fun, and they were having a good time.

"Sounds like I'm going to have to fly over and meet him one of these days. Is this serious, El?" Faith asked pointedly, and Eloise laughed.

"Now, Mom . . . going skiing with him doth not a marriage make."

"That's good news. For now at least." She was young, and it was still too soon. But Eloise was sensible, both girls were, and she wasn't likely to fall head over heels after three months, although you never knew, Faith reminded herself. It was certainly the most serious involvement she'd had in a while. "When did you have in mind?"

There was another pause. "I . . . ah . . . well, actually, he invited me from the twenty-first to New Year's Day." It was out.

"Christmas?" Faith sounded stunned. "You wouldn't come home?"

"I don't really have enough time. We can only take that week off, and the weekends on either end. We're closed that week, so if I come home, I'd miss out on skiing with him. I couldn't go. I sort of thought . . . I was hoping maybe you wouldn't mind . . . I feel kind of mean doing it, but I'd really love to go." It would be the first time that both girls wouldn't be home for the holidays.

"Gee, sweetheart, I was really looking forward to your coming home. It won't feel like Christmas if it's

just the three of us. Do you think you could come home
a little earlier, and maybe go to Saint Moritz on the
twenty-sixth?" She was clutching at straws, but it
brought tears to her eyes to think of her not coming
home. It felt like a tremendous blow to Faith.

"I can't get the time off," Eloise said, sounding
stressed. "It's okay if you won't let me, Mom . . . I understand. . . ." But she sounded upset at the thought. It
was obvious that she wanted to go to Saint Moritz with
Geoff, rather than come home. And now Faith felt like a
monster if she didn't agree.

"Can I think about it for a couple of days? Dad just
left for L.A. this morning, but I'd like to talk to him."

"I already did," Eloise blurted out, and Faith was
shocked again. Alex hadn't said a word to her. There
was always complicity between those two. They were
allies against everyone else.

"You did? What did he say?"

"He said it was fine with him." That really upset
Faith. He had given her permission, without even discussing it with Faith. It seemed a mean thing to do, particularly knowing how much Ellie coming home for
Christmas meant to her mother. It also made her the bad
guy if she said no.

"I guess there isn't much for me to say," Faith said,
feeling sadder than she allowed herself to sound. "I'd
like you to come home, and we've been looking forward
to it. But I don't want to keep you from doing something
fun. It's really up to you, sweetheart."

"I'd like to go," Ellie said honestly, and Faith felt it like a physical blow.

"Okay, I understand. But I don't want you doing this every year. I want Christmas to be sacred for all of us. I want both of you to plan on coming home. You get a pass this year, but plan on being here for Christmas next year, no matter what. If need be, you can bring Geoff, if he's still around."

"Don't worry about that, Mom," Eloise said, sounding relieved. "And thanks . . . I've got to run." She was off the phone seconds later, and Faith sat in her study feeling crushed, as tears rolled down her cheeks.

She was losing them, there was no denying it. They had grown up. And it could only get worse. Boyfriends, husbands, jobs, friends, trips. A thousand things were going to come into their lives now to sweep them away from her. And the thought of not having Ellie home for Christmas nearly broke her heart. What was more upsetting was that Alex had endorsed the plan, and never told Faith what he'd done. It had undermined her, and put her in an awkward spot. And as she turned off the light in her study and went upstairs to bed, she wondered how she was going to get Ellie's Christmas presents to her, there was barely enough time. She just hoped that Zoe didn't get any ideas when she heard. Faith couldn't help wondering if the dissent between the two girls over the Thanksgiving holiday had spurred Eloise not to come home. It was hard to say. Or maybe it was just life. It was what she had to expect now. But the change was painful for her. Perhaps for Faith most of all.

It was only as she turned off the light that she remembered Brad was coming the next day. She had been looking forward to it, but Eloise's call had put a damper on everything for her. It would be good to see him of course, and he always reminded her of her brother Jack. But his visit was no substitute for Eloise coming home for Christmas. There was no substitute for that, and nothing to soothe her sense of loss. Her heart felt like a bowling ball as she climbed into bed.

8

FAITH WAS THINKING OF CALLING ZOE THE NEXT MORN-
ing to tell her Ellie's plans. And then she decided not to
after all. Zoe was studying for exams that week, and self-
ishly Faith didn't want to give her any ideas. There was
no question in her mind that she wanted Zoe home. She
didn't want her deciding to go skiing in Vermont, or go
to the West Coast with friends—since she was still eighteen and Faith could still control what she did. Christmas
was Christmas, and she wanted her home. She decided
to tell her about Ellie going to Saint Moritz later in the
week, unless for some reason the girls spoke to each
other first. But they seldom called each other. The time
difference complicated things, and they lived in very
separate worlds. Faith was still upset, however, that Ellie
had called her father first, and that he had endorsed her
plans without discussing it with Faith. It made her feel
shut out, and as though they were in collusion with each
other, which to some extent they were. It was the nature
of their relationship and who they were. They were both
quiet and secretive, and somewhat uncommunicative,

and as Faith thought about it, she realized that she had forgotten to tell Ellie she had confirmed the two classes at NYU. But she had been so bowled over by her plans not to come home, that it had slipped Faith's mind. Maybe Alex had told her, although Faith doubted it. He wouldn't have considered it a piece of good news. And if he had said anything, Faith was sure that Ellie would have commented, even if only to disapprove. She was very definitely Daddy's girl, and had just proved it once again.

For the rest of the day, Faith was busy with errands and things she had to do. She bought paper to wrap their gifts, groceries, and a list of things Zoe had asked her to pick up before she got home. Faith was home by four, and in the bathtub when Brad called. She smiled as soon as she heard his voice. It was the way she used to feel when she heard from Jack.

"Hi, Fred. I'm at the hotel. I just got in. What do we have planned?"

"Nothing I know of. I'm all yours. Alex is in L.A. It worked out perfectly. Do you want me to fix you dinner?" She had bought a few extra things in case he wanted her to, but he laughed.

"What kind of big brother would I be if I didn't take my kid sister out for a decent meal? How about dinner in SoHo or something like that? Or would you rather stay uptown?"

"Anything you like." She smiled delightedly. It was good just to hear his voice. "All I want is to see you."

"I'll figure something out. I'll pick you up at seven-thirty. There's an Italian place I used to love in the East Village. I'll ask the concierge what he thinks."

"I can't wait to see you." She was smiling when she hung up, and she realized that the prospect of seeing him took some of the sting out of Ellie's defection. The thought of the four of them not being together for Christmas had really upset her. And she realized that Brad was going through the same thing, or worse, with both his boys in Zambia. It was depressing. Gone the days of putting out cookies and milk for Santa and hanging stockings by the chimney. Celebrating Christmas without either or both of her children was a daunting prospect.

But she had put Ellie out of her mind again when Brad rang the door at seven-thirty. She was wearing black slacks and a black cashmere sweater and a big red cashmere coat, and high-heeled black suede boots. Her shimmering blond hair was pulled back in a neat ponytail and she was wearing big gold earrings.

"Wow, Fred! You look like one of Santa's helpers!" He put his arms around her and gave her an enormous hug, and lifted her off the ground as he did it. It was the same thing he had done when they were children. And when he set her down, he took a step back to look at her, and smiled with pleasure. "You look terrific. All the boys in law school are going to fall in love with you."

"Hardly. I'm old enough to be their mother." He looked terrific to her too. He had a slight tan from playing tennis in California, which made his eyes seem more green, and his dark hair looked thick and well groomed. He was lucky, time had not touched his hairline. And his body looked powerful and muscular even in the suit and coat he was wearing.

"You don't look like anyone's mother, Fred. Are you ready for dinner? I got a reservation at a place the concierge recommended. He thought you'd like it."

"I don't care if we eat hot dogs in the subway. I'm just glad to see you," she said, as she locked the front door. He had a cab waiting for them, and he took her hand as he led her across the sidewalk. He was in great spirits, and happy to see her.

She settled next to him in the cab, and they chatted on the way downtown. They were having dinner in SoHo. She told him about Ellie's call the day before, and her own disappointment over it.

"It sucks, doesn't it?" he said honestly. "I hated Thanksgiving without Dylan and Jason. It was our first holiday without them. And Christmas won't be much better. Pam has planned a new form of torture. A dinner on Christmas Day for a hundred. With luck, I'll be in jail, visiting a client. I don't care where the boys are next year, I'm going to see them. I should have done that this year. Maybe you should all go to Saint Moritz and surprise Eloise." Faith laughed at the prospect.

"I bet she'd love that, and so would the boyfriend. At least we'll have Zoe. I haven't told her yet, I didn't want her getting any bright ideas like her sister." But Zoe was younger. At eighteen, Faith could insist that she come home. At Eloise's age, it was harder to do, particularly if she had the approval of her father. "She called Alex before she called me, and apparently he told her it was fine with him. I didn't want to be the heavy, so I agreed. He never even told me." Her complaints about Alex weren't new to Brad. She'd been sharing them with him for the past two months. He thought she was getting a raw deal from him, and always had, but he had been cautious so far in how he voiced it. He didn't want to offend her. But his point of view was very much what Jack's had been, and her brother had always been outspoken about how much he disliked Alex.

"It's amazing how kids play games, isn't it? And our mates along with them. Pam told them not to worry about coming home from college for Christmas one year, because she wanted to go on a cruise without them. She didn't even tell me till she'd bought the tickets, and by then they had other plans. I was seasick for two weeks on the cruise from hell, and I told her the next time she did that, I'd divorce her." But from what Faith could see, she was still doing what she wanted. "The boys were ecstatic. They went home with a friend from Las Vegas, and spent the holidays with a couple of showgirls. They still talk about it as their favorite Christmas." He grinned and she laughed along with him. Just seeing him and being with him reminded her in a nice way of her brother. It was the best Christmas gift of all being able to see him, and not just send e-mails. He had been remarkably devoted for the past two months, and this time neither of them had any intention of losing touch with the other. They had come to rely on their constant communication, by phone and e-mail.

They chatted easily on the way to the restaurant. He talked about his latest cases that had come in, and as they drove past NYU, he reminded her optimistically that she would be there soon, at the law school, and she smiled. It was easy just being with him, and talking about things. She admitted to him how hurt she had been when Ellie said she wasn't coming home.

"It's hard, Fred," he said, looking gently at her, "we have to be pretty thick-skinned. It's not easy watching them grow up and go away. I can't believe how much I've missed my boys this year. But it's their job to try their wings, and ours to let them fly away. Tough stuff, I know," he said, taking her hand. They held hands comfortably until they reached the restaurant. And she was startled by how cozy it was. It was an adorable little Italian place. The waiter gave them a table in a quiet corner, and she and Brad settled in. She dropped her coat over the back of the chair, in case she got cold. And Brad couldn't help noticing again how pretty she was. "I forget what you look like sometimes," he teased. "When I get your e-mails, you're ten years old again in my head, or at the most fourteen. And then suddenly, when I see you, you're all grown up."

"It's funny. It happens to me too. In my mind's eye, you're always about fourteen and I'm twelve. Remember the time we put the frog in Jack's bed?" She laughed just thinking of it, and so did Brad.

"Yes, I do. He damn near killed me for it. He put a snake in mine the next time I came over, as revenge. I hated those corn snakes of his."

"Me too." They ordered dinner then, and a half bottle of white wine. It was the perfect place to have come, it was quiet and pretty, and peaceful just sitting there with him. And with Alex away, they had all the time in the world.

"So what do you think will happen now, when you start classes in January?" In both their minds, the LSAT prep class didn't really count, although it was hard work. Brad asked with curiosity, after they finished their salad, and waited for the main course, "Do you think Alex will get used to it, or go berserk?" He didn't know about the LSAT class she'd been taking so couldn't object.

"I think he'll complain. But the truth is, we hardly see each other. We barely speak. He comes in, eats dinner, goes to bed. And a couple of days a week he goes on business trips. He wants a lot less attention from me than he thinks," she said practically. She had it all worked out in her head.

"And what about you?" Brad asked pointedly. "What do you want from him, Fred?" It was the kind of question Jack used to ask her, and that she seldom asked herself. Faith was a woman who made few demands, and admitted to few needs. She had taken care of herself emotionally for a long time, just as she had as a child, with the exception of Jack's support.

"I don't need much," she said quietly, lowering her eyes and looking down at her hands. "I have everything I want," she said, glancing back up at him.

"I didn't mean materially, I mean what do you need from him to make your life work?" It was a question he had recently asked himself.

"My life works the way it is. Besides, Alex isn't someone who's open to meeting other people's needs." He was shut down, and had always been. It was something she had accepted about him for a long time.

"How nice for him, if he can get away with it. Who's there for you, Fred?" The question was blunt and to the point, as Faith shrugged. For a variety of reasons, she had isolated herself in recent years. She had needed time to grieve Jack's death. And she had focused all her emotional energies on the girls in their last years at home. Alex hadn't enjoyed socializing with her much in recent years. He was consumed by his work. And particularly since Jack's death, she had drifted away from her friends. She had become very solitary, which made her all the more grateful for Brad's friendship now. It was easier to let him in because he was part of her childhood and had been so close to Jack. In some ways, she had not yet recovered from her brother's death.

"All I really need are my kids. They're always there for me." She had reduced her needs to that, and it was all that mattered now.

"Really? It doesn't sound like Ellie's on that team, if she's going to Saint Moritz over the holidays. She's meeting her own needs, although that's standard behavior for one's kids." He was blunt about what he saw, and it bothered him that Eloise was so kind to her father, and so hard on Faith.

"She's young," Faith said rapidly, willing to make excuses for her, as she was for everyone else, and always had been. Where others around her were critical, Faith always made an affort to excuse and forgive. She was generous to a fault.

"The truth is that most of the time anyway, our kids aren't there for us. It's not their job to be. They're too busy putting together their own lives," Brad said philosophically. "But it kind of makes you wonder sometimes who's there for us, if anyone. It's great if you have a big family, brothers and sisters, a supportive spouse. But if not, who does that leave? It's not a trick question, by the way. I don't know the answer to it myself. I was thinking about it on the plane on the way here. Pam is so busy with her own life, and her own concerns, I'm not sure if I needed her, she'd be there. That's a hell of a realization to make. I had to go to the hospital for a checkup recently, just ordinary stuff, but they asked for the name of who to call in an emergency. I put down my secretary's name after I thought about it. Because I figured if they called Pam, she wouldn't take the call. It was kind of a wake-up call for me."

"What are you going to do about it?" she asked, as

they set down a big juicy steak in front of him, and grilled sole in front of Faith.

"Absolutely nothing," he said honestly. "But occasionally, it does me good to face reality. I used to have a lot of illusions about what marriage should be. And the truth is, it never was. Not ours in any case, and not my parents'. They hated each other for years until they got divorced. They did a lot of ugly stuff to each other when they did, and they hardly talked for years afterward. I never wanted to have a marriage like that, and I don't. Pam and I don't hate each other, thank God, I'm not sure what we feel for each other anymore, if anything. We're friends, I guess, or something like that. Or maybe just strangers who live at the same address." It was a painful admission to make, but he had resigned himself to it years before, just as Faith had made her peace with the way Alex treated her, and how little he involved himself in her daily life. But she hoped that he would be there for her if she ever got sick. But failing that, he offered very little in terms of daily involvement and support. He was more interested in his own life, and had been for a long time. She couldn't even remember when it had gotten that way, or how different it had been before. Probably not much. She had just been busy with the girls, and hadn't had time to observe how absent he was. Even when his body was there, his heart and mind were not.

"You know," Faith said thoughtfully, "it's more of a statement about us than about them. Their needs are being met, or they are living out their fantasies about marriage, or their histories. Neither of them seems to need much from us, or wants to be particularly involved. We see it differently, and want more, I guess, but we're willing to accept the little they mete out. What do you suppose that says about us?"

"I used to think it made me a good guy. Lately, I'm not so sure. I think it's more about cowardice and maintaining the status quo than about much else. I don't want to make waves. I don't want to fight with her. I never want a divorce. I want to finish my life the way I started it, on the same path, with the same house, the same wife, the same job I have now. I think I hate change, because of the way I grew up. My parents were constantly threatening each other, one was always about to move out. I grew up worrying about what was going to happen, and then finally it did. I don't want to live like that now. I don't want any surprises like that."

"Neither do I," Faith said with a comfortable sigh. It was nice talking about it with him. She used to do it with Jack, but there had been no one to fill that role since he died.

"We pay a high price for it though," Brad commented as he finished his steak, and set his knife and fork down on his plate. Faith had only eaten half of her fish, but she had a small appetite, which was reflected by her tiny figure. "You sacrifice a lot when you compromise, especially when you're willing to let someone else set the terms. I guess I must figure it's worth it, or I wouldn't do it. The price of peace." He was remarkably honest, and she admired him for it. He knew what he had given up, and he seemed comfortable with it. In its own way, his was not unlike her life. Except Alex was a little more dictatorial with her than Pam was with Brad. They seemed to have solved it by going their separate ways. She and Alex still shared a life, at least most of the time, even if they didn't communicate much, or share their thoughts. She hadn't confided in him in years.

"It's lonely sometimes," Faith said softly, as though afraid to say the words. It was something she seldom even admitted to herself, but felt safe saying to him now. She felt safe with him, and always had.

"Yes, it is," he agreed, and took her hand in his again. It was wonderful being with her. "Do you miss Jack as much as I do, Fred?" he asked after a long moment, and she nodded and looked into his eyes, hers were brimming with tears.

"Yes, I do, especially at this time of year. I don't know why. I miss him all the time. Christmas shouldn't be different from any other time, but somehow it is."

"I don't miss Debbie though," Brad commented honestly, and Faith laughed.

"God, no. She was such a bitch. Talk about sacrificing everything for peace. I'll never know why Jack put up with her. She was awful to him. I don't know how many times she left him, or threatened to. She'd have driven me insane. At least Alex goes his own way, and does his own thing, and it sounds like Pam does too. Debbie was constantly in his face."

"He was crazy about her though," Brad reminded her. "I couldn't figure it out myself. I think it's one of the reasons he and I saw less and less of each other. She hated me, and I wasn't too fond of her. It kind of got in the way with me and Jack."

"You know, she walked away without ever looking back," Faith explained as she sat back in her chair against the red coat, which looked like a giant flower engulfing her. "Her lawyer let us know she was getting remarried and moving away. She never called. She never wrote. I never heard from her again."

"That stinks," Brad said, and Faith agreed.

"Much as I dislike her, I wish Jack had had kids with her, or with someone at least. It would be so wonderful to have his children now. This way, there's nothing left . . . just the memories . . . and not much else," Faith said, fighting back tears again, as Brad squeezed her hand.

"We have each other, Fred. That's what he left us. All the good times we shared, all those memories, all those years when we were kids." She nodded in answer, and for a moment couldn't speak.

They had cappuccino after dinner, and decided to skip dessert. And Faith was surprised when Brad looked straight at her. "Do you suppose there are any good marriages, Fred? I wonder sometimes. When I look around at the people we know, I don't think there's a single one of them who has something I'd want. It sounds cynical, but I'm beginning to think no one's dreams ever come true. We all kid ourselves about what we're getting when we start out, and how it'll turn out, and in the end, we all end up like you and I. Making compromises that cost us a hell of a lot, and being grateful for our kids and old friends to get us by."

"That's a sad way to look at it, Brad. I like to think that somebody out there is happy. I have friends who are. At least I think they are. I can't say I'm not. I just don't have what I thought I would with Alex. It's different, that's all." And she didn't say it to him, but her faith sustained her, and added another dimension to her life. She had always been very devout, as was Jack. Brad had always admired them both for that, and envied them their faith.

"I think you're kidding yourself, Fred. We wouldn't be e-mailing each other for old times' sake, if we had what we want in our marriages. Our kids wouldn't be the hub of our lives to the extent that they are. We might even be happy when they finally grow up and go away. What do you think you have with Alex, Fred? What would you say, honestly? I think I had a friend and a business associate in Pam, and now that we don't work together we're just friends, if that. We're roommates, and not much more." Listening to him, it sounded sad to her, but he seemed comfortable with it. He was remarkably honest, both with her and himself. He had few illusions left, and no dreams.

"I think Alex and I are friends," she said thoughtfully, though he thought she was being overly generous, from all he'd heard from her. But she didn't delude herself

that they were still in love. They were not, but they had
been once. Or at least, she had been in love with him. She
was no longer sure how much emotion Alex was capable of. Probably less than she had once hoped. "We support each other. No, that's wrong," she corrected herself,
"I support him. And he provides for me. He's a good father to the girls, he's responsible. He's a decent human
being." She was struggling to find more, and having
trouble coming up with words to describe what he was
to her. He was solid, she could count on him. But he
didn't give her much emotionally, and hadn't in years.

"See what I mean? It's not exactly what you thought
marriage would be, is it, Fred? When I take a good look, I
see the same thing. But just like you, I wouldn't change it.
I don't think there would be much point. I think the conclusion I've come to is that you get what you get, and you
make the best of it. But the truth is, it leaves a lot of holes
in your life to fill. You fill it with kids, with friends, with
work, with dreams, with fantasies, with regrets, with
whatever works. But no matter what you fill it with, or
how hard you try to kid yourself, the holes are still there."

"That's a tough way to look at it," Faith said, a little
shaken by what he'd said, but she couldn't disagree.

"I'd rather be honest with myself. When I wasn't,
I was desperately unhappy, and constantly trying to
make my relationship with Pam into something it could
never be, and her into someone she never was. Once I
accepted what it was, and wasn't, and who she was in

my life, and who she could never be, I think I finally made my peace with all of it."

"Is there someone else in your life?" she asked openly. It was a question she would have asked Jack, but there had never been for him. He had been too obsessed with Debbie to ever cheat on her, although she had cheated on him, and he had been devastated by it when he found out. But no matter what she did to him, he had always taken her back. Faith had always felt that her brother had taken forgiveness and loyalty to an insane degree, where his wife was concerned at least. But it was also what she'd loved in him.

"There was someone else once," Brad answered as candidly as her brother would have. "I think Pam suspected it, but she never made an issue of it. I don't think she wanted to know. But those things can't go anywhere. They frustrate everyone if you want to stay in your marriage, which I did, and still do. People get hurt. I never felt right about it, and I never did it again. It's easier this way." He seemed at peace with his situation as it was.

"Would you divorce Pam if you fell in love with someone else?" Faith asked, curious about him now. What he had said over dinner fascinated her, and he was equally intrigued by her, and what made her tick, now that she was an adult, what compromises she had made, in comparison to his own.

"Never," he said, looking absolutely convinced. "When I married Pam, I meant what I said. For better or worse. Until death do us part. I'm not going to make the same mistakes my parents made. I owe it to my kids, and even now that they're grown up, relatively, they don't need all the misery of parents who hate each other, won't speak to each other, and destroy everything they ever built. I just wouldn't divorce her. And I'm not going to fall in love with anyone else. I wouldn't let that happen again."

"Neither would I," Faith said quietly, although she had had no opportunities, but she wouldn't have taken them if she had. For religious reasons if nothing else. But mostly out of respect for her marriage. "I feel the same way about it you do," she concurred. "All you do is trade one set of problems for another. There are no perfect lives."

"We're a sorry pair, the two of us," he laughed, as he paid the check, and then he looked at her seriously. "I'm glad we found each other again, Fred. You're like a gift in my life. You suddenly make it all worthwhile . . . like a gold coin you thought you lost years ago, and find in the back of a drawer, and not only is it as beautiful as it once was, but you discover it's become even more valuable than it used to be. I love talking to you, and e-mailing you, and getting e-mails from you. You really brighten my days."

She smiled at him, grateful for what he said. And she felt the same way about him. "It's your fault I'm going back to school. When I'm doing homework at three A.M., I'll blame you," she teased.

"When you pass the bar, you can leave Alex and come and work for me."

"Now that would make his worst nightmares come true!" She laughed, and they left the restaurant arm in arm. It was after eleven o'clock by then, and he had to get up early the next day.

"Have you got time to see me tomorrow?" he asked, as they walked down Prince Street, and he hailed a cab.

"Sure. Alex is in L.A. until the end of the week. And Zoe isn't due till the weekend. I'm a free woman, and I've finished my Christmas shopping," she said proudly, as he made a face.

"I haven't even started mine. I have to do it when I go home." In his case, it meant a quick stop at Tiffany for Pam. She loved jewelry, and she usually told him exactly what she wanted and had seen recently, to make it easy for him. And it was too complicated to send anything to the boys. He was going to bring them gifts when he went to visit them in the spring. And other than that, he wanted to buy a watch for his secretary, and could do that at Tiffany too. His shopping was of the male variety, done in one or two stores, in under an hour, on Christmas Eve. "Do you want to have dinner again tomorrow night? I think there's a dinner for the conference, but I can duck out of it. Why don't I pick you up at six o'clock? I'll talk to the concierge again and see what he recommends. I thought tonight was pretty good."

"I thought it was great. My fish was perfect, and I loved the wine." She hadn't even finished one glass, and Brad laughed at what she said.

"You still eat like a bird, Fred. It's a wonder you don't

starve to death." But she had always been like that, even when they were teenagers. Half the time, she just nibbled invisible quantities of food, and then she'd surprise everyone by eating two hot dogs and a banana split. She had loved banana splits when she was a kid.

He put an arm around her in the cab, and she cuddled up next to him comfortably on the ride home. It was cozy, and she felt safe just being with him. He nourished a deep inner part of her that had been hungry ever since Jack's death. It was a part of her that Alex had never fed.

He got out of the cab and told the driver to wait when they reached her house, and he watched while she turned off the alarm and let herself into the neat little brownstone house.

"I'll see you tomorrow night. I'll call before I come, and let you know what we're doing. Do you want to go someplace fancy?" He would have taken her anywhere she wanted, but she was quick to shake her head.

"I loved tonight. I don't care if we do pizza, or pasta, or burritos. I just want to hang out with you," she said, and he gave her another hug as she beamed. The evening had been everything she wanted it to be.

"See you tomorrow!" he called out the window, as he drove away in the cab, with a wave, and she closed the door and locked it. And as she walked up the stairs to her bedroom in her big red coat, she had a sense of peace that she hadn't had in years.

9

BRAD PICKED HER UP, AS PROMISED, AT SIX O'CLOCK THE next night. All he had told her was that they were going for a simple dinner, and to dress warm, which she had. She wore a big down coat, and a green turtleneck sweater the same color as her eyes, black velvet pants, and fur-trimmed boots. It had gotten cold that day.

"So where are we going?" she asked when he picked her up. He had given the driver the address before she got in.

"You'll see," he said mysteriously.

They stopped at Saks Fifth Avenue, and walked across the street, and she realized then that they were going to Rockefeller Center, to eat dinner, and watch the people skate around the rink. They sat at a table right in front of the big picture window, and it was fun watching people twirl and do pirouettes and do camel spins, and others stagger around and fall down. Everyone looked like they were having fun, and there were lots of kids among the adults.

"Remember when the three of us used to go skating

in Central Park?" Faith asked with eyes full of happy memories and a broad smile. He had thought of taking her there, but decided on this instead. He thought the Wollman Rink in the park would have reminded her too much of Jack, as it would him. They had had so many adventures together, and he had loved them all. Being kids in New York then had been fun. They had lived on the Upper East Side, in a real neighborhood just north of Yorkville, and he and Jack had gone to the same school.

"Obviously I remember," he said with a superior expression. "That's why we're here. I thought maybe after dinner, we'd take a spin. Or a spill as the case may be. I haven't skated in about twenty years. They don't iceskate much in California." The three of them had gone skating as kids at least once or twice a week. Jack had even been on the hockey team at school.

"You mean skate? Here?" She looked surprised and amused, but she loved the idea. "That would be fun!"

"I'm glad you think so too. You can pick me up when I fall flat on my ass."

"Don't count on it. I haven't skated since we were kids." She had taken the girls skating frequently when they were small, but sat on the sidelines and watched.

"Good. Then we're evenly matched."

They ordered dinner, and Faith realized she was rushing through it so they could get to the ice. He had timed it perfectly. They had a six-thirty reservation, and finished punctually at eight o'clock, just in time for the next session. They went into the locker room to rent

skates, while a man on the Zamboni was cleaning the
ice. And by the time they had the skates on, the session
had begun.

Faith ventured out gingerly onto the ice before Brad.
She felt unsteady at first, and wondered if it had been
too long. But by the time she had gone around the rink
twice, she was surprised by how confident she was beginning to feel. Brad was skating alongside her by then,
unsteadily initially, but like her, he found his sea legs
faster than he thought. They had both been fairly decent
skaters once upon a time. And within half an hour, they
were skating around the rink happily hand in hand, and
having a great time.

"I can't believe I can still do this," Faith said, feeling
surprisingly competent, with bright pink cheeks and
her hair flying in the wind, as she looked up at Brad. She
was glad she had brought gloves with her, after his
warning to dress warm. She had had no idea what he
had in mind, and wondered if he wanted to go for a long
walk, or something equally sedate. She had never anticipated this, but was thrilled he'd thought of it. It was
like a time warp into their past.

"You're still pretty good, Fred." He had no sooner
said it than she took a spill on the ice, but he gave her a
hand up as they both laughed, and took off again.

Two hours later, they were both exhausted, but
delighted with what they'd done. They turned in the
skates with regret, but Brad admitted that if he had

stayed on his skates for another hour, he might have died.

"I must be getting old," he complained unconvincingly, but he didn't fool Faith. "I'm going to ache from head to foot tomorrow."

"Me too, but it was worth every minute of it," she smiled. She hadn't had as much fun since she was a child. It had been a terrific idea. "God, do you remember all those times we went skating with all your friends, and you guys let me tag along. You were always trying to chase girls, and I was always screwing it up for both of you. I used to do it to you on purpose, because I had such a big crush on you. I was about twelve or thirteen."

"So how come I didn't marry you instead of Pam? Dumb, I guess," he teased. There was no romantic overtone between them and hadn't been since they were kids in their early teens.

"I think I got over the crush when I was fourteen," she laughed. It had actually been sixteen, when he went to college and she discovered other boys. But until then, for about eight years, she had thought the sun rose and set on Brad. And now that they had found each other again, she still did.

They walked slowly up toward Fifth Avenue, glowing from the cold, and feeling the exercise, but they were both relaxed and at peace. And as they stood on the corner, looking for a cab, Faith looked up at St. Patrick's Cathedral and had an idea.

"Do you want to go in and light a candle for Jack?"

she asked solemnly, and the look in her eyes nearly broke his heart. She lit candles for him at mass several times a week.

"Sure." He hadn't been to church in years, although he had gone to church with her and Jack and their mother when they were all kids. He was Episcopalian, but he liked the pomp and ceremony of the Catholic Church, and had taken communion with them once or twice to see what it was like in a Catholic church, and was surprised to find it was no different than in his. The Catholic Church had always seemed more mysterious and impressive to him. And Jack dared him to go to confession once, and he was surprised by how kind the priest had been.

There was a lot about Catholicism that had always appealed to him, although he had drifted away from his own church too in recent years. Faith still went to church regularly, but Alex wasn't religious, and resisted it energetically, and she had never been able to sell it to her kids. It was something she did on her own, but she had gone more frequently ever since her brother died. Instead of once or twice, she now went several times a week. It gave her a sense of communion with him, and of peace. It was the only way she had found consolation from his death. Brad didn't say anything as he followed her across the street to the church.

It was just after ten o'clock, and the doors were still open. There were beautiful Christmas decorations and poinsettias everywhere, and the church was spectacularly lit. It was an impressive sight, as they walked in, and just stood there, looking around.

There were altars to individual saints all along the sides, and banks of candles in front of them, and the main altar stood at the end of the central aisle, straight ahead. She made the sign of the cross, and side by side, they walked to the front of the church. It was almost as though she could feel Jack walking with them.

They slipped quietly into a pew, and sat there for a while, and she knelt and prayed, for Jack and her mother, and Charles, and her daughters finally, and then, still on her knees, she turned to smile at Brad. He had never seen her look more beautiful. It was almost as though there were an aura of peace around her, and a look of great tenderness in her eyes.

"I feel him here, with us," she whispered. They both knew who she was talking about, and Brad nodded, with tears in his eyes, and then knelt next to her.

"Me too." And then he bowed his head and closed his eyes.

It was just like the old days, skating together, and going to church. The only one missing was Jack, but it didn't really seem as though he was.

It was a while before they both looked up, and then walked past the main altar, to the smaller ones in honor of the saints. Faith genuflected down to one knee as they crossed the center of the church. And he followed her to the altar of Saint Jude. He had always been her favorite saint.

She slipped a five-dollar bill into the slot, lit a candle for Jack, and then held the burning stick toward Brad so he could light one himself. It had always seemed magical to him, as though something as powerful as that could only result in good things, and they stood side by side for a moment, thinking of her brother, in silent prayer. And then he took her hand, and they walked slowly away. They stopped just before they left the church, and Faith dipped her fingers in the holy water, made the sign of the cross, and smiled up at him.

"Thank you for coming here with me," she whispered. She'd been to church earlier that week, but it meant more to her now, because he was here, as though their combined prayers were more powerful, as though it meant more to pray for Jack with him.

Brad was silent as he followed her outside, deeply moved. It had been years since he'd been to church, and he was surprised by how much it had just meant to him, or maybe it was just going with her, and the memories it stirred, of the three of them.

"Do you still have your rosary?" he asked, as they walked down the steps of St. Patrick's hand in hand. He felt even closer to her than he had in a long time, as though she were his sister now too, his blood, and not simply his friend.

"Yes."

"Do you still say them?" He had always been fascinated by it when she was a young girl. He liked the rituals and the pageantry. Jack used to tease him about it and say he should convert and become a priest.

"Sometimes. More in the last few years, because of Jack. Sometimes I just stop in at church and pray for him." Brad nodded, not wanting to ask her why, or just what exactly she thought it did. For him, it was enough that she wanted to, and that it made sense to her. It always had. She had even said once or twice as a little girl that she wanted to be a nun. But Jack hated the idea and told her to forget about it. And as time went on, and she grew up, she was far more interested in having babies and getting married, which seemed healthier to him.

"Do you and Pam ever go to church?" she asked as they stood on Fifth Avenue. It was time to take her home, but he hated to leave.

He smiled at her question. "Pam is a confirmed atheist, or agnostic, I'm never sure which. She firmly believes there is no God." He said it simply, without judging her. It was just who she was, and what she believed. His own beliefs had always been a little vague as to their form, but he did believe in God.

"How sad," Faith said, and Brad smiled down at her. There was something so pure about Faith sometimes, he loved that in her, and had when she was a little girl. "What about the boys?"

"I don't think they're sure, or care much either way. I haven't exactly taken their religious life in hand. I just figured they'd do what they want one day. I haven't been in church in years. Do you and Alex go to church?"

"He's Episcopalian like you, and never goes. I don't think he's an atheist. He just hates going to church and thinks it's a waste of time. He thinks it's something women do. And the girls never want to go, except to light a candle for someone once in a while."

"I always thought that was magical, when we were kids. Like making a wish. I always believed all prayers were answered. I think your mother told me that they were." She had been a deeply religious woman, which had gotten her through a lot of her unhappiness being married to Charles in the early years, and her first husband before that, although she never admitted to being unhappy in either case. There had been a lot of secrets and denial in Faith's family in those days.

"I used to think all prayers were answered too," Faith said sadly. Other people's, if not her own.

"And now?" Brad looked at her intently.

"Sometimes I'm not so sure."

"Because of Jack?" he asked softly, looking into her eyes in the crisp December night, as their breath shot out plumes of frost in the cold air. She nodded in answer. "You know, it's funny. I'm not religious. I never have been. I never really went to church, except with you two and your mom, when we were kids. But I still believe what she told me, about all prayers being answered."

Faith looked sober as she pondered what he'd said. "I wish I were as sure." Life was no longer as simple as it had seemed then. Even in the worst moments of her life, she had relied on her faith.

"I still think they are." There was a lump in his throat as he said it, and she couldn't tell if the tears in his eyes were from the cold or something else. "And I think Jack would think so too."

Faith didn't answer him, she only nodded. She tucked a hand in his arm then, and they walked slowly up Fifth Avenue, not saying a word.

10

BRAD LEFT NEW YORK ON FRIDAY AFTERNOON, THE DAY
after they'd gone skating. He called her in the morning
to tell her how stiff and achy he was, and how he could
hardly get out of bed in his hotel. But he had never had
a better time. He wanted to stop by the house and say
good-bye to her, but as it turned out, he didn't have
time, and had to rush to make his plane. He called her
from the airport instead.

"I wanted to give you a hug and wish you a Merry
Christmas, Fred," he said sadly. He was disappointed
not to see her one last time. "I had such a good time last
night. The best ever. We'll have to do it again the next
time I come to town," but he had no plans. And he seldom came to New York anymore, except for conferences
like the one he'd attended. When he worked for his
father-in-law's firm, he had come all the time.

"I had a great time too," she said, feeling nostalgic. It
had been so wonderful seeing him, and now that he was
going back to California, it was like saying good-bye to
part of Jack again. "I'm glad we went to St. Patrick's."

"So am I. Maybe I'll go light a candle for him sometime in San Francisco. I believe in that. It still seems special."

"I know," she nodded. "I'll light one for you at midnight mass on Christmas Eve. Usually I can get Zoe to
come to that with me." It made Brad think he should do
that instead of Pam's Christmas dinner. But on Christmas Eve they didn't do much. They usually had dinner
at her father's, and then came home and went to bed.
With the boys away, they had decided not to have a
Christmas tree that year.

"When is Zoe coming home?" He had forgotten, but
he knew it was in the next few days. And Alex was due
home the next day. Brad had come into the house the
night before for a few minutes, when he dropped her
off. And Faith had shown him the study where she kept
her computer and wrote him e-mails. It was a small cozy
room full of photographs and what she called sentimental debris. But he liked seeing where she wrote to him.
He could visualize her that way.

"Zoe will be home tonight," she answered him, when
he called from the airport. "Things will get crazy after
that. Kids in and out of the house at all hours, clothes
everywhere, and pizzas delivered in the middle of the
night."

"I really miss that these days," he said, sounding sad.
He would have liked to see her again. "I'll call you over
the weekend. I'll be in the office both days. Take care of
yourself, Fred."

"You too. And thanks for two wonderful evenings. I loved it."

"So did I." They announced his plane then, and he had to go. "Light a candle for me the next time you go to church. I can always use some extra help."

"I'll do that. Have a good flight," she said as he hurried off the phone, and then she sat, thinking of him. It was so odd having him back in her life, and wonderful. It was a real gift. Seeing him had been the best of all possible Christmas presents, except if Ellie had come home. She still had to tell Zoe her sister was going to Switzerland for the holidays. But all she could think of now was the time she had just spent with Brad, and what it had meant to her. Their conversation over both dinners had been meaningful, and she had loved skating with him. It was amazing how easily they still opened up to each other, just like the old days, only better, because they were wiser now. It was so comfortable talking to him. In some ways, he was even easier to talk to than Jack had been. They had always disagreed about things like their mother's marriage, Faith had seen her as lonely and unhappy all her life, while Jack thought Charlie was a decent guy and his sister was too critical of him. And they had never seen eye to eye about their respective mates. She hadn't liked Debbie, and he had hated Alex. But there were no loyalties at issue with Brad, and they saw most things the same way, from the same side. It made her sad to realize how much he had compromised in his marriage. And she felt sorry for him. Pam sounded like the wrong woman for him, but it was obvious that he was entrenched for life. It was noble of him, but seemed misguided somehow, to her at least. But he might have said the same thing about Alex. Neither of them were easy marriages or mates, but they were whom and what they had chosen, and had decided to stand by. She respected him for it, and at the same time, pitied him.

She sent him an e-mail that night, thanking him for the dinners, and the skating. And just as she sent it, Zoe walked in, with four suitcases, her tennis racket, a camera bag, and her computer under one arm. She dumped it all in the front hall and walked into the kitchen. She was pouring herself a glass of milk as her mother walked in.

"Welcome home." Faith put her arms around her and gave her a warm hug, and offered to make her something to eat, but she said she'd had a sandwich in the airport on the way home. She helped herself to some ice cream, and sat down on the kitchen table with a grin, as Faith smiled at her.

"This is a sight for sore eyes. It sure is good to have you here." She was home for three weeks, and Faith was thrilled.

"Feels good to be here too," she grinned, polishing off the vanilla ice cream. "When's Ellie coming home?" she asked as Faith's face clouded visibly.

"She's not. She's going to Switzerland, to Saint Moritz, to ski with Geoff and his family."

"Are you serious?" Zoe looked stunned. "Is she

going to marry him?" It was the only reason she could think of for Eloise not to come home, meeting her in-laws, or staying in Europe to get engaged.

"Not that I know of. She just wanted to do it for the fun of it."

"And you let her, Mom?" Zoe couldn't get over it. The holidays were important to Faith, and Zoe couldn't imagine her mother letting her older sister off the hook that easily, but Faith wouldn't have, if Alex hadn't said she could.

"She called Dad first apparently, and he told her it was all right with him. So I let her get away with it this time, but I told her next year is mandatory. So don't get any ideas." Faith wagged a finger at her, and Zoe grinned.

"Don't worry, Mom. I'm not going anywhere. But it'll be weird not having her here." Zoe looked sad suddenly. It was hard to imagine Christmas without her sister, even if they didn't always get along with each other. It was going to seem very strange, and a little sad.

"I know it will," Faith agreed. "You get to be an only child for three weeks." Zoe's face brightened at that.

"Actually, that sounds pretty good. Where's Dad, by the way?"

"Flying home from California. He'll be back in a few hours." He had called from the airport to say he was coming home a day early, and said he was bone tired.

"I just wondered," Zoe said as she picked up the phone. Half an hour later, she was in her room, unpacking and dropping clothes all over the floor, her computer was set up, the front doorbell rang three times, and her best friends from high school had arrived. A pizza followed suit an hour later, and by the time Alex came home, there was loud music playing, the girls were laughing, and Zoe said they were going out. Utter chaos reigned, and Faith looked ecstatic, as Alex walked into their bedroom with a groan.

"We've been taken over by Martians," he complained. "The pizza delivery boy was going out as I came in. There was someone else delivering Chinese food, Zoe just borrowed a hundred dollars, and there are about two hundred girls in her room. I'd nearly forgotten what it's like when she's home. How long is her Christmas break?" He looked exhausted and desperate, and Faith had just turned off Zoe's tub before it overflowed. But she loved the life Zoe brought to the house. It made Faith feel alive again just having her there.

"She'll be home for three weeks. How was your trip?"

"Exhausting. But peaceful by comparison. Do you think we could ask her to turn down the music, or should I just wear earplugs for the next three weeks? Was it always like this?" He looked overwhelmed.

"Yes. That's why I'm so bored when they're not here." And then she looked at him, as he set down his briefcase, and collapsed in a chair.

"You didn't tell me you talked to Eloise about not coming home for Christmas." She tried to keep accusation out of her tone, but it was obvious nonetheless that she wasn't pleased. And she hadn't talked to him all week while he was in L.A. He had never called, nor had she.

"I must have forgotten to mention it," he said, looking vague.

"You could have said something to me before you agreed to let her do it. It put me on the spot when she called."

"Is she coming home?" He didn't look so much guilty as concerned. Another body in the house at this point would have driven him insane. He'd forgotten what the girls were like when they were home.

"No, she's not. She told me you had told her she could stay over there. It didn't leave me much room to tell her she couldn't go to Saint Moritz, without looking like a real shit. So I said she could."

"It'll be fun for her," he said, taking off his shoes.

"I told her she can't do it again. I want the girls home for Christmas every year, no matter what, and if we don't set the precedent now, they never will. There will always be something more tempting than coming home."

"She'll be fine," he said, placating her.

"I know she will. But I'll miss her anyway," Faith said, as the music in Zoe's room went up several decibels, and they heard a door slam.

"I won't," Alex said honestly. "Besides, they didn't get along over Thanksgiving anyway. I figured it might do them good to be apart for a while."

"It might have done them more good to see each other and make up," Faith said stubbornly. She believed in the closeness of families and all that that entailed. And as she listened to him, she was reminded of all that she and Brad had said for the past two days. There were times when she and Alex were at opposite poles. In fact, most of the time.

"Do you suppose you can get Zoe to turn her music down? I'm going to go nuts if she keeps this up for three weeks," he said, looking miserable, as he went to take a shower.

"Do you want dinner?" Faith asked over the din, as he paused in the bathroom doorway with an anguished expression.

"I ate on the plane. I just want to go to bed. Those kids will probably be up all night."

"She said they're going out. I'll ask her to keep the noise down."

"Thanks," he said, and closed the door. There had been no kiss, no hug, no affectionate greeting. He had simply walked into the room and begun to complain about the noise. She couldn't blame him for reacting to the disruption, but it would have been nice if he'd had something to say to her after being away for three days.

She stopped in to see Zoe and her friends a few minutes later and asked them to try to hold down the noise. There were two pizza boxes sitting open on her bed, while two of the girls ate pizza and watched TV, and Zoe dried her hair. And there was an assortment of

Chinese food waiting in the kitchen downstairs. Zoe had come home at full steam.

"Your father's going to bed in a little while, Zoe," Faith said quietly. "Maybe you guys could tone it down a little bit."

"We're going out soon, Mom," Zoe shouted over the hair dryer. "Three of my friends are coming over in a few minutes, we'll eat something here, and then we'll go out."

"Don't forget to turn off the TV and the stereo when you go downstairs."

"I promise." She did as she said, but when they finally thundered downstairs, Faith found Zoe's curling iron and her hot rollers blazing on the bathroom sink, and she had forgotten to empty the tub. It was useless to point it out to her. She always forgot anyway. She had also left two candles burning in the room, which worried Faith. She was always afraid they would burn down the house. Candles were a constant battle between them, and Zoe always accused her of being paranoid.

"Did they go out?" Alex asked hopefully, as Faith walked back into their room. He was in bed with a book, in pajamas, with freshly shampooed hair.

"No, but they will soon." She didn't tell him about the candles and the curling iron. She knew he would be frantic too. At Zoe's age, there were times when she had the body of a woman, and the mind of a child.

When Faith went downstairs to check on them, they

were eating Chinese food out of the boxes, and laughing hysterically. There were seven of them by then. And for an instant, she was almost relieved that Ellie hadn't come home to add her chaos to theirs, although she would have enjoyed it anyway. But Alex wouldn't have.

"I thought we'd go buy the Christmas tree tomorrow," Faith said over the others' heads.

"I can't, Mom. I'm getting my hair cut tomorrow, and I have to see my friends." It was a tradition Faith loved sharing with her. But things were very different these days. Their traditions seemed to be vanishing in thin air. "I'm sorry. Can we do it next week?" Christmas was only nine days away.

"Do you want to do it on Sunday?" Faith asked hopefully.

"I can't. I'm going to a party in Connecticut."

"If I buy it, will you decorate it with me?"

"I promise," Zoe said, as she gave her a hug, and the doorbell rang again. Four more girls arrived, and it was another half hour before they all left. Zoe promised to be home at a decent hour, but didn't say when. And Faith stayed in the kitchen to clean up the mess. She didn't want to complain about it on Zoe's first night home. It was easier to do it herself, and it didn't take long. And when she went back upstairs to see Alex, he was sound asleep. She turned off the light, and went back downstairs to her study. The house seemed suddenly peaceful and quiet, and she smiled to herself. In spite of the noise and the mess, she loved having Zoe home. This was the life she had reveled in for twenty-four years, and it was nice having it back again, even if only for a few weeks.

She sent an e-mail to Brad, although she knew he was still on the plane. He was probably almost back in San Francisco by then. It was the second e-mail she'd sent him that day.

"Dear Brad," she began, "well, chaos reigns. Music to my ears. Hair dryers, curling irons, pizzas arriving, Chinese food, giggling girls, rap music, stereos, TV, ice cream oozing down the counter to the kitchen floor. Zoe's home. And out again, with her friends. Alex came home from California in the midst of it all, and went to bed. He's asleep. She's out. I'm enjoying the onslaught, and by the time she leaves, I'll be off to school myself. How are you? Hope you had a good trip. It was wonderful seeing you again. I loved skating and both our dinners, and going to St. Patrick's with you. Come back soon. I miss you already. Interesting too to share our views on marriage and relationships, compromises, and the way things turn out in the end. We never used to talk about stuff like that when we were kids. Can't remember what we used to talk about. I think we just laughed a lot. I used to talk about this stuff a lot with Jack. Funny what we've ended up with, isn't it? Not the way it was supposed to work, but just the way it is. As long as the kids are around, I don't really mind. It's harder when they're away. Then you are more aware of what you've got, and what you don't.

"I wanted to buy the tree with Zoe tomorrow. She can

spare me an hour in three weeks. We might have to put
the tree up for Easter this year. Guess I'll buy it by myself. It's okay. As long as she's here. This house is like a
tomb when she's gone.

"Don't work too hard this weekend. Talk to you soon.
Love, Fred."

She sat at her desk for a couple of hours, answering
correspondence after that. And at midnight in New
York, she had an e-mail from Brad.

"Hi . . . just got home. Turned my computer on, to
write to you, and there you were. Send me some of that
noise. I have the other side of that coin, bicycle pumps
and skateboards in the front hall, single tennis shoes
floating all over the house. Incredible racket from con-
flicting stereos and TVs, and my underwear always disappears. How can they wear all my shorts and take all
my socks? Cars parked on the sidewalk outside the
house. A cluster of young males devouring everything
in the fridge. I miss it all. I wish mine were home too.
Enjoy every minute of it! I enjoyed every minute with
you, Fred. What a gift to have found you again, after all
these years. I'm sorry I lost you three years ago. I promise it won't happen this time. You're too good to be true.
Why didn't I snatch you up and keep you when you
were fourteen? I was pursuing girls with big boobs and
no brains in those days. The bigger the better. Jack
would have killed me anyway. Better this way. I love
you as a friend, little sister. Thank you for bringing so
much sunshine into my life. If your mom were still alive,

I'd go thank her for everything you are. Probably no thanks to her. You just are who you are. I'm going to go fall into bed. Wish I were there to decorate the tree with you. Give Zoe a hug from her mom's oldest friend. Don't kiss Alex for me, he wouldn't understand. And take care of you, Fred. Only nine more days till Christmas. Eight till I shop. Love, Brad."

Faith smiled to herself as she read it, and then finally went upstairs to read in bed. She wanted to wait up until Zoe came home, which she did at two o'clock. And Faith went to kiss her goodnight. She looked happy and excited to see her friends, and her best girlfriend from high school had come home to spend the night with her, which was fine with Faith.

"See you in the morning, girls," Faith said as she closed the door, and then opened it again. "No candles, please. I'd like to try not to burn the house down before Christmas, if we can manage it. Okay by you?"

"Okay, Mom," Zoe looked amused. "Goodnight."

Alex was snoring when she slipped into bed beside him, and she turned to look at him as she turned off the light. She could never have had the discussions she'd had with Brad that week, not with Alex, he wouldn't have seen the point of it. And he would never have waxed poetic over the lovable chaos of his children in the house. He wouldn't have skated with her, or gone to St. Patrick's with her to light a candle for Jack. Why was it that one could do things like that with friends, and never with the men in one's life? Alex was solid and serious and reliable, and they had been married forever. But he would have dismissed her out of hand if she had tried to talk to him about the sacrifices one made in marriage, or the compromises one had to make. He would never have understood, and wouldn't have wanted to. She and Alex talked about other things, like children, and business, and his latest trip, or something she'd heard in the news. But she couldn't have shared her philosophies with him, or the dreams of her heart. That was just the way it was. There was no point musing about it, or regretting what she didn't have. And now she could talk to Brad. Just as he had said about her, he was a gift in her life.

She turned the light off then, and five minutes later she was asleep. And when she woke up the next morning, Alex was gone. He had gone to seek refuge in the office and catch up on his work. Faith was getting out of the bathtub and reaching for a towel, when Zoe walked in.

"Wow, Mom! Where'd you get that bruise?" Zoe looked shocked, and Faith looked down in surprise. She hadn't even noticed it. There was a long black and blue mark on her hip.

"What? . . . Oh . . . that . . . I must have gotten it skating the other night," she said, drying herself off. Although the bruise looked impressive, it was barely sore.

"You went skating? Since when do you skate?" Zoe looked surprised.

"Since I was about five. And not in a long time. Don't

you remember? I used to take you skating when you were little, in the park." Jack had even gone with them once or twice. But Zoe had probably been too young to remember.

"Yeah, I guess," Zoe said vaguely. She had been more interested in ballet, and horses after that. "So who did you go skating with?" She couldn't imagine her skating alone. That seemed weird.

"An old friend of Uncle Jack's. We grew up together. He came to New York for a couple of days, and we went skating for old times' sake. It was fun."

"What's he like?" Zoe looked interested, as her mother got dressed and they chatted. It was all part of what Faith loved about having her at home. It was company for her.

"He's a nice man. He reminds me a lot of Uncle Jack. We've been sending each other e-mails for the past two months. I ran into him at Papa Charles's funeral. He lives in San Francisco, and is a criminal defense attorney for kids. Heavy stuff. Felonies, that kind of thing. You met him at Uncle Jack's funeral but you probably don't remember him." The girls had met a lot of people that day, and they'd all been upset. Zoe looked amused.

"Do you have a crush on him, Mom? You look so cute when you talk about him."

"Don't be silly. I've known him all my life."

"Weirder things have happened. Does he have a crush on you?"

"Nope. We're just good friends. Kind of like sister

and brother. We talk about a lot of stuff, and have a lot of the same ideas. Probably because we grew up together. I guess that helps."

"Is he married?" Zoe was intrigued by him. It sounded exotic to her. She couldn't remember her mother ever having a close male friend, although she knew some married women did. She also didn't think her mother had affairs, even though she thought her father wasn't nice to her. Zoe thought it would have served him right, and maybe been good for Faith. She was open to all possibilities, far more so than Faith.

"Yes, he's married. He has two sons, twins. They're working in Africa for the year. They're about Ellie's age."

"Maybe she'd like to meet them sometime. Are they cute?" He had shown her a photograph, and they looked just like him.

"I think so."

"Then they're probably not cute," Zoe said, and walked back to her own room.

It seemed odd to Faith that Zoe was so intrigued by Brad. And a little while later, Zoe left to get a haircut, and Faith went out to buy the tree. She bought a tall wide one that would look nice in the living room, and they delivered it that afternoon. She was decorating it when Alex came home, and he stood watching her for a moment, and then sat down, as though the project didn't involve him. She was up on a ladder, hanging brightly colored balls on the top branches. She'd struggled with the lights for an hour before that.

"Want to help?" she asked hopefully. Zoe was nowhere in sight, and hadn't come home yet.

"Looks like you have it in control," he said, and then disappeared. He hated decorating the tree. She always did it with the kids, but those days seemed to be over. The kids no longer had time, or the interest in doing it themselves. It took her another hour, and then she stood back and looked at her work with pleasure. The tree looked beautiful, and festive. She put on a CD of Christmas carols, and went to look for something on her desk. And when she did, she saw that she had mail. She hadn't checked her computer all day.

"Hi, Fred. Depressing day. Had to share it with someone. Got a call from a couple, saw them a little while ago. Their fifteen-year-old daughter is accused of killing their six-year-old son. From all I can gather, she is mentally ill, though not obviously so, but clearly she is. She may be tried as a result, though I think I can get a sanity hearing for her. She'll probably go to an institution for the criminally insane. Tragedy for them. They're destroyed. Some Christmas gift. The pictures of the little boy broke my heart. I'm going to see the girl tonight. She's being evaluated now. Some days I don't love my job. Can't do much to fix this one, or to help them, except pretty technical stuff. Sorry to bum you out. Hope you're having a decent day. Better than mine. Did you get the tree? I'll bet it looks beautiful. And you too. I liked your red coat. Did I tell you that? You look great in red. And on skates. More soon. Love, Brad."

He sounded so down, she answered him immediately.

"I'm so sorry about the case. Sounds terrible. The ultimate nightmare, it will be like losing both kids for them. How awful for all concerned. I'm really sorry that landed in your lap. All is fine here. The tree is up. Looks pretty good. Zoe escaped all day. A six-hour haircut spared her tree-decorating duty. She'll be home any minute, I'm sure. Have to start dinner. Just wanted to say hi. I looked so good on skates, I now have a bruise from my hip to my knee. Zoe was horrified. Told her where I'd been and with whom. She was impressed. Hope you meet her again next time. Take care. Try to cheer up. Love, Fred."

Zoe walked in as she was sending it. Her hair looked great, and she'd had her makeup and nails done too.

"Wow, don't you look glamorous." Faith smiled at her, still sitting in her desk chair.

"Who are you writing to?" Zoe looked curious, and beautiful, and with her makeup done, she looked surprisingly like Faith as a young girl.

"Brad. The friend I told you about," Faith said easily, and Zoe grinned.

"Mom, are you in love with him?" Zoe looked serious, and Faith shook her head.

"Certainly not. We're just friends."

"Are you having an affair with him?" She was determined to make more of it than it was, but she was intrigued by it.

"Of course not. He's a friend. That's it."

"I think you're in love with him, Mom," Zoe said with a dogged look. "You should see your eyes when you talk about him. They sparkle and light up and dance."

"You've been smoking crack again, Zoe Madison," her mother teased.

"Nope. I think I'm right. You're in love."

"And you are the silliest person I know," Faith laughed.

"Does Dad know? About him, I mean."

"I think I mentioned him to your father. He wasn't particularly interested. He doesn't have the wild imagination you do, thank God. Nor does Brad, fortunately. I had a crush on him when I was a kid, and I got over it when I was about fourteen. That was about a hundred years ago. So, no, I'm not in love."

"Maybe you should be," Zoe said seriously. "You're pretty miserable with Dad." Zoe said it matter-of-factly and Faith looked horrified.

"I am not! That's a terrible thing to say."

"Well, it's true. He never talks to you. He isn't nice to you. He never even kisses you, or gives you a hug."

"Your father isn't demonstrative in front of other people," Faith defended him.

"So what do you do? Wake him up when he's asleep

three hours before you go to bed every night? Mom, I'm
not stupid. And look at how he talks to you. You deserve better than that." Zoe was sincere, and Faith was
shocked. It horrified her that her daughter had observed
all of those things, and had come to the conclusions she
had, at eighteen. But none of that made her in love with
Brad. But it distressed her that Zoe had such a dismal
view of their marriage, and worse yet, it was close to the
mark. But it hurt hearing it summed up that way. It dis-
posed of their marriage like so much trash. Obviously,
in Zoe's eyes, and even in Faith's sometimes, their marriage was not a success. But Faith had ways of looking at
it that made it seem tolerable, and better than it was.

"What you're saying isn't true, Zoe. Daddy and I are
happy together. We understand each other. This is comfortable for us."

"No," Zoe denied what her mother had said. She
knew better and so did Faith, but she was not willing to
admit the truth, either to Zoe or herself, except maybe to
Brad. "He's comfortable, you're not. How can you be
comfortable with someone who puts you down all the
time and won't listen to you? You're better than that,
Mom. All you ever do is make it work for him. Maybe
one of these days you'll find someone who's nice to you,
and leave him. I wish you would. For your sake. Ellie
would have a fit, but she'd get over it. And I'd be happy
for you." She had it all wrapped up, and all the loose
ends tied, much to her mother's dismay.

"Zoe!" Faith put her arms around her and held her

tight. "How can you say all those things about your father?" She was horrified, at Zoe's perceptions, if nothing else.

"Because I love you, and I want you to be happy, Mom. And you're not. I'm glad you're going to school. Maybe you'll meet someone there." She seemed hellbent on Faith finding a new man.

"Zoe, I don't want to meet anyone. I'm married. I love your father. I'm not going anywhere."

"Then you should. Maybe this guy Brad." She was determined to pair her mother off with someone else, and Faith was appalled by the idea.

"No, not Brad," she corrected her quickly, "he's like a brother to me."

"Then what do you talk about in your e-mails?" She was still curious about him.

"Just stuff. You and Ellie, his kids, his job, my going to school. My brother Jack. His wife, your dad."

"Sounds pretty good. What's he look like? How old is he?"

"He's tall, green eyes, black hair, cleft chin. Forty-nine."

"Is he cute?"

"Yeah. I guess he is. I don't think of him that way, he's like family," but what she had just said wasn't entirely true. She had noticed this time, and at Charles's funeral, how handsome he was. But she didn't want to admit that to Zoe, or she'd go berserk, and come to the wrong conclusions.

"Do you have a picture of him?"

"No, I don't."

"See, you just did it again!" Zoe looked victorious suddenly.

"Did what?"

"Your eyes sparkled when you talked about him. I was right. You're in love."

"Zoe Madison, stop behaving like a nut."

"You'll see. I'm right. Maybe you don't even know it yet. But you are."

"I have known him for thirty-nine years. It's a little late to fall for him now."

"It's never too late. Maybe he'll leave his wife."

"Maybe you should stop getting crazy ideas, and relax."

And with that, Alex walked downstairs and stuck his head in, with a disgruntled look. "Haven't you started dinner yet, Faith? I'm starving. It's nearly seven o'clock."

"I'm sorry, Alex. I'll start right now. I'll do something quick." He nodded and disappeared to his own study and closed the door, as Zoe glared at her mother. She hated the way he talked to her.

"Why don't you tell him to get a slave?"

"Zoe!"

"Why doesn't he cook dinner, or take you out? He could take you somewhere."

"He works hard. He's tired. He was gone all week. He was in the office all day today."

"And you did the tree. You cleaned up my room, thank you, by the way. You made me breakfast, you're cooking him dinner. You don't exactly sit around eating bonbons and watching TV." Faith laughed at the image, and Zoe followed her into the kitchen with an irritated look.

"Are you eating here?" Faith asked as she checked the fridge. She had steaks for all of them.

"No, I'm going out. I think you should too." Alex looked like he was in no mood to take her anywhere, and Faith didn't mind cooking for him. She'd been doing it for twenty-six years, and no matter how unfair Zoe thought that was, Faith had no problem with it. "Why doesn't he take you to the movies?" She was right, they hadn't been in months, and seldom went, not more than a few times a year. But Alex didn't like going to the movies, and he was tired most of the time when he came home.

"You're worrying too much. First you think I'm having an affair, then you think Dad doesn't take me out enough. Why don't you think about something else?" She was organizing dinner while she spoke.

"I think you should have an affair with Brad," Zoe whispered to her, and then gave her a hug and went upstairs. Faith shook her head as she put the steaks under the grill, and smiled to herself, looking amused. Zoe was a great kid. And it was a totally insane idea.

11

THE WEEKEND FLEW PAST WITH ZOE AND HER FRIENDS
flitting in and out of the house. Faith cooked meals for
them, paid for pizzas and cabs, changed beds and
washed towels, helped pick out clothes and French-
braided hair, and waited up at night for her to come
home. She was relieved when Zoe took a train to the
party in Connecticut, instead of driving, and that night
Zoe came home at three A.M.

Faith felt as though she were running interference,
because in the chaos and the noise and the mess, Alex
got increasingly nervous, and he and Zoe were constantly at each other's throats. He hated her music and
her language, the boys who dropped by, the mess they
all left, and the way her friends dressed. He thought
they looked like homeless people, and the music they
listened to was obscene, which in fact, some of it was.
But Faith was used to it, and tolerant of all the fashions
and foibles of eighteen-year-olds. More than once during the Christmas vacation, Zoe declared her mother
"extremely cool."

Ellie called from Saint Moritz on Monday night, and Zoe was out, but Faith was relieved to know that all was well. She was having a fabulous time skiing, had met lots of people, and she said that Geoffrey's family was being extremely nice to her. She sounded happy, but much to Faith's relief, not madly in love. Listening to her talk about everything she was doing, Faith decided that maybe Alex had been right, and it had been worth making the sacrifice of letting her stay over there. She was having an exceptionally good time, more so than she would have had in New York.

"You were right," Faith said to him graciously that night over dinner. "She's having a ball."

"I usually am right," he said without hesitation. "I'm right about your going to school too. It's going to be a colossal mistake." Faith didn't want to discuss it with him. She didn't want to have a fight with him, but he didn't back off as he looked at her. "Have you come to your senses about that yet, Faith?" She didn't know why he'd brought it up now, but it made her feel anxious. She was taking the LSAT in a little over a week, and still felt guilty, concealing it from him.

"No, Alex, I haven't. I'm starting in three weeks." She had paid the tuition out of her own money. Her mother left her a little when she died the year before. All of Jack's had gone to his widow, and he'd left his insurance money to her as well. She had taken it all with her when she'd disappeared. She'd left a box of his favorite possessions for Faith, and taken the rest.

"You'll regret it," Alex continued, as Faith tried valiantly to change the subject, and failed. "You may even flunk the first term."

"I really don't want to discuss this with you," she said bluntly, finally, and he stopped talking to her for the rest of the meal. And afterward, he went upstairs to read. She was discouraged about it while she did the dishes, and after she finished clearing up, she sent Brad an e-mail.

"For heaven's sake," he said when he answered only minutes later, as usual he was at his desk, when the signal came that he had mail. "What is he talking about? You had better grades in school than Jack and I did. You graduated Barnard magna cum laude. Doesn't he know who you are? I flunked the bar the first time I tried to pass it. I'll lay you odds you pass it the first time. Why doesn't he get off your back? Just tell him to fuck off the next time he says it," Brad said, sounding irritated. "I believe in you, Fred. Now you believe in you too. Love, Brad."

"I guess he's still mad about my going back to school," Faith replied. "I was hoping he'd be over that by now." It reminded her of all the things Zoe had said. She hadn't told Brad that Zoe had accused her of being in love with him, and thought she should be, if she wasn't yet. She wasn't sure he'd have been amused. And it was as far from the truth as you could get. She loved him as a friend, just as he loved her. But it was hard for a girl Zoe's age to understand. The beauties of platonic friendship. At her age, it was all about sex.

"I'm tired of Alex picking on you," Brad said when he responded again. "How can you live with that without getting worn down?"

"I'm used to it. He doesn't mean it. That's just the way he is," she defended Alex in her next e-mail.

But at Brad's end, things weren't all smooth sailing these days either. The holidays seemed to bring out the worst in everyone. Particularly Pam. She was going from one party to another, and she wanted Brad to go with her, and he was too busy in the office, nor did he care about the social events she loved. He had long since told her that he'd prefer she went with one of her friends. But at certain times of year, she insisted that he go with her. Particularly during the opening of the social season in September, and at Christmas. Pam was going to cocktails and dinners and dances, benefits and openings and holiday parties. He couldn't begin to keep her social calendar straight, nor did he want to. He was doing things that were far more important to him. He had a short trial the week before Christmas, which ruled out everything else for him. But it created enormous tension between them. Pam was not amused.

"For God's sake, can't you get your paralegals to do the prep work? Do you have to do everything yourself?" He had just told her he couldn't go out again that night. He had been in the office till two A.M. the night before—it was an escape for him—one he loved.

"I can't leave this kind of work in the hands of some-one else, Pam, and you know that."

"Why not? I do. I go to court too. My paralegals and my assistant do half the work."

"You're not trying to get kids off from murder charges. There's a difference. There are lives in the bal-ance here."

"As a matter of fact, you're right, Brad. Ours. I'm sick and tired of your never being around." She was fuming, as she paced in front of him in a blue sequined evening gown. She looked stately and beautiful, and the look in her eyes would have terrified most men, but not Brad. He was used to her, and her tantrums. They no longer impressed him as they once had. Although they were fearsome to watch at times.

"I thought we came to an understanding about this years ago," he said, looking exasperated.

"You said you'd come to at least some of the events, if they were important to me."

"But not when I'm preparing a trial. I can't. Simple as that." He refused to be intimidated by her. She had been doing it, or trying to, for a long time.

"Why the hell not? What about your little bleeding-heart girlfriend? Doesn't she expect you to go out with her once in a while?" Brad was shocked by what she'd just said, and narrowed his eyes at her.

"What was that? What are you talking about?" He looked mystified.

"I saw one of your e-mails to her the other day, about

what a gentle soul she is, and something about going to church with her. Since when have you been religious? What is she? A nun?"

"More important, what are you, Pam? What are you doing snooping through my computer? That's a pretty lousy thing to do."

"You left it open while you were out in the garage. So what's that about?"

"She's an old friend from my childhood. Her brother was my best friend. Jack. This is his sister, Faith. And we're friends. Nothing more than that. I don't owe you any apologies or explanations. I had dinner with her in New York, and yes, I went to church with her."

"How pathetic. Are you sleeping with her?" Pam spat at him. They hadn't made love in years, and scenes like this were why, as far as Brad was concerned. And he was certain that Pam had cheated on him several times over the years. He was smart enough not to ask, and he no longer cared.

"No, I'm not sleeping with her, if it's any of your business. I don't ask about your life." They had stopped sleeping with each other by tacit agreement. He just wasn't in love with her anymore. It was like making love to a machine. Pam was all about ambition and drive. After a while, Brad felt as though he were making love to a computer, or his desk. He just couldn't anymore. He preferred to be celibate than to make love to her, although she was convinced that he had affairs. As sexual as he had been with her in the beginning, it was inconceivable to her that he hadn't had sex for years. It was one of those sacrifices he had made, that he and Faith had talked about, although he hadn't explained that aspect of his life to her, and didn't intend to. It wasn't appropriate information to exchange.

But Pam looked shocked by what he had just said. Something in his eyes made her stop and stare. "Are you in love with her?"

"Of course not. She's a friend. Nothing more. I've known her since she was a little kid."

"If you're not sleeping with her, and you went to church with her, then I'll bet my ass you're in love with her, Brad."

"Does it have to be one or the other? Can't we just be friends? And that doesn't explain what you were doing in my computer. I don't go through yours."

"I'm sorry. I just happened to see it. Your letter was on the screen." He wondered if he had said anything unpleasant about her, though he suspected not since Pam hadn't commented on that. "She must be somewhat pathetic if she spends her life in church."

"What she does is none of your goddamn business. Now, let's get back to the point here. I have to work. I'm not going out. And frankly, after all this bullshit, I wouldn't go anywhere with you anyway. So find yourself some other poor slob to push around. You know plenty of guys. Find one who wants to take you to parties every night. I don't." And with that, he slammed out of the room, and went back to his study. He had come home to get something to eat and pick up a file. He sat down at his desk for a few minutes and found that he was shaking. He felt violated by Pam reading his e-mails, and talking about Faith the way she had. Faith had nothing to do with her, and he had done nothing wrong. He was outraged that Pam would accuse him of sleeping with Faith or even suggest that he was in love with her. It was nothing of the sort, for either of them. They had enjoyed the sacred bond of friendship for nearly forty years. Something that Pam knew nothing about. There was nothing sacred to her.

He stormed back to the office half an hour later, with a severe case of indigestion and a headache. No one on the planet could make him angrier than Pam. She had a knack for driving him out of his mind. She was stubborn and unreasonable and aggressive. And if he let her, she could argue with him for hours. He was still upset when he got back to his office, and finally decided to call Faith and see if she was home.

As it so happened, Alex was out at a business dinner, and she was home alone. She was pleased and surprised to hear him, and he calmed down almost instantly the minute he heard her voice.

"I'm sorry to bother you," he apologized, and she could hear that he was stressed.

"Are you okay?" She sounded worried about him, and he smiled. She was everything Pam wasn't. She was gentle, sensitive, cautious, thoughtful, generous of spirit, and nurturing in every possible way.

"I'm just tired. And grumpy," he explained. "I've had a bad day. How was yours?" He felt guilty for burdening her, particularly about Pam. But it was nice having her shoulder to cry on. He hadn't had that kind of support and comfort in years, if ever. And for the past two months, she had been there for him unfailingly.

"It was fine. Alex and Zoe are out, though not together. And I was actually enjoying a quiet evening at home. I'm running the Motel 6 here. I just keep washing towels and changing beds, and blowing out candles, hoping the house doesn't burn down. But it's nice to have her home. Tell me about your bad day. What was that about?"

"I lost a motion at a hearing this morning, and I really needed it to get a continuance on a trial. I'm not ready, and I need to round up more witnesses, or this kid is going to get screwed. My secretary is out sick, which is driving me crazy. And I went home for an hour, to have some dinner, and had a fight with Pam. No big deal. Just a lot of little shit."

"What was the fight about?" Faith always listened to him, and she did it well.

"She wants me to go to ten thousand goddamn parties. She goes to two or three a night, and I just don't have the time or the desire to play prince consort. She knows I hate that stuff, and once we get there, she disappears anyway. My only purpose is for her to make an entrance. I don't have time for that bullshit, Faith. I'm constantly in trial, or preparing one. And these kids need me to do it right."

"Did she back down?" Faith asked calmly, and he took a breath and slowed down. He had gotten all wound up, telling her about the argument with Pam.

"Eventually," he said, and then he got annoyed again. He had been debating about telling Faith, and saw no reason why not. He had nothing to hide. "She read one of my e-mails the other day, which really makes me mad."

"I don't blame you." Faith hated that kind of intrusion too. She was a very private person and didn't even like her kids reading her e-mails, particularly from Brad.

"Apparently, it was one of the ones to you. I think it was thanking you for the time you spent with me in New York. There was nothing particularly inappropriate about it, it just annoyed the hell out of me." And then he laughed, "And she said I was in love with you. She's a little off the mark."

Faith smiled as he said it. "Zoe said the same thing to me the other day. Or at least she asked me. She wanted to know if we were having an affair."

"What did you say?"

"That we weren't. She was very disappointed, and said she thought we should. She said I deserve it, and so does Alex, after the way he treats me. I thought that was an interesting statement coming from her."

"She's right. He doesn't do a damn thing for you, Faith. He never seems to take you to dinner or a movie.

It sounds like all he does is work, and sleep and complain . . . like me," he suddenly laughed at the portrait he'd painted. "I guess Pam should be having one too, except in her case, she probably is."

"Are you serious?" Faith sounded horrified. He hadn't told her they no longer slept with each other. There were some things he didn't say, even to Faith.

"I don't ask. I figure it's none of my business anymore." It was all he wanted to say on the subject, but she understood what he was saying, and was surprised. He didn't look like the sort to give that up, but one never knew what happened behind other people's closed doors. "In any case, what I do is none of her business. And I don't want her casting aspersions on you." He felt protective of Faith, and didn't tell her about Pam's comment about their going to church. He knew it would have offended her, and he was right. "I'm sorry to call and complain, Fred. As I said, I'm just tired. And she made me mad as hell." It was nice having someone to vent with, and they talked for a while, before he went back to his preparations for the trial. And she was happy to have talked to him, so he could let off steam. As always, they both felt better when they hung up. She went upstairs to take a bath and get ready for bed. And he sat at his desk for a few minutes, staring into space and thinking of her.

It struck him odd that Pam had accused him of sleeping with her, and Zoe had asked her mother the same thing. Odder still that they had each suggested they were in love with each other. As he had said to Pam, it wasn't even an option, for either of them. All they had ever been was friends, since the beginning. And the fact that he enjoyed her company now didn't change anything. She was the same person in his life now that she had been as a little girl, when he was helping her climb trees, and painting her braids green. Or was she? It suddenly made him think of how much she meant to him, and how he had come to depend on her in the past two months. And as he thought of it, he got a vision of her skating next to him at Rockefeller Center, and lighting a candle at the altar of Saint Jude in St. Patrick's Cathedral . . . he had never seen a more beautiful face in his life. She was luminous as she stood there praying. And suddenly he wondered if Pam was right . . . and if she wasn't, perhaps she should be. And then with a tired smile, he shook his head. He was imagining things. He wasn't in love with her. No matter how beautiful she had been as a child, or was now, she was his friend, nothing more.

And in New York, Faith was thinking the same thing as she sat in the bathtub, asking herself the same questions. And she came to the same conclusion as Brad. They were being foolish, both Pam and Zoe. She and Brad weren't in love with each other, Faith reassured herself. They were friends, more than that, they were like brother and sister. It was all they wanted, all they needed from each other. Just friendship. Besides, if it had been more than that, it would have spoiled everything. And Faith wanted to avoid that at all costs.

12

THE MORNING AFTER BRAD'S ARGUMENT WITH PAM, HE was on his way to work. He drove past St. Mary's Cathedral on Gough, and had a sudden idea. He had an appointment at nine o'clock and didn't have time to stop, so he gave his secretary a note when he got to the office, and she promised to get the information for him. She slipped him a piece of paper with an address an hour later, when he was on the phone talking to the district attorney's office, and he signaled thanks and nodded his head. He went out to do the errand at eleven o'clock. It took him longer than he thought, but he was back by one.

He wrote Faith a note, and had a small box on his desk, and asked his secretary to Federal Express it to New York. At least he had one gift done. All he had to do now was go to Tiffany and take care of the rest, and he was planning to do that the following afternoon.

Faith and her family's plans for Christmas were very traditional. They were having an informal dinner together on Christmas Eve. Faith usually went to midnight mass by herself, or with Zoe, if she could talk her into it, and they had a more formal dinner the next day, on Christmas night. They opened presents on Christmas morning, and spent the day hanging around the house. The day had been more exciting when the girls were young, but it was still a day that was important to all of them.

They talked to Ellie in Switzerland on the morning of Christmas Eve. It was dinnertime for her, and she sounded emotional when she heard them all on the phone. It was her first time spending Christmas away from them, and it was harder than she'd thought it would be, although everyone in Saint Moritz had been wonderful to her.

"We miss you, sweetheart," Faith said when it was her turn to talk to her.

"Why don't you come to London after New Year's, Mom?" Eloise asked, sounding very young, and home-sick for her family.

"I can't, sweetheart. I'm starting school. I'll have to wait now till I get a break. Or maybe you can come home for a long weekend."

"I didn't know you'd actually decided to go." She sounded disappointed, which confirmed Alex's objections to her plans, that it would interfere with him and their family. There had been no time to tell her since she'd signed up. Their last conversation had been all about her going to Switzerland with Geoff and his family for the holidays, and Faith had forgotten about her own news.

"I start classes in two weeks," Faith said, expecting to be congratulated, but Ellie sounded upset.

"That's such a mean thing to do to Dad." She sounded disapproving, and Faith was hurt by what she said. And it was hard to talk about it with Alex standing next to her. She knew Zoe would be upset by her sister's reaction too. It wasn't very generous to Faith.

"We talked about it, and I think he's made his peace with it," Faith said calmly. She didn't want Christmas to be as disrupted by her plans as Thanksgiving had been, and she wanted to get off the subject as soon as she could. "More importantly, how are you, sweetheart? Are you having fun?"

"I miss you all so much. It's nice, but I'm homesick for all of you. More than I thought I would be. We're going to a big party tonight, and we're going tobogganing afterward. It's kind of scary, but it looks like fun."

"Be careful," her mother warned. "Don't do anything silly!" She worried about her, almost as much as she had when she was a child. No matter how old the girls were, it was still her job. She passed the phone on to Zoe then, and the two sisters talked for a long time. Faith was relieved that they seemed to have made peace. And Zoe had said that she missed her several times. Alex was the last to talk to her, and he had very little to say, but it was obvious from the tone of his voice and his choice of words how close he felt to her. It was a bittersweet moment for all of them when he finally hung up.

"It's so weird not having her here," Zoe said, looking sad. And then she turned to her mother. "Can I go to London to visit her the next time I have a break?"

"That would be wonderful," Faith smiled at her younger daughter, "and if I have a break then, I'll come with you. Otherwise, you can go alone, and I'll go when I can."

"It's ridiculous for you to be bound by 'breaks,' Faith. You should be able to visit your daughter whenever you want. That's exactly what I meant," Alex said, and then walked off. And Faith said nothing in response. She just hoped she could juggle all the balls she needed to, to make her home life and her school schedule work. It was going to be a challenge for her.

The three of them had dinner together that night, as planned. Faith cooked duck for them, with a recipe she'd gotten from a friend. It was a delicious meal, and afterward Zoe went out. Alex lingered at the table for a while, and made an attempt to talk to her, but neither of them had much to say. The lines of communication had been down between them for so long that it was hard to reestablish them on command.

"Are you going to church tonight?" Alex asked offhandedly, as Faith put out the candles and started putting things away.

"I thought I'd go to midnight mass," just as she always did. "Would you like to come?" He never did, but she always offered it to him. Zoe had said she would meet her at the church if she could. And Faith didn't press the point with her. She was going to St. Ignatius on Park Avenue.

"No, thanks," Alex declined her offer, and went upstairs to read. Even on Christmas Eve, there was very little spark between them these days.

Faith was puttering around her study at eleven o'clock, getting ready to leave for church, when the phone rang, and she was surprised to hear Brad. It was eight o'clock for him.

"Merry Christmas, Fred." He sounded friendly and warm, but she thought a little sad too. It was a hard time for everyone, a time to remember what you once had, hoped you would, and all your lost dreams.

"Thanks, Brad. The same to you."

"Did you get my present?" They hadn't talked in several days, and their e-mails had been short and quick. It was a busy time for both of them.

"I did," she smiled. It was a small box wrapped in Christmas wrap, and it was sitting on her desk. It had come in a Federal Express envelope, and she'd been saving it for Christmas Day. She had sent him a set of antique leather legal books that were beautifully bound. "It's sitting right here. I'm saving it till tomorrow."

"That's why I called," he sounded pleased. "I wanted to be sure you opened it tonight."

"Are you sure?"

"Positive. Why don't you open it now?" He sounded excited and she laughed in anticipation.

"I love presents. This is fun. Did you get mine?" she asked as she took the paper off carefully and sat looking at the small flat white box. She couldn't imagine what was inside. Nothing about it gave the contents away.

"I'm saving it for tomorrow too. But I wanted you to have yours tonight. Go ahead, open it, Fred." She carefully lifted the lid on the box, and gave a short gasp at what she saw. They were beautiful antique rosary beads he had gotten in a religious store. The Hail Marys were beautiful old citrines, and the Our Fathers and the crucifix at the end of them were cabochon emeralds, and there were tiny rubies on the tips of the cross. They looked as though they had been handled and loved for a long time. She had never seen any as beautiful, and he had been pleased with what he'd found, and hoped they would mean a lot to her.

"The woman said they're Italian, and they're about a hundred years old. She said they'd been blessed. I wanted you to have them for church tonight, Fred," he said in a soft voice, and there were tears in her eyes. It took her a long time to say anything. "Fred? . . . Fred? . . . Are you there?"

"I don't know what to say. They're the most beautiful thing I've ever seen. Thank you with all my heart. I'm going to use them tonight. I'll say a rosary for you," she smiled. There was a wonderful old-fashioned quality to her, in spite of the way she looked. She had solid values, and a passion for her family, a deep respect for her church. She had grown up to be even better than he ever thought she would. "I'll light a candle for you too. And for Jack."

"Maybe I'll light one for you."

"Are you going to church?" She sounded surprised. She didn't think he did.

"I thought I might. I've got nothing else to do. We're having dinner with a few friends in a little while, and Pam's father is here. But by eleven o'clock, we'll be all through. I thought it would be nice to go." He was thinking of going to St. Dominic's, a beautiful old Gothic church, with a shrine to Saint Jude, which he knew was her favorite saint. He had asked the woman in the religious store about where to go, when he bought the rosary for Faith. "There's a church nearby with a shrine to Saint Jude. If I go, I'll light a candle for you there."

"I can't believe you sent me these," she said, looking at the rosary again. It had a wonderful smooth feel in her hand, and all the settings were yellow gold. There was a little satin pouch to put it in, to protect it in her purse. She had never seen one as beautiful in her life. "I guess my old wooden ones can be retired," she said. It was a gift that meant the world to her.

They talked for a few minutes. All he'd been able to do was leave a message for the boys. There was no direct line to the game preserve where they lived. And they obviously hadn't been able to get a line at the post office, because they hadn't called home. It made the holiday even harder for him, not to mention the tension that existed between him and Pam. He felt like a stranger in his own house these days. As always, she had invited people to dinner whom he didn't know well, and her father had a way of monopolizing the conversation and making it all about him.

"I'm glad you're not working tonight," Faith said, holding the rosary beads in her hand. It made her feel closer to him.

"I figured I'd better stick around and make some points, before I start an all-out war." There was no purpose in doing that, and Faith agreed. And she knew that the next day they were having a huge dinner, in black tie again. "I think Pam must have been married to a concert musician in another life, a conductor maybe, she always wants everyone in black tie, if not white. It's not exactly my cup of tea." He was happiest in old cords and jeans with turtleneck sweaters and hiking boots, although he looked handsome in a suit too, as she'd seen in New York. "I'll think about you tonight when you're at church."

"I'll have your beautiful rosary in my hand the whole time, and I'll be thinking of you." There was a warm bond between them that scarcely needed words.

She glanced at her watch a few minutes later, and told him she had to leave for church, or she wouldn't get a seat. The midnight mass was popular, and the church was usually filled. And she knew Brad had to join his family and guests for dinner anyway.

"Thank you again for the beautiful gift. It's going to be my very best one."

"Merry Christmas, Fred . . . I'm glad you like it . . . thank you for everything you've given me in the past two months. You've been the best gift of all."

"You too," she said softly, and a moment later, they hung up. She went to say good-bye to Alex, but he was asleep in a chair, with a book. And a few minutes later, she walked out the front door, wearing her big red coat, and hailed a cab.

And in San Francisco, Brad made an effort to talk to everyone in the room. He was wearing a blazer and slacks, as was his father-in-law. Christmas Eve was always informal at their house, although all the men wore ties. And Pam was wearing red silk pajamas, and high-heeled gold sandals. She looked festive and beautiful and statuesque. She was a handsome woman, but every time Brad looked at her he saw who she had become. She was tougher and harder and stronger than he would ever have dreamed. He had bought her a narrow gold and diamond necklace with a matching bracelet and ring, and he knew it was the kind of thing she would wear a lot. But he was far more excited about the rosary beads he had sent Faith. They had more meaning to him. And to her.

They were seated at the table in the dining room by the time the mass started in New York. They were

having a traditional English meal, with roast beef and
Yorkshire pudding, and plum pudding and hard sauce
for dessert. But he was distracted as they started eating,
and his father-in-law toasted everyone with Napa Val-
ley wine. All he could think of was Faith on her knees in
church, as she had been at St. Patrick's when she'd gone
with him.

"You seem a little out of it tonight," Pam said when
they finally got up. "Are you okay?"

"Just thinking about a case," he said, looking vague,
and she met his eyes.

"Or your friend in New York?" She knew him better
than he thought. "Did you send her an e-mail tonight?"
she queried. She looked like a huntress going after her
prey, and he shook his head. He hadn't e-mailed her, he
had called her instead.

"Don't make more of that than it is, Pam. It is what it
is. She's an old friend."

"I know you better than that. You're a hopeless romantic, Brad. That's just the sort of thing you'd fall head
over heels into, especially if it's a hopeless case."

"Don't be silly." He tried to brush her off, but what
she said sounded right. He had been a hopeless romantic years before, when he met Pam. But she had stamped
it out of him long since, or so he thought. He didn't believe what she was saying about his feelings for Faith.
He was smarter than that. And Pam was just being terri-
torial and defending her turf. She wanted to make it

clear that she still owned him, whether she wanted him or not, or he her.

Their guests all left around eleven o'clock, and Pam's father had a car and driver pick him up. He didn't like to drive at night anymore. And as Pam and Brad walked upstairs, Brad looked at his watch.

"Do you have a hot date?" she teased. She was on his case a lot these days, although he had noticed her flirting with several men that night. She didn't hesitate to do that in front of him, or even kiss them on the mouth. She did whatever she liked, no matter what she said to him about Faith.

"Actually," he said casually, "I was thinking of going to church."

"Oh my God. You don't have a mistress. You've lost your mind. Why on earth would you do that?"

"I think it's a nice thing," he said calmly, trying not to be annoyed by what she said.

"If you get religious on me, Brad, I want a divorce. Another woman, I can handle. A religious freak, I can't. That would really be too much." He had to smile to himself, wondering what she would think if she knew he had sent rosary beads to Faith. That was about as religious as it got, but he had known how meaningful it would be to her, and was thrilled it had been.

"It's a nice tradition, and I miss the boys," he said honestly. It had been a lonely holiday for him. They were the only allies he normally had in his own house.

The dinner with her father and friends had been painful for him, but he had been a good sport. He always was.

"I miss them too, but I'm not running to church. There must be other ways to deal with it," she said, as she kicked off her shoes, and dropped her earrings on her dressing table.

"To each his own, I guess," he said, left their bedroom, and walked downstairs. He didn't need her approval to go to church. "I'll be back in an hour," he called up to her as he put on his coat, and she came out of their bedroom barefoot and half dressed with a grin.

"Give me a little warning if you're planning to become a priest."

"Don't worry, I will." He smiled up at her. "No danger yet. It's just mass on Christmas Eve. I think I'm safe. Merry Christmas, by the way." He stood looking up at her for a long moment, feeling sad, wishing he still felt more for her, but he hadn't in a long time, and neither had she.

"Thanks, Brad. You too," she said, and disappeared.

He took his Jeep out of the garage, and drove to St. Dominic's at Steiner and Bush. It was a large beautiful old Gothic church, and as he walked up the steps, he could see a cluster of tall pine trees on either side of the main altar, banks of poinsettias, and the church was mostly candle-lit. The shrine to Saint Jude was off to the right, and there were rows of candles there as well. He decided to go there first, and he lit candles for Faith and Jack, and he knelt for a moment, thinking of her, and his old friend. He didn't know what prayers he should say, or even how, all he did was think of them, and wish them well. And he was grateful that some unseen force had brought Faith back into his life.

He took a seat in a pew toward the rear of the church, and was impressed by the beauty and pomp and ceremony of the midnight mass. And when they sang "Silent Night" toward the end, there were tears rolling slowly down his cheeks. He wasn't sure why, or whom they were for, or even what he was crying about. All he knew was that he was deeply moved. And when he went home that night, he felt lighter than he had in years. It was an odd sense of peace and joy and ease. He smiled as he drove home, and for an odd moment, he felt as though Jack were riding in the car with him.

13

ON CHRISTMAS MORNING, FAITH AND ZOE AND ALEX exchanged their gifts. Zoe had bought her mother a terrific leather backpack to use at school, and a long wool scarf so she'd look like one of the kids. And Alex had bought Faith a pretty gold bracelet at Cartier. She had given him a new suit, and some shirts and ties. And she'd given Zoe tiny diamond studs for her ears. All their gifts to each other were a great success. And their Christmas dinner was peaceful and uneventful, although they all admitted they missed Eloise. Faith had cooked a turkey, with her famous stuffing that they all loved, but somehow three at the dining table seemed a little sparse. They tried to call Eloise, but she was out when they called, and by the end of the day, Faith was feeling a little sad. She didn't like the idea that her family was shrinking, even for a year, although Ellie had promised that she'd be home for the holidays next year.

And Brad called her right after they finished dinner, to thank her for her handsome gift. She answered the phone in the kitchen, while she was cleaning up. Alex and Zoe were sitting in the living room, drinking coffee, and talking, and admiring the tree. It was a rare civilized moment between them and Faith was relieved. She thought it might be Eloise when she answered the phone, and was surprised to hear Brad.

"Thank you for my wonderful books. They're incredible. They're going to be the best-looking thing in my office, Fred. Thank you so much." He had been very proud of them when he unwrapped them, and very touched. And he had been careful to open them when he was by himself, to avoid unnecessary comment from Pam.

"They're not as beautiful as my rosary beads," she said happily. It had been hard to find the right gift for him. She didn't want to give him anything too personal, and everything else she'd looked at seemed wrong. The books seemed to strike the right note between them. They were special and valuable, but not too intimate, almost like a symbol of what existed between them, although she had known him long enough to be outrageous if she chose, but she thought she had better not.

"I went to church last night," he volunteered. "At St. Dominic's, and I lit candles for you and Jack at the altar of Saint Jude. He's your guy, right?"

"He's my guy," she smiled. "That's really nice. Who'd you go with?" He had told her Pam was an atheist, and she couldn't imagine that she had gone too.

"I went by myself. What about you?" But in truth, he

felt as though he had gone with her and Jack. He had felt their presence with him during the entire mass.

"Zoe met me at church. It was nice, just the two of us. We walked home afterward, and it started to snow. The perfect Christmas Eve."

"How was Christmas dinner?"

"It was okay. It's kind of small with just the three of us. I'll be happier when Ellie's home next year. What about you?"

"The entire state of California is coming to dinner in black tie in two hours. I can hardly wait. It's so intimate and meaningful. Really kind of touches your heart to see a hundred near-strangers stampeding through your living room, shoving hors d'oeuvres down their throats and guzzling champagne. It really reminds you of the true meaning of Christmas. It's a shame you're not here." She laughed at the description, and couldn't even begin to imagine it. As quiet as their Christmas had been, his seemed even worse. "Pam has a real knack for creating intimate gatherings that make people feel special for being here," he teased, wishing he could be there with her, although that certainly would have been awkward and hard to explain, even to her.

"Maybe you can just give in to it, and have some fun, and not expect it to be anything more than it is," she suggested, trying to be helpful.

"That's kind of what I do. That, and a lot of white wine. These gatherings are a little tough to stomach if you don't drink." She had noticed he drank very little when they had dinner, so she could hardly imagine him getting drunk, even in self-defense. "What are you doing tonight?"

"Going to bed."

"Lucky you. I'll call you tomorrow, or send you an e-mail." He was going back to work the next day, and he was relieved that he was. He had had enough of the holidays, without the boys they meant nothing to him.

"Merry Christmas, Brad. Have a nice time tonight. You may be pleasantly surprised."

"Maybe so," he said, sounding vague, and thinking of her.

They hung up, and she cleaned up the kitchen, and as she was finishing Zoe came in, and asked for some money to go to the movies with her friends.

"Just take what you need out of my purse," she said as she dried her hands, and hung up the apron she had worn over a black silk dress and a string of pearls. She had worn her blond hair in a French twist, and looked like a young Grace Kelly when she did. She pointed to the handbag she had left on one of the kitchen chairs the night before, when she came home from church. Zoe fished around for a minute, and then looked up at her.

"What are these?" She was holding the rosary beads from Brad. They had fallen out of the little satin pouch and were loose in her purse.

"They're rosary beads," Faith said matter-of-factly. She'd had them in her hands at mass the night before, but Zoe hadn't noticed them.

"I've never seen them before. Where'd you get them, Mom?" Zoe was curious. As though she had a sixth sense.

"They were a Christmas present from a friend."

"A friend?" Zoe made a face, it sounded like an odd story to her, and then she understood. "Omigod, don't tell me that guy you grew up with sent you rosary beads, Mom?"

"It's not exactly a shocking gift. It seems pretty respectable to me."

"Yeah, if the guy is in love with you. No one else would even know to send you something that would mean that much to you . . . and they look expensive too."

"They're antiques, and you have a twisted mind. The poor guy tried to send me something religious and respectable, and eminently appropriate for Christmas, and you interpret it as a sign that he's in love with me. I love you, Zoe, but you're sick." Faith smiled innocently at her.

"I am not. I'm right. You'll see. Actually, that's a pretty cool gift." Zoe looked impressed.

"Yes, it is. But do you suppose that you could readjust your thinking to accept the idea that I'm married, I love your father, and no one else is in love with me? That might be a wholesome twist."

"Maybe, but it's not true. This guy is crazy about you, Mom. Look at that, those are emeralds and rubies on that rosary, even if they are little ones. He must be a pretty cool guy."

"He is, and a good friend. I hope you meet him again one day."

"Me too." She put the rosary beads back in her mother's bag, and helped herself to twenty dollars, for the movies with her friends.

"I'll cash a check tomorrow and give you some money. And by the way," she came over to give her daughter a hug, "I love my backpack and scarf. I'm going to be the coolest kid in school."

"Yes, you are, Mom. And all the boys are going to fall in love with you."

Faith rolled her eyes. "You're obsessed." The whole concept of Brad falling in love with her seemed silly to Faith. And offensive in a way. It disregarded the gift of his friendship and made it seem less than it was, and it was very important to her. She had no sense that he was in love with her, nor she with him. They were just very, very good friends, whether Zoe believed that or not.

Zoe went out a few minutes later, and Faith went to sit with Alex next to the tree. He was sipping a glass of port, and relaxing, lost in his own thoughts.

"Thank you for the nice dinner," he said to Faith generously.

"Thank you for a beautiful bracelet," she said, giving him a kiss on the cheek, but as always, he didn't respond. As far as Alex was concerned, displays of affection belonged in bed, at their appointed hour, and nowhere else. Anywhere else, they embarrassed him. And they no longer happened in bed very often either anymore.

"I'm glad you like it," he looked pleased. "I love my suits, and shirts, and ties. You have terrific taste. You always pick out better things than I could pick out for myself." It was a nice compliment, and they had a nice time sitting by the fire. He said he had had a nice chat with Zoe before she went out, which they both knew was rare.

Alex and Faith spent a surprisingly pleasant evening together, and they went upstairs after a while. It hadn't been an exciting Christmas for any of them, but it had been a pleasant day. They watched television for a while, and Alex had been thinking of making love to her, but he fell asleep in front of the TV, and she smiled at him. They had such an odd life. They weren't old, either of them, but they led a life of old people. Sometimes she felt now as though her whole life lay behind her, and not ahead.

It was the same feeling Brad had when he went to bed that night. It had been an exhausting evening for him, playing host to a hundred people he didn't give a damn about, and playing consort to Pam, in her endless social ambitions and endeavors. He couldn't even begin to imagine spending the rest of his life doing it, and yet he knew he would. It was what he had signed on for twenty-five years before, and where, whatever it cost him, he was going to stay. But living it was harder and more depressing than he had ever dreamed.

14

FAITH TOOK THE DREADED LSAT IN THE WEEK BETWEEN
Christmas and New Year's. It was as hard as she had
feared, and she had no idea how she'd done. In the pit of
her stomach, she was afraid that she had done miserably, and Brad tried to reassure her when she called him
afterward. He was the only person in her life who knew
she had taken it. She didn't even tell Zoe where she'd
gone. But at least it was behind her now. Another hurdle
crossed. And all she could do now was hope she'd gotten a decent score.

Zoe left for Brown on New Year's Day. She was starting school the next day, and she hated to leave. She had
had fun with her friends over the holidays, and she always hated leaving her mother, although Faith had reason to be excited herself. She was starting school the
next day.

Alex was painfully silent at dinner after Zoe left, and
Faith knew why. He was still annoyed with her for going back to school. Zoe had made a big fuss over her before she left, and Faith had her backpack and her school

supplies ready for the next day. They were in her study, all ready and waiting on a chair. She went downstairs to check everything again before she went to bed. She hadn't been this excited since she was a little girl.

She'd had an e-mail from Brad that day, wishing her good luck and telling her how brilliantly she was going to do. She wasn't sure of that, but she was really excited to be going back to school. She knew it would be hard, but she was finally doing what she wanted to do.

She was up at dawn the next day, and dressed by eight o'clock, when she made breakfast for Alex. He left at eight-thirty, as he always did, and he said not a word to her. He wanted to be sure she knew he still disapproved. It was hardly a secret to her, or to anyone in the house. He simply glowered at her, and closed the front door.

She made herself another cup of coffee, and kept looking at the clock. She was going to leave at nine, and take a cab downtown. She didn't have to sign in until nine-thirty. And she was just picking up her backpack, and getting ready to leave, when her laptop came alive and told her she had mail. She clicked it twice, and was surprised to see it was from Brad. It wasn't even six A.M. for him.

"Play nice in the sandbox, and have a great day! Be a good girl, and call me when you get home. Love, Brad." It was sweet of him. She hit the reply button quickly, and set down her backpack again to answer him.

"Thank you. You're up very early! Not just for me, I

hope! I'll call you. . . . Pray that the other kids aren't mean to me. I'm scared. But excited too. Have a nice day. Love, Fred." It was Zoe who had always been scared that the kids would be mean to her at school, and they never were. Faith was more afraid that she wouldn't do well in the classes she was taking. It had been a long time since she'd been at school.

She hurried out of the house then, and took a cab to NYU. It was confusing when she arrived, but she had a sheaf of papers telling her what to do, and where to go. They were remarkably clear and accurate, and she found her first classroom with surprising ease. And the class was even better than she thought. It was called "The Judicial Process." It was fascinating, and the professor was interesting and challenging. She was exhilarated by the time they stopped for lunch, and she had another class that afternoon on constitutional law. She was going to school two days a week. She knew it would help her for law school in the fall, and the first one seemed like a terrific class to her.

She was exhausted when she finally headed home that afternoon, but it was the most interesting day she'd had in years. The professor of her Judicial Process class was a woman, and about Faith's age. She would have loved to stop and chat with her, but she felt shy about it, and she knew she had to get home after her Constitutional Law class. It would be four o'clock by the time she got back to the house, and she couldn't dally at school.

She set her backpack down as she came in the front

door, and was already thinking of the assignments they'd been given. They were both challenging and would take time. The phone started to ring almost as soon as she walked in. She was still wearing her coat. It was Zoe.

"How was it? Do you like it, Mom?"

"I love it! It's even better than I thought." She was happy and excited, and Zoe was irrepressibly proud of her. They talked for half an hour, and finally Faith said she had to go. She still had to organize dinner for Alex, and she wasn't sure what she had in the house. But as soon as she hung up, the phone rang again. This time, it was Brad.

"I can't stand the suspense, did you like it?" was his opening line, and she smiled.

"I loved it. I have great professors, it seems like the people in my classes are intelligent. The time flew by, and the homework is terrifying, but I think I can handle it." She let out a little squeak of excitement and he grinned. "I really love it! I just got home."

"You're going to do great!" he said, thrilled for her. It was exactly what he had hoped for for her.

"Thank you for your e-mail this morning." He didn't tell her he had set his alarm at five-thirty so he could send her off in style. "I was scared to death."

"I figured you were. That's why I didn't call. I didn't want to give you an opportunity to fall apart, so I sent the e-mail."

"That was smart."

"I'm so pleased for you. Is the homework tough?"

"Sounds like it, but I think I can handle it, as long as I don't get buried in outside stuff, like dinners I have to do for Alex. That'll be hard."

"Good thing you're not married to Pam." They had had another huge bash on New Year's Eve. Faith and Alex had stayed home and watched TV, as they always did. And Brad said he envied them. "So what's next?"

"I work my ass off, and hopefully get into law school for the fall." Alex was still having a fit over it, but she was slowly forging ahead, and feeling more confident after her first day of school. "I'm going to apply pretty soon."

"Where?"

"Columbia, NYU, Fordham, New York Law School, and Brooklyn Law. I don't have a lot of geographical choice, it has to be in New York."

"Too bad you can't come out here," Brad said with a smile.

"Alex would be thrilled. He'd really love that. A wife who comes home from school for vacations. Although sometimes, I wonder if he'd notice if I were gone. Maybe I can hire a stand-in to do my job," whatever that was these days, mostly it involved dinner, breakfast, the occasional dinner party, and as little conversation as possible, and once in a great, great while, making love. It was hardly a full-time job anymore.

"I would love to hire one to do mine," Brad laughed. "He could do all the black-tie dinners, and opera and

symphony openings. Boy, would I love that!" They both
laughed, and Faith looked at her watch.

"I'd better get organized, or Alex will have a fit when
he gets home. Whatever goes wrong from now on, will
be because I'm in school. I have to be on extra-good behavior now. Perfect dinners, everything on time, dinner
parties worthy of Julia Child and Martha Stewart, I can't
screw up now." She had been thinking of making him a
special dinner that night, to prove that she could juggle
it all, but she no longer had the time or the desire.

"That's a lot of pressure on you," Brad said sympathetically. "Maybe you don't have to prove quite so
much to him. It's not like you've done something really
terrible," he said pointedly.

"In his eyes, I did. I'll send you an e-mail later. I've
got to figure out what I'm doing for dinner. And then I
have to do my homework."

"You're a good kid," he smiled.

"You too. Thanks, Brad." She hung up hastily,
checked the fridge, and decided to run out and buy
something Alex really liked.

By the time he got home, she had stuffed sole in the
oven, she was making asparagus with hollandaise, and
a wonderful rice pilaf from a recipe by Julia Child. And
she served it all impeccably, proud of herself for pulling
it all together in record time. Alex made no comment
about it, ate his dinner quietly, and did not ask her how
school had gone. Faith was more than a little stunned.

"Do you like the fish?" she asked, angling for a compliment from him. She thought it was one of her best. "It's a new recipe I found." She felt like Susie Home-maker making the perfect dinner for him, and still managing to go to school, even if it was the first day.

"It's fine," he said without expression.

"How's the hollandaise?" She knew it was just the way he liked it, and the asparagus was just right.

"A little thick," he commented, and then she realized that she didn't have a chance. Whether he liked the dinner or not, he had no intention of telling her, and she felt anger rise up in her like a head of steam. But she said nothing, and afterward just cleaned up after the meal, without saying another word to him. It had been a lousy thing for him to do. He was not going to concede anything, which seemed like ridiculously childish behavior to her. Now that she was back in school, he could make the best of it, and deal with it. But apparently, he had no intention of making it easy for her. And as she put the dishes in the dishwasher, and he disappeared, she was enraged. She stormed into her study and took out her schoolbooks as soon as she was through. And she sat there until one o'clock doing the two assignments she'd been given. She was finished by the time she went to bed, and had finally gotten over being angry at Alex. And now she had no work to do the next day. She had everything in control.

He didn't speak to her at breakfast the next morning either, and she was irritated with him.

"It's all right, Alex, I'm not going to school today. You

can talk to me. You don't have to punish me till tomorrow." More than she realized, she was still furious with him for the way he had treated her the night before.

"I don't know what you're talking about, Faith. That's a ridiculous thing to say."

"It's a ridiculous way to behave. We're adults. You don't like the fact that I'm going to school, okay. But I'm trying to make it the best it can be for you. You don't have to make it impossible for this to work. You're punishing yourself as much as you are me."

"You did this, Faith. You know how I feel about it. If you don't like my reaction, you can withdraw from school." Simple as that, as far as he was concerned.

"Is that what this is? Blackmail? You're hardly going to speak to me, and make life miserable until I quit school?" He didn't answer her, and her voice was raised. It wasn't how he liked to begin his day. Nor did she. "I guess that's one way to handle it. Not very mature, to say the least. Do you think you can give me a chance on this? And at least see how it works before you start punishing me? I've only been there one day. I mean, how bad could it be?"

"Bad enough. You shouldn't have signed up in the first place. The whole idea is absurd."

"So is your attitude," she blazed at him, which was rare for her. They were off to a very bad start to her school career. And law school would be even worse. But that was his whole point. He wanted to stop her before she got that far. But she wasn't going to give in that easily. If anything, it strengthened her resolve.

"I think your behavior is deplorable," Alex said to her icily, as he picked up *The Wall Street Journal,* and walked out of the kitchen. He hadn't touched his food, and neither had she. It was a great harbinger of what was to come in the months ahead.

She e-mailed Brad about it that afternoon. He answered her that night. He'd been in court until five o'clock.

"Dear Fred, sorry it took me so long to answer. Long day, minor victory for one of my kids. Listening to you talk about Alex drives me insane. He is living in the Dark Ages. How the hell does he get away with this stuff? We should send him to boot camp with Pam. She'd shape him up in a week. He's just going to have to suck it up and get over it. You can't give up your life for him. It's just so wrong for you to do that.

"Can you concentrate on school with him pulling all that shit? You'll have to try. Just do the best you can. You can't be perfect all the time, no one is. Just do your best. But know that there will be screw-ups, and exams, and nights you can't get dinner on the table and do your homework. Like it or not, he has to live with it. If you drop the ball now, or give in, you'll regret it forever. I know Jack would have said the same thing. He would be so thrilled about your going back to law school. He always thought you should. Said you had more natural talent for it than he. Did he ever tell you that? He told me many times, especially while we were in law school, and he kept thinking he'd flunk out. Hang in, Freddy baby . . . you're gonna win! Love, Brad." He always made her feel so much better, and she was grateful for his encouragement. She needed it desperately, and Alex continued to make her life miserable for the next month.

Faith was juggling homework assignments, minor quizzes, taking care of the house, cooking for Alex. And Zoe and Brad were keeping her afloat. It was eminently "doable," and she knew it. She could manage both marriage and school. She had even managed to complete her law school applications. And much to her amazement, her LSAT scores had been in the highest range possible. She was hoping that her scores would compensate for the fact that she hadn't worked or gone to school for the past twenty-five years. And her current grades were straight A's.

The hard part was being iced out by Alex, and the grim atmosphere he created at home. He was overwhelmed by his own resentment for her going back to school. And all it did was get worse as the weeks rolled along. And in early February, she ran into a real crunch. They announced in her Judicial Process class that they were going on a field trip to Washington for four days. It wasn't required, but it was strongly recommended, and the professor advised her to go. There was a paper due afterward, for extra points toward her final grade. She talked to both Brad and Zoe about it, and they both thought she should take the trip. The problem, of course, was Alex. Faith hadn't even had the courage to tell him about it. She wanted to make up her own mind first, before he put pressure on her not to go, which she suspected he would.

It was the week before the field trip when she finally told him what it entailed. He was entirely silent when she explained it to him at the end of dinner. She had had a stomachache all through the meal, waiting to talk to him. As usual, they had eaten without saying a single word. Ever since she'd gone back to school, he made no pretense of maintaining good relations with her. He had become more and more blatant about shutting her out.

"So that's the deal," she summed up. "I'll be in Washington for four days. I can leave you frozen dinners, and I don't know what your travel schedule looks like these days. Are you going anywhere next week?" She hoped he was, so her absence wouldn't create a crisis with him. That would simplify everything.

"No, I'm not," he said bluntly, staring at her as though she had just said she'd been arrested for armed robbery and was going to jail. "I can't believe what you're doing. You're masquerading as a student, when you have responsibilities here."

"Alex, be reasonable. Our children are grown up and gone. We're adults. What do I do here? Nothing. I cook dinner for you at night. I have nothing else to do all day. I was dying of boredom before I went back to school." His charade had gotten more ridiculous every day. It was all about his ego and controlling her. He wanted to know that he could make her do what he wanted. But he had pushed it too far, even for her.

"I'm sorry you're so bored being married to me, Faith."

"I didn't say that. I just don't have a lot to do anymore. You know that. It's not a secret. You wanted me to take bridge lessons and take classes at the museum. This makes more sense."

"Not to me."

"What about Washington?" she said, cutting to the chase. He had said it all before, and she was tired of listening to it, and lying in the dirt on her face at his feet, apologizing to him. It was getting old, to her, if not to him.

"Do what you want."

"What does that mean?" She wanted to know from him how high a price she would have to pay. How angry would it make him, how severely would she be punished? She would probably go anyway, she had decided, but she wanted a glimpse at the price tag before she did.

"It means that you do what you want in any case. Go ahead and do it, at your own risk and peril." It was a thinly veiled threat, and as usual, it pushed a button with her.

"I'm so tired of this, Alex. I haven't committed a crime, for God's sake. I haven't been unfaithful to you. I haven't abandoned you, or our children. Why the hell do you have to act as though I did?"

"You're insane," he said with a look of disgust as he stood up, and prepared to leave the room.

"If I am, you're making me that way."

"Don't blame me if you don't like the consequences of your actions."

"Okay, I won't," she said firmly. "I'm going to Washington. I'll be gone for four days. You can call me if you need me. And I'll leave you all the food you can eat."

"Don't bother, I'll eat out," he said through clenched teeth.

"You don't have to. I'll leave you dinners for four days. Then you have a choice if you want to eat in or out." He didn't say another word, just turned on his heel and walked out.

She didn't even e-mail Brad or Zoe about it. The scene had been so humiliating and frustrating, she didn't want to tell anyone. She was dealing with it herself. And the morning she left, she said good-bye to him, and he didn't answer her. He just continued reading his newspaper and acted as though she didn't exist. If it was designed to make her feel guilty, it had the opposite effect. It just made her angry, and relieved to be out of the house. She felt as though she'd just been let out of jail when she walked out with her backpack, one small duffel, and her computer in its case over her arm. She was taking it with her, to work on, and so she could communicate easily with Zoe and Brad. But it felt great to leave.

More than half the members of her class were going

on the field trip. They met at La Guardia and caught a shuttle to Reagan National Airport in Washington, D.C. They were staying in a small hotel on Massachusetts Avenue that was full of foreign students and minor businessmen from overseas. Just being there seemed exciting to Faith, and late that afternoon, after spending time at the Smithsonian and the Library of Congress, she was thrilled she had come. And she already had an idea for the paper she was going to write when she got home. She started making notes for it in her hotel room that night, and plugged in her computer to work for a while, after they had dinner in an Indian restaurant. She had spent an hour talking to the professor, it was the woman she liked so much, and she got into a fascinating discussion with some of her fellow students about the Constitution and the validity of the laws it upheld. It led to a heated battle about the First Amendment, and by the time Faith got to her room, she was exhilarated and inspired. She was typing rapidly on the computer, when it signaled her that she had an e-mail. It was from Brad.

"Hi, Fred . . . so how's the Judicial Process? Have you done away with it yet? Having fun? I love D.C. Had a girlfriend there when I went to college, she was the daughter of the French ambassador. Used to visit her there, never had so much fun in my life. Tried to fix Jack up with her sister, but he was so outrageous, he scared her to death. So what are you up to? Nice people? Good prof?

"All is well here. Busy days. Trial next week. My secretary informs me it's Valentine's Day next week. The day when you remember someone you love, and realize they've forgotten you, or something like that. Flowers and chocolates. Hay fever and cavities. I seem to be losing my spirit of romance. I would take Pam out to dinner, except she would probably bring two hundred friends and insist I wear black tie. I figure I'll work, and tell her I forgot. She'll probably forget too. I'm rambling. Back to work. Keep in touch. If you run for president, let me know. You'll get my vote for sure. More soon. Love, Brad."

She loved hearing from him. He always made her laugh, or at least smile. And his blurb about Valentine's Day reminded her that she wanted to send candy to the girls. She was sure Alex wouldn't mention the day to her, he never did. They were hardly in Valentine mode anymore, particularly lately. The day no longer meant much to her.

The rest of the trip to Washington was fascinating, and continued at a brisk pace. They went to museums, libraries, universities, gathering data and information to illustrate their course. And it was only on the last morning that they ran into a major snag. They still had a final day to complete, and a last night. But the teacher got an emergency call, her mother had been taken to the hospital. She'd had a stroke and was not expected to live. She got the call on her cell phone, and was understandably upset and said she had to leave. She urged the others to complete the day and remaining night. They weren't due to go home until the following afternoon. It was Friday morning by then anyway. And they weren't due back in New York until late Saturday. But by the time she made the announcement, Faith realized that she had completed all she had to do. She had more than enough for her paper, and more than half the group decided to go home. Without their leader to direct them, they rapidly lost steam. Some of them decided to stay without her, but Faith was among the group that opted to leave at noon. It also allowed her to spend the whole weekend with Alex, which she hoped would redeem her after being gone for three days. He hadn't called her once, or returned her daily calls, since she left.

She picked up her things at the hotel, and took a cab to National with five of her classmates. They caught a shuttle home, and were back in New York at two. It was perfect. She could get home, organize her papers, and cook him a nice dinner as a peace offering. She stopped at the market on the way home, and let herself into the house shortly after three. She was carrying two bags of groceries and set them down in the kitchen, along with all her other bags and belongings. She felt like she had been gone for weeks. And as she looked around the kitchen, she was surprised to see that it was admirably neat. She wondered if he had eaten out every night after all. And as she set the bags down on the floor, she noticed a pair of shoes under a chair. They were high-heeled black satin pumps, and she didn't own any like them. But more surprising, as she picked one up and looked at it closely, was that it was several sizes larger than hers. Her heart began to pound when she saw it, and with a sick feeling in her stomach, she walked upstairs.

The bed in their bedroom had been hastily made, with the bedspread thrown over the unmade bed. And when she pulled it back, she almost instantly spotted a black lace brassiere, and as she looked down, there was a matching pair of thong underwear, seemingly hastily discarded on the floor. She was suddenly overwhelmed by a sick feeling, and sat down on the bed, feeling faint. This couldn't be happening to her. There was no way to explain it, except for the obvious. This wasn't a houseguest, or a daughter, or anyone she could explain to herself. Alex had had a woman in the house while she was gone. And when she walked into her bathroom, there were cosmetics all over her dressing table, of a brand she didn't wear, and there was long black hair in the sink. There was no way she could paint a prettier picture for herself as she saw another pair of shoes, and a sweater hanging on the towel rack. And all she could do, as she looked at two dresses and three unfamiliar suits in her closet, was cry. It hadn't even been a one-night stand. Whoever the woman was who was staying with Alex, she had obviously moved in for the entire four days.

And then with a sudden feeling of terror, she realized that they would be coming back that night, maybe even that afternoon.

Without even thinking clearly, she ran down the stairs, after throwing the bedspread over the bed the way it had been, and leaving everything else undisturbed. And she was careful to turn off the lights. She ran back into the kitchen, grabbed all her bags, including the two bags of groceries she'd purchased, and left the house. She dropped the two bags of groceries into a trash can on the street, and hailed a cab, with no idea whatsoever where to go. There was no friend she wanted to confess this nightmare to, no place to take refuge, and with no idea what else to do, she asked the driver to take her to the Carlyle Hotel two blocks away, and sat in the backseat and cried.

"That's all?" The driver looked at her, confused. It was so close, she could have walked.

"Yes, yes," she said, in total disarray, "just go." She was terrified that she would run into Alex and the woman as they came home. But the worst of all was that it was her home too. He had defiled their home, and their bed. All she could think of as they drove up Madison was the sight of the brassiere and the thong. And all she wanted was to die. It was the ultimate payback for her trip to Washington, if that was what he had intended. But what she also realized as they stopped at the hotel, and the doorman opened the door for her, was that this couldn't have been a new woman to Alex. He wouldn't have moved a stranger into the house for four days. He must have been having an affair with her for a while. Faith felt sick as the doorman asked her if she was checking in, and she said yes.

She didn't want to confront Alex and make a scene. She was going to stay at the hotel, and go home Saturday afternoon, as planned, which meant that Alex and the woman, whoever she was, were going to be cozily ensconced in her house. All she wanted was to check into the Carlyle and throw up.

She asked for a room, and was lucky they had one, since she had no reservation, and told them she would be there for one night, or at most for the weekend. They signed her in, handed her a key, and a bellman carried her Washington gear upstairs. She was clutching her computer as though it were the Sierra Madre treasure, and her last link to the real world. But she didn't plug it in when she got upstairs. She just sat on the bed, sobbing, and it was dark outside by the time she stopped. She didn't even know what time it was. And when she glanced at the clock, she saw it was six o'clock. She couldn't even call Zoe to tell her. She didn't think it was fair to turn her against Alex. She had to sort this out for herself. It just didn't seem possible. But it was obvious to her now that he was having an affair. After all his coldness to her, all his fury and accusations over her going back to school, all the icy unkindness he had showered on her for so long, all the distance, all the silence, all the indifference to her as a woman, he was sleeping with someone else. And the worst part was that she was more devastated than angry. She was beginning to wonder if she should have stayed and confronted them both, but she didn't feel up to it, and she needed time to gather her wits.

It was eight o'clock in New York when she called Brad. She was going to discuss it with him calmly. She wanted his brotherly advice, just as she would have called Jack if he were alive. And she knew from Brad that Pam had had several affairs, and he had strayed once. She expected him to be calmer and more worldly about it than she was, and maybe he would tell her not to get upset. But as soon as she heard his voice, she started crying again, and couldn't even form words. She just sobbed uncontrollably into the phone, and for a minute he didn't know who it was. It wasn't unusual for him to get hysterical calls from potential clients, or their parents, and for a second he thought it was one of those, and then realized with horror that it was Faith.

"Fred? . . . shit . . . oh my God, what is it? . . . come on, baby . . . talk to me . . . tell me what it is. . . ." He was afraid that something might have happened to one of her kids. "Fred, sweetheart . . . please . . . try to calm down . . . take a breath . . . tell me what happened . . . are you hurt? . . . are you okay? . . . where are you?" He was getting more desperate by the second, and she hadn't made sense yet.

"I'm in New York," she croaked, and then dissolved into sobs again.

"Come on now, try to tell me what happened. Are you hurt?"

No . . . but I wish I were dead. . . ." She sounded like a little girl, and all he could envision was the little eight-year-old he had known and loved, with blond braids and no teeth, when they first met.

"Are the kids okay?" That was his worst fear for her, it was what all parents feared most. He prayed that wasn't it.

"Yes . . . I think so . . . it's not them . . . it's Alex . . . ," she said, still crying, but she could get the words out now, and Brad was relieved by what he had heard so far, except for the fact that she was so desperately upset. He wondered if Alex had had an accident, or maybe a heart attack, and had died.

"Is he hurt?"

"No, I am. He's a total shit." Brad suddenly realized they must have had a fight, and it wasn't as bad as he had feared. But it must have been a lulu, for her to be in the state she was in. He had never heard her like that. He wondered if he had beaten her up. If so, Brad thought in anticipatory fury, he was going to nail him himself.

"I thought you were in Washington. What are you doing in New York?" He knew she wasn't due back till the next day.

"The professor's mother got sick, and she had to leave. So I came home early." She was still crying, but coherent enough to talk to him at least. He was panicked over her.

"Then what?" He was anxious to hear.

"I went home."

"Did you have a fight with him?" Brad waved his secretary away from his desk. She was signaling that he had three calls waiting, but he didn't care. He wanted to talk to Faith, without interruptions. Everyone else would have to wait, or go to hell. His priority was Faith.

"No, the house was empty." Suddenly, real panic overtook him. Maybe she'd run into an intruder, and been raped.

"What happened, for God's sake? Fred, you have to tell me." She was driving him insane. He couldn't help her if he didn't know what had put her in the state she was in.

"He had a woman there," she said, and blew her nose in a wad of Kleenex from the box next to the bed.

"She was in the house when you came home?" Brad was stunned. Alex didn't sound like the type, from what she'd said.

"No, her clothes were. There were shoes in the kitchen, her clothes in my closet, her stuff all over my bathroom, and her underwear in the bed. He's been sleeping with her!" It certainly sounded like it to Brad. There weren't many ways to explain what she'd seen. "It was disgusting . . . there was a thong . . ." She dissolved into tears again, and he couldn't help but smile in sympathy for her. Poor kid.

"Poor baby. I wish I were there. Where are you, by the way?" She had obviously gone somewhere to call. He couldn't imagine she was sitting in the house, waiting for them to come home.

"I'm at the Carlyle. I took a room for the weekend. I don't know what to do. Do you think I should go home and throw her out?"

"I don't think that's such a great idea. First, you need to calm down. And then you need to figure out what you want to do. Do you want to divorce him? Leave him? Do you even want to tell him you know? If you don't, maybe it'll just blow over." That was what he had always done with Pam, in the interest of saving their marriage. But she had been smart enough not to bring them home. If nothing else, he thought what Alex had done was just plain dumb.

"What if he's serious about her?" Faith sounded distraught.

"Then you have a major problem." But they both knew she did anyway. Their marriage had been unhappy for years, and Alex had just severed the last thread, along with any respect she'd ever had for him. He had broken her heart with the thong. She felt like she'd been hit by a bus. And then Brad had a thought. "Do you want me to fly in? We can hash this out before you go home. I can take the red-eye tonight if you want, and come back tomorrow night."

"No . . . it's okay . . . I have to figure this out . . . what am I going to do?" She wondered what Jack would have said, but she had the feeling that whatever it was, Brad would say pretty much the same thing. They were very much alike in their views.

"I think you really have to figure out what you want before you confront him. This is your show now, Fred. You've got the ace here." She hadn't thought of it that way, but she wasn't convinced.

"Maybe not. Not if he's in love with her."

"And if he isn't? Do you want to stay married to him? Can you forgive him for this? A lot of people do, so don't be embarrassed if you want to just forget about it. These things blow over eventually. Most of the time at least. It's usually just a passing thing." He hated what Alex did to her anyway, but he was trying to be fair to her, and not get her more worked up than she was. Other people had forgiven their spouses for affairs before. He had Pam, and she him. It all depended on Faith's point of view.

"How could he do this to me?" She was having a typical reaction for anyone in the situation she was in.

"Stupid probably. Bored. His ego needed a boost, he was feeling old. All the same dumb reasons everyone else has for doing that kind of stuff. Most of the time, it's not true love. Just true lust."

"Great. He doesn't even look at me anymore, and he is sleeping with some woman in a thong. She has long black hair," she said, remembering the hair in the sink, and Brad smiled, and wished he could give her a hug. She needed one desperately. "Maybe she's really young."

"I can guarantee you one thing, sweetheart. You're more beautiful than she is. And it doesn't matter if she has a beard and wears a toupee. He's probably just having some fun while you're away."

"Meanwhile, he acts like I committed a felony because I went back to school. And I've been eating shit for a month to make it up to him, and scraping around on my hands and knees. Maybe this is his idea of revenge."

"I'm almost sure it has nothing to do with you. It's about him. Screw him. Let's worry about you. What do you say you wash your face and order a cup of tea from room service, or maybe a drink? I'll call you back in half an hour, and we'll try to figure this out. All I want to help you decide is what you want to do. What I think is irrelevant here."

"But what do you think?" she wanted to know.

"What do I think?" he said, trying to stay calm. "I think he's a complete son of a bitch, and a pathetic little prick, but not just because of this. He drags you around by the hair constantly, in one way or another, he freezes you out, you're lonely all the time, and now he does a dumb thing like this. Personally, I think he should be shot. But if you want to stay married to him, I support you a hundred percent. Because I don't love him, you do, and I'm not married to him." He respected her marriage, and her desire to stay in it, as much as his own. Although he wished she had left Alex years before, for her sake.

"I'm not sure what I feel for him anymore. Right now,

I hate him, and I feel humiliated and stupid and un-loved. I don't know if I love him or not. I just thought I'd always be married to him, now I'm not so sure." A door was opening that seriously frightened her, and she felt desperately insecure.

"Well, don't make any rash decisions until you figure that out. I'll call you back in half an hour." He had eleven urgent phone messages waiting for him by then. He answered seven of them, asked his secretary to take care of the others. It was six o'clock for him by then, and fortunately he knew Pam was going out with friends.

Faith had ordered a pot of tea, and had splashed cold water on her face by the time he called her back half an hour later. But she had no idea what she was going to do about Alex, and just thinking about him in their house that night with the woman in the thong made her feel sick.

"How are you doing?" he asked sympathetically.

"I don't know. I feel weird." And she sounded it. Like she was disconnected, and tired.

"What kind of weird?" He was suddenly worried she might have taken some pills, or done something else to herself. But she was more sensible than that.

"Just weird. Disillusioned, betrayed, screwed over. Numb. Sad." She couldn't think of any other adjectives, but he was relieved.

"Oh, that kind of weird, that's fine. You should. I've been thinking about this, Fred. I think you should prob-ably tell him what you know. If you don't, it'll just poison you. Let him figure out how to clean this up. But don't do anything you don't want to do. I'm just telling you what I think."

"I think you may be right. I don't even know how to tell him what I saw."

"That's the easy part. He knows. This isn't news to him, just to you."

"I guess that's true."

"The news flash here is that you know. Of course you can call him tonight, and give him a heart attack, and tell him you're watching the house. That ought to give him a little jolt," he said evilly.

"He's not answering the phone." She had tried all week.

"Well, that's smart at least. He'll probably be pretty hostile when you tell him you know, whenever you do. Guys don't like to get caught flat out, and one way or another, he'll try to make it your fault."

"How?"

"You've been neglecting him, you don't love him anymore. He thought you were having an affair, although it's not likely he'll accuse you of that." She was squeaky clean, and he figured Alex knew it too. "Maybe he'll say it's because you went back to school. Whatever it is, he'll try to lay it on you to absolve himself."

"Do you suppose he's serious about this girl?" Faith sounded panicked at the thought, as though she was afraid he would throw her out of their house. She couldn't even imagine what she'd do. But Brad knew that couldn't happen to her. If anyone had to leave the house, it would be him.

"That's hard to say. Probably not. My guess is she's just a piece of ass. Sorry to be so blunt. She could even be a hooker."

"I can't imagine him doing that, Brad." But the underwear certainly looked like it, although lots of people wore underwear like that these days. Even Faith's kids. "I don't think that's his style, a hooker, I mean."

"You never know. I hate to think of you sitting in that room, worrying about it all night. I don't suppose you'll get much sleep."

"Maybe I'll get up in the morning and go to church. I have your rosary beads with me." She was going to need more than rosary beads now. She was going to need a cool head, and maybe a good lawyer. Brad just wished he were there.

"You need to think this out quietly, Fred. Just figure out what you want before you make any moves."

"I think I want to know what's going on, who she is, what she means to him. I want to know the truth."

"If he'll give it to you. He doesn't strike me as the type. I think he'll do everything he can to accuse you, and then shut you out to protect himself." Brad knew the species well. He had seen a lot in his years, among clients and friends and associates, and he had made some mistakes himself, though none as foolish as this.

"I think you're right," Faith agreed. "Thank you for listening to me. I'm sorry I'm such a mess." But she sounded a lot better than she had when she first called. He thought someone had died.

"You scared me to death. I thought something had happened to you, or one of the girls. This is pretty lousy stuff, but at least everyone's alive."

"I'm not sure I am," she said, sounding depressed.

"You will be once you sort this out." It was after seven o'clock in San Francisco, and after ten in New York by then. "I think you should take a bath and go to bed. I'm going to go right home. If you need me, call. You can call at any hour. I'm here for you, Fred. I just wish there were more I could do."

"You did everything you could. You did what Jack would have done. All you can do is talk to me, and you did. I have to figure this out for myself," she said, sounding terminally sad.

"You will, Fred. I know you'll do the right thing."

"What am I going to tell the girls if we break up over this? I don't think they should ever know."

"Why not? You didn't do it. He did. He has to face the consequences of a very stupid move. It's not your job to keep it a secret for him. You don't owe him that, Fred."

"Zoe will hate him for this." And Ellie would find some excuse.

"She hates him anyway," Brad said practically, "and I'm not so sure she's wrong. He hasn't been much of a father to her, nor much of a husband to you, from what I can see."

"It hasn't been great," Faith admitted, "but it's just

the way it is." It brought his mind back to the conversation they'd had the night they had dinner, about the compromises one made to stay married, when things didn't turn out the way you'd hoped. He wondered if it was going to be worth it to her to stay married to Alex in the end. At any price, to keep the peace. He hoped not, but he didn't want to influence her. He had no right, since he had done pretty much the same thing. He'd been turning a blind eye to Pam's affairs for years. It was easier that way, for him at least. But he thought Faith deserved a better break. And he probably did too, but he preferred not to rock the boat, and maintain the status quo.

"You sound beat. Try to get some sleep." He was sure she wouldn't close her eyes all night, and so was she. But he thought she should try. "Why don't you call down for a massage? They probably have somebody who could come up even at this hour."

"I'll just take a bath." She wasn't used to pampering herself. Only everyone else. It had been that way for years.

"Call me at home, if you want. I'll be home in ten minutes."

"Thanks, Brad . . . I love you, big brother. . . ." She really did.

"I love you too, kiddo. We'll get you out of this mess . . . one way or another. It'll sort itself out. You'll see."

"Yeah. Maybe so," she said, sounding wiped out. But

she didn't sound convinced, and neither was he. Alex
was the unpredictable element in the piece. It was hard
to know how he was going to react if Faith confronted
him. Badly, Brad suspected as he drove home. He would
have liked to give him a swift kick in the ass for what he
had just done to Faith. It would have been one for the
home team.

15

FAITH TOSSED AND TURNED ALL NIGHT. SHE FINALLY dozed off around four o'clock, and woke again at six. She got up, and watched the sun come up. It was a beautiful sunny day, and she had never felt worse. All she could think of was Alex and the woman with the long black hair sound asleep in their bed. She wasn't sure she would ever be able to sleep in it again.

She ordered a pot of black coffee at seven o'clock and put on a sweater and a pair of jeans. She went to the seven-thirty mass at St. Jean Baptiste on Lexington Avenue, and she held Brad's rosary beads in her hands, but she couldn't concentrate enough to say the prayers. She just knelt and stared into space. And when the mass ended, she walked back to the hotel. She didn't know what to do with herself all day. She wasn't due home till four or five, and she was afraid to go for a walk or leave the hotel, because she might run into them.

Brad called her when he got up. It was eleven o'clock for Faith, and he was worried about her, but she sounded all right. She said she was going to play it by ear when she got home. She just had to see how she felt, which Brad thought was reasonable.

"Just don't take any shit from him," he reminded her, and for the first time since the day before, she smiled.

"I won't. I promise."

"Call me when you can." He was going out to play tennis with a friend, and he had promised to do an errand with Pam. She wanted a new stereo system for the living room, and he had said he would look at some with her. But he was carrying his cell phone, and told Faith to use it if she called the house and he was out. He was entirely available to her, and he didn't give a damn what comments Pam made. It was easy enough to explain to her, although he didn't think he would. He had nothing to feel guilty about, and neither did Faith. Their friendship was entirely clean, and completely pure. Unlike some of Pam's. He thought Pam might even feel sorry for Faith if she knew. She hated it when women were taken advantage of, or abused, and she would have told her just how to let Alex have it right between the eyes, better even than Brad could. But he was doing his best on her behalf.

Faith languished in her room all day, and at five o'clock, she called the bellman to carry her bags, and had the doorman call her a cab. She had too much stuff with her to walk the two blocks to the house. She let herself in with a shaking hand as she turned the key. The lights were on in the hall, and there was no sign of Alex. She assumed he was upstairs. She put her bags down in the hall, and walked slowly up to their room. The bed

was made, and everything looked impeccable. She figured he must have made the bed himself. She wondered
if he had had the decency to change the sheets, but she
didn't look. He was sitting in his favorite chair by their
bedroom fireplace, reading a book. He was the portrait
of innocence itself. And he didn't even have the grace to
look up at her, as she stood watching him. And for an instant, she felt a wave of disgust and hatred and hurt
wash over her. She had to fight back tears.

"You're late," he said, without looking up, and she
couldn't believe his nerve. She didn't answer him, and
he finally glanced up at her. She hadn't moved since she
walked in. "How was the trip?"

She didn't answer his question, but proffered one of
her own. "How was your week?" He could read nothing on her face, nor she on his.

"Long. Difficult. We had a lot of work."

"That's nice," she said, and sat down across from
him. And as she did, she knew that she couldn't go on
with the charade. She had to tell him the truth, as she
knew it, whether or not he did.

"What did you do in Washington?" He could see
something in her eyes, but he didn't know what it was.
He kept talking to her while he tried to figure it out.

"What did you do in New York?"

"I told you," he said, sounding irritated, "I worked.
What do you think I did?" He was about to go back to
his book, but stopped short at what she said.

"I'm not sure. I came home yesterday, Alex. We finished earlier than planned."

"What do you mean you came home yesterday?" He looked stunned. But he made no admission of guilt.

"The professor's mother got sick and she had to leave, so some of us came home. I got in at two o'clock. I stopped to buy groceries, I thought I'd make something you really liked, and I came home. You know, kind of like Goldilocks . . . who's been sleeping in my bed? Whoever she is, she has fairly big feet, long black hair, and wears a thong." His face went pale, but he said not a word for a long beat.

"Where've you been since yesterday?" he said accusingly, trying to turn the tables on her. Brad had warned her about that, so she was prepared. She wasn't buying it.

"I went to the Carlyle as soon as I figured out what you were doing here. I thought I'd spare us both the embarrassment of making a scene in front of her. What's happening, Alex? Who is she? How long has this been going on?" Her eyes never left his, and he had never seen her that way.

"That's irrelevant." If he could have denied her existence entirely, Faith suspected, he would have. But there was no chance of that with everything she had seen. "If you weren't jaunting around pretending to be a kid, going to school, things like this wouldn't happen." It was exactly what Brad had predicted he would do. He was trying to blame her for what he'd done.

"Does that mean when you go on business trips, you

expect me to screw around, and it's your fault? That's pretty much the same thing."

"Don't be ridiculous. I have to work for a living. You didn't have to go back to school."

"And you think that gives you license to cheat on me? Wow, that's certainly one way to look at it."

"I told you you were taking a risk when you went back to school."

"I didn't realize your cheating on me was the risk you meant. We're playing for high stakes here, aren't we?" She was furious but she still didn't know what she wanted from him, or what the outcome would be. Neither of them was backing off and he was still trying to blame her. And as she looked at him, he got out of his chair and paced around the room.

"This is all your fault, Faith," he accused without batting an eye. She couldn't believe her ears. "If you hadn't been such a damn fool about going back to school, this would never have happened. You threw our marriage out the window the day you did."

"No." Faith had white heat in her eyes and faced off with him. "You threw it out the day you brought that bitch into my bed. How dare you do such a thing!"

"How dare you speak to me that way! I won't tolerate that from you, Faith." He was trying to fight fire with fire.

"*You* won't tolerate it? How do you think I felt when I came home and found her underwear in my bed and her hair in my sink?" There was very little he could say to that, but Faith wasn't prepared for what he said next. But he wasn't willing to let Faith have the upper hand.

"I'm moving out," he said, and then walked into his bathroom and slammed the door. She could hear him slamming and banging in his dressing room, and twenty minutes later, as she sat on a chair looking stunned, he was carrying a valise. She didn't say a word to him. She couldn't even think of what to say.

"Where are you going?" She looked devastated. This was a nightmare come true. And suddenly she was wondering if it was her fault, if she had been too hard on him, if she was to blame because she'd gone to school. She didn't know which end was up anymore.

"I'm going to a hotel for the time being. You can call me at my office if you want to speak with me." She wanted to tell him that her lawyers would, but she didn't want to jump the gun, just to have the last word. She didn't even know if she needed a lawyer yet, and she didn't want to ask him if she did.

"Are you in love with her, Alex?" Faith asked pathetically. She knew she'd hate to hear it from him if he was, but she wanted to know.

"It's none of your goddamn business whether or not I am," he said viciously. Not once since she'd confronted him had he apologized to her.

"I think I have a right to know. Who is she?" Faith sounded calmer than she had. There was so much she wanted to know.

"You lost your rights in this marriage, Faith, when

you put our marriage on the back burner and went back
to school." It was a ridiculous thing to say, and even Faith
knew that. He was being spiteful, irrational, and cruel.

"Are you telling me this is the first time you've been
unfaithful to me, and it's all because of me?"

"I'm not saying anything. You'll hear from me when
I've decided what I want to do." It was incredible, he
was threatening her. He had turned the tables on her.
And he was walking out. But she was the one who had
been wronged, and that much was clear to her.

She didn't say another word as he clattered down the
stairs, banging his bag along the wall, and a moment
later, she heard the front door slam. She knew nothing
more than she had when she got home. All she knew
was what she had seen in her bedroom the day before,
and nothing more. He wasn't about to enlighten her. She
walked around the house aimlessly for a while, looking
stunned. Half an hour later, she called Brad.

"How're you doing, Fred?" he asked sympathetically. She didn't sound good to him, but she wasn't sobbing this time. Her voice sounded very small.

"He moved out."

"Are you kidding?"

"He said it was all my fault, because I went back to
school, and it's none of my business who she is, or what
she means to him."

"I told you he'd blame you." But Brad hadn't expected him to move out. He had been cornered like a rat,
and it was the only defense he could use. Escape. It was

a shabby thing to do, and he said as much to Faith. "I'd like to tell you you'll be better off, but I'm sure you don't feel that way right now."

"We've been married for twenty-six years. I'm beginning to wonder if I even know who he is."

"You probably used to, Fred. Things change. We don't always notice it, or want to acknowledge it." The truth was, he was right. Alex had closed the door on her emotionally years before. She had chosen not to notice it, and to just live with things that way. But sooner or later, what she had ignored had come home to roost. And then she had another frightening thought.

"What am I going to tell the kids?"

"Why say anything, for the next few days at least? They won't know for a while, unless he tells them, and he probably won't. Let the dust settle. He may come back when he calms down. Getting found out may have forced him into a position he doesn't want to take. He may just slip back in if he doesn't lose too much face."

"Do you think he will?" Faith sounded hopeful, which nearly broke Brad's heart. He didn't want her being buried alive with a man who treated her the way Alex did. If only on behalf of Jack, he wanted better for her. She deserved so much more than Alex gave.

"He might. Just try to relax. And maybe you should call an attorney tomorrow, just to protect yourself. I'll see if I can find you someone in New York. I'll call some friends who do family law out here and see who they recommend. I'm so sorry, Fred. You don't deserve this. And it's not your fault. I hope you know that."

"I'm not sure what I believe." She wasn't sure yet how she felt. More than anything she felt dead.

She moved into Zoe's room that night. She couldn't bear the thought of sleeping in her own bed, whether he had changed the sheets or not. Brad called to check on her late that night, and Pam commented when he got off the phone. She hadn't seen him look that upset in a long time. Not since one of their kids had been seriously sick.

"What was that all about?" She had just come in from dinner with friends, and he had stayed home, allegedly to do some work. But she knew perfectly well that he just hadn't wanted to go out with her and her friends.

"A friend in distress."

"It must be pretty bad for you to look like that. Anyone I know?"

"No, it's okay. Marital problems." Pam wondered if it was Faith, but she decided not to ask. Brad looked too upset for her to question him. She was smart about things like that, and she backed off.

And by noon the next day, Brad had e-mailed her the name of an attorney in New York. Faith called him and left a message, and was relieved when he called her back. She explained what had happened, and the attorney asked her if she wanted to hire a private investigator to see if they could find out who the woman was. And much to her own surprise, she said yes.

She felt like she was swimming underwater for the

next few days. She went to school, talked to Brad. She hadn't heard a word from Alex, and the attorney called her back on Friday. She was stunned to hear that he knew who the woman was. She was twenty-nine years old, divorced, had a child, and was a receptionist at the investment banking firm where Alex worked. According to some of the secretaries who knew her there, she had moved to New York from Atlanta the year before, and she and Alex had been involved for the past ten months. Ten months. It had nothing to do with her going to school. He had been cheating on her for nearly a year. And just listening to the attorney, Faith felt sick.

She made an appointment to come to his office the following week, but she still had no idea what to do. She didn't know if she should divorce him, or ask him to come back. They hadn't talked all week. She didn't even know how serious he was about the girl. And not knowing what else to do, she called Alex at the office that afternoon. And was relieved when he took her call. She was afraid he wouldn't even do that, but he sounded anything but pleasant when he heard her voice.

"Do you want to get together and talk?" Faith suggested, trying not to sound as angry as she felt. What the lawyer had told her that morning had knocked her off her feet. But so did Alex's response.

"There's nothing to say, Faith," he said bluntly, and tears sprang to her eyes again. She had spent a week crying on and off. It was almost the way she had felt when Jack died, only that was worse. But in its own way, this was like a death too. It was about loss, of faith, of hope, of dreams, of trust, and maybe even their marriage.

"We can't just walk away from this, Alex. We have to at least talk." She tried to sound calmer than she felt, so she wouldn't frighten him off.

"I have nothing to say to you," he said, as though he still felt it was all her fault. And she took a breath, and a leap that would have horrified Zoe and Brad. But it was all she could think of to do. In the face of his endless criticisms, she always felt as though she should make the effort and the sacrifice, no matter how unfair or unwarranted. It was her childhood haunting her again, trying to be the perfect little girl, and never quite measuring up anyway.

"What if I give up school?" It was the ultimate sacrifice, but she wanted to save her marriage. It was too much to give up without at least trying to salvage it. And if that was the issue for him, then maybe she had no choice. She didn't want to trade a law degree for a marriage of twenty-six years.

"It's too late for that," he answered in a strangled voice, and Faith felt the room reel.

"Are you serious? Do you want to marry this girl?" It was the only reason she could think of for his not coming back. She had been a good wife to him. Her only "mistake," if he wanted to call it that, was going back to school.

"It's not about this girl, Faith. It's about you."

"Why? What did I do?" Tears were rolling relentlessly down her cheeks.

"Our marriage has been dead for years. And I feel dead when I'm with you." She felt his words like a physical blow, they were so cruel. "I'm fifty-two years old. I want a better life. We're all through. The kids are grown up. They don't need us together anymore. You want to go to law school. I want a life too." He made it sound like he had been planning this for years. And she had walked right into his trap when she went back to school. What he was saying to her was like ripping out her heart. She had stayed with him out of loyalty, and respect for their marriage. And all he was doing was waiting for a second chance, without her.

"I never realized you felt like that," she said, in a choked voice.

"Well, I do. We both deserve more than this." He was right, but Faith would have never grabbed for the brass ring, at his expense. She had had every intention of staying with him, no matter how difficult it was. He had none of that loyalty to her. "I've already called a lawyer. You'd better find one too." She didn't tell him she already had. This whole disaster was moving with the speed of sound, and if nothing else, she wanted to slow it down. She thought he was making a colossal mistake.

"What are we going to tell the girls?" She could only imagine the spin he was going to put on it. It was going to be all her fault. And she had no intention of telling them the sordid story about the girl. It was too humiliating, but would have explained everything. And she was sure that, like her father, Ellie would blame her.

"We'll have to figure that out," Alex answered her. "Get a lawyer, Faith. I want a divorce."

"Oh my God." She couldn't believe she was hearing those words. "How can you do this, Alex? Didn't our marriage mean anything to you?"

"No more than it did to you when you decided to stop being my wife and become a lawyer."

"How can you compare the two?" She suddenly understood the appeal of the girl in the thong. She was twenty-three years younger than Alex, and a receptionist. She didn't have a major career. He could control her, and he had lost some of his hold on Faith. He couldn't forgive her for that.

"I don't have to justify anything to you, Faith. You brought this on yourself." Part of her believed him and the rest of her wanted to scream, it was so unfair, and a moment later he hung up. He didn't even tell her where he was staying, and she suddenly wondered if he was living with the girl. Anything was possible now. Faith felt as though she had lost her entire world in a single week, and she was crying softly when she heard the front door slam. She jumped, and couldn't imagine who it was, until she heard Zoe's voice.

"Hi, I'm home!" She had come home as a surprise, and Faith didn't know what to do. She didn't know how to explain Alex's absence, and she wasn't ready to tell her about the divorce. She hadn't even absorbed it yet herself.

Faith quickly wiped her eyes and hurried into the hall with a wide smile. But she had a wild-eyed look, and she hadn't combed her hair all day. And there were deep circles under her eyes, from not sleeping all week.

"Hi, Mom," Zoe said, as she dropped her bag on the floor of the front hall and then took a closer look at her mother, with worried eyes. "Are you sick?"

"I had some kind of stomach flu, and I've been feeling rotten all week."

"That's too bad," Zoe said sympathetically, "you sound like you have a cold too."

"I do." Faith was quick to agree. The truth was that she looked as bad as she felt. And it was going to be agony trying to keep the truth from Zoe over the weekend, but she was also relieved that she was there. It gave her something to hold on to, and to anchor her reality to. Her entire life had begun to feel surreal.

"Where's Dad?" Zoe asked, as she checked the refrigerator. There was hardly any food. Faith hadn't shopped or eaten all week.

"He's out of town. He's in Florida." It was the first place that came to mind, and Zoe nodded. The story was plausible to her. Her father went away a lot.

"We need groceries. Sorry I didn't call. I thought it would be fun to surprise you, Mom. I'm sorry you've been sick." She turned to her mother with a smile.

"I'll be fine." Zoe nodded, and didn't think much of

it, and then was surprised to see her mother's night-gown in her room and her bed unmade when they went upstairs.

"Who's been sleeping in my room?" She looked startled as she saw her unmade bed.

"I didn't want to keep your father up with my cold, so I slept in here. Sorry, sweetheart, I'll make the bed right away."

"I thought you said Dad was away." Zoe looked suspicious. It was obvious that something was wrong, and she wondered if her parents had had a fight.

"He is. But he only left today. I was going to move back to our room tonight." But the big pretty yellow room all done in flowered chintz looked like a hellhole to her now. She couldn't imagine sleeping in it again.

"How come he left over the weekend?" That was unusual for him.

"I think he was afraid he wouldn't get in. They're expecting a big snowstorm in Chicago at the end of the week. He was going to a very important meeting, so he left early to be sure he'd get in."

"Mom." Zoe sat down on the edge of her bed and pulled her mother down next to her. In all her eighteen years, she had never seen her mother in such distress or so confused. Not even when her brother's plane had crashed. Zoe had been fifteen years old then and remembered it well. Her mother looked dazed and in total disarray. "You said he went to Florida. Mom, what's happening? What's wrong?"

"Nothing," she insisted, as she started to cry. It had been the week from hell, and she was falling apart. And she didn't want to tell Zoe anything yet.

"Tell me the truth, Mom. Where's Dad?"

She knew she had to say something, if not the whole truth. "We had a little fight. It's nothing. I'm just upset, that's all. It's not a big deal." But it was, and she knew she'd have to tell Zoe the truth at some point. She hated lying to her. "Okay, we had a big fight. A very big fight," Faith admitted, blowing her nose, as Zoe kept an arm firmly around her. Her sympathies always lay with Faith.

"How big?"

"Very big. He walked out."

"He left?" Zoe looked shocked, and was suddenly glad she'd come home. Her mother was a total mess. "He walked out?"

"Yes." She had to fight to hold back sobs.

"Why?"

"It's too complicated to explain. I really don't want to tell you about that part. You have to trust me on that." Zoe decided to respect her mother's boundaries, for the time being at least.

"Did he blame you?"

"Of course," Faith said, blowing her nose again. "Who else can he blame? Certainly not himself."

"Is he coming back?" Faith started to say yes, and then stopped and shook her head as she cried more.

"Holy shit. He's not? Are you sure?" Zoe looked stunned.

"He just told me he wants a divorce." Zoe was suddenly not just her daughter, but her best friend. And she was afraid to burden her, but Zoe seemed to be holding up a lot better than her mother was.

"When did all this happen?"

"A week ago. I'm sorry I'm such a mess."

"What a bastard he is," Zoe said about her father. It confirmed everything she'd thought of him for years, and then she looked at her mother again. "Does Ellie know?"

"No one does. I just talked to him half an hour ago. He moved out on Saturday, and he just told me he wants a divorce. He says he has a right to a life too, and he feels dead being married to me."

"What a shit!"

"Don't talk about your father that way."

"Why not? He is. When were you going to tell us?"

"I don't know. This is all pretty new. I've just been sitting here crying all week."

"Poor Mom. I'm so sorry . . . I wish I'd known . . . I'm so glad I came home. I don't even know why I did. I just missed you this week."

"Me too," Faith said, as the two women hugged and she cried helplessly. And then Zoe took over, and tucked her into her bed. She went downstairs and made her some soup and scrambled eggs. She was shaken by the news she'd heard, but not as badly as Faith. All she wanted to do now was take care of her mom.

She climbed into bed with her when she came back upstairs, and they hugged and talked and watched TV.

And when Brad called late that night, she told him that Zoe was there, and he was relieved. She told him what Alex had said, and he sounded grim at his end.

"What a son of a bitch he is," Brad said, sounding disgusted, and when Zoe left the room to go brush her teeth, Faith whispered what she knew about the girl, and that he'd been involved with her for nearly a year.

"I know you don't believe this now, but maybe this is for the best, Fred. You'd have never left him, and he'd have ruined your life." But it was twenty-six years. A lot to lose in a single week. No matter how difficult he was, or how cold, she couldn't imagine a life without him. "I don't want to bother you if you're with Zoe. I'll call you tomorrow. Get some sleep."

"I will." Zoe had told her to sleep with her in her bed, and Faith was relieved. She couldn't imagine ever sleeping in her own bed again.

"Who was that?" Zoe asked when she came back from brushing her teeth. She felt like a mother taking care of her child, instead of the reverse.

"Brad Patterson."

"The rosary guy?" Faith nodded, still looking sad, and Zoe smiled. "Maybe now you can marry him."

"Don't be silly. He's like my brother, he practically is my brother, and he's married. And I'm still married to your dad." But they both knew now that it wouldn't be for long. Faith couldn't even fathom it, as she lay in bed with Zoe that night. And she finally fell into a deep troubled sleep.

16

Zoe went back to school on Sunday night, and they talked all weekend before that. Faith was still in shock, and in spite of how miserable she was, she never told Zoe about the girl. She just said that her father said he wanted a more exciting life than he had with her, and he was furious that she had gone back to school, which was hardly news.

"Those are stupid reasons to get a divorce, Mom. Do you think he's having an affair?" Zoe said sensibly. But Faith didn't give away what had started it. In spite of everything, she was still loyal to him.

"I really don't know," was all she said.

But she felt better by the time Zoe left. And she saw the lawyer Brad had recommended the following week. He told her everything she needed to know, and showed her the report from the private investigator. The girl's name was Leslie James. And a photograph they'd included showed a very pretty girl. She was tall and shapely and looked like a model, and had long wavy black hair, which Faith already knew. She had a five-year-old daughter, the report said, and she was well liked in the office. The romance was apparently an open secret at Alex's firm. The other secretaries in the office thought they might get married, but Alex had never said as much to anyone.

Faith felt as though she had been kicked in the stomach by the time she left. She was a beautiful girl certainly, and very young. She was eighteen years younger than Faith, which was yet another blow.

She was sitting in her study, staring into space, when the phone rang. It was Brad, checking to see how the meeting had gone.

"It was fine. I saw the report. She's a beautiful girl, Brad. I guess I can't blame him." She sounded mortally depressed.

"I can. The guy's a fool. You're beautiful too." More so than anyone Brad knew, inside and out.

"Thank you," she said politely, but she didn't sound convinced. She felt as though her whole life had caved in, and it had. She and Zoe had laughed over the fact that she had missed Valentine's Day entirely. It had disappeared into the smoke of her own private hell. She hadn't even remembered what day it was, and she no longer cared. But Zoe had gotten the chocolates her mother had sent. And so had Ellie in London, after a slight delay.

"I have some news for you," Brad said, trying to cheer her up. He had been worried about her for more than a week. She was sounding depressed, and he knew she'd been struggling in school, but at least she went.

"What's that?" she asked, feeling half dead. She felt as though she were hanging somewhere in outer space. Everything about her life suddenly seemed unreal.

"I have to come to New York for a couple of days. I have some work to do there. I was hoping you'd have dinner with me. We can just go out for pizza if you don't feel like getting dressed."

"Now that is good news," she said with a sad smile. Even seeing him wasn't the joy it would have been only weeks before. But it was pretty good. It was something to look forward to. "When are you coming?"

"This weekend actually. I have to see a couple of attorneys there, to consult on a tough case. I'm coming in late Friday night. I can be at your door on Saturday morning, and maybe we can go skating in the park."

"I thought you had to work," she said vaguely, and he smiled at his end. She wasn't as dead as he thought.

"I do. I'll work it in. But I'd love to see you. Save me Saturday night, Fred. I'm going home on the red-eye Sunday night. It's a quick trip." He had concocted it entirely for her. He was worried sick about her, and he told himself he owed it to Jack. He wanted to go to New York to take a look at her and make sure she was all right. He didn't have to see anyone, but he told her he did, just so he would have the excuse to come and visit her. It seemed like the least he could do.

And by the time he arrived in New York, Faith had

survived another week since Alex's perfidy. Their lawyers had contacted each other, and things were moving
ahead. They hadn't told Ellie yet, but Alex had said he
would call her over the weekend, and Faith dreaded the
reaction from her. It was easy to guess that no matter how wrong her father had been, or how cruel, she
would side with him. But since she was closer to Alex,
Faith agreed that Ellie should hear it from him. Especially since Zoe had heard it from her. She knew she
couldn't have convinced Ellie to see it her way anyway.
Faith only hoped that Ellie would try to see her side too.

Brad decided to stay at the Carlyle, so he would be
close to her. And he arrived at the house on Saturday
morning, at nine o'clock after he had showered and
shaved. He had been so tired he had actually slept de-
cently on the plane. All he had told Pam was the same
he'd told Faith, that he had to meet with two attorneys
in New York about a tough case. And Pam hadn't ques-
tioned it. And in the end, neither did Faith. He had been
afraid that she would object to his coming, if she
thought it was just for her. She didn't want to impose on
him more than she already had.

And he was worried when he saw her open her front
door. She looked very pale and very thin, in a black
turtleneck and black jeans, no makeup, dark circles, and
her straight blond hair was hanging straight on either
side of her face. It was obvious that she had lost weight.
But she smiled as soon as she saw him and gave him a
warm hug. She didn't look as shell-shocked as she had

sounded on the phone at first. She just looked tired, and very sad.

She toasted him English muffins, made coffee, and scrambled eggs, and they sat in the kitchen and talked for a long time. And afterward they sat in the living room, and he made a fire. She was still sleeping in Zoe's room, and was beginning to think she always would.

"It's so weird," she confessed to Brad, "I feel like I did after Jack died. I feel like everything's different and will never be the same again. Twenty-six years of my life just went right down the tubes."

"I know, kiddo. It's the shits. You'll get used to it after a while. And it will be better one day. It's different than Jack. This gives you a chance to have a better life. Alex was killing you slowly. You're the one who deserves to have a life, not him," Brad said quietly as they sat by the fire. He had asked if she wanted to go skating, but she said she was too tired, and in truth so was he. It was a long way to come for a weekend after a busy week, but it was worth it for her. He was glad he had come, and so was she.

"What time do you have to work?" she asked, and he almost forgot, but recovered before she noticed it.

"Around four o'clock. Maybe five. I only need a couple of hours with them, but we just couldn't cover it on the phone, too many files." He figured he'd go to the hotel and take a nap, and then meet her again for dinner.

"You didn't come just for me, did you, Brad?" she

asked suspiciously with a familiar smile, and he laughed.

"Hell, no. I love you, Fred. But I wouldn't come all this way just to mend your broken heart."

"Good. You've got better things to do with your time than worry about me."

"I say that to myself every day," he teased. "Actually, you're worth worrying about, Fred. You got a rotten break, kid. I think your first rotten break was the day you married him."

"That's what Jack always said." But there had been rotten breaks much earlier in her life too, which had set the stage for her accepting far too much pain from Alex.

"Jack was right. About a lot of things."

He took her out to lunch, and they went to a deli nearby. She picked around at an egg salad sandwich, and he nagged her until she ate half of it. And he shared a bowl of matzoh ball soup with her. It was one of his favorite things about New York.

"They just don't have matzoh ball soup like this in California," he said, and she grinned, and looked more like herself. It was comforting just being with him.

They went for a long walk afterward, and wandered into Central Park. The trees were still bare, and the park looked gray, but the air and the exercise did them both good. It was midafternoon before they went back to her house, and she made him a cup of hot chocolate while he started another fire, and wondered if she was going to keep the house. He didn't want to upset her by asking her. It was a nice place, but he thought it would do her good to move on. But it was too soon to say it to her.

"What were you looking so serious about?" Faith asked as she handed him the steaming cup of hot chocolate with marshmallows on it. It had been one of their favorite things when they were kids.

"I was thinking about you," he said honestly, "and what an amazing woman you are. A lot of women would have handled this whole thing differently, and told their kids what he did. You're always so fair to everyone. Pathologically decent and kind. That's a nice thing to be." But they both knew it came at a high price to her.

"Thank you," she said, smiling quietly at him. Her brother had been that way too. They were instinctively good people, and had always been. But they had been through a lot too, before their father died, and even afterward. There were things about both of them Brad had never known. He had always admired them for their kindness to people, and their tolerance, and honesty, as well as for the bond they shared. When other kids lied, Jack had always told the truth. And the one time Jack knew that Faith had lied to him, he had given her hell. She had been about ten years old, and Brad still remembered the big tears rolling down her cheeks when Jack had scolded her. She didn't look much different than that now, and it had been the vision he had had of her for the past week. Thinking of her that way, in tears, was what had brought him to New York to see her. He couldn't stand knowing how unhappy she was, and not at least doing something to help. And it meant the world to her just to see him and talk to him. She respected everything he thought and said. And she trusted him as much as she had Jack.

"How are you feeling, Fred?" he asked with a look of concern as he lay sprawled on the carpet in front of the fire. He looked very much as he had as a boy, with the same cleft in his chin, and endless legs. And his hair was nearly as dark as it had been then. Even sitting close to him, Faith could hardly see any gray.

"Better, thanks to you." It made him doubly glad he had come. She looked better than she had that morning when she opened the door. Happier, and more at peace. "Not quite as weird. It's going to take time to get used to this. It's going to seem so strange not being married to him." She had been married to Alex since she was twenty-one. It seemed like an entire lifetime to her.

"You may get to like it eventually. How are you holding up at school?" He had been worried about that at first.

"Not great. But I haven't flunked out yet. I think it'll be okay." She was going to apply to law school soon.

"Don't you have to go to work?" she asked, worried about him. It was nearly four o'clock, and he didn't seem in a hurry to go anywhere. He was relaxed and content, lying close to her.

"Yeah, soon," he said, without glancing at his watch. He was getting sleepy from the hot chocolate and the warmth of the fire, and the sense of well-being he had with her. "Life is strange, isn't it? We grew up with each other, and we had every opportunity to fall in love, and never did. Instead, I married Pam, whom I have absolutely nothing in common with, and you married Alex, and he treats you like dirt. It would have been so much simpler if we'd taken a good look at each other and fallen in love way back then. Nothing is ever simple, is it, Fred?" He was looking into the fire as he said it, and then looked up at her with a sleepy smile. But there was something deep and sad in Faith's eyes. There was so much he didn't know, especially about what had set the stage for Alex to treat her as he had.

"It never works that way," Faith said with a sigh. "We all have to go find other people and complicate things. We marry complicated people, and then we think we've done it right. If you marry someone in your own backyard, you feel like you've failed somehow. Too easy, I guess. And there was more to it than that for me." She wondered if Jack had ever said anything to him about their father, but suspected he had not. It had been their secret shame for their entire childhood and a significant part of their adult lives.

She had never told anyone else about her father molesting her, and threatening her about it. She had never felt able to tell Alex, and had always been afraid he would hold it against her somehow. She had discussed it with her therapist at length years before, and with Jack, and her conclusion had always been that Alex wasn't up to it. His own childhood had been cold and unemotional, but relatively normal otherwise, and circumspect. She didn't think he could have understood her father doing something like that, without blaming her for it, which would have broken her heart. But she felt differently about Brad. She knew she could tell him anything. What he had offered her, and always given her, was his unconditional love.

"Complicated is never the right thing," Brad said simply, as he watched her. He could see something painful come into her eyes. "Are you okay, Fred?"

"Yeah. I was just thinking about some old stuff. Ugly old stuff actually. But I think it's always been a big part of my life with Alex, in an unspoken way. I think it's why I let him call the shots and be so hard on me at times. I suspect I always thought I deserved whatever he dished out to me." Her eyes were speaking volumes to Brad, and he held her hand tight, as though sensing that she was facing old demons with him, and within herself.

"Why is that?" he asked softly, as she lowered her eyes, and then looked up at him again. It was harder to say the words than she had thought it would be, even to him.

"There was some pretty bad stuff that happened when I was a kid. Jack knew about it . . . not at first, but he found out eventually. It was hard for him too." Before she even said the words, Brad suspected it, and tightened his grip on her hand. He didn't know how or why he knew, but he did. And she could sense his acceptance even before she spoke to him.

She took a breath finally, and dove in. She wasn't sure why, but she wanted to share it with him. Faith wasn't even aware of the tears rolling down her cheeks, as Brad's heart nearly ripped out of his chest as he watched helplessly. He was just as helpless as Jack had been. Jack couldn't stop it at the time. And Brad couldn't take the memory away from her now. All he could do was be there for her, and as always, he was.

"My father molested me when I was a little girl," she said barely audibly. There was no sound from Brad as he waited for her to go on. "He started when I was about four or five, and did it until he died, when I was ten. I was too scared to tell anyone, because he told me he'd kill me and Jack if I did. So I never told. I tried to tell my mother years later, when we were adults, and she never believed me. Jack found out the year before Dad died, and he threatened him too, if he told. I think it was part of the bond between us. Jack was the only one who ever knew. But I always felt guilty about it, as though it were my fault and not his . . . as though it made me less than everyone else . . . or worse . . . it was hard to forgive myself for it," she said in an agonized voice, "but finally I did. I think, without even knowing it, that was Alex's hold over me. I felt he had the right to treat me badly or be critical or unkind . . . I didn't think I deserved better than that. I played right into his hands." She had looked down for a moment as she explained it to Brad, and when she looked up, she could see that he was crying too. He said not a word to her at first, but pulled her into his arms, and held her tight. Everything he didn't say was in his powerful grip on her. It was a long moment before he could find words for her.

"I'm so sorry, Fred . . . I'm so sorry . . . what a rotten thing to carry around with you all those years. I don't know why, but I just suddenly knew before you said anything. I'm so sorry that happened to you. It doesn't make you less . . . it makes you more . . . a million times more. What a sick, cruel thing to do to a little girl. Thank God he died."

"I used to think that too, and then I felt guilty for that. It happens to a lot of kids, I guess. It's a lonely, scary place to be."

It had impacted her entire life, affected whom she chose to marry, and how she dealt with him and let him treat her for all those years. But Brad's reaction was exactly the one she would have hoped for when she was finally brave enough to speak up. Brad never let her down, unlike Alex, who never failed to disappoint her at every turn and had for so long. Somehow telling Brad and feeling his arms around her vindicated her. She had finally told someone, and he accepted her in spite of it. She was free at last from the chains that had bound her for most of her life. It was an incredible gift he had given her, and they sat there in silence for a long time, as he held her. He was the friend and brother she had always loved, and knew he was, and when she pulled away from him at last, he smiled at her.

"I love you, Fred . . . I truly, truly love you . . . what an incredibly wonderful human being you are. And what a goddamn shame you married that asshole instead of me. I really blew that one, kid." But everything he had said to her that day had been right for her. Telling him had been one of the best things she'd ever done. It was like holding up a mirror, and seeing herself in his eyes. What she saw was the good person who was not to blame for any of it. Not a victim either, or a bad little girl. It was a proud woman who had survived, and deserved love and good things to happen to her. It was exactly the key she needed to unlock the last door to freedom. He had freed her, and she had freed herself. Finally.

"Thank you, Brad. I guess things work out the way they're meant to. You'd probably have been bored if you'd married me." Faith smiled again. "Besides, marrying you would have been like marrying my brother. Incestuous, to say the least." Maybe it was better with him like this, as best friends.

"That's what I always thought. Jack told me I should go out with you once, when we were in college, and I thought he was nuts. You were like my kid sister. I was pretty dumb in those days," he said sheepishly.

"No you weren't." They sat and talked for a while afterward, easily and comfortably. And then finally he glanced at his watch. He hated to leave her, but he had to, to keep up the charade that he'd come to New York on business, and not just to see her. He didn't want to leave her after what they'd just shared. All he was going to do was lie in his hotel room for two hours, and watch a basketball game, or sleep. But he knew he had to stick to his story, and leave her for a while. He felt closer to her than he ever had, but tried to look casual as he stood up.

"Where do you want to eat tonight?" he asked with a yawn.

"You're going to be a ball of fire at your meeting, if you don't wake up." She laughed, and he grinned and shook his head. "What about Chinese?" It was as though nothing untoward had happened between them. They were closer than they'd ever been.

"Sounds good to me. I forgot to bring a tie. I figured I'd buy one if you wanted me to wear one to take you out."

"I figured you'd come in black tie," she teased, after all his complaints about Pam. All he'd brought was a sport jacket, a pair of slacks, a pair of jeans, and some blue shirts. It was a good look, and he looked handsome as he rolled down his sleeves and pretended he was going to work.

"I'll pick you up at seven o'clock. How's that?" he said, planting a kiss on the top of her head and pulling her close to him.

"Is that enough time for your meeting?" She seemed surprised.

"That'll be enough. We only need to discuss one kid."

"Must be a very special kid for you to come this far to discuss him for two hours," she said, as she walked him to the front door. He had said just enough, not too much, and not too little, about the revelations she'd made to him.

"He is," he confirmed, and then hugged her tight before he left. He walked the two blocks to the hotel, and thought about all she'd said to him, what an amazing woman she was, and what a fool he'd been not to marry her. He wished now that he'd taken a different fork in the road than he had years before. But there was no turning back now. All he could do was make the best of it, and acknowledge the mistake to himself. He couldn't even acknowledge to her that he'd made a mistake. But he looked pensive and sad as he walked into the hotel, thinking of the horrors she'd survived, the love she lavished on everyone in spite of it, and how lucky he was to be her friend.

And all Faith could do was thank God she had finally had the courage to unburden herself and tell him about her father. And Brad had been the right one to tell. It had only strengthened the bond they shared and the love she felt for him. A thousand-pound weight she'd carried for a lifetime had been lifted from her heart.

17

FAITH AND BRAD WENT TO CHINESE DINNER THAT NIGHT.
He told her about the meeting he'd had, and invented
all of it, or borrowed it from a case he had in San Francisco. But all he'd done at the hotel for two hours was
sleep. She never suspected it, and was fascinated by the
case he described. And after that, they talked about their
kids. He was dying to see his sons, and she was anxious
to talk to Ellie, after Alex did.

"How do you think she'll take the news?" Brad
asked, looking concerned.

"I'm worried that she'll blame me," Faith confessed.
"God knows what Alex will say to her, but he felt that
since I told Zoe, he should call Eloise."

"She's old enough to be fairly sensible about it," Brad
said optimistically.

"Yes, she is, but you never know. This still feels like a
nightmare in every way. I can't even wrap my mind
around the idea that it's over. Two weeks ago, I was still
married, and I thought everything was fine." In actual
fact, it had been sixteen days. "It is kind of like when

someone dies . . . you keep thinking, two days ago they were alive . . . three weeks ago . . . two months . . . and then one day, you look up and it's been years." They were both thinking of Jack as she said the words.

"Do you want to go to church tomorrow?" they both said at the same time, and she laughed.

"I'd like that a lot. St. Patrick's, or something in the neighborhood?" she asked.

"Let's go to St. Patrick's," he suggested. "I feel like that's our church," he said, and offered her a fortune cookie. Hers said she was virtuous and patient and had wisdom beyond her years. His said he was going to make an excellent deal.

"I hate fortune cookies like that," Faith complained. "I always did. They're so boring. I like the ones that say 'You will fall in love next week.' Mine never say that. I guess now I know why."

"Why is that?" he asked with gentle eyes. Something about her touched him to his very core. She touched his heart.

"Bad luck," she said, thinking of Alex. Everything that had happened in the past two weeks felt like bad luck to her. Very bad.

"Sometimes bad luck is followed by the best luck of all," he said quietly.

"Is that a fortune cookie, or did you make that up?" Faith teased, and he noticed that she looked a thousand times better and more relaxed than she had that morning when he'd arrived. She had eaten and exercised, and as always, he'd made her laugh.

"I made it up. But it's true. Sometimes when the worst things happen to you, you don't know it yet, but they're actually making room for great things in your life."

"Has that happened to you?"

"No, but it has to some people I know. A friend of mine lost his wife four years ago, she was a wonderful woman and he was heartbroken. She died of a brain tumor in six months. And he met the most incredible woman I've ever known. And now he's happy with her. You never know, Fred. You have to believe. It's that thing we talked about . . . answered prayers . . . you have to believe that now. You're in for a bumpy stretch of road for a while, and then it'll get better again. Maybe better than you know."

"I'm glad you came to New York," Faith said, without answering what he said.

"So am I," he took her hand across the table and held it tight. "I was worried about you. You sounded terrible for a couple of days."

"I was terrible. I'm better now. But I guess it'll get nasty for a while. I don't think Alex will play nice."

"Probably not. Judging by what he's done so far." And then Brad had a thought. "Do you want a banana split?" It had been her weakness as a kid.

"Now?" She smiled at him. He had been so good to her all day and all night. She felt utterly spoiled and

comforted, and loved. It really was like being with Jack.
Even better sometimes. "We just ate like pigs."

"So what? They have great ones at Serendipity. I'll
share one with you."

"It's a good thing you don't live here," she said,
laughing at him. "I'd be as big as a house. Yeah, what the
hell. Why not?"

He paid the check and they hopped in a cab, and
went to East Sixtieth Street. The place was jammed, it
was Saturday night, but they found a small round table
for them under a Tiffany lamp, and Brad ordered a banana split and two spoons. It arrived with whipped
cream and nuts, and chocolate sauce, and strawberries,
three flavors of ice cream, and bananas hanging over the
edge of the bowl, and they dove in. Brad couldn't believe how much she ate, particularly considering what
she'd already had.

"I'm going to get sick if I don't stop," she threatened,
and then had two more bites. She could never resist a
banana split.

"If you're going to get sick on me, then you'd better
stop. Friendship only goes so far," he warned, and they
both laughed. It had been fun. They were laughing
about stories from when they were kids. He reminded
her of when she had played a trick on them and told
their girlfriends they were out with other girls. They'd
almost killed her when they found out. She'd been mad
about something and did it to get even with them. They
were fourteen and she'd been twelve. "Why the hell did

you do that?" Brad asked with a grin as he paid the check.

"You wouldn't take me bowling with you, so I was mad."

"Jack got so mad I thought he was going to strangle you."

"Yeah, me too. That's because he really liked the girl. I don't think you cared that much about yours," Faith said, looking amused.

"I don't even remember who it was. Do you?"

"Sure. Sherry Hennessy. And Jack's was Sally Stein."

"You have a hell of a memory. I had totally forgotten Sherry Hennessy. She was the first girl I ever kissed."

"No, she wasn't," Faith said with a knowing look. "Charlotte Waller was. You were thirteen."

"Oh, you brat!" he said, suddenly remembering perfectly. "You were spying on me, and you told Jack. I didn't want him to know because he had a crush on her, and I didn't want him to be upset."

"She told him anyway. She told half the neighborhood."

"No, she didn't. You did, you little shit." He had forgotten it, and was laughing as they walked out of Serendipity and up the steps to the street.

"Well, yeah, I helped. But she broadcast it fairly effectively herself. She thought you were a big catch."

"I was in those days," he said, pretending to strut.

"You're still pretty cute," she said, tucking a hand innocently into his arm. "Considering how old you are."

"Watch that!" he warned, and then suggested they walk to her house, to walk off the banana split. She thought it was a great idea, since they had eaten so much.

"I feel like I'm going to explode."

"You're the size of a mouse, Fred. It's a shame you never grew."

"I always thought so too. I hated being short."

"You look pretty good. For a girl." It was the kind of thing he used to say to her, when she was a kid. And she felt like one with him tonight, reminiscing about people they had forgotten, and cared about so much when they were young. It was funny to think about them again, and wonder where they went. They had both lost touch with all of them. Particularly Brad when he moved away.

They strolled slowly up Third Avenue, talking about the people they had known as kids, and remembering faces and names that neither of them had thought about in years. They turned west when they reached Seventy-fourth, and a moment later reached her house.

"That was stupid of me to let you stay at the hotel. I should have invited you to stay here. I'm sleeping in Zoe's room. You could have slept in mine."

"I'm fine where I am," he said with a yawn. "What time is church tomorrow?"

"We can go whenever you want. They have a lot of masses at St. Pat's, we're bound to catch one. Why don't you come for breakfast?"

"I'll call you when I wake up. Maybe I'll come over around nine, or ten." She let herself into the house with her key, and it seemed lonely and dark. She turned to Brad with a smile.

"Do you want to come in for a glass of wine?"

"I'll never make it back to the hotel if I do. I'm beat. I'd better get some sleep, and you too." They were both tired, and full. It had been a nice evening, and her revelation early in the day meant a lot to him. What she had shared with him was an enormous gesture of trust.

"I'm glad you had that meeting to come to," she said gratefully. The weekends had been hard so far, and would be for a long time.

"Me too," he said, and gave her a hug. "Sleep tight," he said, and watched to make sure that she locked the door and turned on the lights once she was inside. And then he walked back to the hotel with a smile. He loved and respected her more than he had any other human being in his life.

18

BRAD CAME TO THE HOUSE, WITH HIS BAGS, AT NINE o'clock, just as Faith got out of the shower. She answered the door in a cashmere robe, and he handed her the Sunday paper as he walked in.

"I'm sorry. Am I too early? I woke up at the crack of dawn."

"That's fine. I'll be ready in five minutes," she said as she hurried off.

"I'll start breakfast while you get dressed." He wandered into the kitchen, as she ran up the stairs in bare feet, with wet hair.

And when she came down the stairs fifteen minutes later, in a turtleneck and jeans, he was clattering and banging, and there was the smell of coffee in the air.

"Boy, that smells good," she said, as he turned with a smile. He was standing at the stove, had muffins in the toaster, and was frying eggs for them both.

"Sunny side up or over easy?" He looked relaxed and at ease, and had made himself at home.

"Up is fine. Do you want me to do that?" She took a step toward the stove.

"I'm making breakfast for you," he said, and then poured her a mug of coffee and handed it to her. He wanted to spoil her before he left, it was the reason he had come. "Do you want bacon? I forgot."

"I don't think I have any, but I'm fine without." She checked the refrigerator, and there was none. She offered to slice some fruit instead. And he allowed her to slice some oranges and peaches for both of them. He had finished the eggs by then. He put them on two plates, buttered the muffins, and added them. She set the table, and he brought the food, and they both sat down.

The eggs were delicious, and he was munching on a muffin as she smiled. "You're a very good cook."

"I'm a great short-order chef. Hamburgers, chili, pancakes. I can always get a job in a diner if all else fails."

"I'll keep that in mind." It was nice having him around. It reminded her of the times when Jack had visited her in college, or on the frequent occasions when he and Debbie were separated. She had always loved it when he came to stay. Although there had always been tension between him and Alex. She couldn't help wondering, as she and Brad finished the breakfast he had made, where Alex was now, and if he was with that girl. Leslie James. Her name was emblazoned in Faith's mind.

"What were you thinking? You looked upset suddenly," Brad commented as he fished the sports section out of the Sunday paper, and handed the rest to her.

"I was thinking about Alex. And that girl. I wonder if they're together."

"Try not to think about it," he said gently, as he picked up his coffee cup and looked at her pensively. "It's weird how lives change, isn't it? Six months ago, who'd have thought that I'd be sitting here having breakfast with you." They had lost sight of each other for a long time before that.

"Yeah, and that Alex would be gone. Before I thought about them, I was thinking how nice it is to have you here. Do you come to New York a lot?" This was the third time in four months. But he had concocted an excuse this time to see her. And he was glad he had. She already looked much better than she had the day before, and far more relaxed. His trip had been worthwhile.

"It depends. I come here sporadically, depending on what conferences I sign up for, and how much I have going on at home. Most of the time, I can't get away." His work was too crisis-oriented, and he had too many clients, to get away much. "I'll probably come through town for a day when I go to Africa to see the boys next month. Pam's coming with me," he said, as though warning her.

"Maybe the three of us can have dinner," Faith said easily, and Brad laughed.

"That would be fun. She already thinks I'm in love with you. If she gets a good look at you, she'll never get off my back."

"I think I'm flattered. But I'm no threat to her. I'm like

your kid sister. She'll figure that out," Faith said confi-
dently.

"Maybe not," he said, and lost himself in the paper.
He stayed submerged for the next half hour, while she
poured them both another cup of coffee and cleaned up.
It was ten-thirty by the time she was finished, and he
looked up.

"Do you still want to go to church?" She didn't want
to push him into anything. She liked going, but it wasn't
a life-and-death matter to her, particularly if he didn't
want to go. She could always go after he left.

"Actually, I do." He stood up and stretched, and put
an arm around her, and it struck her again how comfortable she was with him, and what easy company he was.
It was hard to believe that he and Pam didn't get along.
He was the easiest man she'd ever known.

"I'll get my bag." She ran upstairs to get her purse
and comb her hair, and five minutes later, she was in the
front hall, getting a coat out of the closet. She put on a
heavy shearling jacket, and a red wool scarf. Brad was
wearing jeans, a heavy sweater, and a warm coat. It was
cold outside, and looked like it might snow.

They took a cab to St. Patrick's, and arrived just in
time for the eleven o'clock mass. Faith genuflected and
slipped into a pew, and Brad slid in next to her, and they
sat quietly side by side for the entire mass. She took
communion and he waited for her, and he noticed at one
point that she was holding the rosary beads he had
given her, and he smiled. And afterward, they lit a

candle for Jack at the shrine of Saint Jude. It was a comforting experience for both of them, and they both looked at peace when they walked outside. During the mass, it had started to snow.

"Do you want to walk?" she inquired, looking up at him. She loved walking in the snow.

"Yeah," he grinned at her, "why not?" He never saw snow in San Francisco, and it was part of what he loved about New York.

They walked up Fifth Avenue and, at Sixtieth Street, crossed over and walked along the outer edge of Central Park. They walked past the zoo, and the playground north of it. Their hair was covered by snow by then, and their faces were red from the cold. It was one of those snows that really stick and seem to silence everything. It felt magical walking along with her gloved hand tucked into his arm.

"I'm going to miss you tomorrow, when you're gone," she said sadly. "This was a real treat. After this, it's back to real life, school, and the divorce. I'm not looking forward to that. Alex is in such a hurry." She was beginning to wonder why, and couldn't help asking herself how much it had to do with Leslie James, and if he was going to marry her after all.

"What are you doing about the house?" He wondered if it was too soon to ask.

"I don't know. He hasn't said. I don't know if he'll let me stay in it, or want me to get out so he can sell it. He paid for it, so I guess he'll try to claim it's his. I don't know how these things work." It was Alex's money that had bought everything they had. And now he was trying to claim it all as his, at least to her. He said all she'd get out of him was minimal support, since she was young enough to go to work. She was beginning to feel as though she had no rights at all.

"If he forces you out, he has to give you someplace comparable to live," Brad said sensibly to calm her fears. "He can't just toss you out on the street."

"I hope not." But even that didn't seem sure anymore. There was no telling what stunts Alex would try to pull. "I guess with the girls gone, I could get a smaller place. But it'll feel so weird to move. We've lived there for eighteen years, since Zoe was born." Suddenly everything was up in the air, and any sense of confidence and security she'd had was down the drain.

"Maybe he'll let you stay and not sell the house," Brad said quietly. He didn't want to upset her. He knew her lawyer would work out the details equitably for her. And they took a small detour into the park at the model pond, and watched the snow piling up on the Alice in Wonderland statues. There were children playing in the snow, and there was just enough for them to slide down the little hills on garbage can lids and plastic saucers. Brad and Faith watched and it looked like fun.

"I wish the kids were still little," Faith said wistfully. "I sure miss all that." It had been such a happy time in her life. Every day had been full, there had been so much joy. She never had time to think about anything except what she was doing with them, or being with Alex at night. She never worried about what the future would bring, she didn't have time to think about it. And she'd gotten up feeling happy and needed every day. It was all different now. They no longer needed her. They had their own lives, and hers seemed so empty now. And on top of it, Alex was gone too. She felt as though she had lost her whole world, and maybe now her house. It was a lot to digest. A lot to lose.

"I miss those days too," Brad said honestly. "It all went so fast. It's silly really, I know we feel old, but we aren't, there are people having first kids at our age."

"Oh my God, what a thought." Faith laughed.

"Would you ever do it again?" She could see that he was serious, and she paused for a moment as she thought.

"That's a crazy question. If you'd asked me that a month ago, I'd have said, hell no, besides Alex would have killed me. He always thought two kids was enough. Otherwise, I'd have had one or two more. Then. Now? Gosh, I don't know. That seems like a pretty crazy idea at forty-seven. The girls would proba-bly have a fit, or be shocked at least. No, I don't think I would. Besides, I'm not even going to be married in a few months. I can't even imagine that now."

"That's my point, Fred. You'll be single again." Just hearing him say it gave her a shock. She still had to pinch herself to remind herself that what had happened with Alex wasn't a bad dream. It was real. "What if you met a guy who wanted more kids? What would you do?"

"Introduce him to Eloise." She laughed, and then grew serious again. "Gee, Brad, I don't know. I'd love to have more kids, but I'm not exactly in the flower of my youth. At my age, I'm not not even sure I could. I know people do. I don't know . . . yeah . . . maybe it would be nice . . . it would be wonderful to have a baby again . . . and it would make me feel hopeful and alive and young. The only trouble is," she said, sobering, as she looked at him, "I'm not. I'm tired and sad and old. And worse yet, alone."

"It won't be like that forever. You'll find someone, Fred. Someone a lot nicer than Alex was to you. You'll be off and running in a few months, and you'll probably be married in a year." He looked depressed as he said it, and she smiled.

"Well, you certainly have my life worked out. What about you?" She knew how unhappy he was with Pam, and how determined he was to stay with her, at all costs. "Don't you want more than what you have?" His life with Pam always sounded lonely to her. But her life with Alex had been too, and she would never have ended it, if he hadn't walked out on her.

"Sure I do," he answered her honestly. "But what I have is what I have. I don't think about it much." That wasn't entirely true.

"Maybe you should, while you are still reasonably young. What if she does what Alex did, ten years from now maybe? Won't you feel like you wasted your whole life, when you could have been with someone you were happy with? Maybe it's worth some thought."

"It's too big a risk," he said, looking straight at Faith. "I know what I've got, however damaged it is. I'm not going to throw it away for a dream that might never come true. Life doesn't work like that. Movies do. Real lives don't. Most people do what you and I have done. They settle for what almost works, and put up with it as best they can. You know that yourself."

"Yeah, I do. I just wonder about it now. Maybe Alex was right to do what he did. I hate it for me. But maybe he finally had the guts to do what we should have done years ago. He did it in a hurtful way, but he's reaching for the brass ring."

"And in his case, I think he'll fall flat on his face, because he did it by hurting you. I don't think you win much that way. You lose. He's chasing some girl in a thong, and kicked you in the teeth on the way out. That comes back to haunt you eventually. If he stays with her, maybe she'll do it to him one day."

"Now there's a cheering thought," Faith said with a small smile. "I don't know what the answers are," she said with a sigh, as snowflakes settled on her eyelashes and stuck to her hair.

He had never seen anyone as beautiful, and as he looked at her, it made his heart ache. He would have loved to turn the clock back about thirty years. But he knew with perfect clarity what he couldn't have. What he couldn't have, and never would, was Faith. And she had no idea the thought had even crossed his mind. She would have been shocked if she had. She had no idea that he even looked at her that way. And he hadn't in a long time, since they were kids. But he did now, when he allowed himself to. Just standing next to her in Central Park, with his arm around her, made him dream of more. But Brad knew better than anyone that it was only a dream.

"You're looking very serious," Faith whispered, and snuggled closer to him. It was getting cold and the wind had come up. "Are you okay?" He nodded and smiled. He loved everything he did with her. Making breakfast for her, talking for hours, going to church, taking walks, even eating the banana split the night before. She had been a golden child, and was even more luminous now.

"I was thinking we should go back to your house and make a fire. And actually, I was thinking about lunch."

"All I do is eat when I'm with you," she complained. But she loved being with him too. And she had been getting hungry while they walked. "We need to stop and get some food. I don't have much in the house. I've been starving myself ever since Alex left."

"That's not going to help," he said practically, taking her hand in his.

They stopped at the grocery store on the way home, and he made her buy enough food to tide her over for the week, and then insisted on paying for it, which she said wasn't fair.

"You're not going to be here to eat all this. Why should you pay for it?"

"Then I'll come back for dinner tomorrow night," he said, as they handed him his change.

"I wish you could stay. It's a shame we don't live in the same town." He thought so too, but he also knew it would eventually create an unbearable challenge for him. He was beginning to feel things for her he had never felt before. And as long as she wasn't aware of it, and there were three thousand miles separating them, he knew he was safe, and so was she.

He carried the groceries for her, and half an hour later, she was making lunch, while he started the fire. Outside, the snow continued to fall.

She made soup and sandwiches, and she had insisted on buying marshmallows and graham crackers and Hershey bars, so she could make s'mores, which they had both loved as kids. Being with him was like a pilgrimage to the past. It made her wish at times that they had never had to grow up. If that were true, life would still be simple for all of them, and Jack would still be alive.

It was nearly four o'clock when they finished lunch, and Brad laughed when he looked at her. They had made the s'mores in the fire. "What are you laughing at?" Faith looked incensed.

"You've got marshmallows and chocolate all over your face. You're a mess." She used her napkin to try and clean it up, and only made it worse. And instead, he took the napkin from her, and wiped her mouth and her chin and the tip of her nose as she gazed up at him with innocent eyes. And as he looked down at her, it took everything he had not to abandon himself to the moment and all he felt for her. "There, now you've got a clean face." Nothing in his demeanor even remotely hinted at the undercurrents he felt.

"Do you want another one?" she asked with a grin, and he groaned and stretched out on the floor near the fire. His legs looked endless to her, and his shoulders were as broad and powerful as they had been when he was a boy.

"No, I don't. I wonder if my plane is going to be delayed by the snow." He was almost hoping it was, although he had to get back. But he would have liked nothing better than to get snowbound with her in New York. He was having feelings he had no idea what to do about. And he knew he had to get back, while he still could. It was so hard knowing she had hard times ahead, and he couldn't be there for her. All he could offer her was his voice on the phone, or e-mails. It didn't seem like enough. He wanted to protect her from the onslaught that he knew instinctively Alex was going to focus on her.

"I'll call and check on your flight," she said helpfully, and walked to the phone in the hall. She was back five minutes later. "It's on time."

"Too bad," he said, with a sleepy smile.

And an hour later, he got up like a sleeping giant from the floor. It was time to go.

At five o'clock, he picked up his things, and Faith put on her coat.

"You don't have to come," he said, watching her. She had no idea how beautiful she was, which had always been part of her charm.

"I know I don't. But I want to anyway. I've got nothing else to do." She wanted to spend as much time with him as she could.

Brad hailed a cab and put his bags in the trunk, and then slid in next to her on the seat. It was snowing harder than it had been when they were in the park, and it was getting dark. But there was no traffic on Sunday afternoon, and they got to Kennedy in record time, in spite of the snow. The Department of Transportation kept the roads clear, and everything seemed normal at Kennedy. The flight was still listed as on time.

She went with him while he bought some magazines, and she bought him a book that she thought he'd like.

"Thank you for feeding me, and taking me out." She smiled gratefully at him. "I had a wonderful time. I'm going to miss you a lot."

"I'll be calling you. Just make sure you behave. Eat, go to school, don't work too hard. Don't let Alex drive you nuts. Do what your lawyer says . . . brush your teeth . . . wash your face . . . don't get marshmallows all over you . . . be good to yourself, Fred."

"You too," she said, looking like a lost child as he hugged her good-bye, and kissed the top of her head.

"I'll call you tomorrow. It'll be too late to call when I get home." He wouldn't be at his house until two A.M. New York time, and he hoped she'd be asleep by then.

"Thanks for everything," she said again, and clung to him. Saying good-bye to him was like feeling Jack slip away from her again. There was a moment of panic, and then a wave of sorrow and despair. She felt foolish hanging on to him, and then finally let go.

He gave her a last hug, and then followed the other passengers down the gangway to the plane, and as they turned the corner, he smiled and gave her one last wave. She stood in the terminal, watching the plane as it taxied away, and then walked outside with her head bowed, and hailed a cab.

The drive home seemed interminable, and the house was like a tomb when she got home. It was still snowing, and the house had never seemed as quiet. She didn't even eat dinner that night, she missed him so much. She just went upstairs and went to bed. And she was sound asleep when the phone rang at two A.M. For a minute, she didn't even know where she was.

It was Eloise calling from London, before she left for work. She sounded agitated, and Faith was still half asleep when she answered.

"... huh ... what? ... oh ... Ellie ... hi, sweetheart ... no, no, I was awake." She didn't know why she always lied when people woke her up, but she always did. It took her a minute to gather her wits, and then she realized it was early for Eloise. It was seven A.M. for her. "Are you okay?"

"Yes, I am," she said angrily. It was obvious as soon as Faith came awake that her oldest daughter was enraged. "I spoke to Dad yesterday," she said importantly. "He told me what you did."

"What I did?" Faith looked blank, and then a tremor of fear ran over her like a cold hand. She wondered what he had said. "What did I do?"

"He told me that you decided you didn't want to be married and go to school."

"He said that?" Faith looked horrified. How could he lie to their children that way? At least Zoe knew the truth.

"Yes, he did. Mom, how can you destroy our family that way, for a stupid law degree? Don't you care about us? Or about him, after all these years? How can you be so selfish and so disloyal?" Halfway through what she said, she had burst into tears, and at her end, Faith was crying too.

"Ellie, that's not how it is . . . or how it went. This is complicated. It's between Daddy and me." Faith felt honor bound not to air their dirty laundry with the girls. No matter how rotten he'd been to her, and was being now, she didn't want to stoop to the same games as he. And she trusted her daughters to see the truth in the end. Faith clung to decency like a life preserver in the storm.

"Don't you think it affects us too? Don't you think it matters to us? We're not even going to have a place to live when we get home. He says you want to sell the house." There was her answer about the house. And as usual, he was blaming it on her.

"We haven't even talked about the house. And no, I don't want to sell it. But maybe that's what he wants. I never wanted this divorce. He did."

"That's a lie. He says you did. He says you forced his hand by going back to school."

"I didn't force anything. I even offered to quit school."

"I don't believe a word you say. Daddy says you've been planning this for a long time, and you told him a year ago that you wanted a divorce." Listening to her, Faith felt sick, and she could see the game plan now. If he could convince them that she had told him that a year ago, it would make more sense once they knew he was seeing Leslie James, if they found out. It was a clever plot. And so far, it had worked. With Eloise at least. And the two vastly different stories would even set the two girls at each other's throats.

"Eloise," Faith said, fighting to stay calm, "I don't want to say your father isn't being truthful with you, but he's not. I never asked him for a divorce. I never wanted to end our marriage. This has been his move, and what he wants. I don't. And I don't want to sell this house. He hasn't said a word to me about it." She felt certain that if she stuck to the truth, without maligning him, in the end Ellie would understand. But Ellie wasn't making it easy for her.

"You're a liar, Mom. And I think it stinks that you're abandoning him. I hope you flunk the bar, and flunk out of school, because you've ruined my life!" And with that, she hung up, and Faith sat there, stunned, with tears rolling down her face. It had been a rotten thing for him to do, to poison Ellie against her. And it was bound to cause tremendous strife between the girls. Because Zoe knew the truth. At least about Alex walking out on her, she just didn't know why. Faith had wanted to protect them from that. And she knew the truth would destroy Alex in his daughters' eyes. And Faith felt that wasn't fair. But Alex knew nothing about fair. What he had done was the cruelest blow he could have dealt, to separate Eloise from her. And now Faith was worried about the house as well.

She lay wide awake in bed for an hour, and then, feeling guilty, she dialed Zoe. Faith knew she stayed up late, and she answered the phone on the first ring.

"Hi, Mom," she said, sounding pleased to hear her mother's voice.

"Did I wake you?" Faith asked nervously.

"Of course not. I was up. Are you okay?"

"No," Faith said honestly. "Ellie just called."

"Did you tell her?" Zoe asked, sounding subdued. She had been upset about the changes in her parents' lives since she'd heard, and she'd had a brief conversation with her dad. But he hadn't said much, particularly after Zoe said she'd spent the weekend with her mom. He had given her the bum's rush off the phone after that.

"No, I didn't. Dad did," Faith explained. She was seriously worried that her own stance for decency and playing fair was going to backfire and damage her relationship with Ellie forever.

"How was she?"

"Crazed. She hates me. Your father told her that I didn't want to be married and go to school, so I asked for the divorce. He even told her I asked for it a year ago," Faith said, blowing her nose.

"Why would he say a thing like that? Is it true?" Zoe sounded surprised. But she was on her mom's team, and had always been.

"Of course not. I think I know why he did it, but that's beside the point. The point is that he made Ellie think that I wanted this, and I pushed him out. That's so unfair." Fair was no longer in Alex's vocabulary and perhaps never had been, Faith realized now.

"So what else is new? Dad never plays fair." Zoe said she had known for a long time that he lied. He had lied to her, about numerous small things. It mattered to her, and had contributed to her not trusting him. "She'll figure it out. You wouldn't be this upset if you were the one who wanted the divorce. That's just plain common sense." But Faith was not reassured. Ellie was being completely manipulated by her father.

"She doesn't even know how upset I am. She never

gave me a chance to talk. She just told me what a monster I am, and that I ruined her life." She didn't tell Zoe
about the house. She wanted to talk to Alex first. She
wanted to know where he stood, because if he forced
them to sell the house, it would upset everyone, not just
her.

"Just let her calm down. I'll talk to her. You can talk to
her when she comes in." Eloise had planned a visit in
March, but now Faith was wondering if she would
come home.

"Maybe I should go over there," Faith said, sounding
worried.

"Let her cool off first. Write her a letter or something.
Mom, she'll figure it out. It's obvious you don't want
this divorce." What wasn't obvious to Zoe yet, and her
mother hadn't said, was why her father wanted out. But
it was clear to her that her mother didn't want to say.
She had a feeling there was more to the story, and as
usual, she was right.

"I feel sick over this," Faith said, relieved that she
could talk to her. Zoe was becoming a friend as well as
her daughter, and she was sensible and wise beyond her
years.

"Ellie always reacts first. And then she makes sense
later on. I think Dad was a total shit for saying that stuff,
but I'm not surprised." And neither was Faith anymore.
There was no limit to the depths Alex was willing to go
to, to destroy her relationship with her daughter.

"I'm going to call him tomorrow," Faith said, sounding agitated. She still thought she could reason with him, which was naïve

"Get some sleep, Mom. Try to forget about it. At least for tonight. Did you do anything this weekend?" She had meant to call her, but felt guilty that she hadn't. She hadn't had time.

"My friend Brad was here from the West Coast," Faith said vaguely. All she could think of was Ellie now. The visit with Brad seemed to have faded like a dream.

"Did he come to see you?" Zoe sounded impressed.

"No, he had business here. But it was nice to see him." Zoe wondered about that, but decided it wasn't the time to tease her mother about him. She had enough on her plate. And whatever his feelings were for her mother, she knew that to Faith, he was nothing more than a friend. But at least he had distracted her for a couple of days. That was something at least.

"Go to sleep, Mom. I'll call you tomorrow. I love you."

They hung up, and Faith lay in bed awake for the rest of the night. All Faith could think of was what Ellie had said to her. And all she wanted to do now was call Alex. But she had to wait till he got to the office. He hadn't told her where he was staying. And finally at six A.M., she got up and e-mailed Brad. She knew he was home by then, and she couldn't wait a moment longer. She wrote him everything Ellie had said. She cried as she typed it. It looked even worse once she wrote it down in an e-mail.

" . . . and what do you think she means about the house? It sounds like Alex wants to sell it. Why couldn't he tell me first? Anyway, I'm a wreck. I feel sick that Ellie believed what he said. How will I ever convince her of the truth? I'm not going to tell either of them about the girl. Ever. It's too humiliating for all concerned. And it makes me seem as low as he if I tell the girls about her. And they would never forgive their father. I'm not trying to poison their relationship with him. Why can't he fight fair? He told Ellie I asked for a divorce a year ago. He probably thinks it excuses his behavior if I wanted out. That makes it sound like he's serious about the girl." She went on and on and on, still trying to be fair to Alex out of some futile sense of decency, and railing at the injustice of it all. Sometimes she wondered if her deep religious beliefs made her too fair. And Alex knew her well, and just where to hit, and how.

"I'm sorry. I'm sounding insane. I'm exhausted, and upset. And it was such a nice weekend. I'm sorry to be a pest about all this. He is being such a shit. Nothing you can do about it, it just helps to talk to you. Thank you for spoiling me, feeding me, being so good to me. I had fun. We always do. I'll let you know what happens here. Have a good day. Love, Fred."

And at nine o'clock, she called Alex. He had just walked into the office and he sounded irritated when he picked up the phone.

"What's up?"

"A lot," Faith said sounding stressed. "I gather you talked to Ellie. That was a rotten thing you did."

"I'm not going to listen to insults from you, Faith," he said, threatening to hang up. "I have a right to tell my daughter anything I want." He sounded instantly defensive. He knew how rotten it was.

"It would be nice if you stuck to the truth. You told her this divorce was my idea."

"Well, it is, isn't it? You tossed our marriage in the trash when you enrolled at NYU."

"I did nothing of the sort. And you brought a woman into my bed. Did you tell her that?"

"No. Did you?"

"No, I didn't, because I want to be fair to you. Alex, you poisoned her against me." She was in tears as she spoke.

"That's what you do with Zoe, isn't it?" he accused.

"No, it's not. You totally lied to Ellie, and made her think the whole thing is my fault. You even told her I asked for a divorce last year, and that's a total lie." He said not a word and there was silence on the line. He had hit way below the belt. "And she thinks I want to sell the house. What's that about?" Her heart raced as she asked.

"We don't have any choice. I want my money out of it. You'll get your half."

"I don't want my half. I want the house, to live in at least. Where am I going to live?" She was crying openly at what he was doing to her.

"You can get housing at NYU," he said nastily, and Faith was appalled. He was the most vengeful man she had ever known. She would never have thought him capable of this. It made her wonder who he had always been. Under his icy exterior, there was no heart at all.

"Are you evicting me?" She sounded panicked.

"My lawyer will discuss it with yours." The way he said it told her he was. He was taking away their home, their marriage, and he had stolen one of their children, with lies. He was destroying her life, just as Ellie had accused her. But Alex really was. And she was worried that the fact that Alex had paid for the house would give her no rights to it at all. She had invested her life and time and heart in their marriage, but the money invested had been his all along.

"Why are you doing all this? How can you hate me so much? Just because I'm going to school? How sick is that?"

"As sick as your walking out on me, to pretend you're a kid." But it wasn't about that, Faith knew, it was about the girl. She suspected that the girl in the thong was at the crux of this. He was the one trying to recapture his youth, and destroy everything they'd had, and her.

"It's all about that girl," Faith accused him, and felt justified doing it. "You're trying to obscure that. What you did was totally without respect for me. And now you're trying to make yourself look clean to our daughters, but you're not. And you know it, Alex. What the hell are you doing? Are you marrying her?"

"I have nothing more to say to you," he said coldly, and without waiting for a reply from her, he hung up. Faith sat staring into space after he did. And then she called her lawyer to ask him to find out about the house, and he promised he would.

It was only then that she noticed that Brad had sent her an e-mail sometime in the last several hours, probably when she was talking to Alex.

"Poor Fred . . . what a turkey he is. Don't worry about Ellie. She'll get it. Kids always do. My parents pulled the same shit on me. It took me a while, but I got it. They were determined to destroy each other, and both sides tried to use me as a hostage. Ugly stuff. You're not doing that. Ellie will see who is. Wait. Be patient. Be cool. Defend yourself against him. Talk to your lawyer. Don't give up the house. He owes you that much. Hang tough. I have to go to work early, and see what disasters came in over the weekend. I had a great time. You are a miracle in my life. Go have a banana split . . . just make sure you wipe your chin. Talk to you later. Love, Brad."

He always made her smile. He always comforted her and now that he was back in her life, he was always there. Faith sat back and read his e-mail again, and felt calmer than she had in hours. And all she could do was thank God for him.

19

FAITH'S CONCERNS ABOUT THE HOUSE PROVED TO BE well founded, or somewhat at least. Although her attorney was slightly reassuring on that score. She heard from him the day after she'd called, as she walked in from school. She was doing well, but having to struggle to concentrate. She was so distracted that the papers she was writing weren't as coherent as she would have liked them to be, and her grades reflected it. But she was hanging in.

She answered the phone as she walked in the door. The attorney didn't have great news.

"You were right. He wants you to move out. He's giving you ninety days." That meant the end of May.

"Oh my God. Can he do that?" Faith went pale.

"Only if you agree. And I don't think you should." She was relieved to hear him say that at least. She had visions of everything she owned on the street. "He owes you half of it for community property, and if you want your money out of it, then you should sell the house. If he wants his half, he can force you out in time, and require you to sell. But he's going to have to make some kind of settlement with you, and if you want his share of the house as part of that, that's what we'll do. I think I can get that for you, Faith, if that's what you want. If not, I can't force him to let you stay and tie up his half indefinitely."

"I want to keep the house," she said in a strangled voice. All she really wanted was not to move, not to change anything, to hang on to whatever she could of a familiar life that had lasted for twenty-six years. She was fighting change as much as she was losing the house.

"We'll take him to court on it. I haven't had any kind of official notice from them about it yet. Let's wait and see what he does. He has to give you time, in any case. He can't force you out until this is resolved."

But it didn't take him long. She had a letter from his attorney by the end of the week. It had been addressed to her lawyer, of course, but it said that Alex wanted her to move out, and put the house on the market as soon as possible. They had given her a few days of grace and wanted her out by the first of June. It was the cruelest thing she could think of, throwing her out of her house. The only thing worse had been bringing his girlfriend home to her bed, and lying to their kids.

Brad was reassuring her as often as they spoke, and she had left half a dozen messages for Ellie, but she wouldn't return the calls. It was an enormous relief when finally, in the first week of March, Zoe told her that Eloise was coming home.

"Why didn't she tell me? She hasn't returned any of my calls."

It came as no surprise to Zoe. The two sisters had had a huge fight on the phone, with Zoe defending their mother, and Eloise defending their dad, each convinced that the other had been handed a raw deal and a pack of lies.

"You don't know what you're talking about!" Zoe had screamed at her in the middle of the night. It had been morning for Eloise. "He fucking walked out on her. I saw her that week. You should have seen the condition she was in!"

"She deserves to be. She's been asking him for a divorce behind our backs for a year. And now she's forcing him to sell the house."

"It's all lies, don't you get that, you moron? That's who he is. He's kicking Mom out on her ass. He wants her out on the first of June."

"The hell he does. He has no choice. He says she wants a lot of money from him. And that's disgusting too. Mom is a total bitch, and it's all her fault. You just don't want to see how evil she is."

"You're blind," Zoe accused her older sister. "You've been brainwashed by him." In the end, they had hung up on each other, and Zoe had the unpleasant task of informing her mother that Eloise was planning to stay with Alex during the week she'd be in town. She was staying in the apartment he had sublet, and refused to stay at the house. She was only going to go there to pick up some things.

She arrived in New York on St. Patrick's Day, and had a week off. It was a full two days before she called her mother, who had been sitting in the house, waiting to hear from her, and feeling sick over it. All she could get at Alex's apartment, once Zoe gave her the number, was an answering machine. And Ellie had returned none of her calls. Faith was so desperate to hear from her that she hadn't even gone to school, but at least she was staying home, studying for exams.

She nearly burst into tears when she finally heard Ellie's voice. But the conversation was brief and to the point. Ellie said she was coming over to pick up some clothes, and she said that she hoped her mother wouldn't be there. For a nearly twenty-five-year-old woman, she sounded incredibly childish to Faith, and needlessly cruel. But she was being tutored well.

Faith was in her bedroom, when Eloise came home. It had taken her a month to move back into her own room. It wasn't practical to live in Zoe's room, and she had finally decided to swallow her pride and her revulsion at sleeping in her bed again. She was lying on it, when she saw Ellie walk down the hall. She had seen her mother too, and said not a word.

Faith walked to her bedroom doorway, and stood watching her. "Eloise, are you going to say hello?" she asked softly, with immeasurable pain in her eyes. Zoe would have killed her sister if she had seen her mother look like that. Eloise was made of sterner stuff, and had a cooler heart.

"I asked you not to be here," she stood facing her mother from down the hall. It seemed incredible that she was unable to distance herself from her parents' divorce, and felt compelled to take sides the way she had. But her father had used her well.

"This is my home," Faith said calmly, "and I wanted to see you. I don't want you pulled apart by this mess. If Daddy is determined to do this, we have to survive, all of us, and we're still a family, whether he and I are together or not."

"What do you care? You're the one who blew our family all to hell, and not him. You're even selling this house, so don't talk to me about your 'home.' "

"I don't want to have to do that, but I can show you letters from his lawyers telling me that I have to get out. He's trying to evict me, El. And I'm trying to stay."

"He only has to do that," she said, sounding like a petulant child, "because you want so much money from him."

"We haven't even talked about that yet. I don't know what I want. Right now, all I want is to stay in this house. I swear to you on all our lives that that's true."

"You're a liar," Eloise spat at her, disappeared into her room, and slammed the door, as Faith stood wondering how her own child could be so hateful to her, so distrustful and disrespectful and unkind. It didn't say much about the way she'd brought them up, or the feelings Eloise had for her. She wasn't a child, she was an adult, and she was using nuclear weapons to destroy her mother. Alex had given them to her, but she hadn't hesitated to use them. It broke Faith's heart to think about the damage she would do. Their family would never be the same again. This was Alex's final gift to them.

Eloise came out of her room half an hour later with an armful of clothes and two small bags, as Faith watched her with an aching heart.

"Why do you hate me so much, Ellie?" Faith asked her quietly. She really wanted to know. She couldn't fathom what she'd ever done to her to cause a reaction like the one she'd had.

"I hate what you did to Dad." For an instant, Faith was tempted to tell her what her father had done, about the woman he'd brought home, and the thong in her bed. But her own sense of decency compelled her not to malign Alex to their children, although the temptation to do so was getting stronger every day, particularly in the face of Ellie's accusations. But she didn't want to drag her daughters into their parents' war. Faith's morality prevailed at all costs, although she felt foolish for it at times.

"I didn't do anything to him, El. I don't know how to convince you of that. It breaks my heart that you have so little faith in me."

"You never should have gone back to school. You

broke Daddy's heart." It didn't even occur to her how unreasonable his position was. She was completely under his spell.

"I'd like to see you while you're here," Faith said, trying to stay calm and not sound as pathetic as she felt.

"I don't have time," Eloise said viciously. "And I want to spend some time with Dad."

"What about lunch?"

"I'll let you know," Eloise said, and then clattered down the stairs and out the door. And as soon as it slammed behind her, Faith sat down on the stairs and burst into sobs. Other than when Alex had walked out on her, and when Jack had died, it was the worst day of her life. She felt as though she had lost her older child. She didn't even have the heart to call Zoe or Brad. She didn't bother to turn the lights on that night, and when it got dark, she went to bed.

What Faith didn't know was that Zoe had flown to New York, and met with Eloise, and the two had had another roaring fight. She thought it was disgusting of her to betray her mother, and to take sides with their dad. They had battled over it for hours, and then Zoe had flown back to Providence. She didn't even want her mother to know she'd been in town, and that she and Eloise were at each other's throats. She was sure it would only upset Faith more.

Faith felt as though she were swimming underwater as the days went by. She was trying to keep her grades up at school, and make peace with Eloise, though her efforts had no results. Ellie went back to London without seeing her again. And within two days of hearing that, Faith was in bed with the flu. She was still there when she was served with the divorce papers. And her lawyer was negotiating with Alex about the house. He was being a real bastard about it and said he still wanted her out. And in the midst of her miseries, she didn't even have the heart to write to Brad. He called her every day to see how she was, and sometimes she didn't even pick up his calls. She just sat staring into space, listening to his voice on the machine.

"I'm worried about you," he said finally, after she hadn't talked to him for four days. He had called her at midnight, and she'd answered the phone.

"I'm okay," she said weakly. She was still coughing from the flu, but had gone back to school.

"The hell you are. You sound tubercular, and you sound miserable." He knew Eloise had gone back to London without seeing her, and it made him sick. She had been completely manipulated by Alex, and he hated what it did to Faith. It was just a very bad time. "You need a vacation. I should take you to Africa with me."

"I'm sure Pam would love that."

"Actually, she would. Especially if you went in her place. She hates third world countries, and she's dreading the trip. I've never seen so much medicine and insect repellent in my life. She's taking a whole suitcase full of that stuff, and packaged foods. Pam doesn't leave anything to chance."

"Is she making you travel in black tie?" Faith asked, laughing finally. He always cheered her up.

"Probably. Actually, I'm flying through New York. I'm meeting her in London. She's going to fly straight there from here. I'm only going to be in town for one day, and a night." This time he really had to meet with an attorney about a case. He was scared to death he was going to lose the kid to a law that could leave him vulnerable to capital punishment if convicted, and Brad wanted some advice from an attorney he respected in New York. He wanted to spend some creative time with him face to face, for an hour or two at least. "Can you have dinner with me, if you're still alive by then? What are you taking for that cough?"

"Nothing much. Cough medicine puts me to sleep, and I have three papers due."

"I have news for you. Dead people don't get good grades."

"I was afraid of that," she laughed. "When are you coming in?"

"Thursday. Figure out where you want to have dinner and make a reservation, unless you want me to cook for you." He was willing to do anything just to spend time with her, and he was relieved that Pam didn't want to go via New York. "I can't wait to see the boys." But as soon as he said it, he realized he had reminded her of Eloise, and was sorry he had brought it up at all.

"I can't wait to see you," Faith said. It had been nearly a month since his last visit to New York.

"Me too, Fred. Take care of yourself." He thought she sounded terrible and was genuinely concerned about her. She had far too much on her plate. And he knew she had the added stress of waiting to hear from law school. But that was the least of her worries, and she didn't expect to hear for another month.

By the time he came to town three days later, she was feeling better and nearly over her flu. She looked thin and pale, and more stressed than she had a month before. But he also knew how upset she was about Ellie, and about the house. It accounted for a lot.

She had decided to make dinner for him, and said she really didn't want to go out. And that worried him too. He managed to talk her into going to Serendipity for a banana split afterward for dessert. And after she ate almost none of the dinner she'd cooked, he was happy to see her dig in. She had greeted him like the long-lost brother he was to her, and literally thrown herself into his arms when he walked into the house, and he had lifted her slim body right off the ground. She was even thinner than before.

"So how long will you be in Africa?" she asked, taking a huge mouthful of chocolate ice cream, and he smiled as he wiped a tiny spot of whipped cream off her nose.

"How come you always get food all over your face?" he teased, and told her he'd be gone for two weeks. He was faintly panicked about not talking to her. He liked knowing how she was, and being there for her. When she wasn't in a total state over the divorce, or something Alex had done to her, they talked or e-mailed each other every day, and had now for five months. She was part of the furniture of his life, and he counted on communicating with her. He not only listened to her problems and concerns, but shared his with her as well. And he didn't like the fact that she wasn't going to be able to reach him. He had given her a sheet of paper with several numbers on it. But they were contact numbers to leave messages for him, and nothing more. Just as he couldn't reach his sons on the game preserve where they lived, she couldn't reach Brad while he was with them. "It's going to be a long two weeks without talking to you," he said mournfully. He could wait in line at the post office for several hours, as his sons did, hoping to get a line. But more often than not, they couldn't. And there was no way he could explain that to Pam.

"I know. I was just thinking of that," she said, looking sad. She had always had friends over the years, women whose children had grown up with hers, or others she was on committees with to do charity work. But since Jack's death, she had become so solitary, Alex had never liked her friends, and it had become more and more difficult to explain why they didn't socialize with them. In the end, she had simply drifted away from them. The only person she confided in now was Brad. And once she went back to school, and now with Alex divorcing her, she had withdrawn from everyone, except Brad. Without question, he had become her best and only friend.

"You'd better behave while I'm gone, Fred," he warned as he shared some of the banana split with her. "Can I count on you to take care of yourself?" He was genuinely worried about her.

"Probably not. But I'll be okay. Maybe I'll hear about law school before you get back. But it might still be too soon."

"Just be good. Eat. Sleep. Go to school. Talk to Zoe a lot." He hadn't met her yet, but from everything Faith told him about what she said, he admired her, and thought she gave her mother sound advice. It seemed strange to Faith too that he was going to London, and Eloise was there, but he couldn't visit her or take any messages to her. Faith made a point of calling her several times a week, just to keep the door open, but Ellie always brushed her off. The conversations were brief and to the point, if she got through at all. Most of the time, Ellie screened her calls, to avoid talking to her mother. It was rare that Faith got through.

They walked back to her house afterward, and he came in for a little while. They sat in her bedroom this time, and he built a fire. He sat in the same comfortable chair Alex always had, and she sat at Brad's feet while he stroked her hair. There was something so enormously comforting about him, and so loving. She couldn't help thinking how lucky Pam was. But then she realized that Pam no longer saw this side of him, nor wanted to. She kept him at arm's length and had for years. And whatever comfort she needed, she got from her friends. While Faith basked in the sunlight of all the unspent affection he had to give.

"I'm going to miss you, Fred," he said quietly, as she leaned next to him, still sitting at his feet, and he reached down and took her hand. They sat in silence that way for a long time, staring into the fire. And for the first time, Faith was aware of feeling something she never before had for him. It was as though she felt a dam opening, and a tidal wave of feelings rushing out toward him. She had no idea what to do about it, or what to say to him, if anything. But when she looked up at him, she looked suddenly afraid. "Are you okay?" He saw something in her eyes, and didn't understand what it was. "Is something wrong?" There was something very wrong, she told herself silently. She had no right to these feelings for him, and never would. All she could do was shake her head. "You looked scared all of a sudden, were you thinking about the house?" Not knowing what else to say to him, she nodded her head. But it wasn't about the house, it was about him. She was suddenly terrified that Zoe might be right, not about Brad, but about herself. She was so happy with him that she suddenly wanted more of him. She was falling in love with Brad. She knew he would be horrified, just as she herself was. The last thing she wanted to do was upset his peaceful life, as hers had been. Whatever it was she was feeling for him, she knew it had to be denied. He could never know.

She was strangely quiet that night, and he noticed it. He was equally cautious about taking advantage of her, and not being inappropriate. He wanted her to be comfortable and feel safe with him at all times, and she did.

It was nearly midnight when he left. He had to get up early the next day. He was going straight from his meetings to the airport while she was still at school. She offered to skip classes and go to the airport with him, but he didn't think it was a good idea to disrupt her life for him.

"I'll call you from the airport in London. And after that, we're just going to have to be big kids for the next two weeks. Think you can?" There was no other choice. But they were both unnerved at the prospect of not being able to communicate for two weeks. Faith knew the bond they had formed with each other was unusual, and had become addictive for both of them. It was going to be a test of their self-sufficiency to manage without it now.

"I'm going to have withdrawals without talking to you," she confessed.

"Yeah. Me too." But there was nothing they could do.

He held her tightly in his arms for a long moment before he left, and hugged her so close, she could hardly breathe.

"I love you, Fred," he said to her just as Jack would have done, and yet she felt so much more for him.

Somehow when neither of them had been looking, Brad had slipped into another part of her heart, and she had to get him out of there again, without him ever knowing where he'd been. It was up to her to do the work, she knew, and she said nothing of it to him, as she kissed his cheek and waved when he left.

Faith was up and left the house by seven-thirty the next day. She walked the two blocks to St. Jean Baptiste Church on Lexington Avenue, in a freezing rain. It seemed suitable punishment to her, and what she deserved. She went to confession before mass began, and spoke in whispers to the priest. She knew she had to confess. She had to tell someone. She had done a terrible thing, and she had only just discovered it herself. She was in love with him, with her whole heart and soul, and he was married to someone else, and intended to stay that way. She had no right to jeopardize his life, his marriage, or his peace of mind. She told herself, and the priest in the confessional, that she had abused the brotherly friendship he had extended to her, and now she had to find a way back from what she felt for him.

The priest gave her absolution, and ten Hail Marys to say, which seemed far too small a penance to Faith. She felt certain she deserved far greater punishment for the feelings she had for him, and the pain and risk she would create for him, if he ever found out.

She said the ten Hail Marys, and an entire rosary, on the beads he had given her, and as she held them in her trembling hands, all she could think of was him.

She was still deeply troubled when she walked home in the rain afterward. And when she got home and listened to her messages on her answering machine, there were two from Brad. He had called before he left the hotel to attend his meeting, and he was thanking her for the night before. His voice was as gentle as it always was, his words just as kind. And as she felt a wave of love for him wash over her as she listened to him, she closed her eyes. She was glad now that he was going to Africa, and that they couldn't talk to each other while he was gone. She needed time to turn the tides of what she felt for him, and to return to what they had once had. She had two weeks to pry him loose from her heart again, and heal the scar.

20

BRAD DIDN'T CALL FAITH BEFORE HIS FLIGHT LEFT FOR London, because he knew she was still at school. But he thought about her as he sat in the airport, and after the plane took off. He just sat staring out the window, thinking of her. Sitting next to her in front of the fire the night before was all he wanted out of life. All he had ever wanted. And knew he would never have. More than anything, he knew he had no right to her. She deserved a good life, with someone who loved her, and would be good to her. He had no intention of leaving Pam, and Faith deserved more than a part of a married man. He would never have done that to her. He was only grateful that she had no idea of the feelings he had for her. But unlike Faith, he had no desire to stamp out the feelings he had developed for her. All he wanted to do was conceal them, and cherish them. Other than what he felt for his sons, she had become what mattered most to him in his life.

After a while, he fell asleep, and slept for most of the flight. He woke for dinner, and went back to sleep again.

And when he awoke finally, just before they landed, he was thinking of Faith again. He had the distinct impression he had dreamed of her all night.

The plane landed just after one o'clock, New York time, and he went straight to a phone and used his credit card to call her. He wanted to say good-bye to her again, before he joined Pam at the hotel. They were leaving for Zambia that night.

The phone rang twice, and Faith grabbed it, and answered in a sleepy voice. It was the middle of the night for her.

"Hello?" She couldn't imagine who it was. And smiled when she heard Brad.

"I'm sorry to wake you," he apologized. "I just wanted to say good-bye again."

"How did your meetings go in New York?" She rolled over in bed, holding the phone, and opened her eyes.

"Great. I got some very interesting advice from my friend. I don't know if it'll work, but I'm going to try like hell when I get back." Faith knew how much it mattered to him. He had lost a trial two months before, and a sixteen-year-old boy had gone to prison for five years. Brad had been devastated, and was convinced it was his fault for not doing a better job.

"I know you will," she reassured him. "What's the weather like in London?"

"Freezing. Cold. Rainy. The usual."

"Sounds like New York," she smiled. In spite of herself, she was glad he had called.

"I wish I could go see Eloise for you. I think I could make her listen to me, I'd sure as hell love to try." But they both knew it was impossible. He was a stranger to her daughter.

"I wish you could. Are you doing anything special in London?" It was strange to think of him with Pam for two weeks. Their lives were so separate most of the time, that she suspected the constant proximity would be hard on him, and maybe also on her. They were almost strangers to each other now. The only common ground they shared was their sons.

"Nothing much. Pam will want to shop. I thought I'd go to the British Museum for a couple of hours. Maybe I'll go with her. But shopping makes me crazy after a while." And then he had a thought. "Maybe I'll go to church, and light candles for you and Jack." The thought of him doing it made her smile, as she lay listening to him in the dark.

"It gets addictive, doesn't it?" she said, and he laughed.

"Yes, it does. The funny thing is I believe in it. It's as though as long as that little light stays on, something special will happen to you, or you'll be safe. I want to give that to you," he said gently.

"You already do. But I appreciate the candles too. I'm sorry I missed your calls this morning. I went to church really early."

"That's funny. I had the feeling that was where you were. You looked awfully serious last night, Fred. Were you okay?" She had been thinking of him and all she felt for him, and she had no intention of telling him that, or she would have to go to confession again.

"I'm okay," she reassured him, "there's just a lot going on in my life these days. A lot to think about."

"I know. That's why I worry about you." And then after a moment's pause, he sighed and told her he had better get to the hotel. "Take good care of yourself, Fred. I'll talk to you in two weeks."

"Take care of you too. And have fun!" she said, and then he was gone, and she lay in bed thinking of him for hours after she hung up the phone. Gouging Brad out of her heart was not going to be an easy thing to do. And watering down what they had until it was just friendship again would be just as hard. She had no idea what to do.

It was after six A.M. British time, when Brad arrived, and by the time he went through customs, called Faith, and got the limo into town, it was nearly nine o'clock. Pam had stayed at Claridge's the night before, and she had already gone out when he walked into the room. She had left him a note, and told him that she would be back in time to leave for the airport with him, and that all her bags were packed. As usual, she had brought far too much.

Brad showered and shaved, ordered something to eat from room service, read the paper, and left the hotel at noon. He went to the British Museum, as he had told Faith he would, and found a beautiful old church on Kingsway, six blocks from the museum, and lit the candles he had promised for her and Jack. He sat in the church for a long time, thinking about her, and what a decent person she was, and how he wished he could do more for her. And then he went for a long walk. He wound up on New Bond Street finally, and wandered into some art galleries. He stepped into Asprey's to admire the silver animals and leather goods, and then he ran right into Pam coming out of Graff's. It was one of the most important jewelers in the world.

"If you tell me you just bought something, I'm going to have a heart attack," he said fervently, and she laughed.

"Just window shopping," she said innocently. She didn't tell him she had bought a narrow diamond bracelet and a new watch. They were sending them home for her, so she didn't have to come clean with Brad yet.

She had a limousine from the hotel, and Brad caught a ride back to the hotel with her. She was looking very stylish in a navy pantsuit and a fur-trimmed raincoat. It was hard to imagine her in Africa. She looked far more at ease in London, in the back of a limousine.

"What did you do today?" she asked pleasantly, as they rode back to the hotel. He smiled to himself thinking how horrified she'd be if he said he'd gone to church.

"I went to the British Museum," Brad said innocently.

"How sensible." She smiled, as they pulled up in front of Claridge's, and the doorman and a bevy of porters ran to their aid. The driver had put half a dozen shopping bags in the trunk for her, and Brad groaned when he saw them emerge.

"I hope you bought another suitcase to put them in, if you're planning to take all that to Africa." He couldn't even begin to imagine what she'd bought. There were bags from Gucci, Hermès, Saint Laurent, and Chanel. Not to mention her stop at Graff's.

"I have room in my suitcases. Don't worry about it," she said, and then marched into the hotel, as the porters followed with her bags. It struck Brad as he brought up the rear how different she was from Faith. She was powerful, confident, didn't hesitate to tell people what to do, and gave everyone the impression that she could have run the world, and would, given half the chance. Faith was infinitely gentler, quieter, more subtle in her approach, and whenever he was around her, Brad had a sense of peace. When he was with Pam, he had the feeling that he was standing on a volcano that was about to erupt. One had a sense of tension and energy that was inadequately confined. And he never knew when her velocity would be directed toward him.

They didn't say anything to each other while they rode up in the elevator, and Pam turned to look at him as they walked into the room. She felt as though she hadn't really seen him in a long time. And in a sense, that was true, even though they existed marginally under one roof.

"It's too bad the boys are in Africa," Pam said as she sat down in a large wing chair in the living room of their suite. She always stayed in luxurious hotels, and took big suites. "I wish they were someplace more civilized," she said, kicking off her shoes, "like Paris or New York."

"I don't think that would be as much fun for them," Brad said, opening a bottle of wine from the refrigerator and offering her some.

"Probably not," she said, and barely took a breath before her next question. She was clever and read him well. She knew he had something on his mind. Although they weren't close, she had remarkable instincts for him. And not always of the best kind. Sometimes all she wanted to do was corner him, and prove she could. "How was New York?"

"Very good," he said, looking pleased. "I got everything I wanted from Joel Steinman, on that capital case I've got."

"That's nice." She was never interested in his work, any more than he was in hers. "How was your friend?" Bingo. She could see it in his eyes, no matter what he chose to say next.

"Faith?" He wasn't going to hide it from her, nor give her the satisfaction of discovering it at some later date. "Fine. I had dinner with her last night."

"Has she figured out yet that you're in love with her?" Pam asked unemotionally. She had everything she wanted from him. Respectability, limited companionship, and the convenience of not unwinding a marriage they had had for years, which it would have bothered her to give up, as much as it would him. Which was why they stayed married. It worked for both of them. But he didn't like the nature of her question, nor her tone.

"No, she hasn't. Because I'm not." Pam had figured it out before he had, but he had no intention of admitting that to her. Secretly, he now knew she was right. But it would have been dangerous for all concerned to admit it to her. And more than anything, he owed it to Faith to protect her. "I told you, we're old friends."

"I can't figure out if you're lying to yourself, me, or her. Probably all three."

"That's a pretty picture you've painted," Brad said, looking annoyed, as he took a sip of wine. Pam was quietly sipping hers and watching him.

"Don't look so uptight," she teased. "You must be in love with her, if you're so defensive. It's no big deal, Brad. We've both been there before. What are you being so sensitive about? What's so sacred about this girl?"

"She's the sister of my best friend, who happens to be dead. And I grew up with her. She's like my kid sister. And I think it's tasteless of you to be making those kinds of allusions about her."

"Sorry if I'm tasteless, darling. You know how I am. I call it the way I see it. And I know you. I think you have a thing for her. No big deal. I'm not sensitive about it.

Why the hell should you be?" She had a way of prying
into his life without tact or sensitivity. It was why their
marriage had finally not worked. One way or another,
she ran roughshod over him. And it was one of the
things he loved about Faith. She was gentle with him.
And with everyone. Pam hit everything with a hammer,
and mostly him.

"Why don't we just drop this particular subject for
the rest of the trip? It'll go a lot better for both of us if we
do." They were about to spend more time alone together, and in close quarters, than they had in years. In
San Francisco, they could get away from each other, and
had their own lives. On this trip, it was going to be like
being Siamese twins. And Brad wasn't thrilled.

They managed to stay out of each other's hair for the
next two hours. Pam took a bath, Brad took a nap, and
they ordered sandwiches from room service before they
left for the airport. It was going to be a long night. They
had a twelve-hour trip ahead of them, and were scheduled to land in Lusaka in Zambia. And from there they
had to take another plane to Kalabo, across the Zambezi
River from Victoria Falls. The boys had promised to
meet them with a van to take them to the national park
where they lived and worked.

Pam disappeared while they were waiting at Heathrow,
she wanted to check out the shops. And Brad went to buy
a book. He tried to call Faith, but she was out. So he left her
a message, sending her his love. He and Pam met up again

half an hour later at the gate, and she handed him a small gift-wrapped box.

"What's that?"

"Present for you," she said, looking apologetic. "I'm sorry I teased you about your friend." Some things were off limits, and she was beginning to think that girl was, which only confirmed what she thought. But she preferred to make peace with him before the trip.

"Thanks, Pam," he said, looking touched, and opened it to find a small Japanese camera with a panoramic lens. It was perfect for their trip. "What a nice gift. Thanks." It reminded him briefly that they had once liked each other, and been friends, but it had been a long time since then. There had been a lot of water under the bridge, and too many disappointments for either of them to rekindle much more than friendship. But for this trip, at least, it was enough.

They settled into their seats on the plane, ordered dinner, and selected movies for their individual screens. Pam took out a stack of fashion magazines she'd brought, and some papers from the office. She was working on some major deals when she left, and her father had promised to baby-sit them for her. He was the only one she really trusted in the firm. Other than that, she relied on herself. In spite of all the other attorneys, and capable people around her, she was a one-man band. Pam didn't work well on a team. And neither did Brad. They had never trusted each other either when they were working together. He handled his own clients, as she did hers, and they had argued constantly about work. It was one of the many reasons he had left. That and the fact that he had felt like he was on a leash, with Pam and her father at the other end. It had been untenable for him. And it was part of why she was so angry when he left. She had lost control of him. Which was one of the things he loved most about working on his own. He was his own man, and no longer answered to her or her father.

They said very little to each other on the trip, and they both looked exhausted when they arrived at the first airport. Neither of them had slept. And as Brad had lain staring at the movies he'd selected, all he could think about was Faith. He would have died rather than admit it to her, but Pam was right. He couldn't get her out of his mind. He worried about her feelings, and her well-being, and what Alex was doing to her. He was afraid Alex would do something really awful to her in his absence. He felt badly for her about Ellie's betrayal. All he could think of were the ten thousand problems she could possibly have while he was gone. And there was no way for her to contact him.

"You look like shit," Pam said bluntly, as they waited for the next flight.

"I'm tired."

"So am I. I hope the boys appreciate our coming all this way. I'm beginning to think we should have waited till they got home." But Brad missed them too much, and they had promised to go. And he had convinced

Pam it would be a great trip. But she was already worrying about the food, and even the bottled water, when
they got on the next flight. And this time, out of sheer
exhaustion, they both slept.

It was morning in Kalabo when they arrived. And
they both woke up at exactly the same moment, as the
plane touched down. There was an incredible sunrise,
and a sky streaked with pink and orange as the sun hov-
ered over the mountains, and they could see herds of
animals gathered on the plains. Brad had never seen
anything like it in his life. The terrain seemed to stretch
out forever, and there were only a handful of roads and
vehicles. And there were half-naked tribesmen standing
near the tarmac, waiting for people to disembark from
the plane.

"Well, here goes," Pam said, looking nervous. "I've
got a feeling we're not in Kansas anymore, Toto," she
said as Brad laughed. She was not a woman who liked
being taken out of her own environment, or the places
where she felt in control. And this was far from being
one of those. But Brad didn't care where they landed, or
what they had to go through to get there. It had been
nine months since he'd seen his sons, and that was
enough for him. He'd have gone to hell and back to see
them.

They walked down the stairs to the tarmac, and into
the terminal to clear customs, which consisted of a bare-
footed man in a shirt with epaulets and a pair of white
shorts. He had a head like an African carving, and he

glowered at them both, checked their passports, and then waved them on. The customs officer had the kind of face and demeanor that would have terrified Pam if she'd been alone. All she wanted was to go back to Claridge's, and then home. The only consolation was seeing Dylan and Jason, but as far as Pam was concerned, being there was a high price to pay to see her sons.

Brad gave a whoop the moment he saw them. They were waiting next to a van outside, and as Pam and Brad and a porter emerged, they hurried toward their parents, and embraced them both. They were handsome and tall, with blond hair bleached by the sun, and faces so darkly tanned they looked like natives. They were identical and looked like Brad, right down to their cleft chins, except for the blond hair that no one had ever been able to explain, except for some unknown distant relative. Brad had always said that there must have been a Swede in there somewhere. They had been towheads as babies and little boys. And Brad realized as he saw them, that they had hair the same color as Faith's. It was yet one more thing to remind him of her, even there.

"You two look incredible," Brad chortled. They had filled out, and from the work they were doing, had developed powerful muscles in their backs, shoulders, and arms. They looked like bodybuilders in their T-shirts and jeans. And even Pam looked excited now that she was here. It was great to see them both.

"You look good too, Dad," Dylan said to his father, as Jason helped load his mother's bags. Only Brad had ever been able to tell them apart. He had always sworn that they looked distinctly different. Pam had never been sure which one she was talking to, and had solved the problem by putting them in different-colored sneakers when they were little, which they had learned to switch later on. But even now, as adults, it was hard to tell them apart. Jason was a quarter of an inch taller, but even that didn't show.

They were full of interesting information and data, as they drove to the Liuwa Plain National Park near the Zambezi River, where they lived and worked. They explained sights as they saw them, named animals as they passed them, talked about tribes who lived in the bush along the road. What they were seeing was exactly what Brad had hoped, and it made him glad they had come. And he realized more than ever what an extraordinary experience it had been for the boys. He knew they would never forget it, and would be hard put to duplicate the experience once they got home. They were due back in July, although they'd been talking about spending a year in London, or maybe six months traveling in Europe, before they went to graduate school or got jobs at home. Pam was determined to pressure them into law school. And after what they were seeing, Brad was no longer sure she had a chance. They had seen a far broader world. The experience had been priceless for them. And neither of them had expressed an interest in the law, nor for working for her later on.

It took them four hours to drive over narrow high-
ways and rutted roads to the game preserve in the national park, and by the time they got there, Pam was
beginning to look unnerved. She had the distinct impression that they were at the end of the world, and they
were. Brad loved it, just as the boys did. She looked as
though she were ready to go home. And it was worse
once they arrived. The employees of the game preserve
lived in tents outside. There were two narrow buildings,
one that served as a large rec room and office, the other
as a mess hall, and there were two tiny cabins for guests.
The boys had corralled one for them, but Brad suggested that he'd rather sleep with the boys in their tent.

"I wouldn't!" Pam said quickly and they all laughed.
There was an outdoor shower, which was actually a
large tent with a hose, and outhouses that served as latrines. It was actually among the more plush of the
game preserves in the region, but it wasn't as fancy as
some in Kenya, which Pam might have preferred. As far
as she was concerned, this was as bad as it got. "Oh my
God," she muttered under her breath, as Dylan opened
a door and showed her the latrines. "Is that it?" she
asked, praying for a bathroom to drop from the sky. The
thought of spending two weeks there nearly made her
cry.

"You'll be fine," Brad said calmly, patting her shoulder, and she shot him a fiery look. "Whose idea was
this?" she whispered to him when the boys went to get
them warm blankets and pillows, and Brad laughed.

"Your sons'. They wanted us to see where they've lived for the last nine months. You'll get used to it, I promise."

"Don't count on it." And Brad knew her well enough to know that she was probably right. But he also knew she'd try. She was spoiled and loved her comfort, but when pressed, she was also capable of being a good sport. And she made the effort for the boys. Although she nearly fainted when she saw her first snake, and the boys warned her that there were flying bugs the size of her fist that would fly across the room at her at night. Just hearing about them made her want to scream, or pack up and go home.

They spent their first night outdoors, sitting around a fire, listening to the sounds of the velvety African night. Brad had never seen anything like it in his life, and he loved it. And the next day, Brad went on a long drive with the boys, over sand roads, to Lukulu, a market town, and Pam stayed at the camp. She didn't want to venture too far. She had visions of their truck being rammed by a rhino or pounced on by a lion, or flipped over by a water buffalo. And she wasn't too far wrong. Some of those things had happened, but for the most part, the people on the preserve knew what they were doing, and by now so did her sons. Brad came back raving about everything they'd seen.

And for the first week, the days seemed to fly by. The only thing he longed for was a phone so he could call Faith and tell her what he'd seen. All Pam wanted was a toilet and a shower. But she stopped complaining after the first few days.

The boys also took them to Ngulwana, on the opposite side of the river from the park, where they had worked digging trenches, building houses, and restoring a disintegrating church. They were currently helping to build a medical office, where a doctor came once a month to treat the ailing and injured locals. The nearest hospital was two hours away in the dry season, in Lukulu, and it took twice as long in the rainy season, if one could get there at all. The only other option was to get there in a small plane. It was not a great place to get sick, Pam commented, and Brad agreed. But he was also impressed by how much work his sons had done for the locals. And everyone seemed to know them and love them. A number of people waved and smiled in greeting as they walked by. And both Pam and Brad were enormously proud of them.

By the second week, Brad had fallen in love with Africa itself, the people, the sounds, the smells, the warm nights, the incredible sunrises and sunsets, the light that was impossible to describe. He never had his camera out of his hands, and he suddenly understood why his sons loved being there. It was magical, and he would have loved to spend a year there himself. And Pam, for all her efforts at good sportsmanship, had eaten everything they gave her, learned to shower in the outdoor tent, still winced when she used the latrines, screamed when she saw the bugs, and much as she loved her sons, couldn't wait to go home. It just wasn't for her. And on the last night, she had a look of joyful relief.

"Mom, you were a great sport," Jason congratulated her, and Dylan gave her a hug. It was Brad who was chagrined to leave. He had spent both weeks sleeping in their tent with them, going on drives with them at night, and getting up with them before dawn. He had seen kills, and stampedes, and a watering hole where sick and old elephants went to die. He had seen things he had only read about or dreamed. It had been a moment in his life he knew he would never forget, and had loved sharing with them. And it had meant a great deal to both boys. They had also had more to talk about and confide in him than they had had in years. They had told him, just as he suspected, that they had no interest in law school, but were afraid to tell Pam. Dylan was thinking about med school, and wanted to come back to work in third world countries with children suffering from tropical diseases, and Jason wanted to do some kind of public health work, on a grander scale, but didn't yet know what. In either case, they had years ahead of them in school, and wanted to get started soon, probably in another year, after they'd applied. But in both cases, law school was out of the question for them.

"Who's going to tell Mom?" Brad teased them on one of their long predawn rides.

"That would be you, Dad," Dylan teased back. "We

figured you have the most experience at giving her bad news."

"Thanks a lot, guys. And when do you expect me to give her this little piece of news?" She had already imagined them working in their grandfather's firm, and had planned that since they were little boys. The only ones who weren't on the same page with her were Dylan and Jason.

"We thought you could tell her after you left." Jason laughed.

"I can hardly wait. I should let you two do your own dirty work. That's part of growing up." But in the end, he agreed. He would tell her sometime after they got home, but he decided to let her recover from the trip first. She had gotten a mild case of dysentery in the past two days, and was increasingly desperate to go home.

She looked like she was being let out of prison the day they left. It had not been her favorite trip, except for seeing her sons. She had been nervous and on edge and ill at ease the entire time. She imagined every possible kind of danger and disease lurking everywhere, and had barely been able to enjoy the sounds and smells and sights. Brad had enjoyed it for both of them, and would have loved to come back, but the boys were leaving in three months. He wished he could have come sooner, so he could have had a second trip, without Pam. It was draining having to constantly reassure her. But he was patient and sympathetic to her fears. It was a big stretch for her. She would have much preferred going to

Hawaii or London or Palm Springs. Africa was just too much. Her nerves were frayed by the time she left, and she hugged the boys good-bye with obvious relief.

"Thanks for coming, Mom," they both said with feeling. And knowing how she felt about it, they appreciated it all the more. Brad respected her for making the effort. The trip hadn't made a stronger bond between them, but it had between him and his sons. He was thrilled to have shared the time in Africa with them.

"I'll see you at home," Pam said, with the emphasis on "home" as they all laughed.

"We'll be back by July," they both said. They had already agreed to come home for a while, before setting off again, either to travel, or take jobs in Europe for a year. Dylan wanted to go to Australia and New Zealand. Jason was trying to talk him into a year in Brazil. In either case, they were obviously not ready to settle down.

"They need to start thinking about law school, or at least apply if they want to get into a good school," Pam complained to Brad as they got on the plane, and he nodded. He knew it was too soon to give her the bad news. She hadn't even left Africa yet. And she looked anxious all the way back to Lusaka, where she sat miserably in the airport, with stomach cramps. She was not feeling well. But she felt better on the flight back to London, and she looked as though she had died and gone to Heaven when they arrived at Claridge's, where they were spending the night before flying home. They were going straight over the pole, and not stopping in New York, and Brad was flying home with her. As far as he was concerned, it had been a remarkable trip, and he felt like a new man. He felt as though he had conquered the world. Pam was just grateful she'd survived.

"I am not going to visit them in Brazil," she said firmly as she climbed into the immaculate bed. She had taken a bath for an hour, and scrubbed her hair and nails. She had felt filthy for two weeks. And she felt like a queen in the enormous bed. She said goodnight to Brad then, turned off the light, and went to sleep, while Brad went to sit in the living room and read. He waited another hour until she'd fallen into a deep sleep, and then he called Faith. She answered on the second ring, and was thrilled to hear his voice. Almost as much so as he was to hear hers. The moment he heard her he wondered how he had survived for two weeks without talking to her.

"You sound great, Fred. Is everything all right?"

"Very peaceful," she said, sounding healthy and calm. It was afternoon for her, and she'd been working on a paper in her study when he called. "How was the trip?"

"Incredible. I can't even describe it to you, it was so beautiful. I'll send you pictures. I want to go back." She was delighted for him. She had worried about him a lot, but had to assume he was okay. She had also wondered, with silent trepidation, if it had been a second honeymoon for him and Pam. She prayed that it would be, for his sake, and an evil, selfish part of her, she told herself, hoped not.

"How were the boys?"

"Fantastic. Big and beautiful and strong, and happy. It's the best thing that ever happened to them. I wish I'd done something like that when I was their age. I wouldn't have had the balls."

"Was it scary?" she asked, sounding impressed, and he laughed.

"I didn't think so. I don't think there's enough money in the world to pay Pam to go back. It really wasn't her trip. She slept in a little hut, and was terrified all night. And she's been sick for the last couple of days. I slept in the tent with the boys." She liked hearing that, and then hated herself for it. She'd been praying about it for two weeks, and had gotten nowhere. She had even spoken to a priest, out of the confessional, and told him about her feelings for Brad. He had told her to pray to Saint Jude, and said that miracles occurred, which only confused her more. The only miracle she needed was to stop having the feelings she did for him. She needed to find the peaceful haven of only being his friend again. She couldn't allow herself to feel more than that, and so far, Saint Jude hadn't helped. Her heart had taken a giant leap the moment she heard his voice. She had even said rosaries about it every day, but using the beads he'd given her, it only reminded her of him. It was her greatest inner battle these days. The outer ones were about the divorce. Alex was making life miserable for her. But she was getting used to it. And she had a piece of important news for Brad.

She let him tell her all about the trip, and then she smiled broadly as she told him she had a surprise.

"Let me guess." He concentrated, reveling in just talking to her again. There was so much he had wanted to share with her, and he couldn't remember it all now. There was too much and he was too tired. "You got all A's at school, in your exams."

"Yes, sort of. Actually I got an A minus and an A. But that's not it."

"Ellie apologized and figured out that her father is a shit."

"Not yet," Faith said, sounding briefly sad.

"I don't know. Give me a hint." But she was too excited to stop at that. She had known for ten days, and was dying to share it with him. She and Zoe had had dinner to celebrate the previous weekend.

"I got into law school at NYU."

"Hurray! That's fantastic. Fred, I am so proud of you!"

"Me too! Isn't that neat?"

"It's terrific. I knew you would. What about Columbia?"

"I haven't heard yet. They send out their letters next week. But I'd rather go to NYU anyway. Besides, I'm already there. And it works for me." They talked about it for a few minutes, and she brought him up to date on the divorce. Alex was still hassling her about the house, but he had already agreed to let her stay longer while they negotiated the settlement. She didn't want spousal support from him, although she could have had it. All she wanted was the house, outright, and some of their investments. In relation to what he had, she didn't want a lot. Her mother had left her enough to get by on. And in a few years she knew she'd be getting a decent salary as an attorney. Contrary to what Eloise believed, she was asking for very little. Even her attorney thought she should get more, but that wasn't Faith's style. As Brad knew only too well, she was decent to a fault.

They talked for nearly an hour, and finally, in spite of how much he loved talking to her, he started to yawn, and she told him to go to bed. He was leaving for San Francisco at noon the next day, and would be back home by six in the evening Faith's time. "I'll call or e-mail you when I get in."

"Thanks for calling," Faith thanked him. It had been an endless two weeks without him, but she had survived. And the good news about law school had buoyed her spirits, in spite of Alex's antics. She hadn't spoken to Eloise in over a week. It was getting harder and harder to talk. Ellie had entrenched herself in her father's camp. And what hurt Faith most, she had told Brad, was the way Alex had simply gouged her out of his life, as though she had never existed, never mattered, and never been his wife. He had simply erased her like so much chalk on a blackboard. He had wiped her off. And no matter how she explained it to herself, it still hurt. It

made it difficult to imagine ever trusting anyone again.
She couldn't even imagine a life with another man, or
dating. All she wanted now was to lose herself in school,
church, and her girls. And the only thing she had to do
now was get her head on straight about Brad. She was
determined to do it. Just as he was about her. No matter
how deep their attraction to each other, and how unknown to each of them, they were absolutely determined to stay behind the boundaries of friendship. And
each of them, in their endless efforts, were getting
nowhere.

21

BY THE END OF APRIL, TWO WEEKS AFTER BRAD HAD GOT-
ten home, Alex invited Zoe out to dinner when she came
home from Brown for the weekend. She was staying
with her mother, as she always did, and she didn't want
to go out with him. But Faith told her that she thought
she should.

"What's the point, Mom?" Zoe looked annoyed as
she hung up the phone. She really wanted to go out with
her friends. "He's just going to talk shit about you."

"He's still your father. You haven't had dinner with
him in a while. Maybe he's trying to bridge the gap with
you." As always, Faith was far more fair about him than
he was about her. He was still continuing to poison
Eloise against her mother, and Faith wanted to go over
to visit her, as soon as she finished school. Their semes-
ter end was only a few weeks away. And Zoe would be
home in mid-May. Faith had invited her to come, if she
went to London to see Eloise.

In the end, Zoe agreed to have dinner with Alex, at a
little French restaurant he had always liked. He was

obviously trying to make an effort with her. She went in a dress she had borrowed from her mother, and she had worn her hair in a French braid. She looked pretty and fresh and young. She had just turned nineteen a few weeks before, and she was getting more beautiful every day. But Zoe was startled when she saw that her father wasn't alone, when she approached the table. There was a woman sitting with him. He introduced them to each other with a broad, happy smile. And Zoe thought her father looked ridiculous. The girl sitting beside him on the banquette was nearly half his age.

"Leslie, I'd like you to meet my daughter Zoe . . . and this is Leslie James." Zoe guessed her to be in her early twenties, although she was slightly older than that. She was wearing a low-cut, tight-fitting dress, and she had long black hair. And although Faith wouldn't have done so, she could have told Zoe what kind of underwear she wore, if she'd been there.

They chatted awkwardly for a few minutes, and Zoe looked uncomfortable, as her father ordered wine. She realized after a few minutes that Leslie worked at his firm. But Zoe thought it was in bad taste to include his daughter on a date.

"Have you worked there for long?" Zoe asked, trying to be polite, and wishing she weren't there.

"About fourteen months. I moved here from Atlanta right before that, with my little girl." Zoe realized then that she had a faint southern accent, and she asked how old her little girl was, for lack of anything better to say.

She hated being there at all. "She's five," Leslie said, smiling and looking very young, as her father looked proudly at his friend. It was as though he wanted Zoe to admire her too, which had been the wrong thing to do. She felt disloyal to her mother just being with them.

"She's a beautiful little girl," Alex added proudly, as Zoe cringed inwardly. "She's adorable." It was obvious that her father had established a relationship with both of them.

"She's learning French. She goes to a French kindergarten. Your father thought that would be good for her." Zoe raised an eyebrow and then controlled herself instantly. She couldn't remember her father ever being that interested in where she went to school.

"That's nice for her," Zoe said, and took a sip of wine. Leslie had asked for champagne. And then Zoe nearly choked at what Leslie said next.

"This is kind of a special night for us," Leslie said with a coy smile at Alex, and he looked mildly uncomfortable. But the idea of taking Zoe out to dinner with them had been his. He wanted his daughters to meet her. "It's our anniversary," Leslie said, tossing her hair back over her shoulder as Zoe looked at her.

"Really? What kind of anniversary?" Zoe asked. It had to be a month or two, which seemed pathetic to her.

"We've been dating for a year. We had our first date a year ago tonight." Alex looked paralyzed for an instant, and then pretended he hadn't heard. There was nothing else he could do, as Zoe stared at them both.

"You've been dating for a year?" Zoe's voice was suddenly a high-pitched squeak.

"Not really," Alex interjected then. "I think Leslie means we've known each other for a year. We met shortly after she came to work."

"That's not true. Tonight is the anniversary of our first date." She looked hurt that he either hadn't remembered or didn't want to admit it, and Zoe's face went pale.

"That's interesting, since my father left my mom two months ago. I guess you guys were going out for quite a while before that."

"Yes, we were," Leslie smiled, and with that, Zoe stood up and accidentally overturned her wine, and it spilled across the table, as Leslie moved back to avoid getting splashed.

"I think that's disgusting, Dad," Zoe said, looking at him. "How could you bring me here to celebrate with you? After all the things you've said about Mom, and about it being her fault, you make me sick. Why don't you have the guts to tell Eloise the truth, instead of poisoning her against Mom? Why don't you just tell her you were screwing around, and had a girlfriend for nearly a year before you walked out on her? It would be honest at least."

Alex's eyes were blazing. He hadn't expected Leslie to give him away. She was obviously not too bright. He was totally infatuated with her, and he had had no clue that she'd do that. "Why don't you sit down and we'll talk about it," he said quietly, while his daughter looked at him with contempt. But he was trapped behind the table on the banquette, and couldn't move.

"No, thanks. I've got other plans," Zoe said, turned on her heel with remarkable aplomb given how shaken she felt, and walked out of the restaurant. As soon as she got out on the sidewalk, she started to run, hailed a cab, and went home. She was crying when she walked in the front door, and Faith was on the phone with Brad. He was talking about a case he was worried about, and she had told him Zoe was going out to dinner with her father. She was startled when she heard the front door slam, and Zoe ran into her study in tears.

"What happened?" Faith stopped talking to Brad to look at her. Her eye makeup had run down her face, and she looked like a little girl who'd been beaten up in school.

"He's a total son of a bitch, Mom. Why didn't you tell me about that girl? Did you know about her?"

"What girl?" Faith looked shocked. "Wait a minute . . . Brad, I'll call you back." He could hear a crisis brewing, and hung up immediately. "What happened? What are you talking about?"

"Dad had a woman with him. Some fourteen-year-old tart named Leslie. She had long black hair and big boobs, and she had the nerve to tell me it was their first anniversary, and they were celebrating it with me. What a fucking disgusting thing to do. Did you know about her, Mom?"

"Sit down," Faith said quietly, and handed her a tissue. "Wipe your face . . . calm down . . . yes, I know about her," her mother said calmly, without volunteering more. He had finally done it to himself. It had been an incredibly stupid thing to do.

"Why didn't you tell me?"

"Because it was none of your business. It was up to your father to tell you, if he wanted to, and I didn't think he would." She didn't offer Zoe any of the details, nor would she.

"Is that why he left you?"

"I guess so. Maybe that, and some other things. He said he wanted a life, and was bored with me. She's a lot younger than I am, that's for sure. And probably a lot more fun."

"She's a total moron with tits. What is he doing with her? And how could he leave you for her? How could he take me to dinner with her?" It had been the most humiliating moment in her life. Zoe had felt cheated and betrayed and used, and what little respect she'd had for her father to begin with utterly disappeared.

"Maybe he's serious about her," Faith said, looking depressed. She felt it as another slap in the face, after many, but this time he had slapped Zoe too. And she hated him for that. His children didn't belong in his affairs. Unless this was more than that, and he was sharing that with them. If so, Zoe would have to adjust and accept Leslie for who she was to him. But it was a little early, to say the least, to be flaunting her.

"If he marries her, I'll kill myself, or him."

"He's not marrying anyone, yet. He's still married to me." But in five more months, he wouldn't be. She just couldn't imagine him introducing that girl to his daughters so soon.

It took her an hour to calm Zoe down, and then before Faith could stop her, she picked up the phone. She dialed Ellie in London. It was three in the morning for her. Faith tried to convince her to wait until she'd calmed down, but Zoe only waved her away. And Eloise must have picked up the phone in her sleep.

"Wake up," Zoe said bluntly, "it's me . . . No, I won't call you back . . . listen to me. Do you know what our shithead father did tonight . . . he just took me to dinner with his girlfriend, who looks about fourteen, to celebrate their one-year anniversary with them. One year! Do you hear me! He's been dating her for a year. And that's why he left Mom! Now what do you think of your hero? After all the shit you gave Mom, you owe her a humongous apology." There was a long silence then on Ellie's end, and Zoe just kept confirming what she'd heard and seen. They argued for a long time, and Faith left the room. She went down to the kitchen and called Brad on the other line. He was still in the office, and she explained what had happened. He whistled at his end of the phone.

"That must have been quite a scene. What an incredibly dumb thing to do. What was he thinking?"

"I guess he's naïve, and he thought he could sell it to

her. She's on the phone with Ellie now. I suspect the shit
is about to hit the fan."

"I'd say it already did," he laughed. "I don't envy
him. Hell hath no fury like girls when they meet their fathers' girlfriends. I think you're about to be avenged.
Couldn't happen to a nicer guy." Brad sounded both
amused and pleased.

"Yeah, I was thinking that too," Faith said soberly.
They went back to talking about his case for a few minutes, and then she got off the phone again. It was only a
minute later when Zoe walked into the kitchen with
a superior look. "What did Ellie have to say?" Faith
asked, intrigued. She was hopeful that Zoe had just provided adequate evidence to turn Eloise around. She
didn't expect her to turn on her father, but maybe she'd
forgive her mother now, or at least try to understand.

"She's coming home this weekend to see you, Mom.
She said to send you her love." Faith smiled. There was
hope. At last.

Eloise came home, as promised, that weekend, and
she spent two days crying in her mother's arms. She
apologized, she sobbed, she begged for forgiveness. She
couldn't believe what her father had done. And she and
Zoe had a major confrontation with him. Faith never
knew exactly what transpired, but both girls stayed
with her that weekend, and when Alex called, neither of
the girls would talk to him. He was in major disgrace
with them, all of which he deserved, as far as Faith was
concerned.

"Do you think he's going to marry her?" Eloise asked, looking panicked, and sitting close to her mom. In the past few days, Eloise's love for her mother had not only deepened, but she had a new respect for her she'd never had before. She had finally discovered and fully understood the decency that was at Faith's very core.

"I have no idea," Faith said honestly. "You have to ask him." But neither of them was anxious to know, and they didn't want to call to ask him.

"Mom," Eloise said finally, in a quiet moment alone, when Zoe had left the room. "I don't think I can ever tell you how sorry I am for all the things I said to you. I didn't understand. Dad always told me I was just like him, and I think I wanted to prove to him that I was, to get his approval and win his love. He never openly said bad things about you, but he somehow implied that he was always right and you were wrong. I learned a lot about myself in the past couple of months, about trust, and belief, and manipulation. I let myself believe that he was telling the truth, and you weren't. I never understood or wanted to accept that you were telling the truth. I was a complete shit to you, I don't know how you can still love me after all the things I said." Tears rolled relentlessly down her cheeks as she spoke to Faith, and her mother was crying too. "I never really knew what a good person you are . . . and how rotten he is. I feel as though I've lost my father now. I'll never be able to trust him again." But Faith hoped she would one day. He was their father and, more than likely, they would eventually forgive him. Or at least Faith thought they should, but that was how she viewed everything and everyone, as worthy of forgiveness, except sometimes herself. The one person she was always hardest on was herself. And what she was hearing from Eloise healed the wounds in her heart.

"I love you, Ellie. I'm sorry this happened to all of us. I don't know why your father did what he did, but he has to live with it now, and work it out for himself." She knew she would never feel the same way about him again, but she hoped that the girls would, for their sakes. It was hard enough to watch their parents' marriage disintegrate, she didn't want them to lose Alex too. They needed him, however imperfect he was.

The two of them left the room arm in arm, and once the furor settled down, the three of them had a nice time. They went out for hamburgers, and to Serendipity for banana splits, and she told them about going there with Brad.

"So what's with that?" Ellie asked, back in the fold again. She held hands with her mother, and Faith was enormously relieved. She had both her girls back. She didn't wish Alex any harm, but she was grateful that Ellie had come around, and had come all the way from London for the weekend. She told her mother she had broken up with Geoff, but she had two new suitors both of whom she seemed to like a lot. But just like Zoe, she wanted to know more about Brad. Faith talked about him a lot, and seemed to think the world of him, but she always insisted that they were just friends.

"I told you, we're friends. He was like my big brother growing up. He was Uncle Jack's best buddy when we were all kids. He's married. And we're never going to be more than friends." She said it so firmly that it always made Zoe suspicious of her.

"I still think he's in love with you, Mom. He has to be. No guy spends that much time calling and sending e-mails."

"He just likes to talk, I guess. But that's it." She sounded sure.

"And what about you?" Ellie asked thoughtfully. "Are you in love with him?"

"Nope. I don't fall in love with married men." She only wished it were the truth, but it was going to be. She had said a thousand prayers, and told herself a million times that no matter how wonderful he was, she could not be in love with him. And one day either the prayers, or what she told herself, would work. It had to. She had no other choice. And fortunately, as far as she knew anyway, he was not in love with her.

"Don't you have feelings for him?" Ellie pursued.

"Purely platonic ones." Faith was emphatic, and inscrutable, to say the least.

"Are you dating anyone?"

"No. And I don't want to." That much was true. She hadn't caught her breath from the agony of her marriage breaking up, and didn't know if she ever would. She doubted it. She couldn't bear the thought of getting her heart broken again. She was happier alone, talking to Brad, and spending time with her kids. "I don't ever want to get married again."

"You don't have to get married," Zoe intervened. "You can just go out, like on a date."

"Why? I'm perfectly happy with the two of you." But they both agreed later on, when they were alone in Zoe's room, that it wasn't a healthy life for her. In the end, they decided that it was probably too soon for her. Unlike their father, who had clearly jumped the gun, sharing his "anniversary dinner" with Zoe. They were both still horrified to have learned that he had cheated on their mother for nearly an entire year, if not longer, while blaming Faith going back to school for the breakup of their marriage. School had nothing to do with it, it was only the excuse.

But in any case, by the time Ellie flew back to London on Sunday night, she had reestablished her relationship with her mother. And when Brad called Faith late that night, after both girls had left, he had never heard her sound happier. At least part of the nightmare was over for her. She had her daughter back at least.

22

ALL WAS WELL IN FAITH'S WORLD IN MAY, WHEN ZOE came home from school for the summer. She had a summer job in an art gallery, and Faith was happy to have a break before she started law school. Her classes had ended at the same time as Zoe's. And Eloise was talking about coming home from London eventually. She was beginning to miss Zoe and her mother, particularly after her recent weekend. And both girls were on bad terms with their father for the time being.

Things got markedly worse when he told them that he and Leslie were planning to get married in October, after the divorce was final. And Faith hated to admit it, but it came as yet another blow to her. She sat and cried in her room for hours when she heard the news. She told Brad in an e-mail the following day but she had been too depressed to call him. Alex was still trying to force her to sell the house, and it was easy to see why now. He was buying an apartment on Fifth Avenue for himself, Leslie, and her daughter. The girls were both furious with him.

It was the following week that Faith was sitting in her study, trying to figure out where to take the girls in August. She was thinking about Cape Cod, or maybe renting a cottage in the Hamptons. Ellie had promised to come home for a few weeks, and Faith wanted to spend some time with them before she started law school in the fall. She was having a lazy morning, going through some papers, and trying to make a decision about the vacation, when Brad called. She had never heard him sound like that, and she realized instantly that he was crying.

"Are you okay? What happened?" She couldn't even imagine a situation that would make him so distraught. He sounded tense and terrified when he answered her.

"It's Jason. I don't know the details yet. We got a message from Dylan an hour ago. There's been an accident. They were working in the village, and a structure fell in. He was trapped under it for seven hours." And then Brad started crying again. "Fred, you don't know how bad the medical care is there. There's only a doctor for a few hours once a month, they're hours from the hospital. I don't even know if they can move him. We just don't know more than that. We sent a message for Dylan to call us. But he has to go to the post office to call, and even if he could get a line, he may not be able to leave his brother." He sounded as though the world had ended, and Faith's eyes filled with tears as she listened to him.

"What are you going to do?"

"I'm going over. I'm leaving in an hour. I have a flight to New York at noon. I'm connecting to a flight to London. It's so goddamn hard to get there. It'll take me more than twenty-four hours to get to him. God knows if he'll still be alive by then." He was in a total panic, justifiably it seemed.

"When do you get here?" It was all she could think of. She wanted to see him. Even if Pam was with him.

"I get in to New York at eight o'clock tonight. The flight to London leaves at ten. I'll have two hours between planes."

"I'll meet you at the airport. Can I bring anything?"

"I'm all set. Pam's packing for me. She can't come now. She has to go to court tomorrow. She's coming right after that," he said, and he didn't mention it to Faith, but he was furious that she wasn't leaving with him. He gave her the flight number, and hung up, and she sat in her study, staring into space, imagining the worst, just as he had. All she wished was that she could go with him, but she knew she couldn't. Particularly if Pam was going to meet him.

And in San Francisco, the subject was under heated discussion.

"For chrissake, call the judge and tell him what happened. He'll put the matter over till you get back. This is more important." He was frantic and livid with Pam.

"I can't do that to my client," she said as she closed his suitcase. She looked as worried as he did, but she felt her responsibility was to her client, which to Brad seemed insane, and was an enormous statement to him.

Even if Jason was all right in the end, Brad wanted her with him. It was the first time in years he had asked her for anything, and this was important to all of them. The boys needed her support, and so did he.

"I think your priorities stink," he said bluntly. "We're talking about your son, not your client."

"Dylan did not say he was dying," she said, shouting at him. They were both on edge, and Brad was dressing while they shouted at each other.

"Does he have to die for you to move your ass and cancel a goddamn court appearance? For chrissake, don't you get it?"

"I get it. I'll be there in two days. That's the best I can do."

"No, it isn't, goddamn it." She was like a mountain he couldn't move, and they were still fighting when the cab came to take him to the airport. But he knew he would never forget the fact that she hadn't left with him, nor forgive her if something happened to Jason. And he knew she wouldn't forgive herself if something terrible happened, but she didn't seem to get that either. She had total denial. "I'll get a message to you once I see him," he said, and left with his suitcase in his hand. He had no idea what she had packed for him.

The flight was an agony for him. He was unreachable on the flight, and he called Pam several times, but she had heard nothing more.

By the time he got off the plane in New York, he looked half crazed. He had run his hands through his hair a hundred times, and he looked frightened and disheveled. And just as she had promised, Faith was there, waiting for him. She was wearing jeans and a white shirt, and loafers. And she looked fresh and clean and pretty. But all he could think of was to hold her close to him, and they both cried as they walked to the nearest restaurant for a cup of coffee. He told her what he knew again, but he still didn't know anything of substance.

They talked aimlessly and held hands across the table, and discussed the endless possibilities. But without further details, she couldn't make suggestions, nor could he make decisions. He just hoped that Dylan made the right choices, and that he was able to get a plane to transport his twin to the hospital if he had to.

"You have no idea how primitive it is, how remote, how impossible to get anywhere. He'd have to travel in a truck over a road full of potholes for two to four hours. It could kill him." The plane was the only hope, if it was available, and they could find it. Faith felt helpless as she listened, just as he did.

It was an endless two hours as he waited to board the plane, and he was grateful that Faith was with him. He called Pam again, and she had heard nothing, and he went berserk when she told him she was going out to dinner.

"Are you crazy? Your son has been in an accident. Stay by the goddamn phone in case someone calls us." She insisted she had her cell phone and Dylan had the number. He hung up, and looked at Faith in despair. "You know, it's times like this when you realize what you don't have, and when you know how stupid you were to think it would be different. It's just more of the same shit it's been for the last twenty years with her." Pam just couldn't be there, not even for her children. And Faith wisely chose not to comment. "I wish you could come with me," he added. He knew how much support she would be, and he needed her desperately. Whatever had happened to Jason, he was terrified he wouldn't survive it. He wanted to be there for him, and for Dylan, regardless of their mother's stupidity, or perhaps even more so because of it.

"I wish I could come too," Faith said softly. But they both knew she couldn't. All she could do for him was be there in spirit, and they both knew after his trip in March that there would be no way for him to call her, only to send her a message via circuitous routes and people. "Let me know something when you can." She would be heartsick for him in the meantime.

"I promise." They announced the plane then and he took out his passport and his boarding pass, and she had to leave him at the security checkpoint since she wasn't traveling with him.

"Brad, take care. Try to relax. You can't do anything till you get there." That was the worst of it, and they both knew his son might be dead when he did. It was beyond thinking. "I'll go to church and pray for him as soon as you leave."

"Light a candle for him . . . please, Fred . . . ," he said with tears in his eyes as they looked at each other. Her

whole heart was his, and there was no way for her to say
it to him.

"I will. I'll go to church every day. Just know that he'll
be okay . . . try to believe that. . . ."

"I wish I could. Oh God . . . if something happens to
him . . ." As much to silence him as to bring him comfort,
without even thinking, she stretched up toward him, and
he had the exact same instinct at the same instant she did.
Without hesitating, he pulled her into his arms, and kissed
her on the lips. And for an instant they forgot the entire
world, as they clung to each other and kissed. She looked
startled when he pulled away, and so did he, but he didn't
apologize to her. She was convinced it was her fault, and
then without saying a word, he kissed her again. "I love
you, Fred." It was the outpouring of nearly forty years of
loving her, and the past seven months of growing ever
closer to her. She loved him too, but even now she knew
that it was something they could never have

"Don't say that . . . I love you too . . . but we can't say
that, we can't do this . . . I have no right to . . ." He silenced her with another kiss, and she started to cry.
"You'll regret this. You'll hate me for it after this is over.
We can't ever do this again."

"I don't care. I need you, Fred. I really need you. And
I love you. I want to be there for you too." He was like
the boy he had been when he had broken his arm when
he was twelve. It was Faith who had held it for him
when her mother drove him to the emergency room,

and he had made her swear she wouldn't tell anyone that she had seen him cry.

"I'm here for you . . . I always will be . . . but I can't steal you from someone else, Brad. That's wrong."

"We'll talk about it later." He didn't want to miss the plane, he couldn't. But suddenly, they had a lot to resolve, and to think about, and he had no idea when he'd see her again. He could be gone for months, and now this would be hanging over them until he came home, and God only knew what horrors would have happened by then. "I just want you to know I may be half out of my mind, Fred. But I'm not crazy. I've wanted to do this for a long time. I just didn't think it would be fair to you." It wasn't, to either of them. It was forbidden fruit, for both of them.

"I've been praying that this wouldn't happen. It's my fault. I shouldn't have . . ." And with that, he kissed her one last time and ran. He looked back over his shoulder once and saw her crying. He waved, and then he was gone. And Faith cried all the way back to the city in the cab. They had done something terrible, she knew that. She had allowed him to cross the line of friendship, not only allowed him, but provoked him to. There was no doubt in her mind that it was her fault it had happened. And she knew that when he came back, they would have to take back everything they had said and done, and promise not to do it again, or they could never see each other again. It was one more grief to add to their worries about Jason. All she could do for him now was pray.

She got out of the cab at St. Patrick's. It was eleven

o'clock at night, and there were still people milling
around, mostly tourists, as Faith stepped inside. She went
straight to the altar of Saint Jude and lit a candle, and then
she got on her knees, bowed her head, and cried. She had
the rosary in her hand that Brad had given her for Christmas. It seemed a sacrilege now to be holding it, after the
sin she knew she had just committed. He was a married
man and they both knew he was going to stay that way.

She knelt for an hour, praying for Jason, and for wisdom and courage for Dylan, and peace for Brad as he
made his way to them. She left the church after midnight, and went home in a cab. She let herself into the
house and walked up the stairs to her room, looking as
though someone had died. She was devastated by
everything that had happened, the terrible news, the
worry, the shock she saw in Brad's eyes, and the terribly
foolish thing she had done, which she knew was so
wrong. No matter how much she loved him, she had to
disappear from his life. She knew that now after praying. Saint Jude was the patron saint of impossible
causes. She had no choice. She was dangerous for Brad.
She stood in the darkness in her room for a moment and
then turned a single light on, as Zoe came out of her
room and stood across the hall, watching her. She hadn't
seen her mother look like that since Alex had walked
out on her months before.

"Are you okay, Mom?" she asked, looking worried.

"No," Faith said sadly, with a look of total devastation.
And without another word, she quietly closed the door.

23

BRAD DIDN'T HAVE TIME TO CALL FAITH WHEN HE switched planes in London. He had to run to another terminal, and he barely made the plane. He had managed to call Pam, but there was no news from Dylan or anyone else. And he sat on the flight to Lusaka looking like a wounded man. Most of the time, all he could think of was Jason. His imagination had run wild with him since he'd heard the initial news and nothing more. And the rest of the time, he thought of Faith, and wanted to reassure her that what they had done wasn't wrong. But there was nothing he could say. She would just have to hang tough and believe in him until he got home. He had no idea what they were going to do, but there was no question in his mind that he was in love with her. He had known it in his soul for a very, very long time.

He slept for part of the flight, and arrived in the morning, and changed planes again, to a miserable egg crate that would take him on the last leg of the trip. And this time, when he arrived in Kalabo, there was no van waiting for him, and no Jason or Dylan. He hired a man with a truck to drive him to the game preserve. But as they drove through the town, he saw what had happened. The roof of the church they'd been restoring in Ngulwana had fallen in, and the steeple with it. Just looking at it, he started to cry.

"A bad thing happened, Bambo," the man driving him said, as Brad told him to stop. "Men got hurt bad. Four of them." Brad nodded. The term the driver had used for him was "Father," a gesture of respect.

"I know. One of them is my son." The man only nodded in answer, as Brad went to look for someone to tell him where the wounded men were. And finally he found one, a tribesman wearing shorts and sandals, with scars on his face. He pointed to a building where the men had been taken. And as soon as he walked in, he saw women crying, and children squatting, and others shooing flies off the faces of the injured men. He found Dylan kneeling beside Jason, among them. Jason was unconscious and there was a tremendous blood-soaked bandage on his head. Dylan stood up instantly and collapsed sobbing in his father's arms. Dylan was so exhausted he couldn't stop crying. The only good news from what Brad could see was that Jason was still alive. But he appeared to be close to death, and Dylan told him that one of the others had died several hours before.

"Has he seen a doctor?" Brad asked, trying to fight panic. He knew he needed to be strong for both his sons, particularly Dylan now, who had been brave and sensible on his own for two days.

"He came yesterday, but he had to leave again."

"What did he say?" Brad looked tense.

"Not much. I tried to get the plane, Dad. But I couldn't."

"Do you know where it is?"

"They said it's probably in Victoria Falls, but no one seems to know for sure."

"Okay. Let me see what I can do." Brad walked into the bright sunshine, not sure where to start, and as though he could hear Faith's voice in his head, he started to pray. He walked to the post office, and asked the only man working there who to talk to about the plane. He gave Brad a number, and told him how to call. It took half an hour to get a local line, and then it occurred to him to radio the game preserve. There was no answer at the phone number he'd been given, and the man in the post office told him where to go to find a radio. And from there, Brad radioed the game preserve, and asked them to radio for the plane. And then he went back to Dylan, standing guard over Jason. He kept swatting the flies off his twin and staring miserably at him. Even with his deep tan, Brad could see that his son was gray. Dylan said he hadn't regained consciousness in two days.

It took another six hours for the game preserve to get the plane. And then they sent a boy in a Jeep into town to tell Brad that it would be at the airport at eleven o'clock that night. If he could get the wounded men to the airport, they would fly them to the hospital in Lukulu. He helped load two men into the Jeep, with their relatives following on foot. And they got a truck for Jason, laid him carefully on a blanket, and put him in the back of the truck, with Dylan kneeling next to him, and Brad in the front seat. They were a motley crew when the plane finally arrived two hours later than they said.

It took nearly an hour to get everyone settled in the plane. And shortly after that, they took off. For Brad, it was like an out-of-body experience, in a totally primitive place, with people who responded at their own pace. The plane was going to land in an open stretch of terrain the pilot was familiar with, and they had an ambulance standing by. Someone had radioed ahead. The ambulance made three trips back and forth with the injured men, as Brad paid the pilot of the plane, and took off with Jason and Dylan. And finally, once they got to the hospital, he knew that Jason would be in halfway decent hands. Most of the hospital staff was British, and there was a New Zealander and an Australian doctor as well. It was easy to see why Jason had wanted to study in the health care field and come back to a country like this. They needed help desperately, and he could make a difference here. If he survived.

After examining him, the doctor in charge told Brad and Dylan that Jason had a head injury of some magnitude, and had both swelling and fluid on the brain. And the only way to relieve it was to drain it. In normal circumstances, it was not a complicated surgery, but setting a broken arm was complicated in a place like this. Brad gave them his permission, and within seconds, Jason was wheeled away, as Brad and Dylan sat together, talking quietly, and watching other people come and go. It was an endless day.

The sun came up while they were sitting, waiting for news of Jason. They were told hours later that the procedure had been done, and he was still alive, but there had been no visible change in his condition so far. And they knew nothing more when the sun set again.

Brad and Dylan took turns sitting by his bedside, and he never stirred. They sat there, never leaving him for three days. Brad felt tired and filthy. He hadn't changed his clothes, showered, or shaved, but he never left his son for a minute. They ate whatever the nurses brought them, and on the third day, he realized that Pam had never arrived. He wondered if she was waiting for them at the game preserve, but there was no way to find out. He finally asked someone to radio there, and the message came back that she wasn't coming. But they had no other details. It was impossible to call her from where they were.

And on the fourth day, finally, Jason moaned softly, opened his eyes, smiled at them, sighed, and drifted back to sleep. For a horrifying instant, Brad thought he had died, and he clutched Dylan's arm, with wide eyes.

But the nurse said he was out of the coma, and sleeping normally. He had made it. He was going to live.

He and Dylan went outside, and they cried and laughed and shouted. It was the best day of both their lives. And the longest week Brad had ever lived.

"You smell like a dead rat," Dylan teased his father, as they sat outside for a long time, celebrating and talking quietly. Someone had brought them some hard cheese and a piece of bread. The hospital was primitive in the extreme, and poorly stocked, but the medical personnel had been terrific, and saved Jason's life.

"You don't smell so great yourself." Brad grinned at him.

After checking on Jason again, Brad asked a nurse and she directed them to an outdoor shower. He had brought his only bag with him, and shared the clothes he'd brought with his son. They were clean at least by the time they went back to Jason, he was awake again and trying to talk, and the doctor was pleased.

"You got quite a blow, young man," the New Zealander said, smiling at Jason. "You must have a mighty hard head." And when Brad took him aside later, the doctor told him it had been a miracle that the young man had lived. Of those who had survived the accident, he had been the most dangerously hurt.

Brad asked later if there was a telephone somewhere, and everyone laughed at him when he said he wanted to call the States. The best they could offer him was a phone he could use to call the post office in Ngulwana, where someone told him they would radio the game preserve, and in turn ask them to contact Jason's mother in the States, if she was still there. It took another day to get an answer from them. They had used the same complicated, circuitous route to call Pam in San Francisco, and she was relieved to know that her son was "okay." It was obvious to Brad from all that that she had never left. And he wondered what she imagined "okay" meant. She had no idea what they had been through. There was no excuse for her not coming, in Brad's eyes. No matter how much she hated third world countries, or Africa when she'd been there two months before, she should have been there. He didn't say anything to either of his sons, but Brad knew he would never forgive her for it. There was nothing she could have done, but she owed it to her boys to be there, and to Brad as well.

And a day later, he used the same circuitous routing of radios and local phones to ask someone to call Faith in New York to tell her Jason would live, and to thank her for her prayers. Brad had no doubt that they had made a difference, and he was desperately sorry that he couldn't call her and talk to her himself, but there was no way he could while he was there.

Three days later, a nurse told them that Jason's mother had gotten a message to them. She couldn't come, but was glad that all was well. She would see them when they got home. It was that message that made the difference to him. Unless she were in a coma herself, there was no acceptable explanation she could

give for not being there. Brad never mentioned it to
Dylan, but he knew that their marriage had died on that
day. They had told Jason that their mom was tied up in
San Francisco, and it was too complicated for her to get
there, and he didn't question it, but Dylan could see on
his father's face how he felt about it, and he tried to reassure him as best he could.

"It would have been too hard on Mom here," Dylan
said gently, and Brad nodded. He had nothing left to
say. They had spent twenty-five years together, and one
always assumed that when the chips were down, the
person you were married to would be there. Even if they
didn't give much from day to day. But when they failed
to stand up and be counted when it really mattered, you
knew everything you had tried not to know all along.
And Brad knew now. Not only wasn't Pam his wife anymore, she wasn't even his friend. It was a devastating
revelation, and a disappointment so enormous in her as
a human being that even if he could have called her, he
would have had nothing to say.

The doctor estimated that Jason would be at the hospital for a month, and they provided two cots for Brad
and Dylan. They sat with him for hours every day, and
then went on walks in the cool of the evening. Brad took
long walks by himself every day when the sun came up.
He had never seen as beautiful a place as this one, and it
was even more so because Jason hadn't died there, but
nearly had, and had been reborn. Brad felt as though his
own spirit had been reborn with him. He suddenly felt

filled with hope and life and promise, the miracle had not only touched Jason, it had touched all three of them. And it was a bond and a time Brad knew they would never forget.

And as he walked home from his long hikes every morning, he found himself not only thinking of his children, and thanking God for them, but he also thought of Faith. He only wished that she could be there with them to see the beauty of the place. She would have seen the splendor of it as he did. And she would have understood what it meant to him.

They flew Jason back to Kalabo a month after he had gone to the hospital. He was tired and wan, and had lost a considerable amount of weight. He was still too weak to travel, but the doctor thought that after a few more weeks resting at the game preserve, and eating properly, he would be able to make the trip home. It was three weeks after they brought him back from the hospital that Jason said he felt well enough to make the trip. The headaches he had had for weeks had finally gone away as well.

It was an emotional day when they finally left the game preserve, and started the long trip home. Brad had gone to the post office twice to try to call Faith, he had waited hours for an outside, international line, and had finally given up. There was no way to call. Nor had he communicated further with Pam. He had too much to say to her to call on a bad line from a remote African phone.

As it had when he'd arrived, it took them two flights to get to London, and Brad had arranged for them to stay there for two days. He had been gone for nearly two months by then. And he wanted Jason to rest and see a doctor in London, before they traveled the rest of the way home. And much to everyone's amazement, when he did, Jason got a clean bill of health. They described the accident, and the procedure that had saved him, and showed them the chart, X-rays, and paperwork that had been sent home with him. And the doctor in London said he was an incredibly fortunate young man. He could have easily died from the injury he'd sustained. They didn't anticipate any long-term ill effects, although they suggested he take it easy for a couple of months. Even Jason agreed with a weak smile. He felt like he'd been hit by a train.

When they got to Claridge's, Jason called his mother, and he cried when he talked to her. And then Dylan told her everything, and after that he passed the phone to Brad. He put her on hold and took the call in the other room. He was no longer even angry at her. He didn't raise his voice. He didn't accuse her of anything. And he didn't want to hear the excuses he was sure she would proffer.

"Thank God he's all right," she said, sounding nervous. And at first, there was silence from Brad's end. He hadn't wanted their sons to hear the conversation, which was why he had gone to the next room.

"What do you expect me to say, Pam?" There were a

thousand rude or cruel things he could have said. But the situation seemed far too serious to him to do that. That would only have made sense if he still cared. And he no longer did. What she had done, or hadn't, had been the last straw for him.

"I'm sorry . . . I couldn't make it, Brad. I got tied up here." As far as Brad was concerned, "couldn't make it" was something you said about a dinner party or a ballet, not a son who nearly died continents away. "I tried, but by the time I could have come, he was all right."

"He's not all right yet, Pam. He won't be for months."

"You know what I mean," she countered. "We knew he was going to live."

"I guess that was enough then, was it?"

"I don't know, Brad . . . maybe I was just scared . . . I hated that place . . . it terrified me, and I've never been good when the kids are sick," she said honestly, but without remorse.

"He nearly died, Pam. I thought he had once or twice." Brad knew he would never forget those moments, nor would Jason's twin. "The worst part is that for the rest of his life, he's going to know that you didn't give enough of a damn to come, when he needed you most. That's a hell of a thing to live with, for him, never mind me. You're his mother for chrissake," even if she chose not to act like a wife.

"I'm sorry," she said contritely finally. "I think he understands."

"If he does, you're a lucky woman. I wouldn't forgive

you, in his shoes. And even if he does, how must it make him feel?"

"Don't be so dramatic for chrissake, Brad. You were there." It was the wrong thing to say to him. All it did was make him angry at her, and turn him off. He cut the conversation short after that. He had nothing more to say.

"Yes, I was. And you weren't. I guess that about sums it up."

"How does he look?" She sounded concerned. It was the least she could do.

"Like he's been beaten with lead pipes. But I think he's happy to be alive. We'll be home in a couple of days."

"Brad," she heard something in his voice that startled her. He sounded completely removed. "Are you okay?"

"Yes, I am," he said firmly. "Jason's alive, that's all that matters. I'll see you when I get back." His voice was ice cold, and as Pam hung up at her end, she frowned. It wasn't that she didn't care about her son. It was just that she hadn't wanted to go. She felt guilty about it. But she had served herself in the end. She always did.

After Brad hung up with her, he called Faith, and was disappointed to find she wasn't home. He called her again late that night, after he had settled Jason, and Dylan had gone out to see some friends. Brad waited till he had time to himself to talk to her. The call was too important to him to do less than that.

"Brad?" She sounded stunned to hear him, as though

he had come back from the dead. He had been away for seven weeks. It was the middle of July. He hadn't seen or talked to her since May. "How's Jason?"

"Doing amazingly well. I missed you, Fred." He could feel all the tension go out of him when he heard her voice.

"Will he be all right?" She had prayed endlessly about him, and gone to mass twice a day.

"He'll be fine." Brad laughed for the first time in ages. He nearly cried he was so happy to talk to her. "If you're going to have a church steeple fall on your head, do it while you're young."

"I was so worried about him, and all of you." She had made a decision in his absence, and so had he. Once she knew he was safe and sound, she was no longer going to talk to him. It had been a painful decision for her. But the scene in the airport when he left had told her all she needed to know. She could no longer trust herself, or him. "How's Dylan?" she asked.

"He was a real hero. We spent some amazing time together. It was an extraordinary time. The doctors said it's a miracle Jason survived. I think I have your prayers to thank for that."

She smiled at that, pleased. "I nearly wore your rosary out."

"I can tell." It felt so good just to hear her voice.

"Did Pam get there okay?" She had no idea what had happened, they hadn't talked the whole time he was away.

"She never came," he said simply, and made no further comment. But Faith could hear all he didn't say. She knew him well, though not quite as well as she thought anymore. A lot had changed on the African plains.

"I see. That must have been hard for you."

"We were okay. I hated not being able to call you. How's everything with you?"

"Fine. Silly in comparison to what you've been through. Alex and I came to an agreement about the house. He's letting me keep it."

"That's big of him."

"I think he feels guilty because he's getting married so soon."

"As well he should."

"When are you going back to San Francisco?" It was odd talking to him, particularly after she'd made her decision. But even hearing him now, she was sure. All the more so, because she could hear everything in his voice that she felt for him.

"We're going back in two days. I didn't want to push Jason too hard. It's a long trip. He needs to rest. I'll call you tomorrow." He was exhausted, and needed to get to bed. And what he wanted to say to her would have to wait.

"Have a safe trip." She had no intention of being there when he called the next day. She was going to leave the phone on the machine. She was going to send him a letter in San Francisco. And nothing he could say to her would change her mind. She knew she was doing

the right thing, for both of them. She wasn't Alex. Or
Leslie. She wasn't going to contribute to Brad cheating
on his wife, or cause a divorce, no matter how unhappy
he said they were. It was a matter of respect, for all of
them, and herself. She had talked about it at length with
a priest, and then made up her own mind. In the end, it
had been the only choice she could make. For all their
sakes.

Brad fell into bed exhausted, and as he had for weeks
now, he fell asleep dreaming of Faith. And in New York,
Faith went to church and lit a candle, to strengthen her
resolve. Just hearing his voice again told her how hard it
would be.

24

THE PLANE BRAD, DYLAN, AND JASON WERE ON touched down in San Francisco on the seventeenth of July. And as Brad turned to smile at Jason, sitting next to him, he saw that his son was crying.

"I never thought I'd come home again, Dad," he said through his tears, as Brad squeezed his hand. He didn't want to tell him he had feared the same thing. But they were home safe and sound. And Pam was waiting at the airport for them. She threw her arms around Jason, and hugged Dylan, and Brad left them to get the bags, without saying a word to her. Pam and the boys chatted endlessly in the limo. Pam asked a million questions, and she kept staring at Jason, as though to make sure he was really there.

The boys were obviously happy to see their mother, as she was to see them. And Brad said very little on the ride home in the limousine. She waited until the boys had gone upstairs, and then she turned to him.

"You're really angry, aren't you?" she asked him bluntly. He hadn't gone near her in the airport, and when she had tried to hug him, he walked away. He wasn't playing the game with her anymore.

"No, Pam. Actually, I'm not. I'm done."

"What does that mean?" She looked stunned.

"Just what it sounds like. It's not up to me to forgive you for not coming to Africa, it's up to Jason. But I know I can't be married to you anymore. We were crazy to stay married as long as we did. Neither of us has been in it for a long, long time. You're not there for me. You're not even there for our kids. I don't want to live a lie anymore. I watched our son nearly die in an outpost of civilization. Everyone says it's a miracle he's alive. Without that miracle, there wasn't a damn thing I could have done to save him. I was sitting there just watching him slip away. I don't know where you were, or why, or why you weren't there. But the truth is, I no longer care, and I never will again. You deserve better than that from me. And I deserved a lot better from you. If we don't have it to give each other, we might as well quit. We should have long ago."

"Brad, this works for us. It always did," she said reasonably, but he could hear an edge of panic in her voice.

"Maybe. For all the wrong reasons. Mostly because we were too lazy and scared to do anything else. That's not a good enough reason to stay married. At least not for me." He had finally let go of what his parents had done. He realized it wasn't about them. It was about him and Pam. And no one else. Not even Faith

"Do you have something better now?" she asked

with accusation creeping into her voice. But it didn't work on him. Not anymore.

"I have no idea. But I know what we don't have. You and I have absolutely nothing with each other, Pam. You know it as well as I do. That's good enough for me. This marriage is dead, and it has been for a long time. It's time to bury it. It died years ago. And I'm no longer willing to die with it. You get one turn here. One. And we've been wasting ours. I figured that out one day at about five o'clock in the morning in an African village with a name I can't even pronounce. And I promised myself that when I came home I would tell you I'm out. It's time to be honest about this."

"You're just emotional because of Jason. It was very traumatic for all of you," she said, hoping to calm him down. She wasn't prepared for what he'd said, although she'd expected him to be upset. But not to this extent. She had counted on his good nature to make him understand.

"Yes, it was traumatic," he agreed calmly. She was getting nowhere with him. "Lucky for you that you weren't there. Except the funny thing is, I feel sorry for you that you weren't. It was the most beautiful experience of my life. And something none of us will ever forget. You missed it, Pam. Completely. You stayed here safe and sound, and comfortable. You missed the boat."

"I know I did," she said sadly. But the truth was, she had felt relieved not to go, and to leave it to him. It had been something she just didn't want to do. "I'm sorry, Brad."

"Me too." And he meant it. "We probably never should have gotten married. But at least we've got great kids."

"Are you serious about this?" It was beginning to dawn on her that he meant it, and the thought panicked her. She was used to being married to him. It was a habit she had relied on for years, but not much more than that.

"I'm totally serious." His face said he was.

"What are you going to do?" she asked in a small voice.

"I'll move out when I come home. I'm leaving for New York tonight on the red-eye."

"What are you going to do there?" She looked suspicious, but he had nothing to hide from her.

"I'm going to see Faith. I have a lot to ask her. And to say."

"I always knew you were in love with her," Pam said, looking both victorious and annoyed, but nothing more. This wasn't about her heart. It hadn't been in years.

"You're smarter than I am. I figured it out not long ago. I have no idea if she'll have me, but I'm going to give it a try. If I'm a lucky man, she will." Pam stood and stared at him in silence and nodded. She could see there was no fighting him.

"Have you told the boys?"

"I thought we'd do that together when I get back."

"How long will you be gone?"

"It depends on what happens." He had been totally honest with her. She knew as much as he did at this point. He felt he owed her that. And it was more than she'd given him. "A few days, maybe a week. We'll see. I'll let you know."

"I'd like to tell my father before we tell the boys."

"That's fine."

"Does she know you're coming?" Pam was curious now.

"No, she doesn't." Pam nodded, and a minute later she left the room. She looked startled and unhappy, but she never shed a tear, or asked him to change his mind. She knew he was gone.

Brad spent the afternoon with Jason and Dylan, and he called the two attorneys who'd been covering his cases. They'd gotten continuances for him on almost everything, except for one minor case that had gone well. He promised both of them he'd be back in another week. And then he had a lot of catching up to do, and he'd have to move. As Alex had done with Faith, although with less grace, Brad was giving her the house. It wasn't worth fighting for. None of it was. They had lived an illusion for too many years. Now he wanted something real.

He told the boys that evening that he was leaving for New York, and they seemed surprised, but not upset. He had spent the last two months with them, giving them all he had. And he hugged them both and told them he'd see them in a week. And he stopped in their bedroom to see Pam, but she had gone out. She had long-standing dinner plans with friends. Brad packed a fresh suitcase, and left for the airport in time to catch the red-eye, and he fell asleep almost as soon as the flight took off. And the flight attendant woke him just before they landed in New York. It was six A.M., and there was a spectacular sunrise over New York.

He was at the house on East Seventy-fourth Street at seven o'clock. He hadn't spoken to her since London, but he assumed she was home. He hadn't wanted to say anything more to her until he saw her face-to-face. And with a feeling of trepidation, he rang the bell. He knew as he stood there that his whole life was about to change, either way.

He was startled to see the twin of the girl he had grown up with open the door. It was like turning back the clock. It was Zoe. She was the image of Faith at the same age. And she looked half asleep, wrapped in a pink robe.

"Hi, I'm sorry to wake you," he apologized, looking slightly nervous, and she noticed instantly how handsome he was. "I'm here to see your mother. My name is Brad Patterson. I just flew in from San Francisco. Is she awake?"

"The rosary guy," she said with a sleepy smile, and pulled open the door to let him in. "I'll go tell her you're here. Did she know you were coming?" She hadn't told Zoe a thing. And he shook his head. "Oh . . . a surprise . . ." And then she looked at him oddly. "Do you want to wake her up yourself?" She thought her mother might like that. And without ever having talked to him, Zoe knew she liked him. He looked like a nice man.

"Maybe I'll do that," he said, accepting her invitation, and hoping Faith wouldn't be upset. He walked up the stairs, knocked softly on the door of her room, and then opened it and walked in. He stood there as she rolled over slowly in bed with her eyes closed. He had never seen a more beautiful sight in his life. And as she opened her eyes, she saw him. For a long minute, she wasn't sure if he was a dream. And he didn't move from where he stood. He just stood there smiling at her.

"What are you doing here?" She sat up in bed in her nightgown and stared at him.

"I came to see you, Fred," he said simply.

"I thought you were going back to San Francisco."

"I did. Yesterday."

"When did you get here?"

"About an hour ago."

"I don't understand."

"Neither did I. It took me a hell of a long time to figure it out. I hope you're not as slow as I was. I wasted a lot of years. I should have run off with you when you were fourteen."

"Jack would have killed you," she smiled sleepily at him.

"Eighteen, then."

"That would have been better." She patted the bed next to her, momentarily forgetting her resolve not to see him again. And he accepted the invitation and sat down.

"I love you, Fred."

"I love you too," she said honestly, "but it's not going to do us much good. I can't see you anymore. Or talk to you. I made up my mind."

"That's too bad." But he didn't look disappointed yet. There was a lot she didn't know. "Why is that?"

"You're married, and I don't want to ruin your life. I prayed about it the whole time you were gone."

"What did you pray for?"

"Wisdom. And courage. The wisdom to know what to do. And the courage to do it when I did. We don't have any choice."

"I'm getting divorced."

"You are?" Her eyes opened wide. "How did that happen . . . or when?"

"I figured it out in Africa, when Pam didn't come. I don't want to live a lie anymore. I can't. I told Pam. I'm done. How does that fit into your plans?"

"I don't know." She looked stunned. "I thought you were married for life." It was what he had always said.

"So did I. It doesn't make sense anymore. We do. That's not why I did it, but it's what I want, Fred. Do you? . . . Could you? . . ."

"Are you serious?" She couldn't believe her ears or her eyes.

"That's why I came. To see you. To work it out. To make plans. Will you marry me?"

"Do you mean that? Are you sure?" But she could see that he was, just as Pam had seen it the night before. There was no doubt in his mind that all he wanted was Faith. She was the woman he loved.

"Stop asking me questions, and give me an answer . . . now!" he said, trying to look fierce, but she laughed. She remembered that face from when he was twelve and she was ten.

"Okay . . . okay . . . yes."

"Yes?" Now he looked stunned.

"Yes!" He reached out to kiss her, and she hopped away from him out of her bed. "You can't kiss me."

"Why not?" He looked upset. "Are you going to marry me or not?"

"I told you I was . . . am . . ." They sounded like kids again, and she had never been as happy in her life, nor had he.

"Then why won't you kiss me?"

"I have to brush my teeth first. Then we can get engaged."

She closed the bathroom door, and he lay on the bed and grinned, as Zoe wandered by, and poked her head in.

"How did it go?"

"Pretty good," he smiled at her.

"Where's Mom?"

"In the bathroom, brushing her teeth." Zoe nodded,

she felt as though she had known him forever. He was that kind of guy. And she'd been hearing about him for months.

"Good luck," Zoe said, and went back to her room, as Faith came out of the bathroom with clean teeth and combed hair, and a robe over her nightgown.

And with that, Brad got up and walked over to her, and pulled her into his arms. "I love you, Fred," he whispered, so she would remember his saying it one day. He wanted her to remember this for the rest of her life, because it was what they had both been waiting for and never had.

"I love you too," she whispered back. And he kissed her for a very long time. It was what they had both hoped and never quite believed. It was the answer to their prayers. Sometimes prayers take a long time to be answered, but the right ones are.

ABOUT THE AUTHOR

DANIELLE STEEL has been hailed as one of the world's most popular authors with over 520 million copies of her novels sold. Her many international bestsellers include *Johnny Angel, Dating Game, Answered Prayers, Sunset in St. Tropez, The Cottage, The Kiss, Leap of Faith, Lone Eagle, Journey, The House on Hope Street,* and other highly acclaimed novels. She is also the author of *His Bright Light,* the story of her son Nick Traina's life and death.

Visit the Danielle Steel Web Site at
www.daniellesteel.com.

Introducing an exciting way to learn more about
DANIELLE STEEL

Visit the Danielle Steel website at
www.daniellesteel.com

DS Finally, a website completely devoted
to Danielle Steel and her books

Log on, and you'll find

❖ *The News Page* featuring the latest bulletins on
current Danielle Steel bestsellers, upcoming novels,
and other news

❖ *The Danielle Steel Bookshelf* featuring all of
Danielle Steel's novels, with excerpts from each one
and a 4-6 minute audio sample from audio editions

❖ *Hot Off the Press* featuring a chapter excerpt from
Danielle's latest bestselling book

❖ *The Screening Room* featuring information on
movie and TV tie-ins

❖ *The Trivia Contest*: win a limited edition of one of
her bestselling novels

❖ *The Guest Book*: add your name to Danielle's elec-
tronic mailing list or send her an
e-mail letter

❖ *The Danielle Steel Scrapbook*: never-before-aired
audio and video interviews, photographs, and more,
available only on the Danielle Steel website

www.daniellesteel.com

Dell